The Lodgers

A Novel

Other Books by A. M. BAULD

Mozart's Sister: A Novel

A. M. BAULD

The Lodgers

A NOVEL

ALCINA PRESS

First published in the United Kingdom in 2023 by Alicina Press.

ISBN 978-0-9550713-1-7

Produced by Michelle Emerson Self-Publishing Services
(michelleemerson.co.uk)

Set in Warnock Pro
Printed and bound by Amazon KDP

Alcina Press, London
www.alcinapress.com
alcinapress@gmail.com

Contents

'But that I am forbid
To tell the secrets of my prison-house,
I could a tale unfold whose lightest word
Would harrow up thy soul...'
Hamlet

INTRODUCTION

I dreamt about my family last night. Colours, smells and sounds, all of them seemed real, if a long time ago. You aren't supposed to be able to look at yourself in dreams, although I saw my face very clearly and could form judgments about my image in a way that I couldn't about others. My nose seemed long in relation to everything else – tick – the rest of me was maybe okay – I slouch and skulk a bit, I have clean hair, I wear my brother's jeans – tick, tick, tick - but in the dream I am watching a blurry image of my grandmother leaning against the kitchen doorway and waving at my mother who is on her third glass of claret, oblivious to anyone's comings or goings.

I can remember Granny turning away with a look of neglect on her face. Her head is slightly bowed, the way a person looks when they're dejected. And here is me, thinking I was invisible in the cloakroom where I'd hidden behind a curtain in amongst the coats.

The dream was the highlight of my rage and my sense that everyone else in the family was *other* as opposed to me. That these others had forgotten my birthday is just one example of their otherness. It wasn't the first time either.

My mother is generally a forgetful person, and it so happens she's afraid of all doors because of the privacy they offer the person on the *other* side – in dreams and in real life. Her solution has been to remove as many as she can from our house, hanging cloth as curtains in place of solid wood. What few doors remain are latched to the walls or wedged back so they are permanently open. In case she forgets.

The curtains are off-cuts she's scrounged from a local upholstery shop where the owner sees her as a human tip for any scraps he can't sell. Their patchwork is calming to a middle-aged married woman who feels trapped by suburban penalties and wants to escape. Curtains can conceal things in a different way from doors, and their mystery is as important to my story as the tapestry was to Polonius and Hamlet. Not meaning to brag, but I've read all of Shakesepeare's plays.

In my dream, I'm tucked behind the most moth-eaten curtain in the house and can hear everything clearly on the other side. It's my eleventh birthday – a long time ago – and no one in my family has remembered to leave any presents at the foot of my bed as they would normally do.

I've been waiting for someone to say, 'Surprise!' or at least sing that awful song. I am hoping if I stay behind the curtain for long enough, they would wonder where I was, which is why I've taken a cold chop and a cold roast parsnip to eat behind my brother's woollen overcoat and the moth-eaten remnant at the top of the cellar stairs.

I was just about to come out of hiding when I heard Granny hissing at me.

'Asp, my poor dear child, is that you in there?'

I say nothing but try to hide my feet by twisting them sideways like a ballet dancer.

'I know it's you,' she speaks in a voice where she's suspicious of anyone under the age of twelve but thinks she's keeping it a secret. 'I saw you out of the corner of my eye,' she says.

Always the corner of one eye, what was in the centre, for goodness sake? Granny was poking the cloth quite viciously for an old lady, and I pulled my feet backwards to avoid her blows.

'It's my shoes, dear. I want my walking shoes.'

The smell of her Number 7 face powder fights with the smell of musty old coats, and I remember how she told me that wearing lipstick was the sign of a prostitute, and yet she, the sly old bag, is never caught without some powder on her nose. I told her I could only find one brown lace-up with two diamond-shaped slits cut across the toes.

Her shoe is sticking out from under a pile of boots next to a second curtain, which conceals the entrance from the cloakroom to the cellar stairs. Granny was all of a sudden in there beside me and quick as a monkey, poking the folds like she found it difficult to stop one action and start on another.

I say all this because I am trying to describe everything that happened in the dream as accurately as I can. I imagine she reached out to snatch her shoe. I'd picked it up but refused to give it to her because I was pissed off that she'd discovered my hiding place and forgotten to say happy birthday.

I suppose I might have accidentally pushed her through the cellar curtain in my annoyance. She made no cry, or at least nothing that my family could hear in the kitchen and nothing that I could summon up in my head.

She must have fallen all the way to the bottom of the stairs as I can still hear the thudding sounds of her body as it bumped against the wood – then the clatter of the shoe. I think I might have thrown it after her in shock, or maybe I just let it fall.

The strangest thing was that in the following silence I remained still - and yet within a minute, there was a second clatter as if her other shoe, which I'd not seen, was chasing after the first one of its own accord.

I fumbled for the light switch on the wall next to the hat shelf and thought, I've got to look down there, and now I cannot, cannot remember doing it. I suppose I ate the pork chop and the parsnip, but I don't remember that either. I certainly can't remember looking down at her, though I've tried since to imagine that I did:

Granny splayed out awkwardly like a punctured rubber doll; her shoes upside down by the coal heap; slipper-socks on her feet; glasses trapped under her nose with one arm bent around her head as if she were looking into her armpit. She's wearing an old custard cardigan and one of her Salvation Army tweed skirts.

You can see knotted fingers through the blue nylon gloves and her hair is unravelled the way it is before sleep, brushed a hundred times to keep the nits away and generally unwashed in case she gets a chill from a damp head. It smells of Granny. Can you smell things in dreams? I've even tried to imagine her Kirby grips scattered on the floor. You get the picture. It's a picture from my memory. I do not recall any of her deadness in the dream as something real and frightening. This would come later.

Without her death in what was obviously a nightmare, subsequent events might have been different. As sure as I am of anything, people, even in dreams, do not die away to be convenient. Their past becomes part of the present and of the future, although I'm not saying that our future is exactly like our past or that I'm setting up an enquiry, already knowing the answer. There'd be no purpose to something so obviously fake.

So. This is my attempt to recall the past to discover something about the present - my family's past and my family's present. I'll begin before Granny died on a September day some years ago when a boy called Jean-Pierre walked up our garden path and became our first lodger.

***

'Words, words, words.'
Hamlet

CHAPTER 1

My full name is Aspen Thrush, but everyone calls me Asp. My brother says the snake part of my name happened in an inspired moment of prophecy because there's real venom on my tongue. He says if I shed my own skin, I'll become a totally alien person and I believe him as what my brother says has a big effect on me.

Most of the fences in the street where we live are broken or non-existent. We have never lived in what the estate agents call a good location! The houses are joined on both sides with front rooms that project so they appear semi-detached, an architectural deceit to suggest the people living there are rich. With three small squares of grey pebbledash above the bay windows, our house is not what my parents wanted but is what our family can afford.

If my story could belong to any neighbourhood, I don't know why I'm spelling out its ordinariness unless it is to say just that. As in all fairy tales, the evildoers have the edge, and happy families is a card game, not a human possibility.

Horror happens in ordinariness. It's how I learned all families are messed up to some degree, and it reminds me that I made a vow long ago to be quiet about who I am so I can find out more about others. (I mean everyone else that isn't me.) All morning

I've been pestering my parents for stuff about our new lodger while we wait for him to knock on our front door. Tension. Apprehension. Scary thoughts. Wild hope.

He comes up the pathway, small and bouncy, despite an overnight bag and a violin case slung across his back. I can see he's got big feet by looking through the spyhole in our front door. These are the last days of an Indian summer, and the curtain over the door has been drawn back to let in the light through two stained glass windows.

***

'Are you the lodger?' asks a thin, cross little girl, eyeing the foreign-looking boy standing on the family doorstep.

'Yes. I'm Jean-Pierre.'

'I thought you spoke French.'

'I do.'

'Mumma! He's here.' The child covered her ears with both hands and shouted to those behind her as she kept staring at the boy.

'Mumma, did you hear me? It's the new lodger. He's called Jean-Pierre, but he hasn't got a moustache or any onions round his neck - and guess what, he speaks English.'

Asp's voice was shrill. She examined the line of fuzz above their new lodger's upper lip and was disappointed he didn't resemble the French boy in Elm's grammar book. If he'd worn a beret or carried a baguette, things might have been different.

What a nasty, noisy child, he thought and wished he hadn't come.

'I'm glad you found us, Jean-Pierre.'

The mother spoke in a low, contrasting voice, staring above her daughter's head from behind the shadows. The sound, almost throbbing, was probably the most noticeable thing about her – and with her thin, scraped-back hair and her mouth a narrow hole revealing yellow teeth, she knew she was plain.

Jean-Pierre looked down at her green Alice shoes, their straps flapping at the sides. 'It is alright,' he began but stopped halfway as if he meant to say more. He could have said the English are unattractive or their houses look damp and windy from the outside. Certainly, their pink skins reminded him of newborn pigs on his grandfather's farm.

'I'm Daphne Thrush. This is Asp, my daughter. Come in, please.'

Again, the low throatiness. But it was more than that. Her prolonged, extruded vowels delayed her consonants in moments of anxiety. After a month, Jean-Pierre would hardly notice.

'Thank you very much. My trunk is at the station. I am early.'

Asp laughed as he squeezed past them into the hallway, and all three tried to make space for the other person. He turned and saw that the mother was nervously tugging at the ends of her cardigan.

'No, no, you're not early,' she insisted. 'We were expecting you. Don't worry about your trunk. My husband can collect it whenever you like.'

'Thank you.'

'Did you come by plane?'

He looked puzzled.

'We live under the flight path,' said the child, pointing back at the sky. 'It's very noisy when you're trying to get to sleep. Granny says the planes' vibrations killed my goldfish because one day, it jumped out of its bowl and died on the breakfast table without anyone noticing. He was called George. I'm called Asp, and I think planes are disgusting.'

'No, thank you, I did *not* come by the plane.' Jean-Pierre unhooked his violin case and lowered his face so they couldn't see his expression. 'I took the train . . .'

'So easy from Waterloo, isn't it? Follow me, Jean-Pierre.' Daphne smiled encouragingly. 'A violin - how nice.'

She picked it up carelessly, tucking it under one arm before he could say either 'it's mine and it's precious and I don't want you to bang it or drop it because this is an eighteenth-century violin made by Bernard Gaudfroy' or that an old man in Geneva who sold cuckoo clocks had given it to him as a present. He said neither because he knew it would sound as random as the child's story about a fish named George, and anyway, it was beyond his grasp of English at this moment.

He imagined what it would cost his parents to pay for his lodgings, weighing cost against their disappointment if he left London without his *baccalaureat.* With a sense of despair, he followed his landlady up crooked stairs painted bright yellow and was tempted to stop halfway, snatch his violin and walk straight down again, but he continued climbing with the child's stare burning into the back of his jacket.

Asp frowned, her eyes narrowed in suspicion and short-sightedness. Since she refused to admit there was a problem with her sight and because the family was also in denial about it, the look had become part of her character. Without her scowl, she couldn't see reliably beyond her own nose and Jean-Pierre, revealing a fine, nuanced understanding of these things, decided to punish her by not turning round as he knew she wanted him to do.

He understood he was also being examined by invisible eyes from behind patchwork curtains on either side of the landing. He knew they were watching him because of the telltale twitches of fabric when he passed, a surreptitious tug and release, the faint sound of someone else's breathing. He might have been making it up inside his head because he was doing something scarily grown up, like taking lodgings for the first time in a strange country, and which could never be repeated. He wasn't sure.

'Here you are. This is your room.' Daphne parted heavy curtains with images of dancing ladies frozen in the folds. She placed his violin on top of a shabby eiderdown and stepped back to allow him the space to look around.

'You see that basin in the corner? You really mustn't drink the water from the tap. If you want a drink, get it from the kitchen. English plumbing. Washing only. Do you understand me, Jean-Pierre?'

He nodded as she laughed in a lonely way, not expecting him to join in, which he didn't. A bedroom smell of dust and old clothes came from an open cupboard, and again, he found himself wondering if he should stay. He stifled a sneeze.

'The bathroom's next door.' It was obvious that his new landlady was struggling to please him. 'Make sure you have a good look round to be certain it's what you want.' Her hand patted the top of his violin case, believing it contained the consolation of a more civilized world inside. 'We'll be downstairs in the kitchen when you're ready.'

Daphne heard him unhook the door behind the curtain as she left and immediately felt offended. *Maybe he won't stay,* she thought as the door closed behind her, and she remembered in a panic that they needed the money for Elm's school fees.

Except for her husband, Henry Thrush, all members of the family had been named after trees or plants. Elm was the eldest child, and until recently, he and Asp had attended the local state school together. But now Elm had started at the expensive private one down the road. There was no money for this and no sense – just years of debts and serial lodgers lying ahead, ruining one set of dreams to feed another.

Daphne's psoriasis would show itself on her scalp in inflamed patches while they considered not the wisdom of what they did but whether they would need two lodgers instead of one when it was Asp's turn to change schools. Beyond that, there was the baby to worry about, but as Leaf was only seventeen months old, they believed they had some time to sort out his future.

'I've left Jean-Pierre upstairs.' Daphne entered the kitchen, her tone of voice implying that the boy's willingness to lodge with them was an established fact and not to be questioned. There they were, the remaining Thrush family, quickly gathered around the table, curious but weighed down by some nebulous sense of the future.

It was an accumulating suspense where they also wondered very specifically if the stranger upstairs would poke around in other rooms, stick his nose in their cupboards, compare the mess, try out each bed like Goldilocks in *Goldilocks and the Three Bears* before falling asleep on the smallest and narrowest.

Outside, the leaves made a dry sound rubbing against each other in the wind as if they had grit on them. It could be heard through the open kitchen window if anyone stopped to listen, but no one did. At the precise moment when the wind dropped, Granny pecked at the remaining strawberries with small jerks of her head as if she were a hen, chopping the rotten bits off them with a carving knife intended for the ham, while the ham, now dry as the leaves, remained uneaten in the centre of the table as they waited for their new lodger to join them.

'Of course we can always give him a month's trial.'

'And then what?' Henry spread a newspaper in front of his plate to fill in time while he waited for his food.

The act of filling in time or saving it was important to him - swallowing beer from a bottle without a glass - listening to the CD left in the record player from the day before and playing it on repeat as he waited for dinner to be served. It saved time. It was like leaving a room when someone asked him a question he didn't want to answer or wearing yesterday's underpants because they were there at the foot of his bed.

The expedience and simplicity of everyday habits bestowed a sense of calm on his uptight soul. Chatter amongst his family was not filling in time but wasting it, something that he felt unconsciously, or he would have to admit he had no interest in what they thought or felt.

'Put that away,' cried Asp.

'I'll do no such thing.'

'It's rude.'

'If I want to read the paper, I'll read the paper.'

'He's coming.'

'No, he's not.'

'He is.' She really wished her father would have a heart attack and die in front of them right now, with his head falling off into the ham. She could go to his funeral and cry real tears.

'Hello, Jean-Pierre.' Daphne pulled out a chair as Henry reluctantly returned his paper to the rack. 'Come and meet the rest of the family.'

Asp noticed dark streaks in the lodger's fingernails that matched the shadows under his eyes. They gave his face the bruised, interesting look that came when you hadn't slept for a week and which she must remember to cultivate.

'This is my husband, Henry. This is my mother, Mrs Pod, but we call her Granny. This is our son Elm, and that's Leaf, the baby in the pram.'

'How do you do?'

'How do YOU do?' repeated Asp.

Henry glared at his daughter while Jean-Pierre examined the boy with white skin and red hair cut like a bowl, who apparently answered to the name Elm. Elm buried his head in his chest and waited for someone else to answer the stranger on his behalf. His chin kept moving from side to side as he swallowed his thoughts.

For a minute or two, there was an uneasy silence as the meal began. His grandmother was pleased to have a new face on the other side of the table, which meant she could tip the strawberries into her lap and swallow them silently one by one while everyone was studying Jean-Pierre.

Henry was absent-mindedly picking bits of ham out of his teeth and thinking about the model aeroplane he would like to buy from a hobby shop six miles further down the A3. Leaf, the monster baby, remained asleep in his pram. Even Asp became equally and uncharacteristically quiet, licking her knife in mirror image of Jean-Pierre, having decided this was an exciting piece of French etiquette that no one had told her about.

Daphne was drinking in the corner and, by the midcourse, sustaining a dinner party flow, talking randomly to everyone, revealing a discomfort with herself that was spawned by periodic self-loathing. General conversation would only begin with some order after the meal.

'I prefer doors to be open. There's nothing Freudian about that. I just don't like them closed. Curtains are somehow friendlier, don't you think?'

Jean-Pierre smiled at Daphne. It was possibly his first smile in their company. 'Are you learning the French at school, Elm?' He was relieved that his words had suddenly translated themselves without effort and was watching Elm's chin slowly lowering itself into a lump of mashed potato where it remained without anyone else seeming to notice. Jean-Pierre thought this must be a nod.

'I don't object to curtains being drawn if a person wants privacy.' Daphne remained sealed in her own world and quite lonely in the way she persisted in living there.

'Elm's shy,' said Asp. 'Go on, Elm. Tell Jean-Pierre you're learning Latin too.

'Curtains make this nice swooshing noise – it's less of a shock than a bang.'

'I've only just started Latin.' Elm's sense of reticence was unique within his family. He had already eaten what was left of the potato on his chin and had moved on to his tie, but his conversational skills were still at a level where his parents felt it safe to give him a mobile phone for his next birthday without worrying about the bill, although there was a new brightness in Elm's eyes when he kicked his sister under the table.

'Really?' Jean-Pierre looked at Elm with interest. 'It's my superb subject, I think. Then the English.'

Leaf, wearing a baby redness of face, was making small, mewling noises in his pram, which were ignored.

'You can always change curtains, but people never seem to change their doors, do they? Don't you agree, Jean-Pierre?'

Daphne turned to their new lodger, who was already weighing whether the boy with hair *comme un ange medieval* was the only member of the family he understood. The father appeared remote, the mother was unusual, the grandmother was a strawberry thief, the baby was ugly and the girl child was rude.

'I try to choose curtains to match the season – you know – heavy fabrics for the cold and light ones in the summer. You can't do that with doors, can you?'

No one was listening. What she said was innocuous enough and that was the problem. Henry would say she was wittering and she was – as lonely as she was embarrassed, her face caught in a beam of butter light with specks of dust floating through the window – a tear dropped into her coffee. She looked like a tired, middle-aged English woman whose drink problem only seemed to worry herself.

'Miss Peters asked me to play the violin at assembly.' Asp waved her fork at Elm, unsure if she were competing with her brother or just filling her own void. Her vow to say nothing about herself and discover more about others was forgotten.

'Perhaps Asp could play duets with Jean-Pierre.' Daphne suddenly foresaw an improvement in her daughter's sight-reading. 'Jean-Pierre is a violinist,' she whispered to Henry, who used to say he only played the spoons in the hope that everyone would laugh.

'Of course, if-you-would-like-me-to-play-for-you, I am okay. I am happy, of course.' Jean-Pierre smiled this time at Elm and sucked the dirt out of his fingernails without any awareness that he was doing it. Asp looked on admiringly.

'Play *with* her,' sighed Henry.

'I prefer maths.' Elm resented being described as shy by his sister and every now and then made a spectacular effort to prove this was a family myth.

'I gave up piano lessons,' said Granny, 'because we didn't have a piano.'

'What happened to the strawberries?' asked Daphne, staring at the empty dessert bowl.

Leaf woke up in his pram and started crying.

'Stop sucking your knife like that, you'll cut your tongue.' Henry glared at his daughter and jiggled the pram until the baby kicked his legs so violently that both booties worked their way down his feet and clung to his toes.

'Jean-Pierre does. I watched him like this.' Asp gave a last lick of her blade and covered her nose suddenly. 'I think Leaf wants changing.'

Henry rattled the pram handle as Leaf's cries went up a notch. The idea that he disliked his own daughter floated into his thoughts and gave him back some belief in his authority.

'Excuse me.' Jean-Pierre was indignant. 'But I have not cut my tongue. Do you have the parmesan?'

Daphne hurried to the fridge in search of cheese.

'We don't say *the* parmesan. We just say parmesan.' Asp examined her reflection in the blade of her knife and breathed on her image until it disappeared.

'The English are not as precise as the French.' Henry poked the baby in various places but failed to shut him up.

'Pardon Mr Thrush. I am unaware.'

It was a modest, unexpected declaration. It was the way he had agreed with something they had said and which changed the way they thought about him, although they didn't realise it at the time.

'Henry,' said Henry. 'Call me Henry, Jean-Pierre.'

'Well, I'm always forgetting the right words in French.' Daphne winked at Jean-Pierre as she placed a lump of mouldy cheese on her lodger's plate and forgot to mention the curtains, to everyone's relief.

'You are always forgetting,' agreed Henry.

'Well, I said I do, didn't I?' Daphne was indignant.

'*I* don't,' said Asp.

'That's because you can't speak any French.' Henry brushed away a winter fly making its drowsy way towards the empty strawberry bowl.

'I do know lots. You don't know anything.'

'*Ou est le crayon de ma tante* was not helpful when I was in Paris.' Granny was staring into her empty lap, remembering her youth, while Daphne slowly shook her head at her mother.

'Shush, Mum,' she said.

'I like programming.' Elm decided to speak up in case no one had heard him before.

'Cool.' Granny looked up, bright-eyed, in Jean-Pierre's direction.

'Young people are always saying "cool". They say it when they've robbed a bank or shot someone dead. "Cool", they say. It's always cool.'

Her cheeks were trembling with a crossness that comes from feeling you have been left behind by modern invention. 'I don't think that's the slightest bit cool.' She withdrew one hairpin from her bun and replaced it sharply. 'Take them to the Antarctic and put them in a swimming costume. That's cool.'

She rubbed the corners of her cardigan together before tucking up a fallen whisp of hair. The wit had gone out of her eyes as suddenly as the anger but not the vulnerability, which remained.

'Would anyone like some more ham?' Unaware there was none left, Daphne was trying hard not to slur her words, recognising that she should change the subject before she changed the baby's nappy.

There was a lot of talking and shouting. No longer stuffy or musty or failed cute. This was potent, perennial family noise. But at some point, without anyone specifically saying so, it was assumed amid the hullabaloo and braggadocio of them all talking more or less at once that because the visitor was still in their midst, he intended to stay as their lodger. The shark that swam with the fish or the fish that swam with the sharks, they would get used to one another in time.

***

'Remember thee!
Ay, thou poor ghost...'
Hamlet

CHAPTER 2

Jean-Pierre quickly discovered that survival in the Thrush family was best achieved by lying low. After violin practice on Sunday mornings with the windows of his room wide open to annoy the neighbours, he spent the afternoons taking photographs of graves in the local cemetery. They were mostly close-ups of headstones, defaced by wind and rain - very old and grey, very English looking.

He liked the way the roots of ivy wrapped their hairy arms around the trees, drawing out the sap in a way that was sculptural and satisfying. He scanned the bouquets of dead roses on the mounds with half their petals scattered in the wind. He could imagine his own funeral at this spot and tried to smell his mother's face cream as she knelt beside his grave. He prodded the ground with a stick, not expecting to stir the bones underneath but feeling the resistance of the earth's hardness.

Asp would discover his photographs of tombs and ivy and wormholes quite early on. He'd stuffed them in a shoe box under his bed on a day when she was snooping. It was the day she had called out, 'Good morning Jean-Pierre,' when he passed by her room on his way to breakfast and he made no reply. Rude. 'Jean-Pierre,' louder, 'Jean-Pierre,' louder, 'Jean-Pierre.' No reply. 'Just rude,' she had whispered crossly under her breath. Arms locked around her knees, sitting up in bed without any clothes on and her curtain drawn completely back, he must have seen her. She had taken her pyjamas off during the night because she was hot, and it was only after he had passed on the landing that she remembered she was naked. She let out a small, inaudible yelp as she thought he would have seen her, followed by a wish to punish him and let him know that she was punishing him for ignoring her. Asp. Oh, Asp.

'Jean-Pierre.'

After supper, the family sat around the table to begin a game of Monopoly, which Asp hated because she never landed on Mayfair.

'Why do you take lots of photos of dead things, Jean-Pierre?'

Everyone turned to look at Jean-Pierre except Asp, who was already looking.

'Do you mean like the graves?' he asked.

'There've been so many deaths in the obituaries,' murmured Granny.

'That's what obituaries are for,' remarked Henry.

'Who's next to follow?' sighed Granny.

'I mean the photos you have under your bed.' Asp was speaking in her child's monster voice. Spitting out her words. She had been working on it for months. 'You know, Jean-Pierre. The statues and crosses and messages on tombstones. *In memory of our beloved Elsie and her rabbit.* Stuff like that.'

Jean-Pierre gave a shrug. He had tried to discuss his new hobby with Daphne on a day when they were on their second glass of red wine after supper, when they were arguing about logical positivism, Jung, the Marquis de Sade, or what made one twin gay and the other not. Neither had a clue about any of it, but knowledge was not required.

Of course Asp knew Jean-Pierre would be upset that she had looked under his bed without him being there. He'd be upset that she'd entered his room. He'd wonder what else she had discovered or if anything in his room was safe from her prying eyes. Planting doubts about his privacy was an excellent way of unsettling him. Of course it would be.

'Are they for Halloween or something like that?' Asp had the whole family's attention and looked pleased with herself. Jean-Pierre put down his fork.

'It's because I like ghosts,' he replied coldly.

'You mean you want to photograph them?' asked Granny.

'You can't,' said Asp. 'You can't take pictures of ghosts.'

Jean-Pierre spread his fingers apart in a fan shape as if his hands had an image of Asp in his room when he wasn't there. His spoken English was now so much better than their French, and after a month, his English teacher at school had informed the rest of his class that he was a gifted student.

'But,' Asp paused, 'you *know* you can't photograph them. Ghosts aren't real.'

'I don't go up to a grave and look for one and go click,' said Jean-Pierre.

'It's really weird, Jean-Pierre,' said Asp.

'I'm not a crazy person.'

'Of course you aren't. What an interesting hobby, dear.' Daphne poured herself some more wine.

'I'm sorry about the Monopoly.' Jean-Pierre turned to Daphne with a grateful look. 'But I can't stay. I have an essay on the second world war.' He stood up from his chair and tucked it in – he always tucked it in – and left them sitting there, arguing over who got the iron, the dog or the boot. He paused to kick each yellow stair on his way to his room and could hear Asp claiming she too had some homework to finish. *Evil has a human face,* he thought.

Downstairs they heard him slam his door so hard that a window on the landing shut with a crash which woke the baby. Leaf may have grown older since Jean-Pierre had arrived, but he was still swaddled in his pram, snug as a plump piglet in a grey stretchy, stained baby-gro. Perpetually sleeping or crying. Trapped into eternal puking infancy by an unspoken conspiracy. It was as if the Thrush family had bought a baby one year and expected it to stay that way the next.

'What were you doing in Jean-Pierre's room, Asp?' Henry popped a dummy into Leaf's mouth and was cooing at his younger son while glaring at his daughter.

'Looking for a ruler. *My* ruler.'

'Do you think Jean-Pierre's trying to photograph ghosts after all?' asked Elm. 'I saw your ruler in your room this morning, Asp.'

Asp was staring at the floor, watching a blob of spit fall from her mouth and land on the toe of her shoe. She knew her brother was trying to make her sound like a liar, and she knew he knew that Jean-Pierre didn't believe there were any ghosts. This was Elm being sly. Elm was her disguised twin conjoined at the head, though Elm's head was more mysterious than hers, being filled with Rice Krispies.

'If you think Jean-Pierre's got something that belongs to you, you should ask him first before you enter his room.' Henry believed he should have been a judge for the crown.

'I suppose he likes nice pictures,' ventured Granny, slipping several hotels and a get-out-of-jail card into her pocket under the table.

'I'm leaving.' Asp transferred her attention from her saliva to her father, giving him the death stare, which he failed to notice.

'I seem to be missing a five hundred pound note.' Henry was shuffling and stacking cards as their banker, another role he would have liked to assume when he went to work each day with an apple and a folded newspaper inside his briefcase and nothing else.

'Has anyone picked it up by mistake?' Henry glared at his mother-in-law.

'I'm off to do homework,' repeated Asp.

'Goodbye then, dear. I'd like to buy the Old Kent Road,' Granny murmured pleasantly.

'I'm not going forever.'

Asp had picked up this habit of permanently sounding cross, convinced her intelligence was buried deep down inside her and that she could only bring it to the surface when she was profoundly out of sorts. Jean-Pierre woke some sort of devil in her. What she hadn't bargained for was his appetite for revenge.

'Jean-Pierre?' Asp rapped neatly three times on his door.

'Aspic?' The sarcasm of the reply was a warning.

'No, it's Asp.' She squinted through the keyhole, not into the abyss but at something light in the corner with a large patch of darkness in the middle. Jean-Pierre's eye, she guessed. 'Can I come in?' Mesmerised by this blinking jelly, she heard him say:

'Why not?'

Darkness was replaced by brightness. It defined the shape of the keyhole. She felt a sense that was new to her, a sense of danger, as the door was opened and Jean-Pierre appeared in a pair of new striped pyjamas, a fountain pen between his teeth.

Ink ran down from one side of his mouth, which he wiped away with small, agitated rubs. It was a while before he removed the pen and stuck it behind an ear. There was such anger in his expression that she felt excited standing there in front of him, wondering whether or not he would try to kill her and if she should run now before he got the chance.

'So what exactly did you take?'

'I don't know what you mean.' She was lying, of course. The trouble was her feet refused to move, and her ankles shook so much they kept colliding with each other.

'I'm making a list of what is missing.'

'What sort of things?'

She wished she'd gone to the toilet. Only it was too late because her panties were already damp, and she knew at some point she would have to take them off and find another pair. Her mother still did her personal laundry, and Asp couldn't remember if any clean ones remained in the linen cupboard on the landing.

'A box of paper clips, a pencil and some postcards. I've only just started.'

'I didn't take them.' A lie. 'Someone else must've. I bet it was Granny. Granny's always taking things from people's rooms.'

'I don't think so.'

He put the emphasis on the 'think.' Somehow she managed to move her feet one after the other until she was sitting on the end of his bed, making herself comfortable against the wall and placing a cushion across both knees to dry the panties underneath.

'Oh well, you don't understand my granny. She's done it lots of times. We have to watch her if she comes on the supermarket shop.'

'But you were the one who looked under my bed.' His accent was more noticeable when he was angry.

'I was looking for something. I was looking for what I thought you might've taken by mistake.'

'*Quoi*?'

'A pencil case.'

'I don't believe you.'

'You sound like a policeman.'

'That's because you're guilty.'

She was certain he was thinking about murdering her. She could turn round now and run. Or scream.

'You've got ink all down your neck, Jean-Pierre.'

'I know. Now leave me alone. I have to do my essay.'

This was not what she had planned. 'Granny's been to prison, you know.'

He said nothing.

She wanted to make sure he would hear her as she added loudly, 'For stealing money.'

He bent down and placed his face directly in front of hers.

'From *whom*?' This time she could see the reflection of her own eyes in his and smell the parmesan on his breath.

'I don't know exactly.' She wriggled uncomfortably.

'Then what *do* you know?'

'Well, I think it was the corner shop. Taking money off the counter, out of people's pockets in the post office queue. You know. Stuff like that.'

Asp leaned back as far away from him as she could – released her breath in little bursts between sentences to avoid the whiff of stale cheese coming at her. 'I think she stole things every time she went to collect her pension book. An' then they took her to court.' The smell was a sweet stench like dead mouse, and it occurred to her that she could end all this interrogation with one quick vom.

'When?' Jean-Pierre exhaled slowly, and Asp leaned to one side.

'Oh, a little while ago. It wasn't the first time either. But I don't know exactly. No one ever talks about it.' She tried staring up at the ceiling and gulping at the air above him. 'I just overheard my dad saying that if she ever got caught again, she'd be stuck in jail forever and if it was up to him, he'd leave her there.'

'But your Granny. She was here on my first day. She is always here.'

He moved towards the window overlooking rooftops and high walls where two cats were padding backwards and forwards in the dark, unable to pass each other and turning away each time they met in the middle. The pause gave Asp time to spring back and breathe again. The trouble was she felt as if she'd swallowed his very being, and she couldn't get rid of the sickly sweet taste, and it disgusted her. She wiped her mouth slowly before replying in the hope it would disappear.

'They only kept her in for a few days. Elm says they must've felt sorry for her because she was an old lady. He said she had a disease or something. Couldn't help it really. He said she'd be dead before they could get her into prison and all that stuff.'

Jean-Pierre could always ask Elm for the truth, but the moment he saw the cats had disappeared and the windowpane was reflecting only dark, glistening shadows, he knew he wouldn't go downstairs and interrupt a game of Monopoly where half the cards were missing.

'Elm knows?' This came after another of his long silences. Elm was the broadsheet of the family. Saint Elm never lied.

'Of course. Only we don't talk about it, like I said. It's not very nice telling the world your granny's a thief.' Asp felt the drama of what she'd said and it excited her. 'Leaf's the only one who doesn't know,' she laughed, flitting between concealment and revelation and unsure which was the more exciting. 'I reckon my mum didn't tell you because she didn't want you to worry about it. I'm just telling you so you don't think it's me that's nicking your things.'

'Nicking?'

'Stealing.'

'Then don't come into my room unless I ask you to.' *Asp,* he thought, *is just like her grandmother, Madame Pod. Mon Dieu.*

'I can give you a key for your room if you like.' She tossed the cushion to one side and started towards the door. 'No one knows I've got it. No one even knows it exists except me. And now you, of course.' She swung her hips, deliberately, rocking them sideways, more comic than erotic - like a half-baked *Lolita* she'd remembered from a film on television, except she was overdoing the swing.

'Show me,' he called, picking up the kimono his mother had given him when he left home and feeling for the five twenty-pound notes he'd hidden inside the lining of its belt. As he counted each one twice, Asp returned to dangle a key in his face.

'See? I told you. You didn't believe me, did you?' she smiled at the money in his hand.

'What if you have another one somewhere?' He made no effort to take the key.

'You won't believe me if I say I haven't.'

'No.'

'So it doesn't make any difference then.' She turned around and walked out, humming to herself softly.

He wanted that key. Other copies, if there were any, could wait. It was this one he wanted because this nasty little girl had offered it to him.

'I'll take you with me,' he called out after her. 'Next time I go,' he added softly, stuffing his money back inside the kimono's belt.

'Next time you go where?' Asp sniffed the air like a small, excited dog about to catch a mouse by its tail.

'If you give me the key,' he was leaning against the door frame, still holding the kimono in one hand and clutching at the curtain of dancing ladies in the other. 'I will take you to the cemetery next time I go.'

'Oh.' She sidled back towards him. 'How do you know I want to go with you?'

'Because now that you've seen the photos, you'll want to see what is real.' He let the curtain drop and plucked the key from her fingers with his.

'When?'

'This Sunday.'

'Promise?'

'We'll ride our bikes.'

'Cool,' and she laughed, remembering Granny. 'It'd better be worth it,' she added, just loud enough for him to hear.

Much later, she recalled his gaze as he waved her out of the room. She thought about it for an hour or so while lying on her bed, trying to go to sleep. It was, Asp decided, a stranger's face that revealed only what he wanted her to see, which seemed reasonable, given that the face was Jean-Pierre's.

***

'Make you to ravel all this matter out,
That I essentially am not in madness,
But mad in craft.'
Hamlet

CHAPTER 3

That Sunday was the turning point in their relationship. It was raining when Jean-Pierre and Asp rode along the towpath in the direction of the nearest graveyard. For most of the year, its headstones were concealed by bush, but this was the beginning of winter and the twigs were already stripped of their leaves. There were no other walkers or random figures on bikes, just a few birds hopping silently in and out of patches of moss.

Slabs and statues gleamed wetly through the lacy branches, increasing a ghostliness that had attracted Jean-Pierre in the first place. A headless cherub stood further back than the rest, with its wings so vast they dwarfed its body and the wall of yew behind. Asp propped her bike against an old sycamore tree, leant across to feel the coldness of the stone and read the inscription below the feet.

'Mary Louise Hutchings, born 1907, died 1918.'

'About your age, Aspic.'

Asp scowled. 'I wonder how she died.' He stared at his watch as if expecting someone to arrive.

'Black Death. I bet it was Black Death. You know, when you sneeze a lot and your skin turns purple because you can't breathe and you die. My biology teacher told me all about tha...'

'There wasn't any Black Death in 1918, Asp. It was... flu.'

'What?' She danced around the plinth three times. 'It's a pity there's no head. I bet it wasn't flu. Do you think it fell off? Perhaps it was stolen. I've had flu and I didn't die.'

The boy turned away, scrabbling at the bark of the trees with his fingers, exposing the orange powdery flakes underneath, rubbing them until they became smooth.

'I want to take some photos from up there.' He pointed at the sycamore where Asp had parked her bike. 'I'll climb that tree, and you can hand me my camera. I want *you* to climb up the statue.'

She collapsed against the stone plinth and threw her head up to the sky. 'Can't do it. Won't.'

He wanted to lash out at her with one of the sticks lying on the ground, but he needed to be calm.

'I'll reach down for the camera. Okay, Asp? You can sit in front of the wings.'

'Why?'

'Because... I want to take pictures of you like that.'

'Told you. Won't.'

He snapped off a branch from the sycamore, concentrating on the pointed end as it dug into the earth, indifferent to the mud that splattered against his chin.

'Are you afraid of ghosts, Asp?' He spoke without looking at her, and any sense of pleasure at being there was now forgotten as anger fed her fear.

'*You* climb it. Go on. You climb it if you're not scared.' Her chest hurt when she breathed. 'I'll take the picture.'

They argued for several minutes in this way until he threatened to leave her to find her own way home. The thought of being stuck with a headless angel and a pile of tombstones scared her, but admitting she was afraid was equally impossible. It seemed forever as she eventually hauled herself up onto the spine of the wings and waved the camera above her head, saw graves below and felt hemmed in by the dead. Even with her eyes shut, they remained there in rows behind her lids. The worms in her mind were whiter than Elm's legs.

'Stay just like that! Don't move.' He was a quarter of the way up the twisting trunk of the sycamore, ignoring the roughness of the broken bark as it rubbed against his trousers. 'Pass the camera, As-pic!'

'Asp, Asp! My name is A-S-P. I'm not a jelly.' She made the mistake of looking down for a second time and dropped the camera, knocking Jean-Pierre's head as he made a grab for it. 'SORR-Y. HELP!' It was not that she was so high up, but each time she turned in a different direction, the act of turning sharpened her fear. 'I hate you, Jean-Pierre!'

'Look at me.' His own face revealed nothing as he rescued the camera from where it was caught on a branch and dusted the lens with his sleeve.

There was a bitter taste at the back of Asp's throat as he aimed at her face and clicked.

'Get me down, Jean-Pierre. NOW. It's... against the law... being stuck up here.' If it had been possible, she would have thrown herself at him and risked the consequences. 'I'm going to be sick.'

'Don't move.'

'Told you. I can't.'

'Stay there.'

'Stop saying that.'

'I'll get down first. I'll catch you.'

'Okay. Go on then. I feel sick. It's your fault if I'm sick all over you!'

She had been a pest from the beginning. He shrugged his shoulders and blew through his lips quietly.

'What if you drop me?' Asp made a small, swallowing sound.

He was silent when he finally jumped, feet together, precise in his movements. As he opened his arms to catch her, she fell, knocking him off balance, shouting and hitting him in feral bursts until he pushed her away, still kicking, still yelping until she found she couldn't breathe. Except she must have been breathing because she couldn't stop hiccoughing, and she saw that the tears that splashed onto her hands had made streaks in the dirt on her fingers, and their wetness was warm and alive. In silence, they picked up their bikes and shook their handlebars and cycled home like strangers on the road.

There would be no return to the way they were before the fall. Jean-Pierre was to stay with his parents for Christmas and the Thrush family would recover from the strain of temporarily living with an outsider by eating too many beef sausages in a perverse fit of gluttony, given that the whole country was in fear of mad cow disease.

When Jean-Pierre returned from France, the family slipped into resentful sullenness, and Daphne continued to boil the ham dry or provide a watery mashed potato that satisfied no one while Granny poured Henry's Christmas cognac on the stewed fruit throughout the day, ensuring that she and Leaf were permanently warm by eating all of it. Jean-Pierre, if he'd been asked, would have argued that nothing fundamental had changed in the Thrush household with the arrival of a new year.

***

'Murder most foul,
As in the best it is,
But this most foul, strange and unnatural.'
Hamlet

CHAPTER 4

It is true that Jean-Pierre always brought out the devilish side of me. Although we never argued openly anymore, and though I took great pains to be sweetie-pie nice to him when we were together, I was always looking for ways of taunting him, wrong-footing him and generally making him feel unsettled without letting him suspect I was the source.

We never talked about sex, the war with Iraq, September 11th or anything that was recent or happening now. It was usually about why Napoleon was a great general, and since I hadn't got past the ancient Romans at school, I thought it was really mean of him to take advantage of my ignorance.

But that's not the only reason I had it in for him on such a sustained level. He implied I was crap at the violin when his playing was always way off the note, and I thought he should have listened to himself. Jean-Pierre had a tin ear. If he had the slightest musical understanding, he would have given up long ago out of consideration for those who had to hear him practise.

One morning I skipped school because it was the annual

swimming gala and I hate crowds. Besides, no one in my family seemed to mind if I went to it or not. Even in summer, the changing rooms were cold enough to kill a verruca, and the pool looked more like a skating rink because there was so much frost in the air.

I knew Jean-Pierre was still at his posh French lycée sailing through his *baccalaureat*, so I unlocked the door to his room for one of my regular snoops. Months had passed since the day we visited the graveyard, but I decided to look for the photos again, hoping that he hadn't taken them back to France last half-term. Just when I was about to give up the search, I noticed his violin lying on the bed outside of its case. I lifted the lid out of habit, as I do my own, and not because I thought I'd find anything inside. You know. Run your fingers idly over the lip of the case. Feel the snap of the clip. Hey presto. The lid's back. It's open. And there they were. Hundreds of them. Stacked neatly along the green velvet lining, tied up in rubber bands.

I'm not sure how many there were, exactly. But each image had the same crazy expression – like a gargoyle with its tongue hanging out and wings above its head. Except it was my face. How dare he hoard me like that, tied up in those little elastic bands next to his violin bow? I grabbed the lot and started ripping. I found the negatives inside an envelope in his rosin box and cut each one into thin strips with scissors from his desk. I shoved them up the chimney inside some tartan socks with little gold studs on the ankles. To punish him, I stole the pins and paperclips from his odds and sods box under his bed before I let it slip several days later that I thought Granny had a spare key to his room after all.

'I'll kill her,' he had said as if he meant it.

'Why?

'Because,' and he hesitated, not because he needed to consider what to say but to add emphasis to what he said, 'because she disgusts me.'

I was thrilled by that reply. The idea that she disgusted him was, well, unexpected, I suppose, and shocking. I didn't question if he meant what he said. I wanted him to know I felt the same way, even though it hadn't occurred to me to think that before now. If I felt cross with anyone in my family, it was usually because they had done something or said something I disagreed with. It had never been a case of their existence being the cause of my dislike. I breathed in deeply before I spoke.

'Me too,' I said.

'Yes, well then.'

I understood from his violent feelings that the missing negatives and photographs had affected him more than I imagined. I also knew by the deliberate way he spoke that he had no intention of telling me any more as he was already turning the pages of the enormous Latin-French dictionary on his desk as a sign I should go. It is also true that I mistrusted Jean-Pierre as much as he mistrusted me.

'She wants to join the Salvation Army,' I said to catch his attention and because it was true. Granny liked the bonnet.

He looked up straightaway, still flicking the pages.

'Granny's leaving home, you see,' I continued, sure now that I had his attention. 'She'd rather live with people who think like her. At least that's what she keeps on saying.'

'When's she leaving?'

'Sometime this weekend.'

I was staring at the hairs around Jean-Pierre's chin. They sprouted outwards like an old lady's. If I thought I could have got away with it, I would have cut them off with the scissors on his desk. I had a thing about scissors. Instead, I asked,

'Do you want to play *Pick-a-stick*?'

'No.'

'Of course Granny keeps saying she'll leave home, but she only ever goes as far as the pond and back. My father says she's welcome to go.'

'Has he asked her to leave?' Jean-Pierre closed his book and lowered his eyelids until all I could see was the dark curl of his eyelashes.

'Of course. Lots of times. But my mum just tells them to stop being so ridiculous.'

Jean-Pierre was now staring at me the way you look into a mirror, without emotion, just staring at me. It was my look. Thief.

'And what does Elm think about your grandmother?'

'No one knows what Elm thinks except Elm. Are you sure you don't want a game?'

'Quite sure.'

That was the end of the discussion. I was satisfied that I'd given him something to think about and left wearing his slippers, hiding them later in the airing cupboard, which I thought was a fairly vengeful, Granny sort of thing to do. I reckon it was the last time we ever talked about her while she was alive. On the following Sunday, she did genuinely fall down the cellar stairs. Just like the dream. Well, almost.I don't know how long it was I left her lying in the cellar, but I do remember Jean-Pierre coming down and finding me crouching beside her. He was, I have to admit this, quite amazing. It was as if he had lived all his life for a moment like it. I was feeling guilty, I suppose, and sorry for what I'd done. I was definitely afraid of the consequences and looked shocked where he seemed – there's no other word for it – exhilarated.

'We'll have to bury her here. We'll never manage to get her up the stairs without someone noticing. We'll have to hide her under the coal.'

'Won't she smell?'

'Not if we bury her properly. No air. No smell.'

And I believed him because I wanted to. It was true the coal heap had lain untouched and ignored in twenty years of modern living. The family stepped around it on the rare occasions when they visited the cellar. Beer and wine were kept in the kitchen for convenience, and long-forgotten dress-ups were stored below in a rusty freezer that was permanently switched off.

The freezer was too bulky to be removed and was wedged behind the supporting pole of the staircase with a pile of family games heaped on its lid. Like so much else in the cellar, these should have been thrown away long ago, being damaged or incomplete – along with Henry's old bike with the wobbly seat, a grey metal filing cabinet containing the previous owner's bank statements, a few unused gardening tools plus a large axe hanging on a back wall. And now dead Granny on the floor.

'People look smaller when they're dead,' I said.

Jean-Pierre swore in French. Something like *'sacre bleu'* or '*merde*'. I may be making that bit up. I don't suppose he really believed that death could shrink someone. He'd have said this was a case of my astigmatism leading me astray - a joke to everyone else except me.

No, I don't know why he then did something so alien as to agree with me. He'd never deferred to me before, but he was silently nodding when he reached up to get two spades off the wall and handed me one of them. There was no question of how did she die, let's call the doctor, the police, my parents or the undertakers. Neither of us thought of saying that Granny had tripped by mistake. Which she could have...

We both worried that no one would believe me. It was just straight into how we could dispose of the body before anyone caught us at it. Extraordinary really, and the strangest thing was that I could remember feeling a surge of happiness that he was taking over. I remember I stopped feeling afraid and started shovelling.

We could hear Leaf crying as usual in the kitchen and my parents walking about from room to room. I heard my brother going upstairs at some point when I paused between shovels, but obviously, no one heard us because we were left undisturbed. I found I could push lumps of coal from one spot to another or make little scrapes around Granny's feet and legs, but I could not bring myself to actually touch any of her body. I left that to Jean-Pierre. In fact, I'm a bit muddled about what happened next.

I'm fairly sure I left the cellar before he had finished covering her up. It was his suggestion. Thank God. I had no desire to savour her dead look in any way. I am not sentimental, but I can sometimes be quite squeamish. There had been a nagging thought at the back of my head that a person who took weirdo pictures of tombstones might make the perfect gravedigger. There was also the scary possibility that Granny might not be quite dead yet, and if this could be so, either as a triumph of will on my part or as a physical fact, I did not want to be the one who buried her alive. Poor Granny. Lying stiff under a pile of coal. Ouch.

***

'There is something in this more than natural, if philosophy could find it out.'
Hamlet

CHAPTER 5

The day Granny disappeared.

Asp was a pain. Let's face it. She was never going to change fundamentally. Maybe an interest in underwear or reading matter. Bach versus David Bowie. Stuff like that. Elm had been lying on his bed more or less since lunch, waiting for his sister to emerge from her sulk in the cloakroom and to come to his room for a bitch about everyone except himself, as she could hardly do that without him chucking her out.

He'd been to a lot of trouble during the night decorating his bedroom with messages on lavatory paper that said *Happy Days Aspirin* and *Beware of the Asp* or *How to Avoid Asphyxia Without Really Trying* and *Hello Babe, I am your Brother for Life.* He had been expecting her since first thing in the morning, and here it was, practically six o'clock in the evening, and she was still hiding. The worst of it was he could have done something while he was waiting – such as design a computer program or make a go-cart. Instead, he chewed the cuffs of his jumper, somehow managing to wrap an empty biscuit tin with a picture of bluebirds on the lid after lining it with tissue paper.

This was to be his present to Asp – a box to store her collection of relics from the riverbed: Roman nails, dead slugs, rusty buttons and the odd stone fossil dragged home in a bucket whenever the tide was low. She hoarded them in a treasure chest under her bed along with her miscellaneous trinkets and would leave them and forget about them until once or twice a year when they were taken out for examination. It was as if she believed the secrets of the world were locked inside each one. He had not yet decided to give her his agate eggs, which he knew she coveted but to which he was still quite attached.

***

Asp did come to my room eventually that day. This all happened a few years ago, so I might miss out some of the detail. She was covered in soot and said something about cleaning Pa's bicycle in the cellar. Fell in the coal heap was her explanation, but I had the feeling this was not the truth. At least not the whole of it. I often get strong feelings about lots of things. People assume I have none because I'm quiet and like computers. Like computers? What a fatuous, inadequate description. Sub-text: must be one of those syndromey people who always plays video games and masturbates in the shower. No artistic sensibilities. Does not drink or shag or burn in hell. Nothing so exciting. Just greasy hair with plastic trainers and an iPad.

'Happy birthday,' I said.

'Is it?'

'Well, I've got something for you.'

'What?'

'This.'

I held out the old bluebird tin for her flotsam and jetsam, and she burst into tears.

'It's lovely, Elm. You know, you're a much nicer brother than any of my friends' brothers.'

'Oh, please.'

'And I really like all the messages and things you've hung up. It must have taken a long time.'

'Hours 'n' hours, but then I've had plenty of time, haven't I?'

'You're so original, Elm. No one except me appreciates you in this family.'

'What about Granny?'

I said this, knowing that Asp liked to believe her feelings were peculiarly hers and were totally more significant because of this. Anyway, she looked as if I'd hit her and started crying again. People often get the wrong end of the stick about Asp. They think she must be some kind of monster because they have such narrow definitions of what is or is not responsible human behaviour. In their terms, there is no justification for her outrageousness, and the trouble is that when she gets pissed off about some injustice, she behaves like the Incredible Hulk on a bad day. It's horrible, and yet, in a way, it's exciting and heroic when the buttons burst.

I have a perfect example. Asp was near the end of primary school, and she hadn't yet spurned the local grammar, or maybe it was the other way around. Neither of us had any real friendships outside of playgrounds, but I suppose everyone has a friend who isn't a real friend, and our lodgers fell into that category. We had our second one - Anne-Marie Dupuis - who was newly arrived for the summer holidays after Jean-Pierre's departure. She and I used to bond by watching Open University maths programmes on Sunday mornings when the rest of the house was asleep. In our hunger for knowledge, we sometimes lost discernment.

I remember Anne-Marie kept on asking if there were any dead rats or mice under our floorboards because there was a funny smell near the hallway. Almost all our lodgers had names with hyphens and would make us practise saying ridiculous things like: '*Ou est Jean-Pierre? Il est dans le jardin avec Anne-Marie et Nicole-Heloise.*' Anyway, I mention the lodgers' names only to secure chronology. It was somewhere in *that* period and not long after Granny disappeared.

A few girls known as 'the local bitches' were hanging around the bus stop around the corner from our house. We knew them all by sight, if not by name. They were getting nasty among themselves and we could hear it on the other side of the road where we were waiting for a bus in the opposite direction. They were picking on the runtiest, scraggiest, most pathetic one among them. Kicking and punching her, tugging the ponytail on top of her head as a way of holding onto her. Laughing at her trainers because they were last year's design and they had the wrong logo or something like that.

'Slag, shit, fuckin' cunt. Bitch-cow, fuck off, yeah, fuckin' slag. Yes-fuck no-fuck.' It wasn't just the yelling that scared us. More the look of menace as they gathered around. I could see the terror on the girl's face through the gaps between their bodies. Like flickers when you pass a paling fence. Asp saw it too. Before Anne-

Marie or I could stop her, Asp was off, zigzagging between cars. Screaming. Not words. Just screaming as she ran towards them. Like she was painted in woad or something.

She was so wild and crazy that she scared them off, and I'm still not sure how Asp knew she could get away with it. The bitches just disappeared, and their victim followed. Vanished before she could get to them. In a matter of seconds, a bus arrived on the other side, and there was no one to get on it and no one to get off. It felt like part of a parable, that great red bus without any passengers, with not one of us going anywhere.

Then Asp waved back at us and grinned. We met in the middle of the road, and as I put my arm around her, I could feel her shaking. It was odd that we never talked about it, never picked over what had happened. If I think about it now, I feel ashamed that I just watched it all from a distance. And yet, if it happened again tomorrow, I suppose things would be the same. I survive by staying outside of most things really, which means I miss out on the excitement sometimes. I admire Asp because she flouts the rules that I obey, or at least some of them, and I think I'm the loser in all of this, not her. That's my opinion.

Anyway, we caught the next bus in the opposite direction, taking Asp with us. I ended up on a seat behind both girls and in front of a man so fat he took up the whole seat. Anne-Marie was busy telling Asp how that sort of outrage would never happen in her little village.

The fat man was eating chocolate biscuits, and every now and then some crumbs would fall down the back of my neck. Although he ate silently enough and made no sounds suggesting he was going to be sick, I had this overwhelming fear that he would throw up any minute onto my head. Instead of moving somewhere else, I sat there thinking about it for the rest of the journey, shrinking into my seat and willing myself, not him, to dissolve into the ether. Ever since, when I travel by bus, I have to stand all the way even if there are empty seats.

***

'Say you? Nay, pray you, mark.'
Hamlet

CHAPTER 6

The same Sunday in June that Granny disappeared – before Jean-Pierre left and before Anne-Marie arrived:

'Asp? Asp, ASP, is that you, dear? Are you with ELM?' Daphne was on her way to Elm's room. Her voice was swelling with each phrase as she came nearer. 'Is JEAN-PIERRE with you?'

'No.' Elm turned to the wall and groaned. 'He's not.'

'Everybody seems to be somewhere you don't expect them to be. Except for your father... and Leaf. I'm looking for Granny. I can't find her anywhere.'

Tossing the black and white striped curtain away from Elm's bed and scratching her head in a continuous, neurotic act of restlessness, her round face looked drawn.

'Have you tried the bottom of the garden?' He'd say anything to get his mother out of the room.

'Good heavens, Asp.' She eyed her daughter with surprise. 'Why the sweep's look?'

In his own room and everywhere, Elm found his mother embarrassing. He could imagine that when she was younger and prettier, though he wasn't sure about the latter, even if she insisted she had been once, she might be gushy or annoying, and no one would notice. But the way she spoke to him now, even more than what she actually said, made him grind the enamel of his teeth. He avoided her as much as he could and told his friends that she must be drunk when she was merely being fatuous.

'Elllllllm.' To Elm, his mother sounded like a vacuum cleaner with the switch left on and no one to push it around. 'I want you to do something for me. I want you to go to the pond and see if Granny's chatting to the ducks. She must have forgotten to come home.'

'Now?' He thought about labels being muddled at the hospital when he was born. He had these thoughts regularly.

'Right now, please darling… Asp? I think you should have a shower and get rid of that soot.' She was holding the curtain up to the light, inspecting it for moth holes before opening the window and thrusting the entire swag outside into the evening air. The material billowed and snapped from behind as she pressed her bulk against its hem and shivered. He had read about mistakes with nametags. This was strangely consoling.

'My petal,' he could hear his mother cooing to his sister as they headed for the bathroom, 'I meant to tell you how grown up you've become. Have you seen Jean-Pierre in the last hour or so?'

Asp's reply was unclear but went something along the lines of 'what do you expect since I'm only eleven?' as Daphne began singing, 'oh where, oh where has the little dog gone, oh where, oh where can he be?' And Elm assumed that Jean-Pierre must be the little dog since his mother treated the entire family as deprived and should-be-grateful pets. None of them paid her much attention, and that was okay because she failed to notice the depths of their indifference. She just kept on fussing until they felt guilty and eventually did what she asked, and afterwards, she would be so pleased with them they'd wish they'd never done it.

Elm grabbed a waterproof torch and left for the pond, although the light was still midsummer, and he could see without a problem. He was afraid she might have tripped and fallen into the water without anyone noticing, but there was no sign of Granny in or out of the pond, and when he returned, his mother was in a panic, talking of geriatric rapes, fatal heart attacks and abductions by aliens.

His father said he would ring the police and ask if they knew anything. Jean-Pierre had materialized in his silent way and was sitting at the kitchen table playing a game of solitaire. Asp, he told Elm, had gone to bed early with a headache and would he, Elm, care for a French lesson right now?

'Yes,' replied the younger boy, unusually happy to retreat for a session of *Ou est ta Grand'mere?*

'Elle est disparue, malheureusement.'

'Quel dommage.'

'Peut-être elle reviendra demain.'

'Oui, peut-être.'

I told Jean-Pierre straightaway that I was not in the mood for French homework. This was a tricky business because I knew he got a concession for his room on the understanding that he helped me with the odd prose and other stuff, like learning the irregular verbs or getting to grips with past participles and the subjunctive. But tonight, he had no interest in me mauling the verb 'to be' or any other verb. There were no excuses on either side. He sat down on the floor in his kimono, which I thought was so cool because it was just black and white checks like a chessboard and nothing else. He leant against my bed and launched into a lengthy monologue about how he liked painting lead toy soldiers before the last day of exams. It was a poetic riff in almost flawless English.

'Do you have any paints we could use, Elm? He produced from his pockets an assortment of miniature metal figures, some white, some pink, but most of them a dull bluish grey. 'I want to finish these before I go home, and I thought you might like to help me.' We painted bloody toy soldiers for most of the night. The world of Voltaire and French grammar was a million miles away. He told me that what he would really like to do one day was to work for Walt Disney, although his father had dreams of him becoming a priest.

'But you never go to church,' I said when he told me this. 'I thought if you wanted to be some sort of monk, you'd show you were keen or something. Before you became one.'

'I didn't say I wanted it,' said Jean-Pierre. 'I said my father did.' The fingers of one hand fluttered across his face like a woman playing with a fan. There was a femininity about the movement, but also contained in such delicacy was the expression of an aesthete. His waving hands and fancy footwork when he jumped downstairs with both feet together very fast or the way he lowered his eyelids as he did now, infinitely slowly when he chose to question something. This contrariness of tempos startled and beguiled me. I'd never met anyone like him.

'You see Elm, my father is a God-drunk. God for him is in everything.'

But I only half understood. I was hooked more by the intense way he talked. Of course I wanted to understand his point of view. No one had ever bothered to sit down and chat with me before apart from Asp, and I was flattered by this new intimacy with someone from outside the family. I sort of twigged that he was trying out ideas without expecting me to question them. They could have been rubbish theories, and I'd still have agreed. I was there to encourage and admire, I suppose. I tried not to disappoint him, and he made a thing of assuming I would understand most of what he said. I was hardly going to admit that I often didn't.

'My father says there's no such thing as free will, you understand. Then he goes and imposes his own on me, which means that I don't have any, but he does. He thinks he's freeing me by denying me any choice.'

'You mean you can only do what *he* wants.'

'*Oui*,' which he pronounced as 'weahhh.'

'That doesn't seem fair.'

Jean-Pierre removed a dribble of paint from the tip of a rifle, revealing a minuscule hole, which he made a great show of scrutinising in silence. He brushed the surrounds, blowing on it carefully before holding it close to the eye, then stretching it at a distance with his arm pointing in the direction of the light above.

My mother, in a Blanche DuBois moment, had fitted economy light bulbs in each room, but even their faint wattage gave the colours an iridescent glow that was beautiful. There was a sort of amazing pointlessness to the detail of these figures, which, unless you have painted toy soldiers, you don't appreciate.

'What sort of things do you like drawing then?' I asked when we were lining up our men and again blowing gently on the bits that gleamed wetter than the rest. I was particularly proud of a foot soldier I had painted with a yellow sword and a gash of scarlet down his side that was intended as blood.

'Old ladies who fall down the cellar stairs. Old ladies that die because you hit them on the head with a hammer.'

'I know. So you draw an egg on their head like in a cartoon.'

'No,' he replied. 'No eggs.'

'Like Tom and Jerry after a fight then. They just... reappear.'

He looked right through me, I thought, and he smiled, even though I could see he was unhappy.

'Everything has gone back to the beginning of the story. Then when it starts again, you wonder if the old lady will have a different accident next time around or the same one.'

I really didn't understand what he was talking about this time. As he spoke, he leaned towards me until his nose was close to mine. 'I'm never going to get married. People can't escape from each other. They always quarrel when they marry. My parents are always quarrelling. Nothing ever changes there.'

'Oh.' I was embarrassed by his closeness, turning over the lead figure with the blood running down its side and trying to decide if I should restore it with a blue splodge. 'What will you do with these soldiers then?'

'Present a battle.' He looked as if he was staring at the world when he leaned back at last. 'Lots of deaths before the resurrection.'

I remember thinking what an odd thing to say, but because he was in the habit of looking at small details from a distance, I believe it made him say unexpected things.

'I understand. You have to bring them back to have more battles.' Maybe I was getting the hang of Jean-Pierre's mind at last.

'If you like. Goodnight, Elm. I'm going to bed.'

'It's... it's so you have a reason to get up in the morning,' I persisted, wishing he'd stay longer, not daring to ask.

'If you like.'

Jean-Pierre was already somewhere else. I think now... and I might be wrong... that he sort of wanted to be closer to me, but he didn't know how. I was his distraction... from studying. I'm not sure I'm right, except that he always used to make a point of brushing past me when we met on the stairs. It was only ever on the stairs... and it seemed that he was the one that was doing the brushing. It never happened with anyone else in the family.

An occasional meeting might be accidental the first few times, I'd tell myself, but it's not something you expect to happen every day. Granny would walk all the way up or down again to avoid passing another person on the stairs because she thought it was bad luck, and I remember when I was on the landing, just before Jean-Pierre's *bacc blanc*, I pressed myself back against the wall so he had enough room to get round and he still jumped into me from several stairs above. Front on, hard.

We both said 'sorry' at the same time, but I didn't mind too much because it didn't hurt. I thought it was funny. It made me laugh. Usually, it was just a hand or an arm against my shoulder, but it was definitely not my imagination or my doing.

'Goodnight,' he said as he left quickly.

And that was that. It was one of the things I liked about Jean-

Pierre. He never bothered with elaborate exits or entrances, despite the bumping thing. He didn't feel the need to explain his actions to anyone.

***

'Give every man thine ear, but few thy voice;'
Hamlet

CHAPTER 7

Daphne telephoned the police the night Granny failed to return from her afternoon walk. Of course she did. She loved her mother despite her annoying habits. She rang the police, the hospital, the National Missing Persons Helpline and the Salvation Army. She rang again the next day and the next. As a child, she had woken up one morning and found there was no one else in the house for no reason she could remember, and ever since, that fear of desertion remained.

She kept on ringing helplines, but the answer was always the same. No news. She telephoned the only other known relatives, Granny's sister Rose in Inverness and her brother-in-law, Hamish, but they had lost contact after her mother had accused Rose of stealing her nine-carat gold earrings from her denture pot.

Henry said he would place an ad in the missing person's section of the local paper. (This was after Jean-Pierre's return to France with a cheque for £500 from the French consulate as a prize for his excellent *baccalaureat.*)

No one responded to his ad asking for information about an elderly lady called Camilla Pod, probably wearing blue gloves, a beige overcoat and a pair of distressed shoes. He forgot to mention that she was also wearing a tweed suit in mid-summer because she was permanently afraid of catching a cold. That might have been helpful. But Henry was not seriously expecting a response. Her few intimate friends were long dead. Who outside the family would care?

Jean-Pierre had been gone for three weeks when the police finally agreed to investigate in earnest. It was also the time when Daphne and the rest of the family began their official mourning.

With the arrival of the law, the pond was drained and the only body that was found belonged to a dead duck. The sergeant assigned to the case seemed in his baldness, notebook, trench coat and fondness for drinking tea without really enjoying it, the epitome of a mild-mannered detective in a police procedural on telly.

Henry, Daphne, Elm and Asp had gathered in the front room in a show of family spirit for their telly police. There was a sense that each one of them was rehearsing lines for a new drama as they chatted haphazardly, trying to remember their script.

'I am staring at her empty chair, and there's that moment when I forget she's gone, and I put out her cup and plate with her knife next to the peanut butter, and I expect her to just walk through the door and join us for breakfast.'

This was Daphne snuffling into her teacup, secretly enjoying the naked wrist of the sergeant sitting opposite her. She had not given up on the importance of sexual feelings or believing that ordinary life should be suspended after a tragedy that was, she argued to herself, not yet officially confirmed. 'We are meant to be a family of six,' she added unnecessarily.

'Plus a lodger.'

'Though he's not with us anymore.'

'We're waiting for the next one to come.'

'Is it possible Mrs Pod might go away without telling you?'

The sergeant looked across at Daphne, writing down something on his spiral pad as Henry answered.

'We barely gave it a thought.'

Not, the sergeant noted to himself, *that they have not given it thought, but barely.* He had yet to get the full measure of the husband and was tired of making small talk in such bleak circumstances to people with whom he was beginning to think he had nothing in common.

'So you thought it unlikely,' he said wearily, closing his notebook before opening it again almost immediately. 'Am I right?' He then reminded himself that every case deserved his attention.

'My mother-in-law is a very old lady without any friends.'

'That we know of,' said Daphne.

Henry moved closer to the sergeant. 'We are a family that keeps to itself. How could she go away? Where would she go?'

He was so close the sergeant shifted his chair into a corner.

'Her own sister does not *speak* to her. We provide the only home she knows. I tell you, there is nowhere for her to go ***to***.' Frustration at being geographically avoided by the sergeant, his fist punched the air, and everyone else looked away out of embarrassment. 'Bugger, bugger, bugger,' he kept repeating to himself as he tried unsuccessfully to read the policeman's scribble until finally, all that could be heard were the snorts of Leaf as he chewed on his dummy. His wife's salty tears kept slipping into her tea, creating a scum on the surface of the liquid. When Henry passed by in his agitated state, she took his hand in hers to remind them both of some notional allegiance. Elm was gnawing at his cuffs, wondering if he could hack into an Interpol computer, and Asp was cutting up the end of her father's newspaper into thin, uneven strips and was staring at her lap. The constable was studying the flock wallpaper, and the sergeant was shaking his head.

'The Salvation Army. That's where she'd go.' Asp's shrill voice took them all by surprise. 'I bet if you ask them properly, they'd have another look and find there's someone just like her with a different name living in their house. I bet she's having soup right now in their kitchen.'

'It's possible,' said the sergeant cautiously.

Asp looked at both policemen and continued scrunching up her strips of paper in both hands. 'She was always going on about how you could tell what soup they were having from the next street away.'

'Yes. Well. She was an observant person, your grandmother.'

The child made him uncomfortable. The sergeant sipped his tea and listened to the sounds of distant traffic. She was filibustering, but he was unable to pin it down. He'd come back to her on his own terms later.

There was something about the way she narrowed her eyes and opened them again very slowly that reminded him of his own mother-in-law. Or was it a spider weighing up a wasp, in which case, which one of them was the wasp? He decided not to believe a word out of her mouth until he had reason to think otherwise.

'Now about your recent lodger, Mrs Thrush.' The sergeant turned towards Daphne to restore his sense of order. 'I mean the one that was living with you when Mrs Pod disappeared. Jean-Jacques or is it Jacques-Jean?' Ridiculous that a child of eleven could have such an effect on him. 'The lodger's gone back to France, you say. Well then – I suppose you have an address you could give me?'

'Yes. Why yes, of course. Jean-Pierre. Jean-Pierre Levin. He stayed with us for his *baccalaureat.* I'll get the address book for you.' Daphne felt her cheeks reddening and wished that they wouldn't.

'Would you like me to write out his address?' asked Henry.

'That's very kind of you, but I can copy it out.'

'Levin. *Levin.* Jean-Pierre Levin. See?' Henry looked triumphant over such a little thing. 'It's between '*Le Monde*' and '*Lobotomies.*' He began prodding his index finger over the relevant spot in their address book. This was Henry playing the pissed-off schoolteacher. 'Got it?' he asked, suddenly bored and wanting to fix one of the servos in his model plane or sustain himself through any further mithering by dreams of perfect flying weather.

'Granny disappeared before Jean-Pierre returned to France.' Elm spoke softly to defuse the significance of what he said.

The sergeant closed his pad and groped at the zip on his briefcase. It was not that he was ignoring Elm. He was giving himself time to think.

'Exactly. That's my point too.'

The sergeant realised he would rather deal with the boy than the girl, being generally more confident in interpreting his own sex.

He stood up to signal the interview was over as Asp bit her lip until she could taste blood. She was trying to sort out in her mind whether or not the sergeant was a clever man. It mattered to her that he was, and she decided that if he turned back to look at her when he went out of the room, she had better watch out.

'Goodbye,' he waved, turning full circle and grinning at the whole family like one of those puppets you have to shoot at a fair. 'WE will do everything we can to locate Mrs Pod – and we'll be in touch.'

'I have no idea why my mother would want to leave us without any explanation,' Daphne whispered, following the sergeant down the front path and holding the sleeping Leaf in her arms. 'She might have caught a bus to Belgium and we'd never know.'

The sergeant turned and caught the end of her smile plus the milk stain on her collar where the baby had posseted. He felt sorry for her in his own way. He was not so brutalised by his job that he could no longer feel pity, and he was pleased he was still an old softie despite the daily grind of pimps, druggies and the generally shifty sperm of postmodern society. He also had a certain tendresse for a maternal bosom, and Daphne's loomed up at him like a sweet promise from behind the baby's head.

'No one is saying that she did, Mrs Thrush.' The material of her dress was so thin he could imagine what was underneath. She looked at him uncertainly.

'The trouble is, I don't know what to think. My mother has

impulses like a child without exactly being in her second childhood. She can be difficult. But I find it hard to accept she might want to disappear from her home without explanation. In a strop.'

'In a strop. Yes, well. Families do funny things in a strop.' He coughed and clutched at the cigarette packet inside his pocket with one hand, opening the car door with the other.

'Not that she was in one, to my knowledge. I believe she was feeling optimistic that day because my husband had promised to build her some bookshelves in her room.'

It was a pity the sergeant thought *that he always had to leave when things became interesting.* He was regretting telling his wife he was giving up smoking. He recognised that his ability to decide to do something and then do nothing about it was pathological. He would pick up the interesting thread of strops another time.

Very slowly, he wound down the window next to where the constable sat fast asleep, nudged him on the shoulder, stirring him awake, not roughly, but in a way that suggested this was a regular pattern. They were an established duo. More a Laurel and Hardy than Tweedle-Dum and Tweedle-Dee, with the constable playing Laurel as he was the thinner of the two and had the face of a marrow.

'Wake up, PC Petrovich. Back to the station. Let's catch some crooks.'

It was strange the way you always came closer to the nub of things when you were shutting up shop. *People let down their guard,* he thought as he waved goodbye to the wife through the open window. 'We'll keep you informed, Mrs Thrush. I'll be back.

I promise.'

'Thank you, Inspector. And Inspector...'

'Yes?'

'I'm sorry. I've forgotten your name.'

'Love, Mrs Thrush. Sergeant Cedric K Love. I am not yet Inspector. Soon though. Soon.'

'The boy, Sergeant Love,' she hesitated. 'I mean, Jean-Pierre.' She found she was shouting across the top of the constable to make herself heard above the street noises from the main road lower down. 'Jean-Pierre – he was a model lodger. I thought you should know that.'

'Thank you, Mrs Thrush. I appreciate that.'

And so the sergeant knew that Daphne realised he thought it was possible her mother had been murdered. 'Anything in our line of work is possible,' he confided to PC Porfiry Petrovich as he leant forward and readjusted his rear-vision mirror.

'A body needs to be disposed of in a humane and hygienic way,' he murmured. They had turned a corner and were passing a funeral parlour. 'It doesn't have to be a silk cushion with a bunch of lilies. Though it still needs recognition – or at least be acknowledged as dead. If you don't have that ritual, it seems to me your life becomes dependent on the return of the person who's missing from it.'

'Yes, sir.' PC Petrovich, half-asleep, was worried that he would miss the start of a contemporary music concert on the car radio.

'Alright then. Let's...' Sergeant Love attempted to cover his bald patch with a length of hair from the other side of his head using his free hand and realised he'd have to let it grow another centimetre. 'Let's talk about the missing person. You need to know whether they're dead or not. Are you listening, PC?'

His constable was huddled over the radio in search of a specific frequency. The blare of changing stations, sudden and violent in their dissonance, was creating its own electronic concert. Sergeant C K Love found himself grinding his teeth and feeling for the packet of cigarettes in his coat pocket.

'I'm listening, sir,' said Porfiry Petrovich.

'This is where we come in, Constable. Can't you turn that bloody thing down? As policemen, you understand, it is also our job to put minds at rest.'

'Not bodies, sir?' PC Porfiry had turned the volume to a whisper. He may have kept failing his police exams due to the number of hours he spent creating avant-garde sound effects, but he tried to remain a policeman while on duty. Even in his daydreams, he invariably began a conversation with a confessed murderer by saying:

'Well, let me tell you, I don't consider it necessary to justify my actions, but I would appreciate it if you could explain to me why you did it in the first place.' And then, when the murderer has confessed, PC Porfiry would arrest him, and the case would be solved.

The sergeant stared at the road ahead as PC Porfiry Petrovich repeated his question. 'So we don't put bodies to rest, sir?'

'Well yes, of course, PC. Sometimes we put bodies to rest. Would you make up your bloody mind what it is we're meant to be listening to?'

The sergeant would say he was more of a Bach and Handel man. 'Sometimes,' he snapped, pressing hard on the accelerator and revving up the engine in his revenge, 'there can be no rest given. It's none of our business, and it's better to let the person we're dealing with find out what's wrong from within.'

The sergeant wouldn't object when his partnership with PC Porfiry came to its official end next month. The constable had turned into an annoying piece of grit recently.

Since the sergeant was to be promoted to inspector, he would be expecting new staff to replace the old. There was a young constable at the Barnes office with an interest in fly fishing who would make the perfect partner. Lah-dah-di-dah-amen.

'If you say so, sir,' replied PC Porfiry, slyly turning up the volume on the radio until further dialogue became impossible and Sergeant Love had, for a second or two, the suspicion that his constable could read his mind.

***

'... if thou
Wilt needs marry, marry a fool; for wise men
Know well enough what monsters you make of them.'
Hamlet

CHAPTER 8

Inspector C K Love and Constable Porfiry Petrovich did go their separate ways over the following months. The separation continued until the inspector's enthusiasm for salmon fishing waned following a bout of pneumonia. War had never ceased in the Middle East. Burglars were still in business. Traffic crimes increased – and the traffic. Pollution was tomorrow's sorrow. What's that? No way. It's existential – although between the departure of Jean-Pierre and the arrival of their next French lodger, the family attic was temporarily reserved for Daphne's artistic ambitions and Henry's model-making – not salvation of the planet.

His wife's canvases were painstakingly layered to resemble frogspawn with interconnecting swirls of mud from the garden and a richesse of paint. This was her tribute to Japanese expressionism. She was fond of saying she couldn't re-paint Rembrandt, but there was no danger of that. Henry's model aeroplanes were, by contrast, smooth and red or dayglo orange plastic, designed to be visible against the sky. They made Henry happy. That summer, his planes were suspended from the ceiling like gaudy, polished bats and providing the family ducked their heads on entering, there was room to move underneath. He intended to fly each one in the park and bring them down with an inevitable crash-landing, repairing any damage in good humour because that was the part he enjoyed most.

Chipping away at a broken tail or packing bits of lead into the fibreglass nose, he would sit on his chair at the top of the house and listen to the indignant chatter of his wife and family. Although he never admitted it, he looked forward to her small bursts of fury more than her rare moments of calm because she seemed less boring when disturbed.

Their separate contrariness was a relief because he felt able to switch off. Her perversity or anger allowed him to concentrate on his ailerons and elevators. It left him free to experiment with what he found most difficult in his hobby, which was the wiring since all the models were radio-controlled. Their baby, still called Leaf, was equally soothed by his mother's rants. He slept through her storms and the sounds of his father's pottering, safe in his pram in the corner of the room. This was meant to be one of those sublime days.

'The trouble is I still don't know what to think. Was it a hit man who got my mother, or was it a hit and run?' Daphne scratched her head and released a shower of white, powdery flakes like flurries of snow. Henry felt a shiver of disgust as they landed on the floor, narrowly avoiding his opened pots of adhesive.

'Like roadkill,' she added.

'Where's the body?' Henry yawned.

'Haven't a clue. Obviously.'

'Someone would have found her by now.'

'Did my mother have another life we don't know about?'

Henry pulled at some levers on his control unit and discovered his batteries were almost flat.

'My batteries need charging,' he said mournfully.

Daphne scraped the worms of dull brown paint on her palate. Along with her other thoughts, at least she understood there was not much point in his going to the park in the afternoon, which suited her just fine. Henry could child-mind Leaf for a change.

'Do I miss my mother? Do I? What I really mean is, am I glad she's not here to remind me of my duty to her as a daughter?'

She scratched at her neck with her nails, sharp, obsessive digging into the skin as Henry turned away to sand his tailpiece. He knew the pointlessness of telling her to stop. A weal formed on the back of her neck, and it was obvious that neither one of them was poised for a good day. It occurred to her that if she kept on like this, she'd have no skin left to scratch. She would apply some of Leaf's cream for nappy rash. Poor Daphne.

The boundaries of who she might be were defined by pain and touch, rarely pleasure. She was jealous of Henry as he lifted the glass fibre casing of his plane to his lips and blew on it, smoothing away any dust with his fingers before he sanded further around the edges, satisfied there were no bumps left on the surface. Henry could be relied on to ignore his own pain.

'She's my mother, yes,' she was saying. 'Well, maybe. *Was* my mother. I've never known for certain. But I wouldn't want her to die alone. Even if we had enough money for a ransom...'

'Assuming anyone asked for one.'

'And if we had it, you'd only want to buy another aeroplane. No. I don't wish her dead. Of course I don't. Do you?'

'Fuck.' Henry knocked over the largest pot of glue with his foot and was scraping up the drips with the heels of his socks. 'Fuck,' he repeated without much feeling as Daphne started up again.

'But if I think she's alive and hiding from us somewhere else, that's easier to deal with. At least I could remind myself how much she pissed me off.'

Henry was distracted by a warm sensation of stickiness in his feet. His toes were glueing themselves to his socks.

'My mother is a very manipulative person.'

'Pass me a cloth.'

She tossed a rag in his direction and watched, irritated, as he removed red and blue striped socks with quick, panicky tugs. 'Are you listening to me, Henry?'

Henry saw how his wife's stomach had drooped like a paddymelon underneath her smock, but he made no connection between the disinterest they felt for one another sexually and her appearance. Instead, he let his glasses slide slowly down his nose and stop in time at a bump on the bridge. It was something his own father used to do in idleness.

'I'm listening.' He wiped his toes with Daphne's rag until his feet were covered in a fast-drying paste that smelt foul.

Daphne patted her husband as she drifted past to collect another canvas and pulled in her belly. 'My mother resented me from the beginning. Was it my fault she was an unmarried mother? I'm not going to be sentimental about this. She is... she was a bloodless figure in my life. She never wanted to be anyone's parent. If I'd been a panda bear, she would have felt the same way. I refuse to feel a fake sense of loss. Can I have my cloth back? Your feet stink, Henry.'

'It's only glue.' He rolled one woollen sock inside the other and stuffed them both into his trouser pocket.

He was admiring the line between the fuselage and the plane, touching and stroking the smoothness of the join as Daphne reviewed her feelings of injustice. She was working on the story of her life to explain her choices to herself, not to Henry.

'I've spent whole years dreaming who else might have been my biological mother.'

'Just like Elm.'

But Daphne wasn't listening.

'And I'm quite sure I don't want to find out my real mother is Aunt Rose. She won't say it directly, of course. She just discards these little hints from time to time about sisters being like peas in a *pod*. Well, that's a joke, haha. I'm nothing like either of them.'

Henry patted the socks in his pocket. If he were Daphne, he'd shut up. She was losing her charm. It amazed him that she never said anything about her father or wondered who he might have been. Odd that.

'I can't think why Mother didn't say, *'I'm leaving for good... I hate washing up,'* or, *'you don't want me here. You're your Aunt Rose all over again. You're pretentious, Daphne, like her. Adieu.* A bientot. *Goodbye, sweetie-pie. Finito.'* What I want to know is how can she afford to *live* without us?'

'She could rob a bank.'

'Don't be stupid, Henry. She wouldn't dare.'

'Forget about her then.'

'I wish I could. Only last month she said, *'Listen to me, only daughter.'* Only? As if that made me precious. *'You're stressed,'* she said. *'I understand. You can trust me.'* Well now. That's a lie, obviously. *'You're going through a bad patch.'* Bad patch! What's that mean? Landfills?'

'Shut up. This is boring.'

'What?'

'I've just come to a tricky point with my servo settings and I can't hear myself think.'

'But you never do think, Henry.' She painted in angry silence for about a minute. *''What you need is counselling,'* she told me. 'Counselling?' I asked. *'Marriage guidance then.'* 'Oh, ha-ha,' I said. 'Now, that's funny.''

Henry removed his glasses and sighed, which she took as a signal to continue.

'A lover does it for free.'

'Does what?'

'Gives you advice.'

'Do you have a lover, Daphne?' Henry rubbed his eyes slowly.

'Don't be silly. I have something far more satisfying.'

'What?'

'If a wife tells her lover that she prefers the inside of her mind to a kitchen cupboard, the lover will think she's fascinating. Until one day, the lover notices that her left tit sags a bit, or he sees her putting too much butter on her toast, and suddenly it's her right tit that sags as well, and bingo, it's all over.'

'So what's more satisfying?' Henry replaced his glasses and shook his head in what Daphne mistook for sympathy. She leaned towards him and smiled, but he wasn't looking at her face.

'Do you know? I only just remembered. We never mentioned her shoes to the police. I mean the ones with holes cut for her bunions. They're missing.' Daphne hesitated, aware that Henry's mind was on his servo. 'Are you listening, Henry? They were her walking shoes. We forgot to tell the sergeant that they've disappeared.'

Henry eyed her tired, middle-aged body and tried to remember who she was. If only their quieter moments when expanded in the bedroom had been more adventurous, instead of twisting themselves with difficulty so that they ended up gently scraping at each other's corns.

When he was asleep, she would tiptoe to the bathroom and take the pink, vulcanised rubber dog bone, which she had cut and chiselled with a kitchen knife until it was just so, wrap it carefully in wadding wool, moistening it with hot water until it became the same temperature as her skin and slip the result inside a small plastic balloon that she reserved in an empty pot of cream for such purposes.

She would, in a moment of shame, turn out the light and shut the door to lie on the cold tiled floor, transporting herself to another world with her furtive rubbing... How would Henry ever understand?

'I suppose what I'm trying to say is,' she was speaking after a minute of unnatural silence between them, 'if those shoes are gone, which they are, she must have intended to go out. I don't believe my mother was kidnapped for a moment.'

'No one said she was.'

'But they might've thought it.'

'Rubbish.'

'Is it rubbish?' Daphne returned to the canvas, stabbing at its thick weave with her unclean brush. She was now reckless with purple. 'You never really listen to me. Except when I say...'

Large splodges of purple paint spilled across the floor and seeped through a crack in the floorboards. Daphne stood in the puddle and dreamed of buying the upholstery shop round the corner with a loan from the bank. She could try selling some of Leaf's smarter babygrows for a start. Almost every shop in the high street was selling somebody's cast-offs.

'As a society...'

Henry sighed. Daphne's anger had lost its edge and with it, scary woman had become... he shook his head... banal... tedious... Crime.

'We've got ourselves into a hell of a mess about the need to work.' Her chin shook indignantly. She glanced at the sleeping baby in the corner. 'Who looks after the children if the parents aren't around? A grandparent? A *missing* grandparent?'

Henry's head sank low on his chest, a family habit if you included Elm. He considered a spot of flying to cheer himself up, batteries willing.

'You don't suppose my mother tried to kill herself, do you?' Daphne made a choking sound. 'Whoopsie. There now, Leaf. My little monster is waking up, I see. Have you sensed that Mummy's going out? What a clever baby boy you are. You just suck away on your new orthodontic dummy until YOUR BIOLOGICAL MOTHER RETURNS BUT YOUR BIOLOGICAL DADDY WILL CHANGE YOUR NAPPY AND MASH YOU A NICE RIPE BANANA FOR YOUR SUPPER. Aren't you a lucky boy?'

A final splash of cobalt violet before realising how much she was in a hurry to be somewhere else. She scraped the remaining puddle on the floor with both shoes. 'We could always divorce, and I could bolt like Mother.'

'Daphne?'

'Yes, Henry?' She closed the lid of her paint box firmly.

'I thought this was your painting day. Where are you going?'

'Out. I'm tearing myself away from my art for a walk.'

'But I'm going to the park in a few minutes. The wind's just right.'

'Well, Henry, your battery's flat, so it doesn't matter. You can watch football on television with Leaf instead.'

Daphne looked forward to stopping at the police station on her way to the river. Henry could pull his weight for once and she could taste freedom already. 'ARE YOU LISTENING, HENRY? Ask Asp to do her violin practice...' Her voice grew stronger and more determined. 'Elm has to tidy his room, but I mean tidy, not a lot of old bus tickets and stale food shoved under the bed. Eggs are in the fridge, dear. BYE.'

He observed the quick, sideways movements of her head as she spoke. He noticed that her cheeks were flushed. He began to feel a faint stirring inside his trouser zipper, despite himself.

'Can you smell something a bit yuck, Henry? I've been meaning to ask you... Ever since Mother left us. Is the smell from downstairs? The cellar, maybe? Or is it just your socks? All of your socks?'

'Sod off, Daphne. It's just glue.'

The warm feeling he'd had was gone. He could hear some slurping sounds of Leaf biting into his dummy, and he scrunched the socks in his pocket even harder, squeezing them through a hole in the lining until they dropped to the floor. He stood on them as his wife was covering her paints with clingfilm and silently wishing the newly promoted inspector would allow his hairy, masculine hand to linger on her palate. Husband and wife, both with their separate and contrary longings.

Daphne climbed down the ladder to the main stairs and felt a small shiver of pleasure at the back of her womb, followed by another. She nearly always felt things twice she said and called them her corn moments. Husband and wife – with their separate, incurable longings.

'Bye, Henry.'

The front door slammed in the wind and the words, 'Bye, Leaf,' came to her as an afterthought walking down the path. 'Christ. You only get one frigging life. I'm not going to spend mine behind a cabbage patch.'

'Why Mrs Thrush, what a coincidence. I was just about to come and pay you a visit.'

She heard the conversation in her head before she reached the police station. It was momentarily unsettling to glimpse another world and have to reject one of them because you can't live in both. She could never decide which to inhabit permanently. She would allow herself to dream a little longer as a treat.

'My mother, you see, Inspector, was a self-deluded woman. She always craved a little glamour. I think she ran away for attention.'

And so Daphne settled into the policeman's chair that smelt faintly of tobacco and sweat. She became almost pretty. It sometimes happens to unhappy wives when they concoct another world in an attempt to forget the one that's real. Husband and wife – with their separate and contrary longings.

***

'A little more than kin and less than kind.'
Hamlet

CHAPTER 9

Hope all OK. Stopping in Helsinki for dry-cleaning and native vodka. Kremlin next.

Camilla/Granny.

The first postcard was of a garish sunrise. There was no date. Address, message and signature had all been typed. It arrived one morning at the end of the summer in which Granny disappeared. The family was waiting for the arrival of their next lodger, Anne-Marie Dupuis. The card was re-read whenever someone came downstairs and saw the picture of a dayglo sun shining over the Gulf of Bothnia where it lay on the mahogany table.

Despite the consensus that the stamp was genuine, ie Finnish, no one was sure it was, least of all Asp. Nor would anyone say why it might be a fake or if they should be puzzled about authorship.

Among themselves, among the police and the cramped, suburban world in which they lived, for the sake of respectability in the eyes of the law, they told people that Granny had not killed herself, that she was not missing or abducted or murdered, but that she was travelling the world and making the most of her geriatric twilight. The fact that she had left home without a passport, luggage and money was curious but not without precedent.

'It's possible,' (Inspector Love was in the throes of one of his increasingly frequent visits to the Thrush family), 'that she has stolen someone else's identity. If you don't want to be found, you can make it very hard for someone to trace you, providing you're not caught breaking any law.'

'It's not impossible to obtain a false birth certificate, national insurance number, driving licence, bank account and passport. The secret is in the planning. She could have arranged her disappearance months or years in advance. Interpol has no lead on this at the moment. The question is, do you want to go to Finland or Russia and look for her there?'

'I don't think so,' said Daphne. 'She obviously doesn't intend to return. I'm not sure she'd *want* to see us.'

Asp groaned, although there was no perceptible pause, no break in the chatter, and the rest of the family, the inspector and his constable, currently PC Petrovich, all watched her leave the table and the room with relief. Elm was busy scooping up the gobs of butter out of the marmalade jar, wondering if he was expected to follow.

'And anyway, I'm not sure my mother *wants* to be found, Inspector. People don't always wish to be rescued.' Daphne eyed the two policemen in her kitchen with uncertainty. 'But I suppose not wanting to be discovered won't stop her from being a missing person.'

'Quite,' sighed PC Porfiry Petrovich with a sweet look of sympathy. They could hear a violin suddenly being tuned through the kitchen hatch. The constable put his pencil down to listen. Asp, so vain about her pitch sense, kept repeating the same two notes in a quest for perfection.

Henry banged a fist on the table and shouted above the scrapes. 'Put it away, will you, daughter? We're having a serious discussion in here. Do-you-hear-me?'

Inspector Love returned to his thoughts on missing persons. The violin kept playing.

'Mrs Pod may have changed her name legally. It happens. It's not uncommon, and it's not a crime, obviously. And yes, you often find that people do it because they don't want to be found. Sometimes they think their families would be better off without them.'

His voice was deliberately pleasant, the way it is when people have to say something unpalatable. It was just that sometimes, he wished he didn't have to say these things.

'That's not true, Inspector.' Daphne looked across at her husband for support. 'She depends on us entirely. Tell him, Henry.'

'Asp, will you stop right now, or I'm coming in.'

'Of course, they're usually trying to escape from themselves, not other people,' said the inspector, turning over Granny's postcard in his hand.

The sound of a violin case being slammed shut in the next-door room.

'Mrs Pod might've changed her appearance or dyed her hair and had plastic surgery.' This was PC Petrovich speaking with his notepad, balanced on one knee. He was meant to be engrossed with copying out the conversation, but the constable's pen had a chain attached to his trouser pocket, and he kept tugging at the chain, wondering when his boss was going to apply for a laptop.

'Well that's just ludicrous, I must say. My mother-in-law's a little old lady, not a criminal... or a film star... and for the record, it's Ms not Mrs. She never married.'

The constable quietly drew a musical note over the 'r' in 'Mrs' as the inspector helped himself to some kitchen roll to blow his nose. 'Is that a new type of cheese you're fermenting, Mrs Thrush?' he asked between sniffs.

'It's definitely not cheese. My wife thought it might be a dead cat in the alley way.' Henry left his chair and was pacing up and down in the space between the wall and the table.

'I've changed my mind about the cat, Henry. You're quite right about cheese, Inspector. Elm found some lumps of parmesan in his coat pocket this morning. I put them in the fridge.'

Henry, unable to contain himself, banged his head against the wall with such violence that he saw small white lights.

'I put them in the fridge,' she repeated, staring at a spot of blood on her husband's forehead, 'but they are very smelly, I'm afraid.'

Elm returned the lid to the marmalade in silence.

'I should throw the lot out because it'll only get worse.' Daphne wanted to mention her mother's missing shoes and the blue nylon gloves, but in her anxiety, she couldn't remember if she had already. 'I – can't seem to find,' she began and stopped.

Perhaps it was the sudden blow to his head, but Henry became unexpectedly excited as he rubbed the blood away on his forehead with a tea cloth. 'The phone might ring in some squalid room somewhere, Inspector.' He waved in the direction of the front door. 'The old girl will be lying dead somewhere, and we'll never know.'

It was possible his wife could have buried his mother-in-law at the bottom of the garden, in which case, he'd throw out a few red herrings to put the law off her scent. He could say Daphne had been digging next to the compost heap at the time Granny disappeared. On and off. Digging for days, Inspector. And then what would he say next? As the idea sprang into his head, he realised he could be having one of those epiphanies where you suddenly realise your spouse could be a murderess, and it might be wiser to say nothing at all.

'Please don't talk about squalid little rooms.' Daphne sprinkled a large spoonful of salt into Henry's tea and stirred it, making small, concentric circles in his cup. 'I believe that my mother will come back, you know. I really do. She is... susceptible to loneliness.'

'Perhaps she's not alone. Perhaps she is living with a friend we don't know about.' Elm spoke very quietly, removing his father's cup from the table and pouring it down the sink. No one was listening to him.

'Hey. Where's my cup?'

'Here. Have another.' Daphne was pouring out a second.

Inspector Love watched the scene being played out between husband and wife and reflected aloud, 'You now have your new identity: you have money from somewhere, you have a passport, you have an untraceable address in a foreign country. You send a postcard to your family from Finland so they don't think you're dead and the police don't think you've been murdered. Yes, it's unusual, but it's possible.'

'What have you done to the tea?'

'Is there something wrong with it?'

There was an unusual and restrained menace in Daphne's voice, which, despite the years of marriage, Henry failed to catch.

'I think Inspector Love and his assistant are leaving.'

The inspector pushed his chair carefully against the edge of the table and winked at Elm. He tapped PC Porfiry Petrovich on the shoulder and accidentally knocked someone else's cup, setting it rattling in its saucer. 'Let us know if you get some more postcards.' He steadied the rim with his thumb before taking Daphne's hand in his, holding it briefly.

'Postcards are a reassurance, I suppose,' she said, smiling back at him, 'but I do wish my mother would pick up a telephone and ring. If she wants to abandon her old life and begin a new one, that's her business, but I'd just like her to tell me that that's what it is. Perhaps we should hold a séance.'

'Not my territory, I'm afraid.'

'This tea tastes like shit.' Henry made a face.

'It tastes of salt.' Daphne made a face back.

'What does?'

'The tea, of course.'

'Or arsenic.'

'Well, I don't think there's much more we can do right now.' The inspector patted the keys in his pocket a little too noisily. 'It's salt, by the way, Mr Thrush. Must go.'

'Thank you for coming.' Daphne imagined a small, select

gathering of friends for a séance. She resolved to bring the subject up again when or if she got to know the inspector better.

'Goodbye, Inspector, Constable.' Henry poured his cup of tea over a dead cactus in the silver cachepot on the windowsill. Daphne was pink with flirtatiousness, and this time he hadn't noticed.

The inspector tapped PC Petrovich on the shoulder with his keys, and the constable rose on cue from his chair.

'Yes, yes, goodbye. Thank you.' The constable shook everyone's hands the way some people do, not knowing when to stop, and because he was a pleasant person. 'I enjoyed the recital,' he smiled, cocking his head in the direction of the music room where Asp had begun playing again. It was a new study for the violin, and she had only learnt the first eight bars.

From that day, the case of Camilla Pod as a missing person was officially closed. The Crown Office issued a statement that no further investigations were being carried out. PC Petrovich was expected to concentrate on a spate of petty thefts within the area. Inspector Cedric Love, as the new Detective Inspector at Special Branch, Central Crime Squad, was another matter.

***

'How do you, pretty lady?'
Hamlet

CHAPTER 10

In a gallery, you're not stuck in your seat with a fixed image. You can walk away and see the shape of what you're looking at from different angles until your brain has adjusted to the scale, or you can come right up to it until it's perhaps as small as you and is no longer a distortion.

Detective Inspector Love was hovering behind Asp in a gallery without her knowing. Both were engrossed by a painting of a giant female nude and were examining the intimate vision of her pubic hair from their different positions.

Several minutes passed before Asp sensed his presence. It was the smell of freshly scrubbed skin and Palmolive soap that made her turn. It reminded her of Granny. Her family, she decided, was always smelling things – good and bad – that might be missed by others without such long noses.

'Oh, it's you, Inspector.'

'What a coincidence. I've been thinking about your family. Have you had more postcards from your grandmother lately?' There was a forced jocularity in the way he said it.

'I thought you'd be the first to know.' She turned back to the painting with a small, unmistakable shrug that said piss off and which he ignored.

'I expect Ms Pod is still in Russia?'

The nude was cropped – a touch of rust-coloured nipple in a corner peeping above the sheet. A line of pubic hair bristling halfway down if you looked carefully. The patient as sitter, the artist as surgeon. Asp liked the idea as much as she disliked the inspector interrupting her thoughts.

'Or Cyprus?'

'Cyprus?'

If they were sitting in a cinema side by side, there'd be a screen and Asp wouldn't have to look at him. Here, if she refused to turn around, it would appear unfriendly. She could see that, but she didn't care. The inspector ignored her question.

'Is your mother here as well?'

'Would you like her to be, Inspector?'

He smiled, showing his lower brown teeth that were broken in the middle. He'd meant to have them whitened when he gave up smoking, but somehow he forgot.

Slowly, she turned to face him. 'I came here with my brother. I've no idea where my mother is.' Her thin fingers fiddled with her French roll, and the inspector wondered why the child was always quite so angry.

'Ah. Elm. Of course,' he said to mollify her. 'The computer genius.'

'It's not just computers, you know. Elm's brilliant at everything.' She stared at his flat round face staring back at hers.

'Of course,' he said again, still smiling.

She was as confrontational as ever, with her T-shirt and jeans ripped at strategic points across her legs and her scrappy hair caught in a bun by a wooden needle. He watched her remove and reinsert it with one quick, sharp jab against her scalp. He could have placed his hand around her waist and his fingers would have met his thumb. Almost.

'People talk about "computers" with an oh-ho-ho sort of sneer in their voice,' she said. 'That's because they don't understand anything about them.'

'I wasn't sneering, you know.' He was trying to apologise. 'Would you and Elm like to share a cuppa with me in the café downstairs?'

'Elm is with the still-lifes.'

'Why don't you go and get him? I'll wait.'

As she hurried past a wall of saints, hands raised in benediction, their halos like smoke rings, she knew she was running to escape. There was a smaller painting tucked away in a corner that caught her attention. It showed two women dressed in luminous blue beside a monk in black. Everything glowed in an enamelled way that startled her. Even the black habit of the monk gleamed back at her.

The women seemed to be asking questions, and the monk was listening to them as he prayed. Asp had rushed past so many masterpieces she was ashamed. Bugger the inspector. She would tell him, when she saw him again, that she was lost amongst art.

Two girls in periwinkle blue smocks brushed past her as she paused. Like the picture. Several years older than Asp, they were chattering quietly to each other as they crossed in front of her, momentarily obscuring the frame from her view. Silver bangles encircled their wrists and made a gentle, melodic rattle. Raffia sandals showed under the hems of their smocks. They could have stepped out of the canvas with their coils of biblical hair and their mediaeval robes. More art than real.

That she'd successfully escaped the inspector and could stop somewhere without him breathing down from behind brought the most exquisite, temporary relief. She moved closer to the image on the wall. It seemed no more than a few inches square. The chattering girls in their blue smocks had disappeared and Asp was swallowed up by a sense of lightness and dark, the hints of another life that might have once been real. Where was Elm?

She pecked at the jumble of thoughts inside her head in a random way. She spoilt her pleasure by pecking too long. She heard the inspector's voice emerging from the monk's mouth and remembered she was cross with herself for promising to share a cup of tea with the police. Was she mad? Why do that? Asp found herself heading towards the exit sign. 'Not yet,' she muttered. 'Not yet.'

Tap tap tap with the heels of her shoes – a stark, echoing noise on the stone floor steps. Like a person cracking nuts in a cell. She was hurrying past relics in glass cages, trying not to tap tap tap as loudly as before in this hallowed space. Elm was not amongst the flowers or fruits.

Perhaps he had discovered their new lodger, Mimi-Saulange, as he wandered from room to room.

'Elm, Elm, Elm, where the fuck have you gone?'

Passers-by were looking at the thin, distracted girl with curiosity. Mimi-Saulange, their new lodger, had threatened that morning to meet them at the gallery. But Asp didn't want to look at paintings with anyone other than Elm. This was holiday time with her brother. And she'd been wasting half of it already with the inspector.

'I would love to see the English art with you.' Mimi-Saulange spoke over a bowl of cornflakes at breakfast. Mimi-Saulange had arrived at the Thrush family home after Emilie-Catherine, who came after Paul-Phillipe, who came after Anne-Marie, who had arrived after Jean-Pierre had left and who (Anne-Marie that is), was supposedly living in New Zealand with a beekeeper. Some stayed a week, some stayed a month, one or two stayed longer. Bed, board and English conversation.

Of them all, Mimi-Saulange was kind both to animals and human beings – a vegetarian with a sweet face and pink chipolata lips. She was already precocious in her commitment to preserving the planet. Within a week, she had done much to transform the quality of Thrush cuisine from the usual dried-up ham to nut rissoles soaked in Cornish seaweed. It was a start. Even Henry did his best not to say, 'Where are the veggie burgers?'.

Asp regularly had her eyes on the French cigarette pants with matching tight sweater or the red tartan mini skirt with a nappy pin, but it was Mimi-Saulange's chipolata lips and midnight curls that would be remembered longer. They were the inspiration for Elm's adolescent dreams and Henry's middle-aged ones, and they clinched her place within the family.

Mimi-Saulange also had a slight lisp and began most sentences with 'unfortunately' or 'fortunately' because she was very fond of adverbs. Despite this oddity, it was agreed she would be a perfect lodger who bothered no one and would be generally admired across the dinner table by all. Daphne and Asp would find themselves inventing flaws for her only to help them forget their own.

It was unspoken and understood that Mimi-Saulange lacked the vocabulary to talk about the profundities of life and death in English, which was either fortunately or unfortunately just as well. On this particular day, Asp hoped that Mimi-Saulange had not made it to the gallery.

'Where the fuck are you, Elm?' she cried as she tap-tap-tapped her way through the different gallery rooms, wearing out her shoes with her tiresome clicks. Some things never changed, except by degree.

Since the day Granny fell down the cellar stairs, or since the day Asp might have pushed her down the stairs, significant time had been marked by the arrival and departure of their various lodgers. Whatever happened in between somehow appeared less memorable.

Time would pass with Asp's daily rehearsal of Lady Macbeth's sleepwalking scene in the conservatory because at some time in the future, she intended to audition for RADA and not just to breathe on plants.

Time was measured with the odd arrival of a postcard, usually of an exotic sunrise, signed 'Camilla' with lots of Xs. Still more time was eked out with periodic visits from the inspector, which Asp likened to her newly acquired menstrual zit since he visited their home once a month and then hung around.

Time was spent on the purchase of a larger buggy for Leaf, who was still wearing stretch-knit baby-gros. But in their school holidays, time was marked by Asp and Elm making trips to the different art galleries or museums. Together.

As Asp hovered among the crowd of people buying postcards in the gallery shop, she spied her brother in the queue. Time was smashed in a kaleidoscope with thoughts over which she had no control.

***

'SOME CRAVEN SCRUPLE
of thinking too precisely on the event.'
Hamlet

CHAPTER 11

'Do you suppose that painters painted larger than life to shock the viewer?' The inspector found a free table in a corner of the cafeteria. He had already ordered pots of tea and a plate with sticky buns.

'Larger than what life?' Elm was cautiously polite.

'I mean larger than real,' continued the inspector, stirring his tea with his spoon as he nearly always did, making small, reckless waves in the hot liquid that threatened to splash onto the table but somehow did not. Policemen spent their lives sipping cups of tea, sorting out what's imaginary, what's real.

Asp said nothing. Elm nodded. The inspector continued stirring. He would feel he'd accomplished something if he could make the girl less angry.

'We were the only viewers in the room, did you notice?' he said.

'I wasn't looking at people.' Asp picked up her cup to warm her hands. 'And anyway, it's not that big a picture.'

She had drawn a pattern of circles on the table with some cake crumbs and wondered what it would be like in hell because if there was one, filled with all the people she loathed in this world, like the inspector, that would be it.

Her brother was regretting that he'd opted for the still-lifes.

'Perhaps, you just get used to the size after a while,' suggested the inspector, reaching out for one of Asp's crumbs and eating it.

'Boring.' Asp rolled her eyes and looked up at the ceiling. 'Yes, really bor-ing. This discussion is dead.'

Her voice was louder than the chatter in the room.

'Surprise is important.' Elm frowned at Asp and kicked her under the table. 'Especially if you've got a thing about being bored.' It was an extra pain the way his sister had her irrational dislikes and how she wanted everyone else to feel the same way.

'Exactly.' The inspector shot Elm a grateful look. His mouth moved sideways like a ventriloquist. It was the way people talked when they didn't want to be overheard.

But Asp was not listening. She was absorbed cutting her cream cake into ridiculously small squares and pushing the leftover crumbs to the edge of her plate, out of the inspector's reach. She was counting her mother's known e-mails to him by the number of crumbs and trying to understand what drew them together as this improbable couple.

A case of virtual love, not virtuous, Elm had said last week when he found one of the emails by mistake on his mother's computer. What with the inspector's obsessive interest in the nude and his obviously displaced lust by word processor, Elm reckoned with Asp that the inspector could be either a dirty old man in a mac or an emotionally deficient peeping tom.

What Asp and Elm had failed to understand was that the inspector's voyeurism never amounted to anything more than unfulfilled fantasy. With his thinning hair and his unhappy marriage, with his dreams of tenderness and of occasional reward that did no harm, Inspector Cedric Love could be middle-aged Everyman.

Dear Daph at Barnes dot, no recent news from Interpol. Pursuing possible lead in Moscow and Cyprus but fear needle in haystack situation. Thank you for the plums. Affectionately yours, cedric.love@specialbranch slash Central Crime Squad slash South West London.com.

Except for Daphne, it is true the family had hoped the police would disappear from their lives after the arrival of the first postcard. But it was not to be. Asp had only recently come to grips with her short-sightedness and double vision by acquiring contact lenses and seeing what was going on around her with new clarity.

She blamed her father's solitary trips to the park for encouraging her mother's infatuation with the inspector. She had her hair tinted an alarming orange with some henna that did little for the condition of her scalp. She was lonely. She would ask Elm or Asp to mind Leaf while she disappeared to the computer room for a private spot of e-mail. This insight depressed Asp deeply as she glared at the inspector sitting opposite them.

The idea that Inspector Love might have deliberately followed them to the gallery or that he was acting with some dark policeman's instinct that had nothing to do with his sexual attraction to their mother alarmed her so much she thought for a second or two she was going to be sick.

Not that Asp had spent these last minutes consumed by nausea or panic that Granny's skeleton might be found and that she would be charged with her murder. Nor was she too bothered by the intermittent postcards that came to the house because in her heart she was sure she knew who had sent them, and it wasn't Granny. What she didn't want was for Elm to discuss his views on things like negative space in art or how many missing, elderly persons there might be in this world. God forbid he would prolong their cups of stewed tea.

'Is that your constable over by that arch?' Asp was studying a man with a face like a marrow sitting a few tables away. He looked familiar.

'Do you mean Porfiry?' The inspector leant forward, tipping his chair the way her father was always telling her not to and smiling with his mouth but not his eyes. Asp squirmed as she saw herself from his point of view.

'Porfiry's not a man for galleries. Music's more his thing.' The inspector chuckled into his second bun. 'He prefers to compose in his spare time… the electronic sort. Sound effects if you ask me.'

'And you're here for the art.'

'Well, yes. But I'm also on duty.'

'Fuck.' Asp dived under the tablecloth. A large poster on the far wall had a picture of a crowd queueing for the exhibition she had just seen. Camilla Pod – Granny – was staring back at her from the throng, wearing an old coat, some gloves and a pair of slippers she didn't recognise. Her small lively eyes followed Asp. The mouth was open in a small round 'O' of surprise.

'Can I help?'

The inspector bent down, and Asp again caught the whiff of soap.

'One of my contacts has fallen out.'

'I've got it.' Elm tapped his sister on the head. 'It's here on your plate.'

He was about to hand it to her when the person who may have been Porfiry Petrovich passed by and accidentally bumped Elm's chair as he left the cafeteria. A tiny bubble of plastic flew into the air and landed on the floor. Dust clung to the surface of the lens like a dirty tear.

'What did you do that for?' Asp frowned at Elm.

'It wasn't my fault. I was knocked.'

'Is this it?' The inspector scooped up the lens with his thumb and forefinger and placed it in the palm of Asp's hand.

'Thank you.'

All three sat down in unnatural silence. Asp struggled for what must have been a minute with lopsided vision. She desperately wanted to go up to the poster and examine it. She felt that Granny was examining her, but she really couldn't be sure. Should she remove her other lens and be blind in both eyes or should she stay half-blind and blurry?

'My mother-in-law tried some contacts once. But she kept on losing them as often as her glasses.'

'I didn't know you were married,' said Elm.

'Most people over forty are.' The inspector toyed with his empty cup and saw his second wife in the bottom of it. 'Do you want to know why I'm here?'

'Yes,' said Elm.

'Maybe.' Asp could see two inspectors in front of her and was blinking at one of them, hoping he would disappear.

'You mean *maybe* you want to know?' The inspector rapped the table in frustration. 'That's not good enough, don't you see? I need your encouragement.'

'NO!' Asp could hear her voice coming from somewhere else in the cafeteria. She kept on hearing things coming from the wrong place. The cafeteria was her mouth. But her mouth was in the exit to the corridor. Her body had disappeared and she was shouting to make sure the inspector could hear her. Everybody in the cafeteria could hear her.

'NO, NO, NO. It's not right, don't you understand? You don't come to an art gallery to be quizzed by the police. We've got nothing more to say – me and Elm. The case is shut – it's over – that's it.'

'I'm sorry you think you're being hounded, Asp. I'd like to think I've become a friend of your family.' He attempted to pat her hand, but she withdrew it sharply, and he pretended not to notice. 'As it happens, the case of a missing person who's still missing can always be reopened. If new evidence emerges, the police will then pursue it.'

'Is this why you followed us here, Inspector? Because you're pursuing it?' Elm looked across at Asp and saw that she was about to insert the dirty contact lens. 'Don't do that, Asp.'

'Hang on a minute,' said the inspector. 'I didn't set out to follow you.'

'Then how'd you know we were coming here in the first place?' Asp was rubbing the lens against her sleeve to clean it.

'I saw you coming. When you crossed Waterloo Bridge, I was on the opposite side. Simple as that.'

'Simple? What do you mean? Creeping up on us like that. What for? MORE STUFF ABOUT OUR MISSING GRANNY?' Asp was trying to blink away one of the two inspectors in front of her nose and was failing. 'Granny's alive. She's enjoying LIFE! What's wrong with that?'

'There's nothing sinister in my being here.' The inspector gave a quick shrug of despair.

'Sneaking up behind us and not saying anything for a while, that's... sinister.' Asp looked to Elm before returning his kick. A bit late for revenge, a bit random – but satisfying.

'Um... Did you think we'd tell you something new, Inspector?' Elm moved his chair out of Asp's reach. 'Because we know nothing. Apart from the postcards that prove our grandmother's not missing. She's just gone away for some reason. People do, you know. We don't have to know why.'

'Well, it was just an idea... that after all this time, you might have thought about why she'd turn up... in a foreign country - without any warning, any plan, any hints.' The inspector hesitated before adding, 'You don't have any theories about it? Any suggestions why that might be?'

Elm scratched his ear and considered.

'The person that used to be a part of our lives is gone. We've stopped pretending her world is the way it used to be. She's changed. We've changed. That's all there is to it.'

'Interesting.' The inspector helped himself to the last bun.

'Are you,' asked Asp, coming back into the conversation, her face paler than usual, her thin long nose even sharper, the sweat from her hands reflecting the light in the room. 'Are you making any suggestions yourself, Inspector?'

'No, Asp. I'm not.'

'They sound like suggestions.'

'I'm just interested to know what you *think* I think.'

The inspector studied them both, one after the other.

'You're implying in a roundabout way that our granny is dead.' Asp spat on her lens, wiping away the grime with her sleeve again and reinserting it in silence. She looked across at the poster and saw that her grandmother had disappeared from the crowd in the photo.

'Is that what you really believe?'

'I think you'd like to suggest it,' she said at last.

'You could say I'm suspicious because it's my job to be like that. But I'm not doing any supposing here, Asp. I'm not accusing – just asking you for ideas. Simple questions. No **body** has been found, and without any evidence that there is one, of course, I'm not going to say she's dead.'

'Well, you're thinking she's dead, even if you're not saying it.'

'Except for the postcards, which we are meant to take at face value, not a hint, not a clue as to where she might be. No arrangements for collecting her pension. No bus pass renewal. Of course that might make sense if we believe she's gone abroad. But no sightings by Interpol of a little old lady answering to her description. Nothing. Just postcards of sunsets or a sunrise from Moscow etc.'

'Helsinki.' Asp heard her voice floating up from either side of her. 'Helsinki, etcetera,' she repeated. The sound was coming from somewhere else other than her throat in a series of echoes that turned themselves into aaaaahs and ohs. And again, it was just her voice in the room that people were listening to. 'You think there might be a body, Inspector. That's just as bad. But you can't spend the rest of your life looking for someone who isn't lost anymore.'

'And as long as you don't suspect we've hidden her somewhere,' added Elm hastily. 'Ask away. Don't mind us then. But of course we'd prefer our grandmother to be alive. Of course we would – we do.'

Asp stood up. People in the tearoom seemed a long way away. The poster was a blur. Poster Granny had clearly left the gallery. Asp was dizzy with the effort of trying to focus. She could see a body sticking halfway out of the coal heap. It had this raw, red, intestinal colour where flesh and clothes merge to look the same. Asp began swaying. A rat sways like that when it's been poisoned. Trapped between the past, the present and the future in her imagination, her voice tore around the room only to whirl back at her. It returned to the same note in repeating loops of real and hopeless misery.

There is something about being caught up in the moment where time stands still that is about as important a human characteristic as can be. Time seems circular. The day does not move into night in a straight line but curves around itself. Time's past is now – the present and the future are suspended. Elm was cradling his sister in his arms. He caressed the top of her head and whispered in her ear.

Strangers hovered above the boy and girl on the floor while the inspector telephoned for an ambulance with a police escort. Some artistic luvvies picked their way like pelicans around the conjoined figures. When the strange looped crying stopped, Asp's wail strayed into their heads, where it remained longer than their discussions about art.

***

'Though this be madness, yet there is method in't.'
Hamlet

Chapter 12

Henry:

Yesterday began as a peaceful Sunday morning in our household. My wife, still in her pyjamas, pressed the repeat button on the CD Player and was listening to Yves Montand singing 'Ah, Ah, Le Grand Boulevard' as she cut crosses on the ends of Brussels sprouts. This pointless exercise took her mind off Asp.

The official story was that Asp had been in hospital for the last week with the stress of too much violin practice and Elm, well, Elm disappeared to Finland for a spot of programming with a Dutch baker he'd met through the internet.

Bubba was looking sweet in his pram, chomping away on a new dummy, and Aunt Rose was on her first visit to our house in years with her husband, Hamish. They arrived with her wheelchair in the boot of their car as she complained that her legs would not carry her for very long without the greatest difficulty.

The French windows were open to let out the moths. A ramp had been hastily erected to make a smooth transition from the house to the garden, and Aunt Rose was reading *Plato's Republic* aloud in the shadow of the apple tree. Hamish was helping me to make Red Baron triplanes and Sopwith Camels out of balsa wood at the kitchen table because that's the only place where we can fit these things. No lodgers as yet.

Daphne panicked about the overdraft this particular summer and decided we needed not one but two paying guests for the next academic year. I was determined not to increase her stress in any way and was tearing up some incriminating bank statements when Uncle Hamish began to count the grains of salt amongst the shavings of balsa. It was, I realised, time for a trip to the park before I throttled him.

'Won't be gone long, Daphne,' I said, itching to remind her that he's her uncle by law and maybe her father, but not mine. As it happens, I'm quite fond of Hamish.

'How long?'

'Half an hour there and back.'

'Take Aunt Rose with you... and Leaf. He needs some fresh air.'

I saw if I protested, she was going to give me a hard time, so I picked up our monster baby and slung him over one shoulder, ignoring the sulphurous smell that was leaking through the baby-gro, and steered Hamish to the car. 'Wait here while I fetch Aunt Rose.' I dropped Leaf into his lap, to the dismay of both.

'We mustn't miss the cricket.' Uncle Hamish's voice came from far away.

'Alright,' I replied, 'in that case, we'll have to eat a late lunch, won't we?' and I shut the door firmly to drown Leaf's whimpering.

'I bow to Nemesis.... For I do believe that to be an involuntary homicide is a less crime than to be a deceiver concerning noble and good and just laws.'

The aunt, when she got going, had a voice like a budgie. It

cheeped all the way from the garden to the kitchen. She was now reading from her wheelchair between the water butt and the potting shed. The sun was beating on her pale pink skin, making it pinker.

'Auntie, I'm taking you to the park to show you the deer.'

'How lovely. Is it the rutting season?'

'Not yet.' I released the brake, grabbed a sunhat from a hook and dropped it into her lap.

'Then I shall take Plato with me as well.'

I watched her fidgeting with the brim of her hat and knew what was coming next.

'Is Daphne joining us?'

She seemed pleased when I said no, humming some child's rhyme as I wheeled her through the house and out to the car. The way she sang, pausing at the end of a line and then starting up again with exactly the same one again, was just like Daphne. 'How much is that doggy in the window, the one with the waggly tail,' repeat. You get the picture. There was more resemblance between Daphne and her aunt than there was between her and her mother.

'Perhaps you'd like me to read you some of my book, Henry. There's a passage describing the habits of deer. Of course it's an allegory for what's natural in matters of gender. Completely fascinating.'

'How's that?' I answered carefully as Aunt Rose tends to be quite sensitive and quick to take offence.

'Here. Just here. Stop a minute, so I can read it to you, Henry.'

'We tried in our argument, if you remember, to make our men like guardians of a flock.'

'Yes, yes.' I was rubbing the sleep out of my eyes.

'Then let us follow this up and give corresponding rules for birth and nurture, and see whether we approve the result or not.'

'How?' Shouldn't have asked the question if I didn't want the answer.

'In this way. Do we think that the females of watchdogs ought to watch as well as the males, ought to hunt with them, and generally share their occupations, or should they be kept indoors in their kennels, on the ground that breeding and rearing the puppies disables them for anything else, while the hard work and all the care of the flocks are reserved for the males?'

'Easy does it.' I was lifting her out of her wheelchair and trying not to bruise the old bird. 'Forget about the sexes. What about the deer?'

'Well, it's obvious, Henry. There's a herd of does to one stag. Just think about it. The stag with his does, the does with their stag.'

Strapping her into the back seat, I suddenly remembered how difficult it is to end one of her discussions.

'It's licensed, serial fucking Henry – the spreading of the seed. Who profits more, the stag with his harem or the doe with her time-share *Bambi*?'

'Yes, Auntie.' I folded the chair and packed it into the boot on top of Leaf's buggy. She looked at me with her head on one side while I tucked a furry blanket around her, the very picture of a frail old lady.

'You see? You see?'

Again, she reminded me of Daphne. 'Hamish will take care of Leaf while I read you the fifth book of Plato.'

I said nothing but feared there might be a sixth.

'We are still evolving, Henry. From now on, I will refer to any symptoms of hysteria as the *male*-strom and this will be my contribution to the language of women's rights – you understand, I refuse to describe any disturbance of the central nervous system as something rooted in the womb.'

Did I say anything at all as I pulled the door shut and turned the key in the ignition? No, I did not, but I noticed as we drove away that the sound of the traffic seemed to have a calming effect on Leaf. He stopped whimpering and blew bubbles that dribbled down his chin and onto his baby-gro, making a damp patch around his collar that kept him cool.

Uncle Hamish was happily reading the number plates on all the other cars within sight, and I could see through my rear-vision mirror that Aunt Rose was asleep with her mouth open. She was making little purring noises, and I thought to myself that only a minute before, she'd been spouting stuff that was two and a half thousand years old and saying it was still relevant.

I felt no specific emotion about anything until I was standing in the middle of the flying field, watching a young boy launch a glider into the air and catch a thermal. He was finding some connection between his brain and the plane, working the remote control box in his hands automatically, just thinking where his plane was going and all the time, searching for better air to keep it up as long as possible.

Uncle Hamish looked up at the boy's plane, its wingspan near six feet, and laughed. It was a miracle, this spontaneous guffaw that came up from his belly and out of his throat in short bursts like a faulty tap. It was a miracle because not even Aunt Rose had ever heard him laughing like that before. I was afraid he might stop, and so I started to laugh with him.

'I prefer kites. Camilla and I had a kite when we were girls.' Aunt Rose turned her head in the direction of Leaf. 'It didn't fly very well.' They both sat quite still, the old great aunt and the old great baby, each one trapped in their different-sized wheelies with their backs to the horizon while Uncle Hamish and I behaved as if they weren't there. It was the first time she had voluntarily mentioned her sister since her disappearance. It must have been the shock of hearing her husband's laughter.

***

I have long thought the most exciting thing about being married to Daphne is the lunch box she makes for me to take to work each day. What she never knew as she carefully spooned last night's cold bolognese onto two slices of bread, polished my apple or poured a tin of Ambrosia rice pudding into a plastic pot, was that I'd lost my job in the city.

As I had no idea what I was going to do instead, I said nothing and continued to catch a train in the mornings. Any train and any direction. If it rained, I'd stay in my seat, travelling up and down the line until it stopped. It made me feel better that way.

The nearest I ever came to meeting up with a ticket inspector was to get a glimpse of one through the glass window of the door to the next carriage. When the weather improved, I would hop off and find an empty bench on the side of the road, outside the local library or in a park, it didn't really matter. I would read the paper, open up my lunch box alongside all the other unemployed, and feed the pigeons. The time of day was irrelevant at this point in my life.

Now I am happy with a cold egg and onion, but Daphne is obsessed with the merits of surprise, and as I stare down at the carefully wrapped parcels of silver foil, it is true I can feel flurries of excitement, wondering what lies within. I am what my daughter would describe as a sad person.

This was the morning after my trip to the park with Uncle Hamish and Aunt Rose. I knew my lunch was going to be the bolognese because we'd had it for supper with the leftover Brussels sprouts the night before, and so unfortunately, there was no surprise. I was in a bad mood generally because I'd seen Hamish waving to me from the platform as I boarded a train heading in the opposite direction from the city. He enjoys studying their comings and goings and was, therefore a potentially calamitous spy.

'Stumm, Hamish, Stumm,' I yelled through the open doors. Two sets of level crossings, umpteen cottages and a number of allotments further on, I got off at Mortlake and caught the next train back to Barnes. The old duffer was standing at the farthest end of the platform, scribbling into his notebook. 'What a surprise,' I lied, tapping him on the shoulder because he seemed oblivious to my presence.

'I'm busy, Henry,' he muttered.

Uncle Hamish was – is – like that. He can say whatever comes into his head, which is why companionship with him can be tricky.

'That's all right,' I replied and, turning away, added, 'I was only going to say that I've lost my job.'

'Were you on the 11.36 Staines to Waterloo just then, Henry?'

There he was, tugging at my sleeve with one hand and shovelling his pad and pen into his pocket with the other.

'Yes,' I said wearily.

'Where are we going then,' he asked, 'as you've lost your job?' I had forgotten how logical he was.

'Do you fancy some spaghetti bolognese sandwiches without the spaghetti?'

He looked at me with vague eyes.

'We're going to have a picnic in Kew,' I said, gently removing his hand from my sleeve.

And we did, catching the 11.46 in the direction of Barnes Bridge. I was on the point of having a nervous breakdown. I kept telling him this, but he didn't listen. I said that it may be the father's main job to protect the son from his mother – and I felt I had done a fairly good job with Elm, but I was worried that I had failed to be of any help or any use to Asp.

The thought was getting me down. That, plus unemployment, school fees, music lessons, a new battery for the car, the occasional model aeroplane and wondering what the neighbours were saying about the unexpected disappearance of my mother-in-law. I told him this long before I could bring myself to explain to Daphne that I was out of a job.

***

'And then it started like a guilty thing
Upon a fearful summons.'
Hamlet

CHAPTER 13

Neighbours. There were two main sorts in the street, with only minor variations among them and both archetypes lived on either side of the Thrush family. Facing them, on the right-hand side, was the old girl who used to chat to Henry on her way back from the off-licence. She would pause at the bus stop to take a swig out of her gin bottle and was, according to rumour, not appearance, pushing a hundred.

He was fond of her. They all were. She measured time not by the day and the night but by the seasons because when you are very old, apparently, normal time is like the aftermath of a car crash. There is no scale by which to judge your breathing - only some crushing stasis, which exists in the blink of an eye before it morphs into something else, leaving behind a sense of panic or belief that you have missed out on the related bits in between. The changes of season are rational by contrast and expectation. They are measured out by what you have time to see around you.

Come the spring, when her front garden was a rug of snowdrops, she would buy Christmas cards at half-price before sitting down to write out the messages for next year's list and sealing them in stamp-addressed envelopes. By the summer, she'd be out there snipping the privet hedge with a pair of scissors or off to the shops with her stick.

Occasionally she'd bring out the secateurs and smarten up the branches of a prunus tree that overhung the street in order to watch the children crashing on their roller skates. At the first sign of autumn leaves, she would draw the curtains of her sitting room windows at the back of the house so she didn't have to look at the encroaching brambles. These she never snipped or clipped and Henry decided to call her patch of thorns *Sleeping Beauty's* paradise.

In winter, when the snow fell on the deranged branches of self-seeded buddleia, the frost made a white film over their twigs. The only apparent life in this back door wilderness, apart from herself and a single, fat tabby, were the cockroaches that scuttled into her kitchen, the pigeons in her eaves, which she fed with whole slices of cut-bread or the hedgehogs and foxes that lived under the holly trees.

Her only visitors were Daphne, Henry, Asp and Elm. It was a redeeming smidgeon of authentic neighbourliness – to offer company to someone who made few demands and kept herself to herself. They understood that her box room was stocked from floor to ceiling with neatly wrapped gifts for those relatives and friends who failed to materialise.

They knew that her winter months were spent unwrapping and rewrapping each one with the cat curled on her lap. When the cat scratched the paper until it was hanging in tatters around the gift, she would reach down to her pile of magazines on the floor and select the most colourful page to wrap it up again.

She had given Henry a miniature bottle of brandy on his birthday and an extra one on the day he installed a cat-flap in her kitchen door. They were delicately aware that these gifts were not a sacrifice but further evidence of her Miss Havisham time warp. There had been street talk of a fiancé in the air force during the second world war. He'd been killed on the day before they were to be married. No one could remember who first told the story and they were reluctant to ask her outright.

For this and other reasons, Henry decided she probably wouldn't notice any change in his comings or goings. Or at least she wouldn't say anything if she did. Should she glimpse him in his garden, polishing the wings of his planes on a Monday or a Tuesday, so be it. It would be the same as a Saturday or a Sunday. Her discretion was dependable, whereas the neighbours to the left were quite another matter. Even the buckles of their boots, permanently undone on the outside, were like the wearers themselves, bloody useless.

These neighbours were the greatest threat to Henry's self-esteem. With their four-by-four Range Rover, their neat gravel garden, seasonal holidays, no mortgage to pay and no apparent children, he occasionally experienced homicidal feelings towards them.

As a venereologist, Wellies One had a large private practice in genito-urinary infections and a line in snappy suits. Wellies Two was the wife who straightened the hair on her head and elsewhere with heated tongs every day because at some profound level she believed her husband or her lover or both would abandon her if her hair were in curls on her head and elsewhere.

'Good morning, Henry.' She spoke through a hole in the fence on the day he sat in the garden to avoid further train journeys. 'Hi there. Having a day off to enjoy the weather?'

He was lying on the long grass amongst the dandelions, nurturing his contempt and jealousy, intending to read in the shade of the horse chestnut tree. It was plain as a pikestaff that he hoped she'd go away, for he kept his head low over his book. Besides, he couldn't remember her real name or her husband's. They were just Wellies One and Wellies Two.

'I hope you don't mind the strimmer noise.'

He turned a page. It was a library paperback, which, until he sat down to read the first chapter, he had forgotten he'd read last year. She could vacuum the grass as far as he was concerned. He couldn't give a toss.

'Excuse me. Mr Thrush? This is Wellies Two speaking. Remember me? I'm your next-door neighbour, wishing to pass the time of day.'

Reluctantly, Henry dropped the book onto his lap.

'I wouldn't strim if I were you.' He spoke slowly, deliberately. 'There's a black cloud over there that's heading this way.'

'Thanks for the tip.' She was frowning at the untidy edges of his lawn, itching to remind him that the wear and tear of the fence on his side was not her responsibility but his, yet reluctant to appear unfriendly because she found Henry quite attractive with his beard and his nice, Mediterranean olive skin.

Her 'little Turk' she would say as she nibbled his ear in a moment of future intimacy. It was one of her enduring griefs that Wellies One was a pale, spotty white with a ring of purple moles on his stomach, a fact she had only absorbed when it was too late to change their wedding plans. 'I haven't seen Asp around for a few days,' she added brightly.

He picked up his book and removed some grass from the dust cover. *Hell lies in the small frustrations that grow like seeds,* he thought.

'Has she gone away on holiday – somewhere nice?'

Drip-drip-drop. The seed is a weed all of a sudden.

He flicked some pages to avoid looking at her small retrousse nose or her perfectly formed white teeth gleaming back at him through the gap in the fence.

'Not exactly.' He hesitated. 'You wouldn't call it nice.' While he tried so hard to think of somewhere plausible to place his daughter before opting for a partial truth. 'She's in hospital, actually.'

'Good heavens. I had no idea. Nothing serious I hope.'

She made a low, murmuring sound and Henry felt his penis shift underneath his trousers and the tag of his zipper flip sideways like a signal on a railway track.

'No. Not serious. Just getting her verrucas burnt off, whatever they do to verrucas when you've got them all over your feet and you can't walk for days afterwards. That's why we decided to have it done in the hospital. Being so close together, it's better that way.'

He silently willed her to look somewhere else as he turned and rolled carefully, tenderly onto his stomach.

'Oh, the poor thing...'

'I've never had any myself.'

'I won't go to public pools.'

'Really?'

'You pick them up in changing rooms.'

He raised his chest slowly from the grass, wondering why, whenever he lied about something, he was never prepared for the development that followed.

'Would you like a Pimm's, Henry?'

'Ah, well...'

'Before the rain comes.'

'Mm...'

'In your garden or in mine?' Her red, pleated lips were pursed around her perfect teeth.

'Yours,' he laughed as their mouths brushed lightly through the gap in the fence. They had become so close to one another.

His affair with Wellies Two began with the sweet scent of winter jasmine floating through the fence. Daphne had popped into the police station with Leaf to have a word with Inspector Love. Elm and Asp were presumed to be at school. Asp was on a home visit or, as she called it, hospital leave. Uncle Hamish was pushing Aunt Rose around the back streets of Roehampton, counting the number of houses with pebble dash on their front facades.

It was the last hot day of summer when Henry confided to Wellies Two: 'I laugh, but I don't smile, so people often think I'm unfriendly,' and Wellies Two had kissed him for the second time through the gap in the garden fence - a gentle, lingering, sweet kiss that was ripe with promise and Henry whispered through her open lips that she should knock on his front door.

It was never an all-consuming, obsessive fling where like rabbits, they were at it every minute but more an idyll on an afternoon when there was nothing else to do and Daphne, Asp, Elm, Leaf, Aunt Rose and Uncle Hamish were not around. Sex lingered in their consciousness as little or as much as the taste of Pimms that preceded it. He liked the hint of wiggle in her hips when she crooked her little finger in front of his nose and led him into her empty house, the laughter in her throat.

Henry took to collecting the stepladder from the cellar and propping it up against the Wellies' fence for convenient access to the other side. He did this on days when everyone else was out. For extra storage space, he cleared out the freezer in the cellar as much as he could, ignoring the odd pack of frozen peas. He repaired the dodgy plug and filled the space with bags of ice for the Pimms that he and Wellies Two would enjoy, reckoning there was enough ice to last for an Indian summer of cocktails and clandestine fucking.

It was from tact that Wellies Two never asked why he didn't go to work, and he never bothered to explain. He had avoided the truth about Asp's illness as she had also avoided mentioning her tryst with a Polish builder – a builder who would turn up from time to time and fail to build anything. Wellies Two was Henry's shameful secret as Jan, the Polish builder, would be hers.

Considering they went through so many bags of ice, it was a miracle they were never discovered. Had they been asked, they probably would have said that when the weather changed, and they ceased to be outdoors quite so much, the habit would wane accordingly, and that was okay.

By the end of September, when the nights were drawing in, and Wellies One was off work with his annual flu, the episodes were significantly fewer. For a short while, there always seemed to be one still night when Henry, finding himself alone in the home, would lie on the grass and open his eyes to discover Wellies Two standing over him, undressed and smiling as in a dream by moonlight with the dying scent of autumn leaves tangled in her hair.

It was a stolen time when you knew the curtains might twitch in the old girl's house on the opposite side when she raised her telescope to the skylight windows or fed the hedgehogs at her kitchen door, where you might miss the various neighbours' silhouettes camouflaged by trees at the end of their garden, but you could, if you wanted to, see two thousand stars in the sky.

***

'GIVE ME THAT MAN
That is not passion's slave, and I will wear him
In my heart's core, ay, in my heart of heart,
As I do thee.'
Hamlet

CHAPTER 14

The inspector sat beside Asp's bed and waited for her to stir. The Thrush family and their elderly relatives from Scotland had been coming and going for the past few days. Now he felt it was his turn for a hospital visit.

Not some devious act of depredation, just sitting there, threatening his haemorrhoids on a plastic stool because he felt responsible for her being there by counting the get-well cards on the wall and trying to forget that banshee howl of Asp in the art gallery. He hadn't reckoned on the mincemeat when the door swung open and a stray orderly plucked a steaming plateful from his trolley to place on the tray by Asp's bed. The inspector hoped he wouldn't catch *MRSA* from just sitting there, smelling its rancid lumps.

'Wakey, wakey.'

A nurse was leaning over Asp's sleeping form. A small watch with illuminated dots was pinned to her baby blue uniform, where it swung back and forth like a pendulum, hitting her breast hard as she pushed the tray and the food into a corner. The aluminium lid covering the food slipped to the floor and rattled into a corner, spinning.

'Wakey-wakey-time. Well then.' The voice slipped smoothly from little girl to bossy woman. 'At least your supper's safe.'

He passed the lid to the nurse as if he had dropped it in the first place and felt in his pocket for a wet-wipe.

'Thanks, Sergeant. Don't scald yourself.'

The inspector was weighing up whether he should correct her or forget it. He did neither. She was punching the pillows like a heavyweight with transparent plastic gloves on her hands, her nurse's fob still in its erotic swing. Asp was silent throughout, still half-asleep, opening and shutting her eyes against the hard electric light because the light, more than the food, was bothering her.

'Look at you – skin and bones. Eat up now. I'll be back with your medicine in a tick.'

She left the room, taking with her the whiff of bossiness and antiseptic, leaving behind the stench of stale meat and their own silent thoughts.

***

'Am I being questioned again?'

Asp tilted her face to avoid the overhead spotlight. She was a small ghost in the shadows.

'No. Not at all. I've come to see how you are.'

'Well, now you've been, you can go.'

'But I don't know how you feel.'

'I'm depressed.'

'Are you?'

'Why are you always asking questions when you know the answer already?'

'But I don't, you see.'

***

'It's a bit difficult to chat if I'm not allowed to ask you anything.'

'No. You're *not* allowed.'

'Nothing at all?'

'Not one word. With anyone.'

'I'm sorry.'

***

The inspector studied his fingernails. He kept his head low, examined how he'd cut each tip below the pads, pressing hard on the soft bits between the knuckles with his fingers to see if it would hurt and when he couldn't bear the pain any longer, releasing them with a whoosh of relief.

'I'm fed up with people expecting me to explain myself,' said Asp.

'Are you sure it isn't you doing the expecting?'

'That's crap. I'm always being asked why or what and stuff like that. Well. I'm not interested.' She flung herself back against the sheets.

He hesitated, too old, too out of it as far as she was concerned. 'Is that it? Do you want me to go away?' Looked across at the young, sullen face that revealed so much unhappiness. He should have sent Petrovich instead.

She kept glancing back at him furtively until he said, quite unexpectedly, 'If you knew my thoughts, if you understood what eats me up from time to time, you'd see me differently.'

'Maybe I don't want you asking any more rubbish questions about my granny.' Her voice, when it came, was toneless. 'Even though I know policemen are supposed to ask questions. And you do. Whenever you see me.'

'Do I?'

Neither of them spoke a word for about fifty seconds, which seemed like a long time in a hospital ward with no one else present but themselves. Asp was the first to cave in.

'Did you know you can tell by the sound of its buzz when a fly is about to die?'

'No. I didn't.'

***

'If you think me guilty of murder, why don't you take me to prison?' She was picking at the loose threads on the bed cover and watching them unravel.

'What a bizarre thing to say.'

'You mean it never entered your head?'

'I've told you before. Why should it?'

'Because you're an inspector who likes to collect lots of dead bodies.'

'I have no bodies right now, and I'm off duty.'

'I'm in a psychiatric ward.'

'I know.'

They were equally uncomfortable in each other's company. Asp, in her restlessness, discovered she had made a hole in the bed cover and could stick her finger through it. The inspector was feeling the weight of self-censorship as he shifted on his stool and considered how to deal with a fragile adolescent.

'You tend to look on the dark side of things when you're locked up.'

'There aren't any locks, Asp.'

'Feels like there are.'

'Listen to me. If I upset you the other day, I'm very sorry. I'm not a monster.'

'What are you, Inspector?'

'You know who I am.'

He leaned forward. Asp slid under the sheet with one finger still caught in the hole as he tried to see things from her point of view, tried even to improve her opinion of him. His present fear was that official worries seemed to thrust themselves upon him the nearer he drew to them. 'Perhaps I want you to know I have some feelings. I can feel sympathy for other people even.'

His hand felt inside his pocket and screwed up the two pages of notes he had written before coming.

'You're upsetting me.' She was watching him from behind the hem of her sheet.

'You're going home tomorrow.'

'Am I? Then I want to tell you something. So we don't have to talk about it anymore.'

'Go ahead.'

'When there aren't any more postcards coming from Granny, my mother'll be the first to tell you. She'll ring you up or else she'll send you one of her secret e-mails. I bet it's an e-mail.'

His hands were resting over the curve of his knees. He listened to her, no longer expecting to be getting somewhere. He was too tired to take offence at any hidden meaning.

'I know, I *know* exactly how my mother thinks. It'll be, "Nothing came in the post last week," and then, "we haven't had a card for a whole month," or, "we haven't heard a word in three months". And that's the moment when everyone'll agree that Granny must have died from old age. Even you, Inspector. As you said, you haven't got a body, so for you to fantasise about her being murdered is pathetic. It's just a – just a sick sort of habit.'

'Have I once mentioned murder? That's not fair. You invent your own obstacles.'

'You're coming here to this hospital, and sitting there in that chair in front of me isn't fair. I can't get up and run away from you.'

'I'm sorry. I suppose I felt responsible. For you being here.' He raised his hands from his knees and folded his arms under his armpits as he breathed in slowly and hoped there was some football on television that night. *She was just a child chattering,* he reminded himself.

'I know that you *think* she was murdered. My point is that thinking it doesn't make it a fact.'

'I'm not disagreeing with you.'

He wanted to placate her even more than before because he was tired. Didn't fancy a scene in the hospital and looked around to see if anyone had entered the room or overheard them. He spoke with exceptional gentleness. 'I haven't said what I think, Asp.'

'Because you won't!'

He watched her rattle the sides of the bed in her fury. She had begun to shout at him, eyes blinking the way they had in the art gallery. He was nervous just remembering.

'Listen, listen to me, Inspector Love. I try to make something nice happen for a change, and it's crap, but that doesn't make *me* crap, does it? Just because I fail to make something halfway decent happen? Do you see my point? There's a difference between an idea about something and what it is.'

He shook his head at her logic as she pulled the tray of food back from the corner and towards her, then pushed it violently to the end of the bed as she smelt the mincemeat.

'I don't have to tell you any more than that.' She closed her wild eyes and kept them shut as she spoke quietly for once. 'You can go now.' So quietly, he wasn't sure if she had.

Standing next to her, telling himself that she had tripped up his conscience, there was nothing more he could think of saying. Not here certainly and not yet. The mince had turned to congealed cement, and small flecks of animated dirt were swirling round inside her water jug. Nice.

He walked down the long tiled tunnel that led away from the wards, whistling Handel's *Largo*, something he did when he was feeling unsettled or not in control of his emotions. He saw vats of steaming mobile dinners, shiny coffee machines, people passing him in the corridors with blank expressions.

The further he walked, the more he felt hot. He stopped by a wall basin to wash his hands, to pass the time, and to spend a good ten minutes scrubbing his nails. Coming towards him from the other direction, he saw the nurse with the bobbing watch, carrying an aluminium lid in one hand, a bottle of pills in the other.

'Goodbye, Nurse.' They drew closer. The starch gleamed in streaks across her dress and her cap. He was an expert at seeing the flesh under the frock and not a million miles away from Henry in his priapic wishfulness.

The nurse nodded back at him, covering the watch with the bottle to stop it swinging as she passed and disappeared down a different corridor.

Was he so transparent, he asked himself as he began whistling again – following the exit signs on the walls until, at the last corner, he collided with Daphne.

'Was that you whistling?' she laughed, and he realised that he was unused to people laughing at him.

'I do like whistling.' She let him place an arm around her. 'My father always whistled when he took us off to the shops to buy sweets.'

Now why did she make that up? She didn't have a father, at least not one she'd known, discounting the possibility of Uncle Hamish on the grounds of incongruity. The lie just slipped out of her as if she wanted it to be real.

'I've seen Asp,' said the inspector.

'And?'

'She was tired, I think.'

'Then I won't disturb her.'

It was a paltry excuse for a mother not to see her sick daughter, a measure of her inadequacy as a parent, and her reply disturbed the inspector in a way he hadn't reckoned with. It was maybe unexceptional that a married man, who's stopped having sex with his wife, still wants it with someone else. It was also a general hankering he had – a fallow interest in every available woman he met. *There were not so many in his path,* he thought sadly, and his interest was expressed as restrained lechery that others couldn't see.

He was standing in such closeness to this woman in the narrow corridor that he had to hold his breath in case she stepped back. He tried to listen to her breathing and wondered if she felt the same way. Not that they would talk about it. This was hardly a moment of grand or even ludicrous passion.

If they had shown any serious interest, whatever was between them would have ceased to exist. In that sense, it was the opposite of Henry's attachment to Wellies Two. Perhaps if Daphne had known of her husband's affair, she might have done something equally robust with the inspector.

'Would you like a lift home?'

'Yes please.'

The longing for romance in some men outlasts their capacity for sex, he thought with bitterness. *It lasts to the grave.* And as they walked to the car park, he kept on sneaking glances at her from side on, noticing that below her chin were the beginnings of a turkey wobble.

He thought about the nurse, Asp, his wife and the woman in the paper shop who had beautiful, liquidy eyes when she handed him his cigarettes. He remembered them all until the images in his head became muddled and Daphne patted the back of his hand, telling him she was glad that both he and Henry were not urban smoothies. He told her she sounded just like Asp, and she laughed and said what else did he expect 'my dear', and that floored him a bit.

He drove her home and felt no more lust of any kind that night. A pity. You see how fragile a thing it is. You want it, and as soon as you get near to having it, you throw it away, and the next day you want it back again. He was well suited to his job. Inspectors are voyeurs of a kind.

***

'It is not, nor it cannot come to good;
But break my heart, for I must hold my tongue.'
Hamlet

CHAPTER 15

Mimi-Saulange Bernard left the Thrush family home after a year to join a convent in Ireland. She would write to them as Sister Marie-Therese Bonaventure and be remembered as their little vegetarian who began every sentence with fortunately or unfortunately.

Anjelica Markovitch from Croatia (via America) followed within days of her departure and was quickly joined by Violette Lepage from Haute Provence. They were to be simultaneous lodgers. Their gut reactions to the Thrush family on first meeting:

'*Merde.*'

'Oh my God. Shit.'

***

'But stay, what noise?'
Hamlet

CHAPTER 16

Asp is out of hospital.

Anjelica had a Caravaggio face and the words 'cock-up' tattooed on her arm. She arrived with her designer luggage in a taxi from Heathrow. That hint of glamour was different for a start. Violette was small and dark with hair that fell to her waist and smelt of violets, which goes to show the power of suggestion. When the habits of the Thrush family life had palled, both girls turned to each other for solidarity. They observed any dips from a distance, drawing strength from their togetherness, ready to kick ass with the rest if need be. Anjelica arrived a few hours before Violette.

'This is the front bedroom which gets the sun in the morning. The other is smaller and at the back of the house, but it has the prettiest fireplace.'

Daphne wanted to sound enthusiastic but could do nothing to change the weariness of her voice, ashamed of the patter and the hospitality that came at a price. She decided to apologise, but it made her sound insincere and she struggled this time to keep it short.

'Of course, Violette will be studying for her first-year bacc. She might want the larger room for her books – computer and printer

– things like that.' Anjelica listened, saying nothing but running one hand lightly across the mantelpiece, feeling the cold of the marble seep into her fingertips.

'You are here to study art, is that right?' Daphne's eyes followed the manicured green nails with a look of longing that said I wish I were at the beginning of my life too. 'You choose,' she sighed.

Anjelica asked if she could think about it. Drifted between both rooms three or four times before deciding she would take the smaller one with the decorative fireplace and the red chimney tops seen in a line of turrets through the window. It was Jean-Pierre's old room, chosen because the walls were set back by a narrow landing, making it the nearest thing to her own island in someone else's domain. She considered asking if she could be left alone to unpack when Daphne removed herself to a hall window overlooking the street before disappearing downstairs.

It was the same morning that Henry sat on the end of the marital bed and announced he had lost his job and bought a new car. It was, he explained, applying his deodorant without removing the cap, the shiny red people carrier on the other side of the street that had been parked outside their house for several days. No one except Henry seemed aware it was theirs or that the family's fourteen-year-old estate car had finally been taken to a knacker's yard for rusty old crates.

'Oh.' Daphne hauled herself up from the pillows and reached out to touch his arm, worried he had spent all his redundancy money on a lorry. She scratched her skull in her anxiety and released a shower of flakes – caught one and tasted it cautiously with the tip of her finger.

A number of inconsistencies from the past week at last made sense: Henry's unexpected appearances and disappearances, his willingness to set the table for the evening meal or his readiness to take Leaf for a walk in his new double buggy. 'In that case...'

It was not her fault that her voice emerged between hiccoughs. The tears forced themselves into her eyelids and slipped down her cheeks. '*You* can collect the French girl with Uncle Hamish.' Hic. *Henry had no concept,* she thought, *no plans for what needed to be done.* Her eyes narrowed to squeeze out the wetness. No concept of difficulty – or what lies ahead. She would have to have any *concept* on his behalf. The trouble was she had none herself.

Henry swung between self-pity and thwarted desire on his way to the airport. It was not true that he had no plans. The idea of a new affair occurred to him when he was halfway along the A3. Not with Wellies Two. That was out of the question. Wellies One had snarled at him last Saturday by the dustbins. And certainly not with a lodger. Never, never, never with a lodger. His wife would smell a rat.

Daphne had been exhibiting all the signs of temporal lobe epilepsy in the last few weeks, complaining of a putrefying stench in the hallway that he personally had mopped and hoovered to shut her up about a dozen times. He tried to enjoy the drive with Uncle Hamish at his side in the front seat. He tried to forget about Daphne altogether. Difficult.

At a red light, he dreamt of small round female bottoms as ripe as apples. He hoped Uncle Hamish would remain motionless beside him and not interrupt his private erotic fantasy. But Uncle Hamish was absorbed by Beethoven on the car radio. How could he remain motionless? They had reached the coda of the first movement of the fifth symphony: *Da-da-da-daah* and Henry realised, sadly, there is an end to everything.

It was at that same moment – that fleeting moment – when Daphne sniffed the dust on her desk in the sitting room and closed her eyes to the pillar of bills, which if breathed on directly, would collapse. She meant to sort them into ordered groups of 'must be paid immediately,' 'can wait ten days,' 'hold back until further notice' and 'chuck.'

The sounds of Anjelica's unpacking could be heard through the ceiling. Asp, home from hospital, was sitting outside in the garden, laughing with Aunt Rose and Elm on a summer's day when no one should be sitting indoors. Leaf was strapped into his bouncy chair on the patio, enjoying the insects weaving above him in the air. Daphne saw it all and put her head down carefully on top of the paper mound and sobbed.

She had failed to tell Henry that she'd handed over her bric-a-brac affairs to the man from the upholstery shop. He had wanted an outlet for some new ceramic pots he was making, and she told herself that selling her shop back to him would give her more time to spend with her daughter.

It was only after the business had been sold and the mortgage for the premises repaid that she discovered there was still not enough money in the bank for living comfortably. 'What a mess,' she wept, what a bloody mess. 'I want my mother,' which is what she unwisely said to herself whenever life seemed a bitch.

'Mrs Thrush,' Anjelica was standing in the doorway pretending not to see her landlady's distress. 'I think there's a wasp in my room.' But Daphne continued sobbing and the girl went away to get rid of it by herself.

There had been another postcard. It arrived in the second post. Was it really years of sporadic postcards from her mother? This one was of a mountain with a rising ball of sun. *W.Y.W.H.* had been typed on the back, and the postmark was Borneo. Kicked behind the front door curtain after Henry and Uncle Hamish returned from Gatwick with Violette, it would remain there unnoticed for several weeks. When eventually rescued, no one could remember if they had read it before or not.

***

'What to ourselves in passion we propose.
The passion ending, doth the purpose lose.'
Hamlet

CHAPTER 17

It was a minor miracle that Violette and Anjelica were drawn to each other from the start. At some point, no one could remember exactly when they decided to stay for two years and not one. If either girl had occasional doubts about the sanity of their hosts, it was expedient to bury them. Daphne's shepherd pies inevitably burnt when she became distressed or anxious. But the girls' close friendship was more than self-serving – it was genuine, and the entire Thrush family remained convinced that they were perfect tenants. And so they were.

For the first time, Daphne, Henry and children found that as individual members of a family, they cared that they would be liked in return. Henry remained out of work and unable to hide his weekly signing-on for unemployment benefit. The family's anxiety about money or the lack of it made them vulnerable to other people's opinions. It was inevitable, this reversal of competence, and it happened without anyone noting the change.

Elm stumbled first. Violette was passing Elm's room when she glimpsed him through the open curtain, body jack-knifed above the bed, a copy of Rochester's 'Fair Cloris in a Pigsty Lay' in one hand, the other somewhere deep inside his jeans.

'Fly, nymph! Oh, fly ere 'tis too late
A dear, loved life to save;
Rescue your bosom pig from fate
Who now expires, hung in the gate
That leads to Flora's cave.'

'What are you doing?'

'Doing what?' He was cursing his mother for the lack of a door as he fell backwards onto the mattress and rolled over onto his stomach.

'I was scratching an itch, if that's what you mean.'

'Do you have *les puces*?' Violette was laughing at him with her pink gums and neat white teeth.

'I haven't any fleas.' Elm was more humiliated than embarrassed as he tried to lie still and appear cool. He would have preferred to have been a puddle on the floor so still you wouldn't see it, but if you did, you'd walk around it or step over it.

Violette took in the dried tomato ketchup on his T-shirt, the unwashed jeans and the holes in the heels of his socks, the whole adolescent male awkwardness. She remembered her own brother lying on his bed in a darkened room, and she laughed again.

'You have nice teeth.' He added but wished he hadn't when she disappeared almost immediately. He thought he might have a shower. This was a significant change. Voluntary washing. It was his first observance of the law that said there is a connection between personal hygiene and being desirable to the opposite sex.

There were times when Anjelica and Violette would sit outside the French windows of the sitting room and have a reflective and delicious bitch in the garden about the oddities of the English. Their chat would clarify what egregious act had gone before and their intimacy and sense of togetherness grew the more they gossiped.

Gusts of laughter would rise to the rooms above, and Elm or Asp would open their bedroom windows to try and catch the gist of what was said but never could, though both girls spoke to each other in English.

Violette had attended an American school in Paris as a child. Anjelica had left Dubrovnik for New York at the beginning of her high school there and had forgotten most of her Croatian. They saw with the eyes of travellers. Sharp and irreverent, merciless. Everything was defined by difference. Different usually meant worse.

Great Aunt Rose found her moment of enlightenment while she was washing pots and pans in the kitchen. She was shrivelled by arthritis, clutching at the wheels of her chair with her twisted fingers, planning a return to Scotland while Asp practised scales in the music room.

Violette just happened to be collecting water for her kettle when Aunt Rose, who loved all things French with a passion, seized the chance to talk about Paris. She asked if it was true there was a mysterious hum that could be heard inside Notre Dame at a certain time of the day. A mystical, sonorous, plangent hum like the howls of dead monks at Vespers seeking peace for their restive souls. A holy, unearthly sound of restlessness.

'Yes. There's a hum,' said Violette. 'It's the traffic from outside. You know – like m-m-m-m-m-onk.'

Aunt Rose looked startled and put the ghosts of the monks back inside their tombs. She tried not to sound disappointed when she turned her face up towards Violette and said that Parisian traffic must be more romantic than Edinburgh's.

Violette looked down at the neatly coiled bun of the elderly lady in her chair. She reached across for the tap and asked if Aunt Rose believed in reincarnation. Asked her while turning the tap on with such force that water splashed across Aunt Rose's lap and onto a pile of washing in a basket next to the wheelchair.

'Ah, si desolée, Madame. Excuses-moi.'

Aunt Rose turned again towards Violette, 'Do *you* believe in reincarnation, my dear?'

'Of course,' the French girl replied.

'Ah, but what do you believe?'

Violette smiled back at her and Aunt Rose felt a wave of happiness.

'Il y avait une fois, you were a very little bird in a cage. *Une canarie, Tante Rose.'*

Tante Rose flushed with happiness. She liked the idea of being very small. It made her sound ornamental, delicate even. Not an old lady with a face of granite like a gravestone, stuck in a wheelchair for most of the day until she would eventually die in a cloud of midges.

'Was I trapped too?' she asked shyly.

The lodger replaced the lid on her kettle, studied the ceiling for a few moments and shrugged her shoulders in that way which gives such weight to indifference. 'Only if you think so.'

'Oh, but I do, I do,' thought Aunt Rose. She was dreaming of her life as a canary in a gilded cage in the hall of mirrors at Versailles. She squeezed the water out of her skirt and watched it spill its glistening, transparent drops to the floor.

'What an interesting young person,' she sighed when Violette left the kitchen, and the sound of an E flat minor scale floated through the kitchen hatch.

'The prison is in my mind.' Aunt Rose was struggling to hold onto her reverie for a little longer. Another scale. And another to pass the time. 'Time is something you worry about in a piece of music,' she thought. 'You have to get it right.'

'Will you help me to my room Asp, dear?'

'Yes, Auntie.'

***

'More matter with less art.'
Hamlet

CHAPTER 18

The great aunt and uncle had returned to Scotland when Daphne suggested Anjelica should inspect her artwork. Claimed she wanted an expert's opinion to take her to another level. What she really craved was praise, and while Anjelica was helping her hang out the laundry in the attic, the older woman dived in recklessly in search of it.

'I suppose that art is no longer about looking at something. More about theory. I am caught up in this insane quest for perfection.'

'And what's your theory, Mrs Thrush? I mean, is that it? Your search for perfection is the art?'

Anjelica turned over a stack of canvases in one corner and decided her landlady's paintings were worse than she feared. The largest of them stood separately from the others on an easel.

Irridescent blobs of green with brownish-wispy bits in the centre were piled in a higgledy-piggledy, arbitrary arrangement. They looked like fish eyes – or frog spawn. But it was true that the painting glittered in the attic light.

A straw hat of the sort worn on holidays abroad was hung over a long black cape on the back of the one fire door in the house.

Henry's model planes were no longer hung from the ceiling but were thrust into another corner under plastic covers like a giant tee-pee.

'You've a Giacometti up there.' Anjelica waved in the direction of the hat and cape.

Daphne tried to see it through her lodger's eyes. 'Art should challenge assumptions, I suppose.' She spoke stiffly but fast, in case the girl, unlike Henry, was hot on concepts and believed that hers were rubbish.

'Sorry?'

'I mean I'm not doing all this as some sort of bourgeois recreation.'

'No, of course not.'

The lodger's voice was soft and reassuring, and Daphne relaxed slightly, tugging at her skirt and withdrawing a safety pin from its pocket.

'I try to startle myself. I paint my life.'

'Oh. Really? How do you do that?'

'Well, I throw blots down an awful lot and wait for a picture to emerge. I'm not deliberately controlling the image.'

Anjelica was silent.

'My brush is my thinker. My thoughts drift separately.'

Daphne dug the safety pin into the top right-hand corner of a blank canvas which was propped up against the wall, apart from the rest.

'You mean you're not in control of what's happening on the canvas?'

'Not consciously.'

'*Not* consciously?'

Daphne frowned. Had she, Daphne, got the wrong end of her brush?

Anjelica arched her back slowly as a cat does, stretching lazily, rippling its body before it moves on to a sunnier spot. Outside the small roof window, you could see the tips of horse chestnuts stretching up to the light, getting snarled in each other's branches they were so close to one another.

The summer coats of leaves were tired round the edges and waiting to drop off, but the light was wonderful. It came from behind them, dappling what it touched with darkness and light, mocking their conversation with its abundance of beauty.

'Yes, yes.' Daphne decided she wouldn't hold back. 'I'm not consciously doing anything, you see. Art is the surprise. Or do I mean the surprise is in the art? I'm aware that I'm trying not to change anything in case I go and spoil it. If it ends up accidentally looking like somebody's vomit, I'm not going to edit it out, don't you see? Because it's meant.'

A jet passed overhead and left a line of white cloud above the skylight. Daphne was shouting, though there was no need for her to raise her voice. The jet had passed.

'I suppose you're going to say then it isn't art.' She hadn't intended to say that. Everyone said that. Daphne prided herself on trying to be original. Picked up the canvas with the safety pin in her distress and held it, frowning underneath the window frame.

Anjelica felt the beginnings of a headache. Her landlady had shouted at her. The moment of pleasantness between them was over. The wet linen she had scooped out of the basket was dripping puddles on the floor and should have been lighter but felt heavier by the minute. The paintings were dreadful without exception. She had wasps in her room. She was homesick for Dubrovnik. Her landlady clearly had no intention of shutting up.

'This is my latest piece. I've called it 'Safety Pin On A Canvas.'

'I see.'

'But it's not, you know. The safety pin is in your head, not mine. I have taken a safety pin and changed it into a chastity belt. It will remain a chastity belt if no one thinks of it as a safety pin.'

Anjelica dropped her basket and rubbed her tattooed arms slowly across her chest. The word 'cock' was scratched on one wrist in faded green ink, the capital letters small and irregular. The 'up,' which followed the 'cock' was invisible from where Daphne was standing.

'Or nail clippings.' Daphne suddenly smiled. 'It could be someone's old nail clippings. It's an act of imagination after all,' and she hummed softly to herself as she pegged the corners of a sheet on a line above their heads and kept on nodding and smiling at her lodger as if she, Daphne, were at last onto something profound.

'Acquiring lodgers was the same as stamp collecting,' she whispered silently and slapped her face with her apron when Anjelica had gone. You hoped they'd increase in value or that some day, someone who knew something about art would simply comment on her work and see it for what it was. Provocative.

The girl was obviously not interested. You could see this by the way she kept her eyes fixed on the floor. She probably wanted to talk about art being energy and energy being part of the cosmic order because that's the sort of nonsense young people talk about when discussing art. Not how men's orgasms are so short as to be insignificant, which is why they have the time and the energy to be great artists. Hahaha.

'Is there a wasps' nest somewhere?' Anjelica had returned looking nervous, her voice strained. 'I keep on discovering them. Could you have a look in my room? I'm allergic to wasps.'

'A whole nest, are you sure? I'll trap them. I won't kill them. I'll just make them want to leave forever. Don't worry.'

Daphne secretly believed that without a sock to darn, a washing machine to fill, curtains to repair, onions to chop and wasps to chase, she'd be bored. If Anjelica had dented her confidence in her art, she had restored it elsewhere. She would be a tolerant, conscientious and benevolent landlady, she was certain.

Triumph would come standing tiptoe on a chair in her lodger's room as she slid one of her mother's postcards underneath an upturned glass before ramming it sharply against the wall. The wasp would crawl around inside with flustered, diminishing loops, and she would release it through the opened window, and Anjelica would be grateful to her for the rest of her stay.

But Daphne caught sight of herself in the mirror - hair thinner than a baby's, so light it floated out from her head horizontally in wisps instead of falling. And eyes – well, she didn't know what her eyes were like. It depended on how she felt at any one time. Sometimes they sparkled and she could see that once she might have been thought pretty. Now she doubted anyone would stop to look at her, and that was okay.

On the landing outside, she was aware that Anjelica was waiting for her by the stairs. The girl was crouching over a large coffee table biography of Picasso. Her black curls so shiny and thick, her face more like a Caravaggio.

'All gone.' Daphne's voice was softly triumphant. 'Can I see your book?'

Asp was standing on the steps below, her violin tucked under her arm. 'Anyone seen Violette? I want her to accompany me.'

'Hello?' Violette appeared from behind a curtain on the landing. 'Sorry. I've got a maths test. Some other time?'

'Well, all right.'

Except it wasn't really. Asp had been trying to attract Violette's attention for about a week. The psychiatrist at the hospital kept asking if there was a special *pal* in her life and to shut him up one morning, she had decided to say yes, lots of *pals*, although it wasn't true. Her friends at school lived in a world she had no desire to enter.

The French lodger was different. Asp frowned and examined her violin. Its wood was dull like an old school desk. A hairline crack had appeared next to the the scroll while she was in hospital and was affecting the sound. It felt breathy, no longer pure. She returned to the music room, scratching an arm as if her mother's psoriasis had invaded her too. Maybe she should ask if she could have a pet. Every year she asked her parents for one – a jumping spider would be nice – and every year she was told no. A cat would keep her company. COULD THEY NOT SEE THAT?

Asp felt detached and calm as she listened to the lodgers discuss their plans for a walk in the park to see the deer. *If I don't have a friend, I'll definitely have a cat,* she thought and placed her bow on the strings, held it, lifted it for a second and pressed down hard, gripping the gut with the hair. 'Much better,' she whispered to no one but herself.

***

'There is a willow grows askant the brook
That shows his hoary leaves in the glassy stream.'
Hamlet

Chapter 19

Henry's insight when it came was less straightforward than the rest of the family's. He was flying his model aeroplanes alone that afternoon and thought he saw Violette and Anjelica as dots in the distance. He felt a small glow of pleasure and importance because they had walked all the way there to watch him fly.

'You see – it's quite simple. The pressure that the wing exerts on the air is equal to the opposite pressure of the air on the wing. It's basic physics.' He'd tell them this in so many words as soon as they caught up, and they would be glad they had come.

But Anjelica danced across the flying field and became trapped in his towing line, and Violette had to cut the nylon thread around her friend's legs with a pair of scissors, ruining his bungee in the process.

'What the fuck?' Henry waved a tangled ball of line and forgot that his plane was still in the air. They giggled as it soared, then stalled before spiralling downwards with the loss of momentum. Too fast and too late for Henry, struggling with his remote control. It crashed into the top of a tree next to some deer that seemed carved into the landscape they were so still. It could not have been worse as far as Henry was concerned. He was afraid of heights. He loathed all deer.

He discovered the trunk was impossible to shake, being solid and wide. His plane was stuck up there for good. There was no foothold for him to climb and the lower branches had been gnawed away by the deer or ripped off by their antlers.

He was worried the girls would hang around to watch him fall if he tried to climb the tree. *Girls are like that,* thought Henry, *they're all sadistic at heart. They wait for you to make a fool of yourself.* No, he was not a misogynist. He was realistic. Joke.

Crestfallen, he sat on a mound of uncut grass, waiting for the deer to move to another patch. The girls had disappeared without his realising they had, so he was wrong about the hanging around bit. He considered what to do next. Thought of copying his mother-in-law and pissing off without a word. Why not? He'd send postcards from Las Vegas, but of course, he never would, never did.

He was glad there was no one left to witness his lonely vigil at the foot of the tree and removed his shoes and socks and stretched his legs, digging his toes in some dog shit by mistake. He felt doomed and dismal. His plane would be a write-off, but he had to shimmy up this bloody tree or lose his precious radio control gear. Shit had tightened his skin, tweaking the hairs on his toes. *Shimmying was out of the question,* he thought gloomily. He was stuffed.

'Oh, Daph,' he addressed a beetle crawling across the bark. Aloud and almost tearful. 'Daph, Daph, Daph,' he repeated with increasing passion as he recalled his last thoughts of his mother-in-law and as he peered into the topmost branches.

'Bloody woman!' He rammed his head against the trunk, beating the sides of it with his fists. A crow flying above squawked in alarm. 'Bloody fucking woman!' he cried even louder than before. 'Oh, Daph, what have you done?'

Henry continued to hurl himself at the bark until there was blood on his knuckles and under his palms, and right at the moment when he felt there was no point to anything anymore, the plane jerked sideways and crashed through the leaves, landing nose first in the earth by his bare feet. The wings were battered at the tips, but the body and the tail were still intact. *Like me,* he thought. *Just like me.*

His hands were trembling as he scooped it up by the fuselage at the join between the wings and carried it back to the car park. His shoes were tied together by their laces and hanging round his neck. He could feel his trouser bottoms flapping against his ankles in the wind, whipping their flesh as he began estimating the cost of his accident. The shit, at least, was dry and odourless. He bent down to brush it off.

***

'What is a man,
If his chief good and market of his time
Be but to sleep and feed?
A beast, no more!'
Hamlet

CHAPTER 20

Leaf was the only Thrush who escaped biblical humiliation. For Leaf, there could be no question of pain transmuted into enlightenment. Nobody expected anything of Leaf, which is probably why he was left alone. Leaf was everyone's oversized ugly doll, a plaything who slept, ate, soiled his nappies and cried.

His obstinate bulk never yielded to the idea that he could grow upwards instead of out. He couldn't talk, he couldn't walk, he couldn't crawl, he couldn't sit up without support, and he never appeared any older, just bigger and heavier. The board games such as Monopoly were not for him, although in his highchair, he became a dab hand at Grab or building blocks that he flung without discriminating against anyone who passed.

Time didn't have the usual meaning for Leaf because it always seemed to be standing still for him, as in *Rip Van Winkle* or an unused metronome. Deep down inside himself, where he lived, no one knew what was going on or why. It was something he had in common with Uncle Hamish, and if Uncle Hamish remained unscathed by criticism and unenlightened, it was because he was not a real Thrush, and he preferred his own world. He too was a type of baby, and babies were a protected species.

Violette and Anjelica grew meanwhile in their importance. The greatest danger they faced was to be absorbed into the family or become inured to their ways as the months passed. Thrush strategies for wooing were straightforward enough.

'Would you like my black skirt? You look better in it than me;' 'please eat my share of pizza/lamb chop /strawberries/ chocolate buttons;' 'let's all go roller-blade in the park, have a swim, walk along the towpath;' 'I've got some free tickets for the new Bond. Want to come?' 'Give me a few minutes and I'll burn that CD you wanted/fix your computer/share my new unchippable nail varnish/have a look at that knotty maths problem.'

There was no limit to their adoring both girls. They believed it important to be the admirers more than the admired. Any exhibitionist fake homicidal thoughts by Asp were buried before they could surface. Any natural longings by Henry or Elm were unnaturally suppressed. Daphne found herself darning the holes in their laundry and washing their sheets not once a fortnight but weekly with pods of lavender.

Henry remained unemployed throughout their stay, quietly playing with his model aeroplanes and somehow holding on to his darkest secret. The dole queue. Occasionally he would sell one of the planes or try to repair broken ones for other fliers in the park. In return, he would receive free car maintenance, a can of two-star petrol, surplus vegetables on their way to rot, the occasional skinned rabbit, one year's supply of disposable nappies and, by mistake, someone's used batteries and an empty tin of anti-freeze.

The money from the lodgers and the sale of the bric-a-brac shop had topped up the family's dwindling funds. It brought a small but vital cash flow that kept the bailiffs from their almost only functional door. Daphne, round about this time, set herself up as a Humanist Life Consultant with PC Petrovich as her first patient. He came in search of a cure for composer's block, willing to try anything. Everyone it seemed was willing to try anything.

When at the end of two years, Violette and Anjelica were standing with their bags packed in the living room ready to depart, they were begged not to go. Violette was to become a medical student in Marseilles. Anjelica was off to Albania to restore mediaeval icons damaged by the war between the Serbs and Croatians. Daphne cried for ten minutes when they left because she said they'd never had it so good, which was true. Leaf cried because his mother cried.

Asp said she'd miss their chatter outside her bedroom window and promised she would have a cat when they returned. If they returned. Elm looked sad and had an exceptionally long shower after they'd gone. Henry said they were the only lodgers who'd ever bothered to come and watch him flying in the park. Both girls parted from each Thrush member with promises to keep in touch.

It was a period when the cellar remained untouched, deliberately avoided by Asp and almost forgotten by the others, when the family, including Asp, seemed to accept the absence of Granny without apparent distress and when Asp was planning to buy a cat from the local pet shop for £1.50 as they'd had a glut of kittens.

If the inspector came to visit, he insisted he came not on business but for pleasure and was quickly rewarded by Daphne when she called him by his name, which was Cedric.

Elm was awarded 'A' grades in all his A levels and would later complete his Natural Sciences degree at Cambridge with a starred first. Asp won scholarships to the sixth form of a posh London school for boys and to the Saturday school of the Royal College of Music before beginning her degree in English at Oxford. Of that, more later…

By the end of Violette's and Anjelica's stay, Leaf had begun saying *'Golly, golly, golly',* and although it was all he ever said, this was interpreted as speech. Wellies Two received breast implants as a joint Christmas present for herself and Wellies One, who it must be said, saw the benefits.

The old girl from the house on the other side died peacefully in her sleep with an empty bottle of gin by her bed, which prompted Henry to say at her funeral that it was the way he'd like to go. In straightforward accession, Asp acquired her cat without having to part with £1.50 at the local pet shop as a fully grown tabby answering to the name of Granny walked through their front door the following day and never left, except to catch an occasional mouse.

***

'O MOST PERNICIOUS WOMAN!
Hamlet

CHAPTER 21

As if their cloying adoration couldn't last a minute longer than the two years in which Violette and Anjelica had lived with them, along came Anastase Besoin for the next academic year. By the simple act of being, Anastase did her best to forestall any more attachment to lodgers.

Despite paying twice as much as Violette and Anjelica, Anastase was so detested by Henry, Daphne, Asp, Elm, Leaf and everybody who lived in the street, there were continual cries of 'Bring back Violette, Bring Back Anjelica,' cries so heart-rending and so constant that it was impossible for their new lodger not to hear them every time she opened her bedroom window.

Without realising it, there were brief, miraculous moments of solidarity in Thrush family life when blood ties did count. Quite soon, Anastase became known as Nasty. It was her suggestion.

On previous lodgers, she would say: 'Where are these froggie paragons then? What made them so fucking perfect, and why did they leave?'

Nasty's English father had disappeared without leaving a forwarding address while she was still a small child, a fact which should have given her something in common with Daphne but didn't as neither knew of the other's loss. Her French Canadian mother fled to Cuba with a Turkish piano teacher during Nasty's early adolescence, and her mother's sister meanwhile dispatched Nasty to England after Nasty disowned her through the courts with an injunction to prevent all future contact.

After rejecting her relatives or being rejected by them, the unhappy girl did the obvious things to assuage her misery by eating herself into obesity and becoming even more repellent to the lean and sanctimonious middle classes of Putney and Barnes of which each Thrush was a poorly disguised member.

That beneath Nasty's blubber was a core of sweetness seemed as implausible as it was improbable. That in Nasty there was something fresh if only they could find it or that in their selves, something stale would never occur to them. To probe would contest the very basis of what they themselves were.

On the day of her arrival, Nasty swore not to be good but to be different. Shades perhaps of Asp, though no one saw any connection between the two adolescent rebels. By the second day, Nasty had forgotten her vow, and too soon, Christmas came and went in a state of protracted despair on both sides.

Daphne retreated to the attic to address her latest piece of installation art, which was her laptop computer. In doing so, she believed she would lance a boil and exorcise her unhappiness.

'There is always a crisis of some description for all people at any given time.'

She typed while looking down at her fingers, pleased that some warts on her knuckles had vanished and pausing only to press 'save' when the screen blinked back at her.

'Ours is the presence of the new lodger, known as Nasty. The following statement is to remind this family never to have lodgers again if we ever can possibly help it:

OUTLINE: Anastase Besoin. Eighteen years old, Canadian female. Application for enrolment at the French Lycée refused eleventh hour. Supposedly saw list of host families on school pinboard; chose ours due to least cost and is taking gap year in our house. Arrives with blue tin trunk containing a year's supply of euros, Canadian dollars and multiple boxes of M&Ms.

DESCRIPTION: Morbidly overweight, average height. Purple hair with white fringe – black nylon leggings at all times.

LIKES: Enemas before bed, peanut butter and tobacco at breakfast. 'Moon River.'

FRIENDS: Ex-drug addict/ dealer – female and currently homeless.

COMPLAINTS SO FAR:

Carved 'I hate Bono' on dining room table. Cost of repairs: £4,000

Cut fringe off Turkish rugs and eyelashes off Leaf's dolls. Cost of repairs: £2.49p.

54) Smashed Christmas fairy on tree after drinking one and a half bottles of vodka; burnt holes in said Turkish rugs. Cost of replacement: £3,000,000. (Turkish rugs believed mediaeval treasure).

Diagnosed sociopath aged four by mother's therapist.

183) Drinks wine at breakfast. Cost: Variable. (diagnosed alcoholic at nine by mother's therapist.

Difficult to gauge grasp on truth - like catching soap in

bathwater. Underlying Munchausen tendencies suspected.

191) Crashed Elm's birthday party with ex-drug addict while stoned. Complains subsequently that English university students are emotionally frigid faggots and that sixteen of them were seen naked on sofa.

208) Returned unexpectedly from weekend trip to Paris same day of departure; claims to have been attacked by nuns.

300) Ex-drug dealer friend says Nasty has stolen gold necklace with locket from stranger in street. Inscription inside locket reads, 'love from Daddy.'

417) Claims family is deliberately starving her with green leaf salads. Maybe true.

699) Expects five-star hotel service in a private house.

Signed: Daphne Thrush, New Year, 200-.

P.S. Have I no friend will rid me of this living fear?

The words had wormed their way out of Daphne's liver. They made tiny perforated holes like a colander inside her body, but this was no time to be ill.

Elm hurried back to his room by the Bridge of Sighs, removing himself from any Nasty fallout, such as Nasty's unhappiness, her disappointment and contempt. Henry hid behind his newspaper, unaware she thought he was a wanker and a pervert. He observed her from the sides of his eyes without turning his head.

She would have preferred an ally in Asp, but Asp was either too snobbish or solipsistic to tolerate a rival.

Unhappily for them all, Nasty's relationship with the family was a misalliance from the start that would have catastrophic consequences at the end. On her bedroom wall, stuck between a newspaper picture of Prince William on a polo pony and a poster for *Terminator* Fifteen, was a scrap of paper with a poem copied out in Nasty's wilful scrawl. Throughout her days as a lodger in their house, Nasty would recite it before she fell asleep.

> Flying High – by Anastase Besoin
>
> *One called Hemp,*
> *The other Weed*
> *Spliff in a drag*
> *O-ver.*
> *Rocked the joint*
> *And dropped the bomb*
> *O-ver.*
> *Fuck-a-duck*
> *Insane man*
> *Massive!*
> *O-VER.*

***

'There is nothing either good or bad,
but thinking makes it so.'
Hamlet

CHAPTER 22

'Henry?' The voice belonged to Wellies Two. Husky. Sexy. Seductive. *Whatever,* thought Daphne bitterly as the second time the 'Henry' was more tentative and more uncertain before it stopped.

Daphne hunched over her laptop and pressed the delete button on her file marked *'Lodgers.'* She plucked a scent bottle from her desk drawer as the front doorbell rang, and this time, she could hear Asp's voice directing her patient upstairs.

There was already a pattern in the way the consultant and her sole client would pass their hour-long session. PC Porfiry Petrovich would start by ducking his head to hide his face, reciting his inner thoughts between lengthy silences. Daphne would consider her responses in the gaps between thoughts while Porfiry Petrovich weighed up the best way to talk about an extremely delicate and personal subject, himself.

It was only his third or fourth visit, and Daphne was reluctant to spoil things by hurrying him up or asking him to speak in complete sentences with a beginning and an end.

She hadn't quite yet discovered what she was meant to do. It was Henry's idea that she should become a life consultant, and if she failed, it was Henry's fault, not hers.

'There's nothing to it.' Henry had no time for resistance that morning. He was late for the park. 'Besides, we agreed. You just listen to people banging on about their lives and make encouraging noises.'

'Well, you do it then,' she replied, knowing that he couldn't hear a word she said as he slammed the front door. She had already capitulated the night before, explaining how she'd manage the therapy part of the life consultancy business – but only because they needed the money. It was agreed between them during an attack of morning sickness that had arrived in the evening - an attack that came and threatened to last forever.

She was too old to have babies, Henry argued with a look of disgust on his face and too young, she snapped, for the menopause.

***

'Ah, Porfiry. Your timing's perfect.' Daphne waved her patient to the futon. It was covered and stapled in black leather to look like a couch. She watched him from her swivel chair, noting that his ears were like exotic shells washed up on a beach, one noticeably larger than the other. Topics up for discussion: police, music publishers, the state of contemporary music, his gallbladder and how many times his compositions had been performed. Once.

They had agreed in the first session that she would address him as Porfiry and not PC Petrovich. It was obvious from the way his eyes rolled when she addressed him as constable that he resented his junior status.

Perhaps, she said, his unhappiness was not so much his lack of promotion or that his compositions were being ignored by the musical establishment but that his personal feelings were contained in a self-limiting box. He had avoided intimate analysis so far in his life and she was curious why not. Wasn't he?

'I am an unhappy person.' Pause. 'I do harm to myself.' Pause. 'But I hope it's something that will wear off.'

'Do you mean your unhappiness might wear off or that you might do less harm to yourself as you get used to the unhappiness?'

'I mean, I'll get used to being shit miserable.' Long pause. 'I'm more than one person, you see. Policeman by day and secret avant-garde composer by night. There's this gap between what I know is the real me and what everybody else thinks I am.'

He was studying Daphne's painting of rain on a boulder when suddenly he closed his eyes. 'I can't say which *me* is the more miserable.'

His eyelashes were so long they curled back on themselves as if too heavy and too burdensome to remain open. After a minute or two, he made an effort to look at her, resisting the inertia that had already set in when he sat down and tried to talk about himself - genuinely trying to explain who he thought he was and what he'd like to be.

'An onion without a heart. That's what I'd like to be. I'd make other people cry, but I wouldn't cry myself.'

Daphne looked down at the notes on her desk and sighed. 'I

see,' she said, knowing full well that she didn't really. Porfiry Petrovich was only getting started.

'When someone walks past me in the street, they could be a murderer, a psychopath, a thief, and nobody knows. It's an exciting possibility I don't think about. I don't have any clear perception of them and they don't have one of me.'

'Yes...'

'I react to events, not to people... like a car parked on a double yellow line or someone waving a gun and running in the opposite direction.'

'Yes?' Again, Daphne wondered if she was up to this life consultancy business. Perhaps she could make her patient a tomato sandwich while she gave it some thought.

'What would it be like,' she asked after some mutual silence, 'if you gave up being one of these two things... Would that make it easier? Would you be less miserable if people only thought of you in one way? Policeman or composer but not both at the same time?'

'I can't stop being a policeman if that's what you mean... it pays the bills... and I can't stop being a composer because I want to compose... so it's a question I can't answer.'

'Are you saying, Porfiry, that one is business and the other's pleasure?'

'I suppose that one is a habit and the other is more a compulsion.'

'Ah.' She considered this as she rearranged the bits and pieces on her desk. She placed a small framed photo of Asp and Elm next to a tiny plastic Russian Babushka and a brass bell in the shape of a St Bernard with a barrel. ' Ting-a-ling, Porfiry. If a habit becomes a compulsion, does that make it alright?'

Porfiry Petrovich looked at her with horror. 'I might look out the window and say, excuse me, Mrs Thrush, I've got to get the licence plate of that car I've seen going the wrong way up your street because I can't help it. It's a habit at that level, I suppose.'

'And that's not a compulsion?'

'Not one I want.'

She rose to remove a loose nail from her collage on the wall and returned to her chair. Resolved to listen more attentively from now on. It was not something that she felt came naturally to her. There was so much for her to learn.

'Of course, I might try to understand why someone commits a murder,' he reflected. 'I don't want to, but I know I have to if I'm to become a successful policeman, which I'm not. If you don't empathise, it's just a process of legalized vengefulness, isn't it?'

'So you're saying that you're vengeful.' Daphne fingered the St Bernard very gently so as not to ring it by mistake.

'Sometimes I get caught up in a desire for revenge.'

Porfiry Petrovich drew himself up from the couch until he was sitting with his legs stretched out in front of him, his face white and bloodless. What Daphne was about to say was not remarkable, but it was what he would remember.

'You know Porfiry – there's a month or maybe a year of purity when you're a young child, and you're told in the school assembly that you must stand up for old ladies on a crowded bus. Then you're told you mustn't lie or steal a biro from a bank either, and for a while, you do everything you're told to do – and so one day, when you are an adult, you forget what you're supposed to do, and that's it. You're corrupted. And of course you feel anxious when you see an unknown policeman from another station coming towards you – because you think you might have done something you shouldn't have... And maybe you have. Is that not so, Porfiry?'

Asp's cat jumped through the open skylight and landed on the patient's lap. It remained stretched across both his knees, flicking its furry striped tail and rhythmically, sheathing and unsheathing its claws.

'Just push her away, Porfiry. She's always coming in here on the scrounge. I think she likes the smell of turps.'

'She can stay.'

'Would a cat make you happy?'

'I've already got a cat.'

'What sort of harm do you think you do to yourself, Porfiry?' She was becoming quite pleased with her line of questioning.

Pause.

'I sometimes force myself to listen to music by other composers.'

'So you don't like their music?'

'No.'

'Because you think it's bad?'

'Yes.'

'You're not jealous.'

'No. They write crap.'

'And you don't.'

'Not really. Mine isn't. CRAP.' The longest pause so far. 'It's just that unlike everybody else, I never get a chance to hear it.'

'So you're cross because they're being performed?'

'Yes.'

'And you're not.'

'Maybe.'

'What do you *think* would make you happy, Porfiry?'

'I'd like someone to say, 'Well done, Petrovich. I think you're in line for a promotion... I'd like to commission you to write an opera.'

'Anything else?'

'No. That's it.'

Daphne smiled at him encouragingly. 'But you can make this happen. I mean, the performances and the police work.'

'I'm only the driver who takes notes and types them up back at the station. I don't get to solve crimes on my own.'

'That's a pity. And the opera?'

His face was animated for the first time – the lantern jaw, the marrow face, the proud poppy eyes, the intensity, Daphne found it strangely affecting. She had once seen a badger like that, blinking in the light of her torch as she stumbled on its hole in the ground late at night. Porfiry was her badger. Her articulate badger for the words flew from his mouth as if he couldn't stop them coming.

'I'd start with the notes, *D-E-A-D*... on contra-bassoon... with drums... some reverb from the back of the hall. A funeral march. Down the aisle.' He was singing now and conducting with both arms in the air. 'It's mostly about Hell. Daaah-aaaaagh-AAAAAAH, followed by six trombones in unison.'

Daphne's knowledge of contemporary music was sketchy, but

she suspected this was cutting-edge funky. 'Like Dante's "Inferno"?' she interrupted brightly. 'The Police Federation might be interested. Maybe they'd commission you. I'll suggest it to Inspector Love.'

At the mention of the inspector's name, he covered his face with his hands, and the cat began to purr. Daphne realised her mistake, but it was too late to undo the damage. His moroseness had returned.

'I don't want any… any pity. I don't want any contempt. I don't want to have any special help. Any concessions.'

He pushed the cat off his lap. He remembered she was offering him help. He was aware that Daphne was looking at him with pity and imagined he saw a tear in the corner of each eye.

'I believe, Porfiry, that you are a very thoughtful person,' she said quietly. 'Very thoughtful. And that being thoughtful makes you too hard on yourself. Sometimes you should sit back and say: "I'm really pretty amazing".'

'I'm doing two very different jobs, which are both difficult in their own ways, and I'm using all of me to do them rather than two distinct me's. Then it doesn't matter if the people who see you as a policeman don't see you as a composer and vice versa, does it?'

'Well… Yes, it does… It means we're back to what I hate most. The idea that I'm treated as two different people.'

'Which of the two is treated better?'

His eyes drifted towards a collage hanging on the opposite wall – it was made up of empty food tins and rusty nails on a background of hessian. A small dolly with raisin eyes and silver pumps on her tiny feet was dressed in a pink tutu and waving a knife and fork in the centre. She saw him blink away what she hoped was a tear of his own until she realised it was something in her own eye that spilled over one lid and then another before it rolled slowly down her cheek.

'I don't know. I don't think either of the two me's is treated with respect. I've been passed over for police promotion so many times. Then I go to concerts and meet other composers, but none of them want to see what I've written. I ask to see theirs. I even listen to their broadcasts.'

'Excuse me, but don't you think you're being a bit wet? If you're being honest with yourself, you're not being very helpful.'

Her words, usually so languid with long pauses in between each one, ran together quickly.

'You see, Porfiry, deep down, nobody is very generous with their respect. Perhaps you expect too much. I mean, you're a very interesting person. How many people can say that they're a policeman **and** a composer? Perhaps instead of worrying about which person you are supposed to be, you should just say you're both. Like ham and pickle.'

'What's special about ham and pickle?' He blew his nose with a grubby tissue from his pocket, and she made a private note to remember to have a box of fresh ones next to her laptop in future. The glasses that she'd taken to wearing on the end of a chain were covered in minute crumbs and could do with a wipe.

'But Porfiry, the point is your two passions complement each other.' She wished she'd thought of it before. This whole tissue thing. She could imagine a week's worth of patients having to blow their nose, except that so far, there had only been Porfiry. Wellies One and Wellies Two had seemed quite indifferent, almost rude, when she'd mentioned the possibility...

'Let's face it. You are definitely being a tiny bit self-pitying.' There was so much for her to say to her badger. She had better lie down on the futon with him in a non-lascivious way. She felt exhausted already.

'Perhaps you should teach night classes in contemporary music. At the police station. Eventually, there'd be lots of people just like yourself and you'd discover both interests go together without splitting any sense of who you are into two bits.'

'But... I don't want anyone else to be me.'

'Ah. You see? At least you're admitting now that you're one and the same person. I think this is progress, Porfiry. We'll talk about it some more next time.'

She was vaguely aware that he was clapping his hands together, which seemed an oddly joyful thing to do.

'And... um... Porfiry?' She was reluctant to bring up the matter of a fee as he moved towards the door with the cat following at his heels and rubbing herself against his trouser cuffs. She suddenly realised she could send him the bill by post, and her eyes widened. 'Maybe you could let me hear some of your music next time you come.'

'Whatever.' He hung his head and nudged the cat to one side. So sadly done, she could have hugged him out of pity.

Then she remembered that the family was going away on holiday the following week and that was about all she could remember or consider.

'When we return from France, we'll have a listen to your music. Next session, Porfiry. Promise. Asp will see you out.'

The life consultant waved goodbye to the patient in a semi-blissful state, although it was clear the patient was still miserable by the droop of his head. He was not shown to the front door by Asp, who was in the kitchen asking Wellies Two to feed the cat while they were away. He let himself out.

After closing the front door and checking that no one was watching, he began hopping down the path, landing in the centre of each paving stone, head down and one right leg held up with his right hand as he leapt to the next square before switching to his left and hopping on his left foot. Like a human pelican about to take flight. 'Bye bye birdie,' he sang.

***

'We go to gain a little patch of ground,
That hath in it no profit but the name.'
Hamlet

CHAPTER 23

The summer holiday was always dicey if it happened at all. Not that they were in the habit of taking one in spring, autumn and winter. A scramble to find the deposit in February had been doomed with both parents still out of work, Asp's psychiatrist not yet paid and Nasty's rent in arrears. They had ditched dreams of a château on the Loire and one week before they caught the ferry across the channel in July, Daphne settled for a converted mill (shed) up a mountain in the Cevennes. As a precaution, brake checks were organised on the red van and Leaf's buggy.

'I've never been to the Cevennes.' Henry spread a map of France on the floor of their kitchen, hitting the green bits with his thumb to make his point. 'You'll be glad I bought a people carrier and not a donkey for up there.'

'Well, we don't want a bourgeois villa with an umbrella and a swimming pool.' Daphne's mistrust of anything new was expressed in her increasing number of sarcastic visions. She had shaved her head as a negative reaction to their giant pod on wheels and decided its colour, a shiny letterbox red was her chief objection. *Silly woman,* thought Henry.

'Speak for yourself, Ma. I want a swimming pool.' Asp's idea of a holiday was to be left on a beach with a bottle of suntan lotion.

'There's no road marked for where we're going.' Elm was planning an escape clause along the lines of must have internet connection or can't come.

'We'll take out five-star travel insurance.' Henry imagined a spot of slope soaring from a mountain top and was showing he was keener than usual.

'It's not a proper holiday if we can't swim.' Asp was sceptical of her mother's fitness to choose either films or holiday sites, having once been stuck with Aunt Rose and Elm in some foreign flea pit with a tin roof, deafened by the rain, forced to watch a Swedish film about a maid in a forest vomming on the ground because she'd been raped. And no subtitles. *Merde.*

'There's a rockpool next to the mill.' Daphne looked pleased with herself. 'I'll write to Jean-Pierre. His family has a second home somewhere near Nîmes. We could visit them. Leaf will love it.'

'I don't think so.' Did Leaf speak?

'Insane. I'll come and see you.' Nasty butted in because she was pissed off that no one in the family had invited her to come along. That she'd planned to leave for a narcotics' holiday in Amsterdam with the ex-drug addict was taken for granted but not discussed.

'We won't know our exact address until the last minute, Nasty.' Daphne could be quick sometimes.

Elm: 'Pack the badminton bats.'

Asp: 'Over my dead body.'

Henry: 'They're in the cellar.'

Asp made some odd choking sounds. 'I'll get them.'

'Shit, man. I'll come with you and have a look around. Didn't know you had a cellar. Massive man. Wait for me.'

Asp decided that she, Asp, would faint. Her chest felt tight to breathe, which was helpful. She prayed for a severe and systemic decline to begin right now. Of course, Nasty might trip on the cellar stairs and die, and besides, there was a precedent...

Elm leapt in. 'There's nothing down there except a pile of old rubbish and a disgusting smell.' He drew closer to his sister. 'Maybe some old tools and badminton bats. Not worth the trouble, Nasty.'

'I can't smell anything. What smells?' Nasty had her hands on her hips and was looking at him oddly.

'It used to smell, I mean. It used to smell like a drain, but it doesn't any more.'

'I'll bet,' said Nasty with a sneer. 'Maybe it was rats? Maybe the smell was their putrefying bodies?'

Asp slipped off her chair, knocking over Leaf's buggy, trapping him underneath it as he vented shrill, piglet cries. She collapsed on the floor as he was snatched up by Daphne and checked over for broken bones.

Faces froze in a tight circle around her head. The second hand of the clock on the wall quivered before it became stuck on six-fifty-nine. Nasty stood with her hands still resting on her hips, arms akimbo, her eyes wide. The word hospital was mentioned in hushed voices. The badminton bats and the coal heap were not.

Asp was breathing in a peculiar way, drawing in breaths and not letting them out, lying at her family's feet, thinking it was a miracle that no one except herself had explored hell in any serious way since the day she and Jean-Pierre had played at being grave-diggers *down there.*

'Asp, dear. Have a sip of water.'

Her mother raised her head and tipped some water down her throat while Nasty watched with interest.

'She's hyperventilating.'

'Dead rats? You're right, Nasty. That's all it was,' said Henry looking sideways at their lodger. 'They must have managed to get in under the floorboards. Sneaky bastards. Elm's right. There's no smell there now.'

'We try not to talk about it.' Daphne looked shiftily at Nasty. 'We try to forget *down there* exists.' She was distracted by the sight of Asp attempting to throttle herself. 'I'm afraid any mention of *it* seems to upset my poor darling daughter. She really does need a holiday.'

'Ugh.' The sound might as well have been 'yuck'. Leaf, the baby of infinite blubber, had hurled a building block at Asp's head. It missed and rolled to the other side of the floor. In rage, he spat his dummy out so that it too landed on the floor, and Nasty kicked it under the fridge with her Doc Marten boot. As he struggled to get out of his highchair to retrieve it, he became stuck.

Tears of outrage and desperation ran down his fat red cheeks. Such outrage and such desperation in his heaving body that everyone was provoked into saying, 'There, there, Leaf, darling boy. It's our fault. We didn't mean to neglect you. Here's another dummy in your favourite colour.' All except Nasty, who pinched him hard on the nose when no one was looking.

Asp announced from the floor that she was feeling much better. The clock chimed seven times, and Elm went up to his room in search of maps with minor roads. Nasty following.

'Bloody hell, Daph. You're not safe with a pair of scissors. Look at you.' Henry sat down in a sweat as his wife cleared the table of dirty plates. She paused to run a hand across the half-centimetre stubble on her skull and dropped a raspberry yoghurt pot on her husband's foot. It splattered halfway up his trouser cuffs, forming small red peaks before it dribbled down into his socks.

'I'm sorry, Henry. Just think of the money I've saved by not going to a hairdresser. We can afford to buy some brandy.'

She kissed him lightly on the lips before cleaning up the mess and before Henry could rub away the feeling of her mouth resting lightly on his. 'You know, you do humiliate me – for no reason,' she added softly. 'You really, really do.'

'Bloody hell, Daph.' They had never been a holding hands husband and wife. Once in a while, they forgot there was still an undercurrent of affection that surfaced at unexpected moments. It had been that way in the beginning. A genuine warmth between them – an acceptance that they were comfortable in each other's company and could forgive each other's lies. Now when the warmth came, it took them by surprise or else it made them laugh.

***

'Let it work,
For 'tis the sport to have the engineer
Hoist with his own petard;'
Hamlet

Chapter 24

aspthrush.blogspot.com

Diary of a Summer Holiday by Asp Thrush

The following notes settle any future arguments about what was done, when, where and why.

Good riddance, Nasty, THE lodger from hell. Thanks for leaving red silk knickers with black lace additions in my sock drawer. Pity so large. Bye bye FOR SURE. Told Elm never mention badminton bats again. (I broke the bats.) No more need to enter cellar. EVER.

House to be locked by Nasty when Nasty leaves for Amsterdam with druggy friend. Nasty pleased we trust her. JOKE, says Elm. Radio left on in case of burglars.

Overnight ferry from Portsmouth to Le Havre. Arrive before breakfast. Hour drive later, lost in dark. Try to find auberge that isn't seedy bar over motorway and notice parents getting bitchy. *'Mind the bend Henry,'* or *'Be sure you're on the right side, no the **right** side of the road.'*

Down a gorge nowhere; driver parent says passenger parent

should walk. Auberge in moonlight seen through trees. Six wooden huts by stream. Next to Sauxillanges. Paradise. Sang *Doh a Deer* on way to restaurant – tune not words. Saint Elm says I can't sing in tune, which **is** mendacious. Elm sucks. Our starter pate *de Grand'mere* (not kidding). No.2 fresh trout from a bucket still with the bones obvs. No.3 Blueberry tart. (Delicious aroma of stew bubbling on stove through the night). Woke up with purple teeth and bits of trout stuck in teeth. Bulimic's paradise. Wish we could stay.

5th July
Leaf car-sick in back seat. Leaf may have eating disorder on top of arrested development. Had to clean up mess. Love Leaf. He's so ugly. Million bales of hay like fat jewels in plastic wrap. Stole three sunflowers for Great Aunt Rose; bicyclist shouted '*voleur.*' You were, said St Elm. I was, said I. No more flat, rural yellow fields. Narrow roads up scary mountains. Elm navigated.

One or two arguments about left, right and should we ask goat lady for directions. This goat lady waits by sharp bend at bottom of steep hill with herd bells tinkling in case of crash. Ma asks in French if she has keys for mill but no reply. She is silent ghost of the Cevennes. Arrive at Mairie and Temple de Lezinier, Chaldecoste and Sainte Andeol de Glerguemort, land of Monsieur and Madame Bertrand, keepers of keys and little Bertrands. Maybe friend there for Leaf.

Discover old mill by pond – our destination. Shown small stone hut where Elm and I will sleep. Halfway up the valley. Not another house in sight. Saw real rats! Big ones. Writhing in wooden box at end of bed. My bed. Ma found toxic pellets of pesticide and placed about a hundred inside box. Elm questioned this. Elm almost vegetarian. Found black slugs in bath. May be leeches. Ginormous. Refused to investigate.

Turned on taps and flushed slugs down plughole. First hours spent distributing pest poison, sweeping up rat droppings, scrubbing mould off cushions. Worried we may kill a rat in real life. Oops. I am also almost a vegetarian. Pa collecting wood from forest for stove. More liquorice coloured slimey crawlies in bath. Wash in pool. Bliss. Float on back. Buzzards squawking overhead. Across the valley, trees like broccoli. In the shadows, bats and more buzzards. Elm testing new battery laptop in shed. This is the beginning of our holiday.

6th July
First morning, parents descend mountain in search of village shop. Car in neutral to save petrol. Goat lady in same spot as yesterday. Still waiting for a crash? Got a funny feeling…

Afternoon: Pa assembled barbecue wrong way round. Elm read instructions. Walked, ate, read, slept, had nightmare about inspector.

7th July
Leaf sick again. Leaf *is* def. bulimic. Pa launched slope-soarer from top of Caldecoste. It crashed. Either too much wind or not enough. No more flying, v. grumpy for rest of day. Put Leaf's bouncy chair by pool. Swam and read sexy passages in my Colette. No idea where others gone. Colette had a cat. Took Leaf in papoose to find waterfall. Saw hippy family in distance. Some sort of picnic on red blanket in a clearing with a donkey. Could be

Famille Bertrand and all the little Bertrands. Smelt pot. All naked and laughing a lot. Pretended not to see them in case they thought I was spy. Why can't we have a picnic? Lots of waterfalls and silvery, granite rocks. Beautiful.

8th July
HAD A PICNIC! No donkey and no pot though. Found wild thyme and mint in crannies. Leaf stung by horsefly and crying six hours later. Elm calmed him down. Read more sexy bits in Colette.

9th July
Slept with Leaf at mill to avoid rats. Slept on kitchen floor next to pair of glow-worms glowing. They glow more when they're at it. Am learning a lot about nature on this holiday. Feel bad about leaving Elm with rats. Forgot to tell him they're not dead yet, just slowed up. Feel bad about that.

Thunder in valley sounds like *Rigoletto,* Act III. Ma got dirt in her eyes from door kicking up dust. Says she's blind. Eyes look like frog's. Read her Balzac because she can't see obvs. Pa says he should be called Balls-ache not Balzac. Bad day for everyone. Storm over and chairs back on terrace.

10th July
We're all bored and sick of each other. Elm says it's alpine claustrophobia. Set off for mediaeval town of Florac in second gear as foot brake playing up. Do you want a present, asked father, slipping into neutral at top of steepest slope to scare mother. Saw goat person smiling in evil way at bottom of hill. Bought some black slip-on shoes for canoeing at Sainte Enimie.

Sainte Enimie, 11th July
Bubba Leaf is left with Famille Bertrand back at Mairie. Elm and I impeccably behaved on river. Eyeless in Gaza parent kept grizzling because stupid other parent got muddled between left and right oar. Amazing how blind can see. One or two crashes. Fell in river going over dyke and acquired Spot-the-Dog bruise while Elm was negotiating rapid backwards. Aged parents more in water than out. We won race to finish. Leaf more cheerful after day with little Bertrands. Maybe dope in Leaf's mashed banana.

12th July
Ate, walked, slept. Found Ma snipping again. Nail scissors for nails as not much hair. Says she feel better when cutting hair. Not mine I said. Not yours, she said. I didn't say, well, try your eyelashes next time.

Trip to Nîmes, 13th July
Been dreading this. Practically HAIRLESS Ma sidles into shed before breakfast to ask Elm for use of laptop. *'A quick email to inspector for any news on Granny.'* Elm replied in sleep. *'Can't be done.'* What a relief. Second nightmare: Inspector Love in canoe behind, shouting through megaphone. Couldn't hear because of noisy rapids.

My boat tipped up and I drowned in dream. Nasty pushing my head under water as I swim to surface. Remember sinking, spinning, thumping head on mud. Kept seeing face with patch on one eye. Nasty, Granny the cat or Porfiry Petrovich. Maybe goat lady. Can't remember any more. Ma woke me and said we were off to Nîmes to find Jean-Pierre. I asked for another cat back home. *'We'll see,'* she said aloud. *'Won't,'* she said under her breath. I heard her.

Fed up with keeping diary.

***

'My tongue and soul in this be hypocrites.'
Hamlet

CHAPTER 25

'Excusez- moi, y a t'il quelqu'un ici?' Daphne stuck her head through an open window at the back of the Levin family's house after unsuccessfully knocking at the front. Her French was almost exhausted. A daisy chain was resting on her scalp. The skin was shining through the stubble in bright sunlight. 'Jean-Pierre?' she cried. They were ragged with heat. The sweat ran down their bodies in a stream, except on Leaf, who kept sucking the salt from his bare arm.

The house had stucco walls with a gravel path all the way round. There was an open back door next to the window with dead geraniums on its sill. Coloured streamers were hanging in front of the door to keep out the flies. Beyond the plastic ribbons and with the light against them, they could see the furred outline of a woman who appeared familiar. As quickly as she appeared, she vanished down a corridor - a shadowy figure that became an apparition in their minds while they squabbled over who she might be.

'Granny. She looked like Granny.'

'That's a sick thing to say, Elm.'

'No it's not. She might be an imposter.'

'It was the goat lady, you dick. Granny's in Borneo.' Asp poked her brother hard in the ribs, winding him as he turned and winded her back.

'I thought the person looked like Jean-Pierre.' Daphne removed the daisy chain from her head with great delicacy and stuffed it in her pocket.

'Maybe it was Jean-Pierre's grandmother. It was a woman, not a man, I tell you.'

'She's dead.'

'Which grandmother are we talking about?'

'Whoever.'

They stood there arguing in the heat and the dust while the dog was scavenging in an upturned bin on the lookout for bones. The darkened hallway promised coolness if only they could step inside.

'I need to sit down because I'm expecting a baby.' No sooner said, no sooner Daphne was squatting by the back door, wiping the sweat from around her neck. Who the apparition might have been was lost with the starkness of her words.

'Really, Daph. We agreed not to talk about this on holiday.'

Henry moved to sit next to her, but she waved him away before shifting onto her knees and resting her hands on the roof of Leaf's buggy. Fingers curled over themselves in a clench. Asp remained still, not sure if she could be the one to say she felt sick, although she did. One of Elm's eyes swung to the right while the other looked straight ahead. In shock.

'Sorry.' In her mind, Daphne's thoughts had already shifted from pregnancy to nail clippings. They were nestling in the pocket of her skirt next to the daisy chain and had been there since the day she'd scooped each one secretly from the waste paper bin in the inspector's office. She didn't know why she'd bothered to collect them in the first place, except that having them there gave her pleasure.

'It's been a long pregnancy.' Henry spoke because no one else did, and Asp snapped back at him.

'We don't need another baby. We've got Leaf.'

Elm found a shadow below the guttering and tilted his head into its dark coolness. 'Leaf might like company.'

'The doctors aren't sure of dates.' Daphne was eying her two older children calmly. 'But I'm quite puffed up around the middle.' She said, patting her stomach.

She remembered how she had put on her best underwear and shaved her legs when she went to Harley Street. It was the first day of Ascot and the surgery was empty. People's minds were elsewhere. She had tried to tell the young man with smooth-shaven cheeks who examined her vagina that, at the moment of conception, it's like the scent of virgins. A nothing smell. A sweet, clear moisture. Not the stench of low tide and rotting fish. It had been the same with all her other pregnancies. She was certain of it. There was no question of doubt in her mind.

The young man had studied his notebook and scribbled in it for several minutes without once looking up. There were no further comments from Daphne or from the young man. A nurse had been summoned to see her out so that she never saw his eyes again. Later that afternoon, she had gone to John Lewis and purchased the newest, zappiest double buggy with fluid suspension and a yellow sheepskin rug in anticipation.

'I tell you, it's been a long haul, this pregnancy.' Henry sighed. 'Longer than Leaf's, and we know that took forever.'

'Rubbish. We're not talking elephants here. Babies aren't cuckoos locked in a clock. They don't pop out on the hour.' Daphne unfolded her legs and slowly rotated her feet to get the blood running into her toes. She was transfixed by the darkness beyond the doorway, thinking it might be the entrance to Merlin's cave. A fly landed on her cheek, which she swiped away without any awareness of what she was doing. 'You have to want babies. You have to want them a lot. Anyway, we've chosen a name. It's *Snow*.'

With her big toe, Asp flicked the fly back into the air and watched as the insect crawled inside the dog's ear with its wings folded.

'Girl?' she asked her mother.

'Don't care, don't know.' Daphne felt the milk seep through her nipples, moistening the front of her blouse and was delighted she wouldn't have to wean Leaf for a while.

'Might be both,' said Henry.

'Twins? You're not expecting *twins?*' Asp looked horrified.

'Not that we know of.' Daphne smiled at her daughter. 'Though, of course, it would be nice.'

'Why not *Snowdrop?*' Elm played with his mother's fingers, loosening their grip against the buggy rail. 'Or if it's a boy, you could call him *Thorn* and say he was a small prick in your side.'

They laughed, the way families can abruptly laugh after they've been tearing into each other, and the scrap of a dog ran inside barking until someone shouted back at it in a voice that was used to being angry.

'Va, va. Tetes-toi.'

The dog ran out again with the fly on his nose. A homunculus of a man came to the doorway wearing a pair of old shorts tied at the waist by string and with nothing on top. He had a thin, wrinkled chest with a snaggle of dark hairs over sun-browned skin and as he parted the plastic ribbons, staring at the odd group in his back yard, a look of understanding slowly crept across his face.

'Aha! Bienvenue. La famille Trush. Toutes personnes. Entree. We expect you. *Venez-ici.* It is well.'

He could have been forty-five or sixty. Lizard lids and a nose so bent that from whatever angle you looked at it, the shape was twisted in profile. Running towards Daphne to embrace her without having to bend at all, he was so very small. And thin. '*Viens, Madame, viens ici.*' He pulled her to her feet so fast and hard she almost toppled over. '*Thierry Levin, le papa de Jean-Pierre.*'

'Of course you are. I can see the resemblance.' Henry steered the buggy through the streamers with the rest of the family in single file behind him. They were following Monsieur Levin into a narrow room on the left of the hall, a room frozen in time for thirty years, a combination of rust and brown, so resistant to change that in a magazine, it would have passed as retro.

A leather sofa and two armchairs with dayglo cushions matched the wallpaper. A glass coffee table dominated the centre of the room, on which was placed the sort of ashtray you see in hotel foyers, plus a neat pile of car magazines and an enormous television zapper. No visible television. Apart from the three-piece suite and the coffee table, the only other furniture was a smart wooden cabinet so highly polished that it picked up the shadows of people walking past.

And yet as bright as it was outside, it seemed like twilight in. It was so very, very dark. And deliciously cool. The air smelt of stale cigars and rosemary. Although the window was open, a wire mesh was stretched across its frame, with bloated flies crawling slowly upwards on the inside, trying to get out. They would struggle to the top and drum their legs against the metal bar before slipping to the bottom to begin their climb all over again. There was no one else in the room and no sign that there had been. The ashtray was clean.

'*Merci pour le message.*' Thierry Levin waved his arms in the air and urged his visitors to sit down and have a glass of lemonade with tiny squares of homemade biscuits, which they did, including Leaf.

'Ah, now this is your *petite Feuille.*' Before Leaf could open his mouth to howl, he had been plucked out of his seat and propped on Monsieur Levin's hip, parallel to the floor, short legs wriggling in protest.

'Is Jean-Pierre here?'

'Oh no. I am quite alone.'

'But…' Asp's voice faltered as her brother's foot came firmly down on hers.

'Jean-Pierre stays behind with his mother in our little home in Peyruis. Always they are there in the summer. They will not return for a month.'

'What a pity,' Henry grabbed the zapper from the coffee table and turned it over in his hands. 'We'll be in London before then. I don't suppose you have a television here by any chance?'

'Really, Henry. We haven't come all this way to watch M'sieur Levin's television.'

'But it's the Grand Prix. You saw the ads. They're everywhere.'

'Well, we haven't come to Nîmes for the Grand Prix.'

'Attendez, Mrs Trush. *Attendez.'*

Leaf still at his side, still waving his short fat legs, their host pounced on the mahogany cabinet and revealed a small grey screen behind hinged doors. *'Attendez.'* He pressed two, three buttons. *'Voila.'*

'Magic.' Henry slapped the sides of the armchair, certain in his mind that the television was warm. The leather made a loud sucking noise like a fart.

'This is terrific. Would you mind if I stayed?'

'Henry!'

'It's the Grand Prix, Daph.'

'We know that.'

'Don't be a spoilsport.'

'M-m-m-grrrrrr.' Leaf's eruption made them laugh, except for Daphne and Asp. *'R-r-r-r-r-r-ugh, m-m-m-m-m-m-rrrrugh.'* He refused to stop.

'You see, Mrs Trush, your Leaf is just like a car.'

A point of view can happen when a character steps outside of himself, looks at the other person and knows how he feels. Monsieur Levin seemed to understand the feelings of their monster baby. Elm, glad they had a chance to be somewhere cool, wondered how to shut Leaf up so they could watch the race in peace.

He'd spent the morning lurking in shadows, zig-zagging across footpaths to step into the blackest alleyways and hovering underneath any roof he could find to avoid the sun. As he settled deep into the sofa, he thought this might be the best bit of their holiday so far.

Daphne looked down at her older son sadly. There was no point in resisting further. Monsieur Levin was pressing her into the larger of the two chairs. Only Asp stood alone. She had seen the back of a picture frame on top of the mahogany cabinet and was longing to turn it around.

She strolled towards the back door, casually seizing Leaf en route. Her father, like brother, had settled back into the softness of the leather, content for the first time since the holiday began. And yet there are always some people within whom there's a well of harmless wickedness that they would like to draw from and express. In the Thrush family, since no one else was perceived as entirely innocent or harmless, that person was of course Leaf.

Transferred from one set of arms to another, he bellowed in outrage. His eyes were invisible behind the corrugations of fat. The puffed-out cheeks belonged to a cherub with toothache. His mouth glistened with saliva. *'M-m-m-m-m-ugh!'* he yelled, wriggling in Asp's arms until she turned back from the door and dropped the baby at her father's feet, where he continued to scream even louder, his cries more piercing than the cars in the race itself.

'I'm going outside. Leaf obviously wants to stay here.'

'I'll come with you, darling.' Daphne rose, kicking Henry's ankle in one fluid movement as she passed.

***

'Lord! We know not what we are,
But know not what we may be.'
Hamlet

CHAPTER 26

'I just wish you hadn't cut it.' The daughter was walking with the mother along a path that led to the other side of the house. 'Or went and dyed it that disgusting puce colour. What on earth? It's... shite. I can't bear to look at you, Mama.'

'Hair grows. It'll fade.' Daphne slipped a hand around her daughter's waist, remembering the physical release she had felt as she snipped her hair within a centimetre of her skull. She'd wanted to go deeper into the shaft, but some sliver of fear had held her back.

'You don't have to look at yourself.' Asp wanted a mother with hair like Pocahontas.

'Well, I didn't expect it to be quite so... so different.'

'I don't understand. You weren't even grey.'

'Not yet.'

'You can't be trusted with a pair of scissors.'

'Your father's already said that.'

'He's right.'

They were looking down at the gravel for signs of fresh footprints.

'I can always fluff it up with the vacuum cleaner.'

'Gross.'

'It's like a blow dry, only it sucks.'

'GrossER.'

'Yes.'

'Hair does grow.'

'You said that before.'

'I need to remind myself.'

Asp created a series of miniature pyramids with her feet on the gravel. Daphne said she wished they didn't argue quite so much.

'Yes. Well then.'

'Asp dear, it was a woman we saw a minute ago, wasn't it?'

'You know it was. Why do you say that?'

'I really don't know.'

'Nor do I.'

The dog, which had followed them, dislodged one cairn of tiny stones with his tail.

'Whoever it was back there had a frilly apron, a pair of flip-flops and hair down to her shoulders. I bet it was the person in the picture frame.'

'What frame?'

'The frame on top of the television. It was turned round, so we couldn't see who it was.'

'He lied to us about being on his own.'

Asp stared at her mother. 'He did. By the way, what did Inspector Love say about your bald look?'

The dog charged through the gravel, kicking pebbles in all directions and smashing the remaining pyramids.

'He said I reminded him of Joan of Arc. After the stake.'

Daphne laughed in a slightly nervous way.

'It wasn't that funny.'

'Do you think we imagined this person in the hallway?'

'All of us?'

'She looked so… I don't know…familiar.'

Asp pushed the dog away from a set of large footprints near the side wall with some more geraniums in pots, which she hadn't noticed until now, their blousy petals still a brilliant blood red.

'Whoever it was that we saw in the hallway wasn't a ghost – it was probably your inspector.'

'You're being ridiculous, Asp. He's not *my* inspector.'

'Nor mine.'

'If you must know, the inspector is on the Isle of Wight. He's having a well-earned holiday with his wife. He never wears skirts. And he's definitely not in the south of France.'

Asp eyed the outline of her mother's belly before turning back to the footprints.

'I don't understand why you have to stay in contact with him,' she said at last. 'I mean, all the time. It's not as if he's going to find Granny and bring her back. All those stupid e-mails you keep sending the inspector. It's pathetic.'

'He takes an interest in our family.'

'Why? Why on earth should he be interested in us?'

Daphne's upper lip trembled as she thought her daughter was onto something she had missed.

Asp leant forward and gently tucked her mother's blouse into the waistband of her skirt.

'I'm not so sure about *Snow* as a name, Mum. It's a bit, you know, crap.'

Daphne leant forward to kiss her daughter on the cheek. The daisy chain and the envelope containing Inspector Love's nail clippings fell out of her skirt pocket, scattering a mixture of dried flowers and the hard, brittle ends of nail in the air.

Not the clippings, not the dead flowers, not even the envelope that fluttered away and was caught amongst the geraniums in a window box were ever thought of again. In Daphne's mind, they had already ceased to exist, while at the back of Asp's was the shocking thought that her mother's bump might be due to nothing more than middle age spread.

Daphne leant against the wall of the house to rest for a moment.

'Look at me. Like an overgrown pumpkin. Does it show too much?'

'It's... insane.'

'You mean massive.'

'I'm talking about lust, Ma! You're too old to be having a baby.'

'I'm not. Or else I wouldn't be pregnant. You'll come round, dear.'

'No I won't. Let's walk.'

They wandered through narrow lanes that were more like footpaths and forgot that they were hoping to find their mystery person. They admired instead the drying sheets strung between buildings or peered through windows at painterly scenes of family lunches with people sitting at long tables with red and white checked table cloths eating crusty bread.

In the shops and cafes, the people inside were gathered around their television sets watching the Grand Prix. Like Elm and Leaf and Henry and Monsieur Levin. As they turned down one alleyway on the edge of the village, they found themselves facing a tall stone villa sandwiched between a derelict cottage on both sides. It was one of those grand, lofty houses that is half townhouse, half château, with its grounds reduced over time to little more than the perimeter of its walls.

An iron fence formed a barrier between the house and the road, with a gravel path leading directly from the gate to a carved wooden door at the top of stone steps and a collonaded verandah on either side. Tall, pale blue shutters, pale as the sky, were closed except where there was a set of open windows at the very top. The front garden was mostly stubbles of dried grass on either side of the path, and around the base of two palm trees, yellow butterflies were fanning their wings on the tips of blades.

'I bet she's up there,' said Asp.

Daphne nodded. An indistinct figure was opening one of the shutters just below some guttering, startling the pigeons who flew outwards into the sky before settling on the fronds of the palm trees. The dog, which had followed them up until now, streaked across the road and squeezed through a gap in the iron railings. It disappeared around the back of the house, and they could hear its excited barking above the passing lorries.

Asp felt she was Judith about to enter Bluebeard's castle in the south of France as she looked longingly at the château door.

***

'And yet, to me, what is this quintessence of dust?
Man delights
Not me – no nor woman neither...'
Hamlet

CHAPTER 27

Asp:
Mum kept complaining of morning sickness and insisted on returning to the Levin house to ask if they had any liver salts. She said I should wait in the shade opposite the château, but the moment she'd gone, I pushed open the iron gates and headed for the front door. It had a heavy ringed knocker hanging from the head of Medusa. I knew it was Medusa because she had snakes for hair.

I knocked three times, waited, and knocked again. I could feel the shudders of the knocker in my fingertips and noticed a splinter of blue paint had sprung back in a curl from the door and fallen to the ground. The door gave way as I pushed at it with my shoulder, then swung back on itself, revealing a wide hallway.

The sound of my own footsteps made me think I was in an empty house until a voice said, '*Viens.*' I could make out a large pair of flip-flops with painted toenails. I don't know why, but my eyes remained fixed on the stone floor and the flip-flops. A second, shorter '*Viens*' and I followed whoever it was to a set of spiral stairs. I didn't see anything clearly until we started climbing up the steps and onto each landing. The door behind us had closed with its own weight and the light was poor.

Whoever I was following climbed without any of the slowing down that happens when you move from one flight to another. Whoever it was, began to talk very fast. In English.

'I saw you, all of you, standing outside.' A mad cackle like Mrs Rochester. 'So I ran away.'

I recognised the voice but not the fake, American drawl. The light was so poor as we climbed, I could only see heels and legs and the flutter of a skirt. The person's back... followed by another coughing fit – it could have come from a man or woman because the coughs had no obvious pitch. It wasn't until we'd climbed the first full flight that I was absolutely sure it was Jean-Pierre chatting away. Reminiscing. Talking to himself. To me. To both of us.

'Explaining to my parents – that was really tough.'

'Jean-Pierre?' I felt weird asking. But, Jean-Pierre... Who'd have thought?

'Of course it's me. You understand, Asp...'

'No I don't.' I shook my head as if I had nits or something, but Jean-Pierre was looking straight ahead.

'My mother, Asp. She always knew I liked girls' clothes.'

'Um,' I answered, but I meant to say, 'really?'

'It's because I dressed up in her clothes if she went out. Then I'd get muddled about the way they were meant to hang in the cupboard, and I'd hang them up the wrong way so she always knew what I'd done when she next looked inside.'

I was tiptoeing very closely behind Jean-Pierre to make sure I didn't miss a word as if I had to catch the past in one finite climb or in the space of a few minutes.

'A secret life isn't easy, Asp. You think you cover up your tracks. You want to say, "this is who I am". But I couldn't and I didn't. So I changed all of that the moment we left England and headed for the *Bois*.'

'Who's "we"? Who else were you with?' We had stopped on another landing to catch our breaths as if something oppressive or darker than ourselves was urging us to watch out, be careful. Jean-Pierre ignored my question.

Instead, he said, 'The Bois de Boulogne. As if I didn't know that.

'It's where I feel at home. Only we didn't stay because I like to move around. We wandered all over the place. Just travelling...'

'Who's *we*, Jean-Pierre?'

Again, infuriatingly, he didn't reply, and we came to a passageway at the top of the stairs that was lined with tall, open windows. I remembered seeing them from the street and one of the pigeons was still resting on the ledge by the guttering. It was eyeing us warily.

I could see the passageway ran straight down the middle of a large attic that was hung with faded tapestries of exotic birds and wild flowers. There were three doors on either side, all of them shut. I thought it was weird for someone to tell their life story in the time it took to climb a set of stairs – and I did all those things you do to startle yourself out of dreams, like pinch yourself or shake your head in case it was just that, a dream.

'I dress up as a woman. I speak in another voice. Do you like my American accent, Aspic? GOTCHA BABE. HOWDIE? YOU KNOW WADDA MEAN? I dress up as a woman.'

I laughed because his accent was terrible and he laughed with me. It definitely felt like a dream, believable until the moment you wake up.

'We get to move all over the place,' he continued. 'The police don't find a person if they keep changing their address. They're just missing persons as far as Interpol's concerned.'

Pacing and stopping and turning back again when he reached the end of the corridor. Jean-Pierre was still laughing. It felt as if I was always studying him from behind as I followed him to and fro – *almost slavishly,* I thought.

'We've lived in Rome, Amsterdam, Venezuela, Helsinki, Moscow, Cyprus and Tokyo. We came to Nîmes for the summer because some American friends of the family own the château, and my father is the caretaker when they're away in Borneo.'

Ah, Borneo – I remembered a dog-eared postcard of a jungle. I remembered it because there was a sun filtering through the leaves and the stamp had said Borneo. I remember it clearly. What is this fear about forgetting and remembering?

Suddenly he opened one of the carved wooden doors in the passageway and led me into a darkened room where he switched on a lamp. The smudge of scarlet lipstick on his face and the faint patch of rouge on each cheek were crudely applied. The blue eyeshadow was glittery. The skin on the face unnaturally smooth. The toes, peeping through the enormous flip-flops, were carefully manicured and painted red. The skirt he was wearing was in need of a clean.

'So they were *your* postcards. I thought so.'

'What did you expect?'

The voice was breathier than I remembered and the twang had disappeared.

'So, there you are. No more postcards for a while, Asp. I'm saving up for the big chop. In Morocco or Colorado. Can't decide which. Are you surprised?'

I shook my head as he began stroking what looked like a padded bra with two small, pointed cones underneath.

'Call me Pierrette. Please call me Pierrette. Please. Please. Please. Please.' He looked at me as if to say, if you do, we can be friends.

'I had my Adam's apple taken out last year. See?' He turned and leaned towards me.

'That's amazing,' I said softly. I could smell the perfume on his neck. A sweet, cloying scent of lavender like an old ladies' smell.

'Just so you know – they scrape off a bit of the cartilage, *et voila*! No bump. Like a girl. But I also want to *be* one. It's a syndrome, Aspic.'

'Sorry?'

'You think you're a woman when biologically you're a man.'

'Was it like that when you lived with us?'

'Yes. Sometimes.'

'But you didn't **do** anything about it.'

'Obviously not.'

'Would changing your sex change who you think you are?

'It might let me become who I want to be.'

'Oh. And you don't mind being stared at?'

'Sometimes. I mind it sometimes.'

'Maybe... less lipstick?'

Pierrette touched her mouth lightly with her fingers as if to check there were no streaks of scarlet in the corners.

'You can't accept I'm different, can you, Asp? That's what this is about. Ask me a question that you really want to ask me.'

'Oh? And what's that?' I said.

'Is it like cutting the tail off a donkey?'

I made small shoving gestures with my hands in the air. 'Oh no. I promise you. I don't – don't want to know… Pierrette.'

'Ah, but I promise you, you do. It's normal. It's normal to be curious. Admit it.'

But I couldn't, naturally, admit it.

'Well, I can't tell you what it feels like because I haven't had it done… But if I ever do, it will be because I want to feel right in my own skin.'

Pierrette tucked a curl behind one ear and drew the curtains back from the open windows so the natural light outside flooded into the room and brought with it a faint breeze. I shut my eyes to protect myself from its enamelled brilliance and listened.

'I want every one of my thoughts… to be in line with my body. I *have* to cross over – or I'll wither away. I want to go to sleep at night and know that in the morning, I'm going to wake up without a penis and everything will be fine… I will be myself.'

Perhaps for the first time, I caught the true sense of her despair.

'You're so lucky, Asp.'

'I suppose you must fancy men,' I said, opening my eyes slowly.

'Oh Asp, Asp, Asp. You ask me that?' Half angry. Half amused. 'Well, I don't *fancy* the ugly ones. I prefer pretty boys and pretty girls.'

And then I said what I said and I wished I hadn't, but I did. 'Are you gay?'

'A ça,' she sighed. 'I'm not straight, Asp. I am not *bendy*. I am human. I am a word.'

'Maybe you just don't like sex,' I said.

Pierrette pursed her lips in a pantomime of shock and we stared back at each other without trying to give anything away, and so I asked, 'Does it cost a lot?'

'$60,000. All in. All out,' and we both laughed again, which was good.

'Can you pay?'

'No. Can you?'

Pierrette widened her eyes so the lashes curled back on themselves in a soft, velvety fringe. I leant forward on my chair until I could feel our breaths on each other's cheeks. She had switched off the lamp, and I heard a loud sniffing and glimpsed the wet streak on her upper lip. It could have been oil or sweat the way it gleamed or no more than a trick of the light where it fell. I wasn't sure.

'I've got a cold. I'm not doing coke.' She kept wiping and rubbing the tip of her nose as if she had been caught out, and I waited while the sniffs turned into a fit of coughing.

'Most of the girls in the Bois do coke. It numbs the pain.' She tossed her head nervously. 'But I'm not going down that road. I'm not a hooker.' More coughing.

'But why do it if it hurts?'

She plucked a silk handkerchief from out of her sleeve as if she'd only just remembered it was there. She gave her nostrils a final, careful wipe, and it was obvious from the slight wince she gave that the wall between her nostrils was paper thin and that it hurt.

She folded and unfolded her handkerchief, squashing it to make a neat square before tucking it carefully into the belt of her skirt and before giving a shrug of fake unconcern.

'*Laisses tomber,* Asp,' she said and placed a hand gently between the small bump-like cones underneath her bra. Her hand seemed to be trying to reach her heart. Patting the space slowly as you pat a baby.

I was moved. Like most people, I dislike uncertainty. The great taboo breakers have an unsettling effect on you. They break down boundaries and push us into places they would otherwise have never explored. I wasn't sure if Pierrette was a great taboo breaker, but I thought she might want to be. She was my friend, and I felt a tear form in each eye because I realised I loved her in my way.

'How is Elm?'

'Elm?' I replied. I wasn't expecting that. 'He's studying natural sciences.'

Her expression softened.

'Always clever. Donc. I'm just surprised he's grown up.'

'And what about me?'

'No. You look exactly the same. Only taller.'

'I'm like Leaf.'

'No. Leaf is a bit – ugly. You are pretty. I like the gap in your two front teeth, and I like your hair that way, Aspic.'

I flicked the ponytail at the back of my head out of embarrassment as it fanned outwards and revealed its silkiness. I hated my *dents du bonheur* – and yet, Pierrette was the most extraordinary person I would ever know, and the truth is I would have suffered a lot more than embarrassment for such compliments.

'Leaf was dropped on his head at birth,' I said. That's why he looks...Squashed...Why he doesn't ever seem to change.'

'No, Asp. He wasn't dropped on the head. He doesn't change because you won't let him.'

Pierrette was leaning over me as if waiting for my reaction, then spoke again as if she had given up waiting and was only now coming to the point.

'Do you ever think about your granny these days?'

'Sometimes,' I said.

'So when a postcard arrived, you'd assume it was from me, not from her – because you thought she was dead. Yes?'

'Yes,' I whispered.

We could hear the sound of our own breaths overlapping in the empty room. I closed my eyes. I thought it strange I was still breathing.

'What if I told you she asked me to send them?'

'I wouldn't believe you,' I answered.

***

'I understand you not, my lord.'
Hamlet

Chapter 28

I know now why terror is called blind. When I first opened my eyes and tried to look into the distance there was a blank, dark space of an abyss where I could see nothing. Pierrette was invisible. It was only after a minute or two of nothingness that I got used to the terror and my own mortal rage. My heart stopped beating quite so fast and an image slowly formed of my grandmother – without life – lying on the cellar floor.

'We buried her,' I said. 'Don't you remember? I told you. I pushed her down the cellar stairs.'

Pierrette was back again. I stared at the blue eyeshadow and the smeared red lips, and the red cheeks that were like a grotesquely grimacing clown, and I began to shake. My friend raised a finger to the tip of her collapsed nose and held it there in silence.

I cried out as if it were the most obvious thing in the world for me to change a belief that had haunted me for the last five years. 'No, no, no,' I shouted. 'YOU PUSHED HER, JEAN-PIERRE.' Not Pierrette, note, but Jean-Pierre. I covered my face with my hands because I was afraid to look at her directly. I cried like a child who covers her face so she can't be seen. 'You were in the cloakroom all the time I was there. You let me think I'd murdered my own granny, but it was you.'

'No, Asp. She tripped and fell by mistake.'

Pierrette sounded like the old Jean-Pierre I used to know – the one who took photos of graves and worms and dead leaves – and me. It was cold and full of certainty.

'You didn't push her, Asp. I didn't push her either. She just fell.'

'You were there all that time, and I didn't know.'

'Yes.'

'In the cloakroom.'

"Yes.'

'And you saw.'

'Yes.'

'And you didn't say anything.'

'I didn't say anything.'

'Why?'

Pierrette drew her chair closer towards me and sat down, our knees just touching.

'Why was I there?' She appeared vague, although she collected herself quickly. 'I was looking for something. Behind the cloaks.'

'It was the photos, wasn't it? The photos you took of me. You were looking for the photos.'

'I thought I'd find them in your coat pocket.'

'I shoved them up the chimney.'

'All of them, Asp?'

'All of them.'

'Burnt, I suppose.'

'I reckon.'

She pushed her nose upwards until you could see the hints of collapsed cartilage between her nostrils.

'The shoes,' I reminded her. 'Granny's shoes. You threw them down the stairs after she fell. You threw one. Then you threw the other straight after. You scared me. You made me think it was Granny's ghost.' I could still hear the dull, thumping sound of both shoes falling, one at a time, all the way to the bottom of the cellar. I'd heard them fall so many times before and always against my will. When I was awake. When I was asleep. *Memory was about what you remember,* I thought. Not what you wanted. My heart ached with these unpleasant feelings.

Pierrette had cupped the raw space around her nostrils with her fingers. There was a calamitous squeal suddenly coming from her nose. Like a whistle when you blow your nose. I wasn't sure if it was imaginary or real.

'You want the truth? The shoes were in the way. I was angry. So I threw them down the stairs.'

'And so you let me think I'd killed her. How cruel is that?'

'I'm sorry,' she whispered back at me.

'Why should I believe you now?'

'Because you want to.'

'And so we both buried her alive.'

'No we didn't *bury* anyone, Asp.'

'You tell me I'm wrong then. You tell me what you remember. Go on. You tell me the truth. That it was someone else and not me – who covered her up with lumps of coal... a crime so... so pointless, so random, so without benefit to the person who killed her. Tell me what happened. Tell me. Tell me. Tell me. Tell me, Pierrette.'

'I took down two old spades off the wall. You picked up some coal from the heap and placed it next to her head. We took it in turns to dig around her body. But I saw your face and I told you to go.'

'You saw my face? What did it look like?'

'Like this.' Pierrette rolled her eyes upwards, opening and shutting her mouth like a fish on a hook. 'You replaced her glasses and I took them off again to close her eyes. Well, I also thought she was dead. You patted her on the arm, and I said, go upstairs, and you said, why? But I told you there was nothing we could do about it. It wasn't our fault. But it didn't look like that.'

'So you started to bury her.'

'Yes. Because I thought no one would believe it was an accident.'

'And I thought I'd killed her.'

'I didn't want your help. I'd changed my mind. Your parents were arguing about something in the kitchen and we could hear Leaf crying.'

'Leaf was always crying.'

'We heard Elm going upstairs, and I knew he was going to look for you, so I told you to follow him and explain you'd been in the cellar cleaning up an old bike.'

'Am I meant to believe Granny recovered the moment I went upstairs?'

'You have to believe me, Asp. I kept on shovelling the lumps of coal. I covered her feet first and I was working my way up when something made me stop. I heard this sound. It went on forever. BRRRRRRAAAAAAAAAAAAAAAAAAAAAAAAAAAAAAA

GH.' But Pierrette was not finished. 'BRRRRRRRRRAAAAAAAAAAAAAAAAAAAAAAGH,' she said again. 'It was like some toxic gas that escapes from a dead body.'

I watched as she clutched the sides of her skirt to stop it from fluttering in the breeze from the open windows.

'There was saliva at the corner of her mouth. She was half sighing, half mewing like a cat. I bent down to cradle the top part of her body. Her head kept lolling on its side. I managed to turn it around, and as I did, her eyes opened. Blinking up. Staring at me. Her mouth formed shapes without any words coming out. But you won't like what I have to say now, Asp.'

What do you mean, now? I wondered without actually saying it aloud.

'Granny said your name after you had left. A-A-A-Asp. It was as clear as that. Of course she made other sounds. I listened carefully to each one. Like GAAAAAGH! But the way she said A-A-A-SP – that was so clear.'

I began to cry and Pierrette put her arms around me as she went on talking.

'I had to prop her up against the wall while I shifted the lumps of coal. I must have spoken for about ten minutes before I noticed that she was nodding back at me. That's when I realised she understood what I was saying.'

'How is that possible?' I said, rubbing my tears away as fast as they came.

'We could go away together, I told her. Escape for good. We won't tell anyone. Not for a while. In case they bring us back. I remember saying, "you can wear your old shoes but we'll get some new ones that won't hurt your bunions and we'll go to France when you're feeling better." I told her I'd packed my bags.'

'And then she nodded?'

'Why not? She didn't shake her head. She definitely nodded. She understood. Of course she did. Besides, I knew she was bored with her old life.'

'You never liked her.' I said this to be spiteful.

'But we needed each other, don't you understand, Asp?'

'Oh, please.' I slapped the sides of my chair the way a person does in despair because they don't believe a word they've heard. 'How did Granny look when you told her your plan?'

'She looked okay, I think.'

'What's that supposed to mean? Granny was okay? She'd just fallen down the cellar stairs, Pierrette. She'd never travelled further than Inverness. How could anyone travel round the world without worldliness? You tell me that. Did she like being with you? Did she like travelling with you? Did you ever ask her if she was happy?'

'No. I never asked.'

'Because if she didn't like any of it, that's – that's such a waste.'

Pierrette's arms shot out from where she'd been holding me. It was as if the idea had never occurred to her.

'How did you live?' I asked.

'We had money.'

'Where from?"

'We had some money. Her money. My money. We made friends.'

'She must have been sick sometimes. She was old.'

'I looked after her.'

'She didn't have very much.'

'We lived simply.'

'What's simply?' I could hear my own shrillness again. My disbelief.

'We moved around. We left our miseries behind.'

'What? You mean you didn't pay your bills?'

'I mean loneliness, Asp. She left loneliness behind. Do you understand that?'

'No.'

'Perhaps, when you see her...'

'See her? When? How?'

'Listen to me, Asp. Listen to me and I'll tell you. But I have to begin at the beginning.'

'Where is she?' I cried, but Pierrette was talking across me already.

'When your Granny could still walk, we used to sit in cafes and listen to strangers talking. She didn't want to be a part of any conversation at first because she couldn't reply. Now she can do a whole sentence with blinks and grunts. Her brain works silently.'

'This is ridiculous,' I said. 'It's impossible. I don't believe you. Even if I want to.'

Pierrette scratched her blouse with her beautiful, languid fingers. She sounded – well, bonkers. It all sounded bonkers.

'The truth is, Granny lost her balance. Maybe she had a sudden stroke. In the cloakroom. But she tripped. And fell. No knocking her over or pushing her down the stairs. She knocked herself out.

There was no murder, Asp.'

I stared back at Pierrette, who was unstoppable.

'I managed to clean the coal dust off her face and get her changed into some clothes from the dress-up box in the cellar. I found a skirt we both liked. It must have belonged to your mother. Bright green with white spots and a zip on the pocket.'

I must have looked stupefied. My mouth was hanging open and loose.

'Really, Asp. It was very pretty. I lost it though. I can't remember where. Do you want me to tell you the rest?'

'Go on.' What else could I say?

'We sat on the cellar stairs for quite a while until the house was quiet. When I worked out what she was trying to tell me, I sneaked out into the street and hailed a taxi from the Upper Richmond Road. I half carried, half dragged her upstairs without anyone seeing us. We went straight out to visit an old, retired actor she used to meet at the pond. No one knew they were friends except me.'

'I'd see him with her, sitting on a bench in the graveyard on Sunday. It was her idea we should find him and when we did, of course he invited her to stay in his house. It all happened so... simply. All she needed – passport, a few papers, a change of underwear, smelling salts, alarm clock – they fitted in her bag.'

'Where's Granny now?' I heard myself asking, but I'd stopped expecting Pierrette to answer me. She was treading water, feeding me details I would piece together later. She was slowing down the narrative to give me time to grasp what really happened as opposed to what I thought had happened.

'ASP! ASP! Are you up there?'

A female voice floated through the window from somewhere outside. Pierrette could see my mother waving at her from the street below.

'Don't worry, Aspic. Your Granny is quite safe where she is,' he said.

'Where is she?'

'ASP! ASP!'

'In Peyruis. With our family.'

'But your father said that's where *you* were. And you're here.'

'Did he say that?'

'Yes. He did.'

'ASP, ARE YOU UP THERE?'

Can I see her?'

'Of course.'

'When?'

'Whenever you like.'

Pierrette smiled. Her scarlet mouth became a widening crack across her face. 'You know something, Asp? My parents have accepted everything.'

Everything? I felt a faint tickle in my throat. The room smelt of damp despite the breeze through the open window. The clamour of the stray dog plus Daphne's shouts had drawn shop owners out of the shadows and into the hot sunlight to discover the cause.

Pierrette, still smiling, left to fetch my mother. I moved out into the corridor and sat by the stairwell to wait. I could hear a female voice humming a nursery rhyme on the other side of a wall close to the staircase. The voice was familiar, although I couldn't place it at first – and then I realised the singing, like some mournful laughing, was coming from inside my throat.

'I'm not going to cave in yet,' I said aloud, interrupting my song and clutching the top post of the stairs because I was feeling giddy. The skirt of my dress clung to my body in the heat, and the wooden floor of the attic was shuddering with the vibrations of steps coming closer. My eyes closed briefly. When I sang again, my voice was strong.

'Round and round...' I rather hoped if a person happened to be on the other side of the wall by the staircase, that person would hear me as I heard myself. I was lost in this thought as my mother's face appeared behind Pierrette on the landing below and disembodied as the Cheshire cat smiled up at me.

It's a fact that since I told my family I wanted to study acting, my mum has worried that my life might be turning into a series of potential audition speeches of the post-modern, ironic kind. Was this just the beginning? Behind the mother's smile was a well of unbearable anxiety.

'Round and round we go.'

Pierrette clapped her hands theatrically. *'Brava,* Asp.'

'It's your turn,' I replied like some dotty Ophelia plucking at the folds of my dress.

And so my mother knew her fears were justified. A cool wind was blowing round the château walls, and the yellow butterflies and pigeons had disappeared from the garden.

***

Être, ou ne pas être, telle est la question.'
Hamlet

CHAPTER 29

Quel désastre. Whatever. *C'est tout.* Must improve their French. Can't be arsed. I need powder for my nose... I am, you understand, a woman-in-waiting. I am NOT mad.

Pierrette is rubbing her chin thoughtfully and waiting for the mother to take the daughter by the hand and leave immediately. She, Pierrette Levin, will go with them of course. And then there is the small, urgent matter of *la grandmère.*

***

'Is't not possible to understand in another tongue?'
Hamlet

CHAPTER 30

Asp delayed her moment of reunion with her ailing grandmother, hanging back with Leaf on the veranda of the Levin house in Peyruis. Her parents and Elm had gone straight to Granny's room to say, 'Hello Mother, Camilla, Hi Granny,' and pretend that nothing out of the ordinary had happened over the last four or five years to explain their separation.

The drive from Nîmes with Jean-Pierre, Jean-Pierre's father and his dog had passed in a general state of shock as they listened to the account of Jean-Pierre's sexual rebirth as Pierrette.

They listened intently to her description of how she'd filched some underwear from Daphne's drawer back in London and learnt that this was the official start of her extensive collection of female underwear.

They heard more disturbing details of Granny Pod – how they would notice that her lips would slope inwards to her mouth instead of outwards – like Popeye. How the hair on her forehead had greatly receded, and her face looked like a thumb. How she had tufts of hair growing from her ears but still could hear a baby crying in its pram. How the eyes might be watery, but she could still see. Or how her body would jerk sideways when she walked, but she could walk. Though dimmed, she was not dim – simply older. They would find her alive, of course they would, but ailing and resting for the present, in bed. A little holiday in Peyruis.

No one in the car reacted with surprise, and Monsieur Levin kept stroking the dog at his side or looking straight ahead throughout the journey as he and Pierrette took it in turns to drive. It was now late afternoon. They arrived in this tiny, perfect French village with the last of the sunlight shining on the olive trees in the Levins' garden.

***

Doctor Oblonsky was the family doctor of Monsieur and Madame Levin. He had hurried from his patient's bedside to join the English guests on the veranda, who had – of course – already been to see his elderly patient the moment they arrived. Briefly…

Mopping the pinpricks of sweat from his forehead with a red and white spotty handkerchief, the doctor wore a straw panama on his bald head with distinction. He was there to give the Thrush family his latest medical opinion on Granny Pod over a glass of Pernod.

Everyone was nibbling some exquisite, mouth-watering, irresistible titbits such as homemade tapenade. It was the treacly scented, voluptuous dark ooze of macerated olives on tiny rectangles of toasted bread that made the English wonder why they weren't born French. Pacing from one end of the veranda to the other, glass in hand, Doctor Oblonsky declared that dementia could follow a stroke. Madame Pod had lasted well, but one could not fight mortal destiny.

For a fraction of a second, Elm could have sworn the doctor had said 'moral'. He raised his eyebrows at Asp and realised he was wrong when he saw her blank gaze back. Pierrette was slapping at flies crawling across the table, her thoughts somewhere in Colorado. Henry was relishing his second *bière*. Monsieur and Madame Levin had finally sat down to enjoy the scene, steeped in temporary relief that this was payback time for the Thrush family's care of their only child. Leaf was snoring quietly in Asp's arms. Daphne was sucking at the tapenade on her knife with furtive darts of her small, pink tongue.

Both families kept on turning with a touch of sycophancy towards the doctor. They were hoping for enlightenment as that is what they were conditioned by their society to do – to be expectant and respectful when someone medical was in their midst. In turn, it fed the doctor's faith in his omnipotence and made him that shade more pompous and theatrical than wise.

'Degeneracy can begin with lapses of memory, mood swings and a struggle to find the right words. In the case of stroke damage, it is harder to assess. It is natural that there should be some confusion in understanding for the person who has had the stroke.

'In the case of Madame Pod, she has spent two or three or four years in what seems to have been a miraculous escape from her predicament. In short, she has achieved an extended autumn, but now, in view of her sudden deterioration, her double incontinence and her apparent apathy, winter has arrived. As her family,' and he waved his glass towards Daphne, 'you must prepare yourselves for the inevitable.'

Sanctimonious pip-squeak, thought Henry after checking out the translation with Elm, who agreed with his father that the doctor was a pompous *git au font.* Daphne appeared overwhelmed by the length of his speech. Madame Levin offered more tapenade on toast. Monsieur Levin expressed his thanks to the doctor and was now studying the Thrush family from a distance, the way one does an alien group – hoping no one catches you as you watch, disapprove or gloat.

Asp had already lifted Leaf out of his bouncy chair for a second, extended visit to their grandmother. Elm was admiring the rows of pink lights like miniature Chinese lanterns hanging at the foot of the olive grove. Fireflies darted in a haze around the trees. Daphne and Henry, uncertain of their French, retired to bed.

***

'Rest, rest, perturbed spirit.'
Hamlet

CHAPTER 31

'Granny?' The grey face on the four-poster was still. 'I was waiting until I could be alone with you. And Leaf. I thought you'd like to see him properly. See how much he's grown.'

The baby stretched his arms out towards the bed, and Asp placed him as close as she dared next to her grandmother's startled face.

'I'm sorry, truly sorry, Granny. Will you try and forgive me?' She bent low to stroke the shrunken figure under the sheet. 'So relieved I didn't... kill you.' Asp burst into tears. 'So glad you're alright.'

Granny: 'All I can say is when I can't see you anymore, you'll be sorry. Freak.'

Leaf: 'Are you talking to me or Asp?'

Granny: 'If you understand what I'm saying, then I'm talking to you.'

Leaf eyed his grandmother with sudden fury. Water was leaking out of the side of her mouth, and her skin smelt funny, and she was being rude about him. Without cause.

'I understand lots of things.' He grabbed the end of her nose between his thumb and fingers, giving it a quick pull.

'Oooh. You nasty little boy. I always thought you were strange in

the head.' Granny's rasping breaths and the hubbub of voices coming from the veranda were the only sounds in the room. Asp seemed to be looking at the faded prints of wild boar on the walls, but the truth is she saw none of it. Her silent tears were self-recriminations that splashed onto Elm's head and then stopped as quickly as they had begun.

'The pianist, Solomon, had a stroke. Did you know that?' Asp was wiping away the tears from her face with her fist.

'No-o-o-o-o.'

'Some musicians were walking past his house, and they could hear him practising the 'Moonlight Sonata' through the open windows. He played it very slowly.'

'OF COURSE IT WAS SLOW. YOU CAN'T PLAY IT ANY OTHER *WAY!*'

'I don't get it. Is this a joke?'

'It doesn't matter if you don't.'

'Does.'

'DOESN'T!'

'I'm fed up with baby talk. How am I s'posed to have interesting thoughts when all I ever hear is itchy-citchy-witchy-coo type rubbish?'

'Which you *speak* so well.'

'Only because everyone expects me to be their little dum-dum. It's become a lifetime's work, staying in touch with my inner child.'

'You mean baby.'

'BuBuBuBuBuBah. Bubba.'

'There. You see? I told you. You can talk if you want to.' Asp bent down suddenly to tickle her brother under the chin.

'Oh, please.'

'If you don't like it, why don't you just speak up?'

'I would, but they're much happier with the idea of me being...'

'Infantile.'

'Babyish.'

'Well, everyone assumes I'm senile, which is almost the same.'

'I'm not so sure. Babies can develop. They aren't stuck in a rut.'

'Except you haven't grown much, have you?'

'Not much.'

'Exactly. By the way, I'm not senile. Just bored.'

'GRRRRRRRR.'

'OK, Leaf, look at me. I want you to put your tongue against your top gum like this, straight after the 'grrrr' part. Watch me. "Grrran,"... And if you sort of smile as you say it... Watch... There... see? You'll be able to say "Grrrranny". Just like that.'

'GOLLYGOLLYGOLLYGOLLY.'

'What I'd really like is a bath with some Epsom salts.'

'Haven't you had a wash since you left home then?'

'It doesn't smell that bad.'

'EEURGH.'

'Granny darling?' Asp leant across the bed and kissed her grandmother on the cheek. She could feel the crepes of skin move underneath her lips. A taste of old powder. 'Do you understand what I'm saying? Are you happy now, Granny?'

Whenever Asp had knelt by the pond in their garden in

England, she would remain there without moving until the frogs returned to the surface of the water to scramble onto the lily pads and sun-bake. She loved that. Her grandmother's eyelids had opened with the kiss – opened, shut and opened again. Just like an ancient frog in a fairy tale with its scarlet mouth revealing tiny vomerine teeth.

'You do understand, don't you, Granny? And you are glad you went away? I thought so. I'm really, honestly glad that you're alive after all these years... of thinking you weren't. Well, you know what I mean. But it's a huge, amazing shock.'

She lay down on her grandmother's bed beside Leaf, indifferent to both their smells because her sense of her own rottenness had eclipsed theirs. The baby's toes were rhythmically pounding the top of her head like a cat's paws in search of milk. She managed to push him further up towards the pillow, but he wriggled down again as she reached out to slip an arm around her grandmother's waist.

'You'd better watch out, Leaf, or I'll post you through the baby hatch for unwanted foundlings. Granny, don't you see? I thought somehow... without meaning to, of course, that I'd killed you and... naturally, I couldn't tell anyone. I had this unbearable secret. And now... now I've got another one.'

Her mouth touched the old woman's spine through the sheet. Her voice was muffled by the cloth. Each time she had a fresh thought, she was obliged to repeat it to be heard.

'I disgust myself. I really do.' She uncurled herself to slap Leaf's feet, covering his mouth with her free hand to stifle his indignant roar.

'Is she trying to tell me that she's murdered someone else?'

'Sorry. I'm choking to death actually.'

'You look very pretty, Granny.' Art has its own rules, she thought as she watched the eyes wobble like milk jellies on a plate.

'Asp. Can you take over the translating for a bit?' Elm was sloping in the doorway. 'What are you doing to Leaf? You'll smother him.'

'Can't you manage on your own?' She pulled the baby towards her, covering his wet face with kisses to stop them both from crying.

'I've been asked by Monsieur Levin to go and look for Jean-Pierre.'

'You mean Pierrette. Look where?'

In the middle of a yowl, Leaf had fallen asleep with his head hanging backwards.

'A miracle. My bad boy-baby. Look where?'

'In the village.'

'I'm coming too.'

'You're supposed to give Granny a bath, Asp. The smell in here is horrible. You might as well throw Leaf in while you're at it.'

'Oh great.'

At which point, Doctor Oblonsky appeared behind Elm as a dark shadow.

'Time for your medicine, Madame Pod,' he said in his rich bass, Russian-sounding French.

***

'For by the image of my cause I see
The portraiture of his. I'll court his favours.'
Hamlet

CHAPTER 32

Elm:
Sometimes I have to watch my sister, not so much when she's with Leaf, although yes, even with Leaf, but mainly with Jean-Pierre. Sorry. Pierrette. When they're together, it's as if there's some malevolent force – not that I have any concrete examples. This is only an instinct. I have those from time to time. Nothing is what it seems to be. I can't help it. Maybe Asp is just that little bit mad and unreliable. Emotionally, I mean.

'Elm! Elm, *cheri.*' It was Pierrette hurrying towards him in a pink and white striped dress that made Elm think of an animated lollipop. Her arms were muscular and covered with fine bleached down. Wrists were smothered with silver bangles. 'Wait there,' she screamed. 'Don't go away, *mon ami.*'

Elm glimpsed the outline of his unwanted erection in the butcher's shop window. White-skinned, English and turbulent as he searched for a corner in which to hide, reflecting that the involuntary rising of the penis is such a hassle for a man. He hurried past the huddle of people outside the patisserie, crossed the road in the direction of the *tabac* and rounded the corner into a square where some small boys were playing *boule*. Pierrette followed.

Her arm stole round Elm's shoulders and lingered there. It was so light in the way it rested below the English boy's neck. They heard the laughter of the street boys, watching them both from a distance.

'Have you come to bring me home, *mon ami*? I'm glad.'

It occurred to Elm that he could throw himself on the ground and spoil the game of *boule* by dying from shame and embarrassment right there. But that was more Asp's style. Instead, he said in English, without a trace of emotion, 'Your father wants you to get some *pastis*.'

'And what do you think this is?'

Pierrette pointed her chin at a mega bottle of *pastis*, four baguettes and a bag of apricots in a straw bag. 'Come. I hate shopping in my own little village. Let's go. They're either rude like those stupid boys over there playing *boule* or they're rude in a more subtle way. The old people say things like, "You remind me of your father," and they laugh. Hey.' Pierrette grinned at Elm. 'I don't think so.' A ball scudded past her feet as she shoved two fingers in the air at the grinning boys. '*Gros beaufs*!' Tossed a flank of hair over her shoulder and walked away at a lick. '*On y va.*'

They were hurrying along a scorched road, passing an old duffer in overalls with a box of heavy tools. He was chewing a cigarette out of the corner of his mouth and his '*Bo' soir*, Jean-Pierre,' was an exclamation of scorn. Pierrette replied, 'bonne soiree' in a fluty voice that was meant to sound nonchalant and made Elm smile. It could have been Rosalind as Ganymede in *As You Like It*, except this was a boy playing a girl. It was a harmless, friendly exchange on a country road. They crossed a bridge over a dried-up riverbed and sashayed between trees.

They tripped through ploughed fields to avoid any conventional pathway and almost dropped the straw bag of groceries. Pierrette dangled her high heels in her free hand, dancing in bare feet through the soil. They left behind them the rumble of a solitary tractor and the thwarted bitchiness of a country village. In her new guise, Pierrette was more fun than Jean-Pierre.

She prodded Elm in the middle of his back with the baguettes as if she read his mind. 'Pierrette sounds better than Zizi, for example. My parents prefer Jean-Pierre. *Bien entendue.*'

'Maybe it's the same for the people in the town.'

'But they're not my parents, and besides, my parents accept me as I am. That doesn't mean they don't have a preference. These nasty little boys should think before they open their mean little mouths. They don't because they don't want to. It's digging in the dirt, which they love to do around here.'

'I'll try to remember,' said Elm, 'Pierrette.'

They both laughed. 'But it's okay if we forget sometimes. *Hein*?'

'Okay,' said Elm.

'And Mr Thrush – Henry. He surprised me. I really thought he'd be – I suppose – hostile. But he's been very polite. He must like my father a lot.'

'It was the Grand Prix and the French beer.'

'And Elm?'

'Yes?'

'Do you remember the lead soldiers?'

'Of course.'

'I've still got some that need painting. Are you interested, *mon ami*?'

The house was visible through the olive grove, and Elm stood still for a moment. He was admiring the spotted light on the walls, the ground, on the trees. He was listening to the drumming noises of the crickets. 'So beautiful,' he said quietly. 'You'll have to forgive me – I'm English. I always talk about the weather before I see or say something else.' In his heart, Elm was partly expecting to see his friend restored to the old Jean-Pierre, but it wasn't going to happen, and so he said, 'I'm sorry. I promised to go for a walk with Asp after dinner. Do you mind?'

Pierrette tossed her head to hide her disappointment.

'No problem. I've a better idea. We can go, the three of us, to our little cinema with the corrugated iron roof.' Her voice rose to a thin falsetto. 'They're showing *Les Diaboliques*. Your sister will love it. Let's hope there's no rain.'

***

'Come my coach! Good-night, ladies; good night,
sweet ladies; goodnight, good-night.'
Hamlet

Chapter 33

Pierrette declared over dinner that she, Pierrette, was in sparkling form as in a mountain stream. Asp recalled how the old Jean-Pierre had rarely smiled or laughed at anything but with his new self, he did both. She looked across at her mother, now glassy-eyed and worse for wear.

Daphne had been working through the wines, regretting the cardboardy hams she had fed their exotic friend in lodging days, inwardly scolding herself for a lifetime of slovenly tendencies and admiring the style, the fastidiousness, the temptations, the glory of the banquet placed in front of her by Madame Levin.

She would have liked to stop thinking, which is why she had drained each glass put in front of her and consumed the remains of Elm's. That Jean-Pierre had become Pierrette or that her long lost mother was alive and an invalid seemed of minimum surprise. In her sodden, mawkish state, Daphne was only faintly worried what the family might say next.

As for Henry, she reckoned he would cope with Pierrette's revelations if he thought Daphne wouldn't. He was busy describing his model aeroplanes to Thierry Levin with exuberant arm movements and lubricated franglais while avoiding all eye contact.

Elm was listening to a peroration by Doctor Oblonsky on the pros and cons of euthanasia, wondering why he always got to sit next to the dull ones. Leaf slept through his five courses while his grandmother was propped up with cushions in a wheelchair, spruced, sweet and smelling of lavender – just like Aunt Rose. As for Asp, she was tending to her granny in her new role as saint.

Above all else, Daphne longed to say: 'What, what, what's this? We've been here before. I know this scene in another form. The forced smiles. Our dinner table. Our house. Ever since lodgers. Never being ourselves. Always pretending to be someone nicer. Afraid to be real.'

'Truth,' she announced in the middle of their raucous din, 'is about solidity and wash noble.' Poor, round-faced Daphne with her empty glass and glazed eyes, her mangled consonants, her small nose sniffing doom – her pauses longer than her words.

'Do you shtill play the violin, Jeanne-Pierre?'

Pierrette shrieked in a fake, girly sort of voice and stole a mussel from Asp's plate. 'I practise every morning without fail.'

'You're sabotaging my seafood.' Asp leapt from her chair and quickly sat down again, loath to rip her party dress made of double-strength baking foil to please Leaf.

Elm and Henry seemed to think this was funny and laughed. Asp sulked over a remaining langoustine and wondered if her relationship with Pierrette was the same as Trilby's to Svengali, in which case, she'd make it clear she'd be Svengali.

'The violin is in his bedroom to be safe.' Madame Levin was

speaking with careful, schoolgirl English. She had been stealing glances at Pierrette – bursting into silent tears when anyone addressed her, which they tried not to do in case they caused more distress.

'Ashp-is-zackly-the-shame.'

'No I'm not,' snapped Asp.

'Your grandmother is a most interesting case. Quite unusual.' Doctor Oblonsky was still keen to be heard. His small pointed beard was thrust upwards by his chin, and he stroked and petted it whenever he was being watched. Elm had the doctor down as a character in a Chekov play, convinced that the main canon of European literature had sprung from the village of Peyruis about a hundred and fifty years before.

'In what way is our grandmother medically interesting, Monsieur *le docteur*?' asked Elm, removing his foot from underneath Pierrette's.

'Travelling the world when you have just had a stroke... is remarkable.'

Granny winked at Elm in her lopsided way. This was as exhausting to watch as it was difficult to execute. Elm winked back.

'And when you haven't any money, it's bloody ridiculous.' Henry had finally caught the gist of what was being said and given up on Franglais to speak in English with a heavy French accent.

'Incredible.'

'*Qu'est ce qu'il dit?*'

'My father agrees with you, *M'sieur le docteur.*'

Elm placed a hand over his glass and quickly pushed it out of

Daphne's reach.

'Excuse me, but we did have money.' Pierrette was indignant and a bit squeaky. 'Just a little. We used to keep it in a box in a safe deposit at Harrods. We took only what was *nécessaire – de temps en temps.*' She tucked a nasturtium flower from the salad behind her ear and renewed her game of footsie with Elm under the table. 'Harrods was very good at sending it to our latest address.'

Daphne slipped slowly down her chair until she was lying on the floor beside their feet. Asp jumped up at the mention of Harrods, declaring it was her favourite store and ripping some crucial strips of silver foil around the arms so that she was forced to sit down again immediately to conceal the damage.

Henry choked into his red paper napkin. The doctor was humming a drifting tune by Tchaikovsky as arranged by Faure. His shrewd Tartar's eyes were fixed on a distant point above his patient's head while he was considering his fee for services rendered so far.

'What box? In Harrods?' Henry was redfaced, apoplectic. 'What rubbish. My mother-in-law never had a penny when she lived with us.'

'Oh yes I had. But I wasn't going to let you have any of it...'

No one at the table, including Daphne, still wrestling with her muddled fancies on the floor, was aware of how they must seem. Their lack of insight, combined with one family's greed and the other's foreignness, lay at the heart of their misunderstanding and turned the occasion into a farce. To Henry, his mother-in-law's reply was a wordless, whooping noise, and both families behaved as if they hadn't heard his question.

Through the fly screens, they listened to the dripping of rain on the leaves. Much louder in the south of France than at home, thought Daphne from underneath the table, where she remained until the feet on either side of her had disappeared and the rain had stopped. A delicious moisture cooled the air, and the only audible sounds were those of Leaf sucking on his dummy or Monsieur and Madame Levin putting dishes into the dishwasher in the kitchen.

The family fades away, beginning from the outside in.

***

'The players cannot keep counsel, they'll tell all.'
Hamlet

CHAPTER 34

Elm was first to mention his grandmother's jewels, furs and monies as they were coming out of the cinema after a showing of *Les Diables* and Asp was thinking she had discovered her definitive audition speech for RADA as a result. Pierrette was encouraging her by re-enacting the scene where an *apparently* dead husband rises out of the bath, removing his fake eyeballs at the moment when his wife has an *apparently* fatal heart attack.

'Oh rough,' protested Asp. 'That's *so* rough. Let me, let me try.'

'Gag a little.'

'Really?'

'Pretend you do it all the time. You do. You know you do.'

'Like this?'

'Not for real.'

'Wasn't that amazing, Elm?'

'I suppose so.'

'You mean you didn't LOVE it?'

'Well, there were *some* bits.'

'What are you talking about? It was fantastic.'

'I got bored after a while.'

'You're not serious. This was A CLASSIC film, Elm!

'Why are you shouting?'

'I'M NOT SHOUTING.'

'It wasn't real.'

'Oh please…'

'I can't believe you didn't think it was great.'

'The actors were real. But they were acting.'

'So?'

'That's my point.'

'Let's go back inside and ask them if we can see it again.'

'What I'd like to know is, does Granny have any money left?'

'Pots.'

'Pots?'

'What do you think?'

Elm had been standing slightly apart throughout, watching his sister as she ran back and forth between a clearing in the trees, flinging herself on the ground, picking herself up, laughing, arguing, appealing to Pierrette and falling down again.

'*Rien, mon ami. Presque rien.*'

'I just thought...'

'That she had some diamonds?'

'It would have been nice.'

'Well she did,' Pierrette insisted.

'What?'

'Your granny had some real diamonds and a few roubles. They were kept in brown envelopes. Inside the Harrods box.'

'And now they're gone.'

'Almost. We had to live.'

'As I said, diamonds would have been nice.'

Elm reached up to an overhead branch and swung himself with all the strength in his arms, making sporadic Tarzan noises from the back of his throat and wondering how many roubles were a few. He continued to sway as Pierrette did the same from the tree opposite, only faster.

Asp eyed them both from where she lay in the grass and decided that no, she wouldn't re-enact a heart attack in French as her audition to drama school because all it required her to do was scream a lot and faint. The excitement she had felt while watching the film had faded and would never return.

She estimated they were about a ten-minute walk from the house but was reluctant to walk alone by moonlight. She jumped up from the ground, dragging her coat across her stomach, hopping in small circles to get rid of a cramp. A loose strip of foil had unravelled from the hem of her dress and was dangling close to her ankles. She bent down and ripped it off, scrunching it into a tight ball in her hand as she peered between her naked legs and tried to see the moon from underneath. 'Come on, you two. I want to go to bed.'

Pierrette slipped from her branch and spoke in low tones to Elm, who had given up swinging to squat on the ground. A minute passed and became five. They were squatting side by side, whispering to each other and excluding Asp from whatever it was they were discussing – the way it happens when three people are together and the balance of attention is skew-whiff.

'Hurry up. I'm cold, standing here, waiting forever.'

Pierrette came towards Asp with exaggerated slowness, wrapping an arm around her and kissing her lightly on the side of her neck. 'There,' she said as if the gesture of intimacy made up for any neglect. 'We're coming now, Aspic. Don't be jealous, *cherie.*'

'What were you talking about just then?'

Elm brushed the dirt off his hands and turned his head away from his sister. 'Nothing. Just stupid things.'

'No, really.'

'Yes, really.'

'Him Tarzan, me Jane.' Pierrette tittered and Elm joined in.

Jean-Pierre never tittered. Pierrette loved tittering. Asp felt disgusted. There was something about the sound that Asp found deeply upsetting and which, if she'd thought about it, she would have said was cheesy and fake. And excluding.

Their laughter continued as they half ran, half walked towards the house on the other side of the woods. Asp followed close behind. They walked fast to beat the cold, and they could hear Asp swearing under her breath that they'd lied to her. She was pressing them to say more, but all they did was laugh in that stupid way, and she felt glad when Pierrette tripped and one of her high heels snapped, so she had to limp for the rest of the way home.

***

'...if words be made of breath,
And breath of life, I have no life to breathe.'
Hamlet

Chapter 35

It's surprising how much ground you can cover when you know there's little time to say whatever's necessary. Asp believed she'd covered quite a lot in her brief encounters with Granny, drifting in and out of consciousness. It's not a comfortable place – the place of the nearly dead, with its fears, deceits, delirium and confessions but at the base of Asp's thoughts was her need for some sort of absolution, which she hoped would be hers.

'Granny dear? There's a look in your eyes that tells me you know who I am, even if you can't see me. You let me wash you with a sponge while you sit in your wheelchair or as you lie on your bed. There might be a hundred different ways to interpret what you say, but I want to be spot on.'

I like to think Granny had forgiven me from the moment I arrived in Peyruis. I saw it in the way she submitted to me when she was in the bathroom. 'I absolve you,' she was saying as I wiped the crevices of her skin. Grunt. Grunt. 'You were a child when it happened. It doesn't count.' Grunt. Powdery grey folds hanging from her bones, she was tiny, tiny, shrunken. I tried to be gentle, balancing her on a bedpan or cutting her toenails so they no longer curved back into the foot like claws. Her surrender made me tender and – more difficult to admit, increased my fascination with her vulnerability.

'We're flying from Marseilles tomorrow,' I said, as matter of factly as I could, having just this minute waved goodbye to my parents, Leaf and the red van. 'Elm and I'll be taking you home.'

'AH-h-h-ew-h-h-h-er-r-r-r-r.'

That's more or less how it sounded – with the vowels elongated and a rushing noise at the end like faint thunder.

'Elm's arranged for you to have a bed on the plane. You'll be tucked up with lots of aeroplane presents like bed socks and eye patches and bottles of water that you spray on your skin to make you feel nice.'

'M-ng-ahhhh-mm-ngh-ah-h-h-h-m-m. Who'll read my horoscopes when I'm dead?'

Her head shook with a beginning and an end to the tremor.

'Jean-Pierre, sorry, I mean Pierrette, is returning to Nîmes tonight and wants to say goodbye. Can she come in now?'

'E-e-e-e-o-o-o-o-o-wh-h-h-h. I don't give a toss. I'd like a glass of water.'

Granny might've lost concentration for a moment, or maybe she was in pain because I'd removed the bedpan too quickly and the sides of her bottom had that burning feeling that comes when they've been rubbed the wrong way. In any case, she said nothing, apart from wind noise.

'Granny, is that alright?' I lowered her as carefully as I could onto the mattress and waited. She may have been just a skeleton, but I couldn't believe how heavy she was. It must have been a few minutes that she lay there, bug-eyed against the pillow – as if she'd gone into a trance to avoid the pain. I was aware that the rhythm of her breathing had changed. It may have been what they call stertorous. I don't know. I make these things up out of my head.

Perhaps she was drowning in her own spit. Each breath was like another terrible sigh. Her jaw seemed quite rigid, and her brown eyes looked strangely blue under their transparent sausage skin. I tried to open her mouth wider with my fingers to release her tongue.

I asked myself, what do you do with the dying when they can't speak and they can't tell you jokes anymore? It's not like you can put them out of their misery just because you feel like it. So you end up kissing them and smoothing their foreheads, and you go on changing their bedpans, and you're afraid because you don't know how long it can last like that. I don't want to be mean about this, Granny, but hurry up and please die right now. Die, Granny, die.

I am not being heartless – just practical. There's no one to look after you properly, and you always said you didn't want to be put into a home. Anyway, Pierrette is off to Colorado for a sex-change. Your daughter's living in la-la land and thinks she's pregnant and Elm and I will be away at university. You wouldn't like it – a safe, dull life with Henry or Aunt Rose and Uncle Cecil. Even Leaf is not much consolation.

I could hear Pierrette tiptoeing around in her flip-flops somewhere behind me. She came to the foot of the bed, her new mascara as purple as her skirt. She ran her fingers in a scale across the sheet and leant low over Granny's face, breathing into her lips like someone giving the kiss of life.

'I think she's dead, Aspic.'

'Are you sure? But she wasn't a minute ago. She was sighing as if she wanted to talk.'

'She was expiring *cherie,* right in front of you, face en face.' Pierrette spoke in a man's voice.

Once more, Asp saw the spades in the cellar and her grandmother lying on its floor. You could never be certain of the truth with... Pierrette. 'Are you sure?' Asp bent as close to the body as she dared.

It's possible that on some metaphysical level, Camilla Pod had heard her granddaughter's despairing thoughts and decided enough was enough. Maybe she didn't fancy the flight back to London while alive or a return to her old life with her dysfunctional family. Maybe she no longer wanted to suck strawberries or cheat at Monopoly. There seemed no point to the effort of lying awake on her bed. It was not safe for her to return to Moscow, Cyprus or Borneo, the doctor had said. Her eyes had turned a dark, unnatural blue. And now, she'd stopped breathing, just like that.

There is a sadness in the room after death – the absent voice, a plant or an object that brings back a memory – the empty chair or, in this case, the bed with a lifeless body lying on it – a sense of loss. Granny had not been present in their lives for the last five years, although her family could think about her as if they were going to see her again at some point. That fantasy was over, and each person in that family, with the possible exception of Henry, would feel the loss in their own way. Even Pierrette, who was not one of them.

'Are you absolutely sure?'

'I'm sure.' Pierrette spoke softly and in a man's voice. 'I will get Doctor Oblonsky.'

***

'Something is rotten in the state of Denmark.'
Hamlet

Chapter 36

'I can definitely smell dead cat.' Daphne opened the front door of their house, testing the air in the hall with the certainty of a retired estate agent. 'I do hope it's not the old girl's cat that's gone and died while we were away.'

Henry was outside unloading their suitcases, and her remark was addressed to him as the only other person present, apart from Leaf, still asleep in his baby seat. 'The place has been locked up for two weeks. What do you expect?'

'Well, you come and smell it then.'

'In fact, this is just like your pregnancy.'

'I beg your pardon?'

'You're imagining it.'

He was tired. He'd been driving for seven hours before the boat crossing and for three hours afterwards in a traffic jam. He was tempted to go off on his own to the pub and leave her to bring in the cases by herself. She had an infallible instinct for getting up his nose. He particularly loathed the way she displaced blame from herself so that everyone else was made to feel guilty.

'You're very cruel, Henry.'

'Why?' He slammed the boot shut and dropped the bags. 'I'm

only telling the truth.'

He walked up the pathway, kicking at the tufts of moss that swelled out of the cracks of tiles, wiping the sweat off his forehead with the back of his hand. 'And don't tell me I smell too. I've had enough.' He pushed past her, fed up with her hysterical pregnancy and a lifetime of olfactory hallucinations, which he believed were pointers to his wife's insanity. He was completely unprepared for the stench that poured out of the hall and had him vomiting on the doormat within seconds of entering the house. As he did so, spewing a half-digested croissant across the tiles, Daphne was already walking down the street in a huff with Leaf in a sling around her neck, missing her chance to gloat and say, 'I told you so.' She, along with at least a dozen other mothers that day, was heading for the nearest cappuccino bar, determined not to return until she'd forgotten what it was that had upset her in the first place.

'It's coming from the cellar.' Henry leant against the open door for support and was talking aloud to himself. He remained in a slump until he was sure nothing was left inside his stomach and it was safe to investigate the hell down there. 'Jesus wept,' he cried from the depths, lifting the lid of the deep freeze and slamming it shut again within seconds. The ice cubes collected for his Pimms as well as several packets of frozen peas, had melted within their bags on the top.

A nest of writhing maggots, pink as the flesh they had eaten and swimming in their own glue, fleetingly obscured the real horror underneath. Three fingers with chipped red nails bitten to the quick were sticking out from behind the sodden pods. They curled over the plastic corners of the bags in a shining rictus, gleaming, stinking to high heaven.

'Anastase Besoin. Anastase Besoin,' he repeated, transfixed by the dismemberment – drawn and quartered, deep frozen and defrosted.

'Daph, Daph, what have you done?' It had to be Daph. No one else to blame. No one as mad as his wife when she lost her rag. No child of his. No one in the family as potty. But his wife. Could she? Would she? Did she? When did she? How could she?

Henry was Hamlet leaping into Ophelia's tomb as he pushed the freezer plug back into its socket. Again he raised the lid, more gingerly this time. Tinnitus in his ears made it difficult to think. He delicately, between his own finger and thumb, tweaked the corner of an ancient, sodden bag of peas, lifting it beyond the reach of the broth of grubs.

A partially eaten hand that otherwise might have been three or four sausages nestled at the top of a plastic food box containing neatly arranged, cannibal portions. Henry closed his eyes and dropped the open bag of peas onto his foot. They lay in a pulp across the top of one shoe for several seconds before he kicked it off and his foot came out of his shoe.

'I could dig up the old girl's garden. I could even throw the bits over the fence. Got to hide them somehow. Give it to the foxes. The police won't think of looking next door.' He had stopped struggling with his incapacity to imagine or believe in the enormity of the crime that had been committed in their absence abroad. There was no time for indignation, though his thoughts were as twisted as the scene that confronted him and as rotten as the air he breathed.

He had already sicked up his vestiges of humanity and kindness on the floor by the front door. Who *they* were, was a mixture of the inspector, the sergeant and other imaginary, more nebulous voices of retribution crowding in his head. Each came flying at him in disordered images.

'Sod off, Daphne!' he cried with passion. 'Sod off!' he cried to all of them – and wept as he struggled to re-insert his foot into his shoe.

Inspector Love and PC Petrovich were stuck up a tree like the Cheshire cat, looking down at him as he stuffed the limbs into a dozen bin bags – grinning in a cartoon bubble that swirled before his eyes and then faded into nothing.

He shook his head and tied the knots of yellow plastic string only to discover he couldn't get a finger through the holes in the gathering at the top. Only then did he pause to open every window in the house and stick his head out of the lower back one in Elm's room. Only then did he let the wind settle on his face as he stared at the old girl's garden next door.

Next door had remained an impenetrable wilderness that was unthinkable to change. Contained between a wall of clipped hedges at one end and Daphne's controlled jungle on the other, this was a place of mystery, brambles and magic. Henry found himself listening to the mournful under-song of several redwings, which had strayed from the bird sanctuary nearby. As he listened, he knew what he must do.

He would lug the bin bags up the cellar stairs and through the house – one at a time; he could manage that – and into the back garden. That was the easy part. He would pause for a moment to recover and adjust his balance with a quick glance round to check he was alone. He would – of course, he would – rip each bag with his fingernails and tip the dismembered bits over the fence to be lost among the old girl's brambles or become food for the foxes.

'And that,' he said flatly, 'will be that.' As for Daphne, if she ever returned, Henry would say nothing to her. Since the first day of his unemployment, he'd become an expert at burying uncomfortable thoughts, if not mortal remains.

'Oh Daph, Daph, Daph! What have you made *me* do?' A solitary, starved tear appeared in the corner of one eye and was just about visible if you looked hard enough at the point where eye and eyelid are joined.

***

'Larded all with sweet flowers,
Which bewept to the ground did not go
With true-love showers.'
Hamlet

CHAPTER 37

There were eleven babies of various sizes in eleven buggies, including Leaf. They were lined up on one side of the room with a surplus of mothers sitting vaguely near their offspring, smoking and sipping cappuccinos. Not a man in sight. The babies had tremulous hands from the mixture of nicotine air and an overdose of caffeine in the spoonfuls of froth their mothers fed them from time to time. Their eyes expressed surprise, distaste, rebellion and suspicion all at the same time, having cried their way to the coffee shop before running out of tears.

The New Zealand waitress was distributing eleven pink and blue rattles, placing them firmly in their plump, palsied hands as each mother discussed the extraordinary benefits of baby classes if conducted in French. Daphne was on her mobile in a corner, slightly apart from the rest. She was distracted by her own conversations with Asp or Elm, who were in Nîmes and with Inspector Love, already on his way to meet her in Clapham. Leaf was hanging upside down on her lap, snoring loudly, the only sleeping baby in sight.

'Ah, the poor, wee bert of a therng.' And the waitress smiled with such great sweetness as she picked up his own rattle from the floor and tucked it under his chin. Daphne was talking into her mobile phone in rapid bursts.

'You're sorry Granny is dead? Well, yes... Inconsolable... Now, let me get this right. Are you saying cherry wood or bronze? ... Oh... You mean self-sealed. How do I... You choose darling... You can see it. She would have preferred cherry, I think... and the insurance? It doesn't? Ah... no. Thought so... Did she ask for me?

'Well, yes, of course I know she couldn't speak... sorry, sorry... D'you want us to come back? It's okay... You'll manage... Pierrette is helping... That's up to you... I'd rather you didn't stay longer than necessary. You'll bring her back. Just you and Asp... with Granny... We'll worry about the cost later. Thank you, darling. Let me have another word with Asp...'

People are governed by what they do and there are always consequences. If fate is ignored, it is through choice, not through some passive, wishy-washy, random, get-out-of-jail card that is given by happenstance to win the game. Surely?

'Asp sweetheart... Are you sure you don't need me? It's... It's absolutely terrible... Yes, I'm glad she didn't suffer... Yes, inconsolable.

'Could I have a small espresso please?

'I understand. And Jean-Pierre – sorry, I mean Pierrette – is flying to where? Borneo? Are you sure? That's ridiculous. Tonight? You mean you're not sure... I see. How can...

'Thanks. And some hot milk on the side? With a glass of tap water... Thanks very much.

'No, I left your father at home. He was in a foul mood and the whole house stank after being closed up for two weeks. I couldn't face it... I don't know why. Dead rats under the floorboards perhaps. Yes, I'll tell him... I've no idea... a trapped fox... from next door... which side? ... Are we talking Wellies Two here? I'll tell him to look. You think what, sweetheart? ... I can't hear you.'

Just occasionally, two or more incidents will occur in life with potentially fateful synchronicity and with one serving to illuminate the other. Daphne turned her face to the wall in a bid for privacy as a funeral cortege passed the shop window in a blur of lilies, red eyelids and black hats behind smoked glass. It processed so slowly down the street that while it was visible, time – it's always going to be like this with time – time seemed to stand still.

Daphne not only failed to see the cortege, but she also missed the four women dressed in black, rising from their benches to leave the coffee shop with the greatest dignity, who, if she had seen their expressions, would have made her understand her own loss.

It was an unconscious blankness on her part, that gulf between chance and choice having made her turn away and miss. She'd blown it.

For several seconds, the only sounds inside the coffee bar were of rattles smashing on the terra cotta floor, teaspoons stirring, machines hissing, Leaf snoring and Daphne's voice.

'Can I have another quick word with Elm? ... He's gone? ... Well, tell him I think that cherry wood would definitely be nice... Did you mention cost? Oh. It doesn't matter if it's sealed or not...

She's hardly going t... What? ... Nothing can get in. Or out. Of course not, darling. How much did you say?

'Thanks. Could I have a spoon please?

'You sound very distant... You are, of course... What? I've no idea... Did you say velvet? ... I see. You both prefer white satin to velvet... I understand.' (Is there a point at which the will of the majority becomes unjust?)

'Love you. I'll ring again when I get home... Leaf's fine... Bye now. Be brave... We'll talk later... It's nobody's fault... You're never old enough to lose your mother... Give my love to Elm... and... do remember to say thank you to the Levins. From your father and me... Yes. Monsieur and Madame Levin. Must go, petal... You too.'

'Sorry. I asked for a teaspoon, not a rattle. Is that a touch of kiwi? Thank you, no, no, thank you, thanks.

'Bye sweetie-pie. Love you... Bye.'

Anxiety made her smell. Anxiety and grief. She could smell her own armpits mixed in with the bitter tang of coffee. She hoped that no one would notice as she pressed her arms close to her sides, still holding her phone. She was angry with herself for her sense of shame when what she felt she should be feeling was grief and nothing more.

'Hello, Cedric. How lovely to see you again.'

***

On the day of Granny's funeral, before the sun was up, a full moon floated across the sky and cast its silver light on a small London street. Two foxes were dancing upright on hind legs, their front paws placed lightly on each other's shoulders. Theirs was a fox trot of such intimacy – with shudders, moans and keening sounds as they turned together in decreasing circles.

After several minutes of being joined like this, the vixen broke away to lie down in the middle of the road. She raised her bottom to the sky, howling like a battered woman. The dog fox danced alone, his tongue hanging out as he listened to her cries and kept his distance for several minutes.

Only when he reached the end of the street where it joins a main road did the dog fox hesitate. He twisted right and left, checking that they were unobserved. Still upright, he trotted back to her, thrusting his body against hers in a series of sharp, erotic jerks.

'Inconsolable. Yes, inconsolable Cedric. I'm inconsolable.'

***

'And where th' offence is, let the great axe fall.'
Hamlet

CHAPTER 38

For Henry, Granny's death was a straightforward rite of passage. For Aunt Rose, it was the same. She insisted her sister's death made room for a new life. As one day would her own. When the brain is dead, she told Hamish, you feel relief when they are allowed to go. Elm wasn't yet clear what he felt. Granny Pod had been absent from their lives for the last five years, and it seemed to him she had died once already.

It was generally accepted that the family had mourned for her in their different ways. Her unexpected 'second' death from natural causes released a floodgate of grief in Daphne. She kept repeating the word inconsolable until everyone believed she was.

For Asp, the finality of Granny's real death in France would induce feelings of intense remorse and self-punishment. She planned to swallow an overdose of pills on the day that she returned to England. (Henry only hurried her decision with his tale of body bits in the freezer and their subsequent disposal.)

Asp would later say that she took the pills because the future always seemed a bit dodgier, a bit messier, a bit more like the past than you expect. Elm said she should realise that horrors can illuminate understanding but that suicide, successful or not, was fundamentally selfish, and she should grow the fuck up. For the second time, Daphne would sit by her daughter's hospital bed – this one in a private ward with a two-way mirror, paid for with a single diamond, a farewell gift from Pierrette.

After refusing to explain her actions and only opening her mouth to receive food from her mother, Asp asked to see Detective Chief Inspector Love of the Central London Serious Crimes Group – alone. Daphne left the hospital as the inspector entered. They did not meet.

Asp's tongue was unleashed from the moment Inspector Love arrived, and in a fit of fury, she confessed to the murder of Anastase Besoin.

'I wasn't going to kill somebody I wasn't fucking mad at. What the fuck would I want to do that for? I killed her because I fucking hated her, and so did everyone else. It's no bloody mystery. Despite what you might think, I don't go round murdering any fucking person just for the fucking fun of it. I had a reason.'

It was the second time Asp had assumed responsibility for the death of someone and revealed a gift for self-torment that was cloned from her mother. She might choose to believe that personal fulfilment is more important than collective responsibility and bugger the consequences, but on reflection, that was more Nasty's style. Then quite suddenly, out of a silence between herself and the inspector, Asp changed the subject back to her own attempted suicide.

'Do you believe in fate?' she asked.

'I believe we can control our lives.'

'I must have swallowed twenty-eight pink and white pills when

I got back home from France. Our father kept on telling us how he'd found Nasty in the cellar freezer, and something in me snapped. I found one bottle of pills in the bathroom. It was Granny's medication from years ago. My mother never throws anything away. Three gulps. All swallowed. Not chewed. Was that fate or was that some sort of super control by my tongue?'

The inspector shook his head. He had no answer, and instinct told him not to interrupt the flow.

'I got a taxi and asked the driver to take me to a bed and breakfast in East Putney because it cost too much to go further, but it would still feel private.'

He listened carefully with his head to one side, scribbled on some scraps of paper and still he said nothing.

'The landlady thought I'd had an abortion because I told her I was tired and wanted to sleep undisturbed. She had a wrinkled, pixie face with dyed orange hair and not many teeth.

'She gave me bacon and eggs with sausages and fried toast and told me to think of it as the breakfast I didn't want the next morning. I laughed. My last meal on death row, I thought. I ate every scrap.'

The inspector looked up from his notes. He couldn't help himself. 'You ate before you tried to kill yourself?'

'Well, yes, I told you. At some level, I must have wanted *not* to die. Shit happens. The food lined my stomach with its grease, and when the landlady found me half dead and hanging off the bed, she stuck her fingers down my throat until I threw the lot up in a bowl. Anyway, I lived and Nasty didn't. Sod's law. I slept for three days after those pills.'

The inspector was busy scribbling again and shaking his head, reflecting on the landlady's fingers.

'I couldn't find a razor in my make-up bag. I reckon if God had wanted me dead like fucking Nasty, he would have helped me to find the razor. So I lived. It's all God's fucking fault.'

So far, the inspector had been writing in fits and starts: 'It is my professional opinion the subject is lying.'

He began filing his nails, a deliberate act of dandyism which made him feel less like a policeman. Head bowed, he was relieved that she couldn't see any expression on his face. He knew he must look odd. He felt odd. He felt like an ant, not a puppet, and he'd got stuck in a spoonful of porridge. The ant was currently drowning. He wanted to go to bed.

On his lap, along with his scraps of paper, was a page of newspaper. The inspector waved it under her nose, but Asp pushed it away and refused to look at what it said.

Decapitated Woman in Suburban Back Yard, by the Chief Crime Correspondent

Police cordoned off the garden of a southwest London house today. The dismembered body of an adolescent female has been found in the back garden of an empty house in the suburbs. Police were called to the scene when builders discovered a sawn-off hand in the claw of a mini-digger they were using to clear the undergrowth. Body parts were removed on a stretcher covered by a red blanket at 10 a.m.

Detectives last night were studying photographs of the victim in reassembled form. Pathology reports suggest that the person responsible would have been heavily bloodstained at the time of the murder, approximately three weeks ago. It appears that the young woman had suffered multiple wounds, being bludgeoned in a frenzied attack before being sawn into sixteen small, joint-sized pieces. Detective Chief Inspector Cedric K Love, who is leading the enquiry, said wounds are consistent with those inflicted by an axe or similar weapon.

Last night, police appealed for witnesses and asked for help in identifying the victim. Detectives are working on the theory that the victim had been killed elsewhere and that the killer had dumped most of the body's remains before making his or her escape. Several black bin liners had been stuffed with sections of the corpse and emptied in a garden overgrown with brambles at the back of a private house that had been vacant for some time. The bin bags were found concealed under some brambles. No arrests have yet been made.

Evidence of fox disturbance has hampered the immediate and positive identification of the victim, who was most probably Caucasian in origin, late teens, estimated as five feet tall, with raspberry-dyed hair. The remains of some black nylon leggings were also found. DNA tests are being carried out and the information checked with the national database.

The gruesome discovery has led to suggestions that there may be more bodies buried in the garden. Police examination of the scene is ongoing and a special squad has been formed to sift information. Forensic officers continue to examine the empty house for clues. Professional counselling has been provided for the two developers who found the remains after buying the house from the local council as an investment. The street has been sealed off, and door-to-door enquiries are being made. Any one who can assist the police with their enquiries should telephone the following number…

The inspector stuffed the cutting back inside his coat pocket along with his scribbles.

'I'm slug slime,' said Asp.

'What did you say?'

'I'm slug slime. You know. The lowest form of life. Is there any lower? I'm the crap that's left behind. The waste.'

'Ah.' The inspector knew just what she meant.

'At least I've left a trail for you to follow. I should be dead. But I couldn't find the fucking razor. I'm sorry, Inspector Love. I'm really, really sorry.'

'I know.' It was a small trick of his to agree with someone unexpectedly, but the tactic sometimes backfired.

'I don't mean I'm sorry I killed Nasty. She fucking deserved it. Although I'm sorry I'm still alive.'

The inspector hesitated. 'Because you're afraid of punishment?'

'Why should I be sorry about anything else?'

'You believe there's a kind of justice in her murder.' He wished he were in bed.

'I didn't give it that much thought.'

As he leant towards her, she moved back to preserve the space between them.

'Trying to kill yourself... It's not a moral restitution,' he said quietly.

This was a knife turned so delicately that you can't hear it tearing the flesh until later when you try to imagine the sound. He told Daphne later that she'd looked straight back at him with those wide, glittering eyes. Daphne had frowned and said Asp must have forgotten to put in her contacts. She often did.

'I'm not going to say any more without a lawyer, inspector.'

Asp wiped her face dry with the back of her hands and buried them in her lap.

'This is not an official visit, Asp.' He extended his arm to look at his watch. It was time to leave.

'This is not an official visit, Asp,' she mimicked. 'It's an unofficial fucking enquiry, though, isn't it?'

'You asked me to come.'

'I did.'

'Well then.' The inspector, remembering how tired he felt, gave a yawn.

'I wanted you to know the truth... That's all. So you can call off the search. There aren't any more dead bodies in next door's garden.'

'That's all you wanted to say? You're certain about that?' He looked doubtful.

'I wasn't expecting them to even find her. I thought I'd be gone before anyone discovered anything.'

'Anything?'

'Why do you keep repeating what I say? I tell you, I intended to be fucking dead before anyone discovered that I'd stuffed her in the freezer.'

'And put her remains into bin bags.'

'I know nothing about fucking bin bags.'

'You said you stuffed her in the freezer. Your words, not mine. But she wasn't found in the freezer, Asp. Someone must have taken her out.'

'Well I bloody didn't. I left her in there so I could forget about her. I didn't know the fucking power was off, did I?'

'I'll tell you what I did. I cut her up into bits and stuffed her into those small plastic food bags you buy for leftovers. Not bin bags. It wasn't for a bloody dustbin... And that's the moment when I first thought about killing myself. After I put the freezer lid down. I really wanted to... I thought about it when we were in France too. But my family...'

She pressed her fingers together in a steeple, one on top of the other, before releasing them. 'Some days I can't – I mean, even *think* about them – and so I imagine different ways... You know...to... It calms me down. Just thinking about it. It calms me down.'

She rotated her thumbs slowly several times, taking care that they never touched each other as they revolved. She did this with cracks on pavements. Never step on one, or else you die...

'Because you think when you're dead, you don't have to worry anymore. Is that it?'

'Because then no one can say I'm getting off scot-free.'

'So this confession of yours is meant to be part of the punishment?'

'Perhaps.'

'I might not believe you. Had you thought of that?'

'Then I wouldn't be punished.'

'You wouldn't have to be if you didn't do it.'

She looked at him without understanding. It hadn't occurred to her that he might not believe her.

'Imagine this then, Asp. You're in a small dark room. Just a cubbyhole. There's a curtain covering the space that you're in with a small hole cut into it. You're holding a lens in your hand that's no bigger than your palm. Light floods through the hole in the curtain and onto the lens. It projects an image onto the wall.'

'And?'

'It's accurate. You can measure it. You can trace it. Catch hold of what is real and define it.'

He had genuinely surprised her, despite his tiredness which was real.

'It's my *camera obscura.* Every policeman has one up here,' and he tapped his forehead with his fingertips.

'What are you trying to tell me?' Asp looked back at him uncertainly. 'That you already know everything about what happened? Are you saying that your picture is different from mine?'

She had one eye on his notes and the other on the door as if expecting someone to come in and take her away. 'You don't have to believe me if you don't want to. It's up to you.'

She leant forward and whispered into his face, 'Sometimes I can't bear to hear myself speak.' She jumped up from her chair next to the bed and walked over to a darkened window in the wall, pressing her face right up against its two-way glass.

'Are we being fucking watched through this?'

'Yes.'

'Who's in there? PC Petrovich? Special Branch?'

'Just some doctors. It's their standard procedure. It's not…'

'A betrayal.'

'I was going to say a police station.'

'Did you have any idea why I wanted to see you?'

'No.'

'But you know now.'

'Yes.'

'So the police work's over, isn't it?'

'There are rules which you follow if that's what you mean.'

'What rules? You've got your body and you've got your confession.'

'So you tell me.'

'So there's nothing fucking left for you to investigate.'

The inspector could feel the beginning of a migraine. He had been recently given command of the Central London Serious Crimes Group. He liked his job. He thought of himself as a thoroughly modern policeman. He liked to gather clues without leaping into judgement. He liked to listen, believing that listening led to truth. He was alert to randomness and the significance of dreams. He was not easily shocked nor easily misled. But Asp genuinely puzzled him. Her story was ridiculous, of course. And he wanted to go to bed.

He stretched his arms and clenched and unclenched his fists like a boxer after he's taken off his gloves. He wanted to say there is some inevitability about any police procedure, a necessary step-by-step pickiness. But this, here in the hospital, as she said, without a lawyer present, was not it. He prided himself on being remorseless and efficient, not a slave to the procedure but sensible with his flow charts. He still believed in ground rules. It was his job to make sure that every detail was logged and, before any arrest could be made, that there was a case for prosecution. His face when he looked at Asp was dull with his tiredness.

'It's not so straightforward. I need to go away and think about what you told me.'

'Need? What do you need to think about?'

'The facts. We need to work with facts. How did Anastase Besoin end up in bin bags in the next-door garden if you didn't put her in them?'

'I told you already. I've no fucking idea.'

'And the blood. Where was the blood?'

'In the cellar. I cleaned it up.'

Her eyes followed his movements around the room, watching him stoop to pick up his notes, which kept falling out of his hands onto the floor.

'I cleaned all of it up. Then I painted the walls before we left to go to France. I'm always painting walls and furniture and stuff like that. No one comments on it. It's just normal in our house. We have to do it every time we get a new lodger. It's like removing the fucking Blu Tack. It's easier than cleaning everything. I do it all the time.'

'And your clothes?'

'I burnt them on the rubbish heap.'

'How did you do it, Asp?'

'With a fucking match.'

'How did you kill her?'

'I told you. I bonked her on the head with a spade.'

'One blow, no struggle. That was it?'

He stopped moving up and down the room and saw that Asp was watching him. 'Did she scream?'

'I think she tripped first and hit her head on the edge of a stair. She yelled a lot, so I hit her fucking hard. And then, I used the electric carving knife. I went and got that from the kitchen.'

'No one heard anything?'

'Only Leaf. He was with me.'

'Ah, Leaf.'

'Yes, Leaf. He was hanging on the wall in his papoose.'

'Why were you in the cellar? You told me once that you don't go down there if you can avoid it.'

'I was getting the badminton bats for our holiday. Nasty followed me down. She was snooping. Now that, Inspector, that should be on your fucking *camera obscura*.'

'What?'

'That she sneaked and fucking snooped. It should be on there.'

Asp sucked in her breath as she remembered. 'Are you trying to trap me or something?'

She stood up and ran around her chair, rattling it from behind.

'You know what? You're grinding away in there, and you think you'll get where you want to be by just...grinding. I want you to go. I want you to go before I fucking disappear with your fucking grinding. Go away right now.'

Like a rabbit in a hat. He wished he could. He would, anyway.

She was shouting, swearing, panting and hitting the air with both index fingers stretched as far as they would go, quivering at the tips.

'Go on. I've said it all. I might start changing things if you make me repeat myself. I don't want to, but I might.'

'OK, Asp, it's fine. I'm going soon, I promise. We're both tired. I'm nearly finished.'

He sometimes worried that his own need for facts might overwhelm the truth, and because he worried about it, he said something that surprised himself and was about to astonish her.

'The law conceals as much as it discloses. Sometimes...' He paused to place an arm around her thin shoulders. 'We hand out punishment for one sort of wrong and ignore another.' He placed it lightly because he worried that she would shrink away.'

'Murder is, however you look at it, a selfish act, a criminal act. But where the person murdered was a monster, it's possible to understand why it happened. It doesn't make it lawful. It doesn't make it just. But it's... understandable. Meanwhile, we wait for the DNA results.'

She curled into a ball on the floor in front of his feet, and he told her that the consultant psychiatrist had suggested she should spend the weekend at home.

The nurse with the bobbing watch arrived to help her pack her things. The inspector was looking down at a few more notes he had scribbled on a piece of paper he had overlooked because it had fallen on the floor by his chair. The note was there to help him write his report for the database, but it was in such a mess he picked it up and shoved it back into his trouser pocket, where it would remain with his other scraps until they ended up inside his wife's washing machine.

He hoped that the nurse would bend down, lean over, and pack the overnight bag at the end of the bed so he could see her fob watch swinging against her starched uniform. It was a moment's prurience on an unimportant scale. It made him feel slightly less headachy until she moved in front of him, and all he saw was her back. She didn't even turn when he slipped out the door to speak once more to the psychiatrist with the bouffant hair.

***

'Let shame say what it will...'
Hamlet

Chapter 39

'That man in the car is our new, near neighbour.'

'Near?'

Elm mistrusted his parents' use of the word 'neighbour', but 'near' and 'new' seemed equally misleading as they could have referred to anyone living in the street who arrived after themselves.

'At the end of our garden. They live on the other side.' Henry pointed, outraged, at the gold BMW parked bumper to bumper with the red van outside their house.

It was the following Saturday after Asp's meeting with the inspector, and she was on leave from the hospital and at home for the weekend. Daphne had plumped for a family visit to Tate Modern to celebrate the news of Asp's nine A's at A level. It would raise family morale. She was also wondering how to tell Henry and Elm that Asp had recently confessed to the murder of Anastase Besoin.

Without being able to pin down why this should be, she was fairly certain Henry believed that she, Daphne, was the one who was guilty, just as she, Daphne, thought that it might have been Elm. Leaf remained unaccused. Leaf, the innocent, was to be left in the care of Aunt Rose and Uncle Hamish, now semi-permanent guests since the day of Granny's funeral.

'A dead body on one side of the house and new neighbours at the back. We live in an exciting street.'

'They don't live in our street. They're round the corner. They just park here because it's free parking.'

'Can we change the subject?'

Asp, on a cocktail of antidepressants, was spoiling for a fight. 'He looks lower middle class.'

Elm was outraged at the snobbery of it all.

'He's got a peculiar haircut. I'd say they're middle, middle class.' Henry saw himself as an anthropologist of a class-ridden society or a post-modern ironist concerned with its divisiveness, but he also had, by stealth, ordered a new plane on his credit card and was feeling excitable.

'No, lower trying to be middle.' Asp believed in nuances.

'Why do you always have to assign class?' Elm's face was flushed red as his hair. 'Why not just say he looks like a dick?'

In scabby conversations, the loudest will claim immunity from the scabbiness. Elm was an expert in small but potent eruptions. It was not a million miles away from the tactics of neighbours steering shopping trolleys into one another in their local, upmarket supermarket. Man gets mad. And madder.

Some believe indignation has its own force. Banana skins or *schadenfreude*, it was the Thrush method of passing time on car journeys. Asp and Henry were the uberbitches reigned in by Elm as the arbiter of what's obnoxious, unfair and inadmissible. This was how they had been with Nasty.

Appalling, thought Daphne whenever she remembered. In the act of remembering, she would feel better for being appalled.

'Did you notice how our new neighbour folds back his wing mirrors? He's too worried about his car. He parks here because it's quieter than round the corner.' Henry blew his horn at the cyclist in front.

'I heard *her* this morning.' Daphne stretched an arm to the backseat and patted her youngest child's foot.

'Who's *her*?'

'His wife, I suppose. I was just sitting in the garden reading my star sign, and I could hear this high, whiny voice in the distance, coming from their conservatory. I couldn't hear him. She kept saying, 'you undermine me. You keep on undermining me. You always undermine me in front of ***.'

'Ah. A proper marriage.' Henry laughed for at least a minute. Genuine haw-haw noises that made his body shake in the seat and made Daphne want to shake *him*.

'She must have been talking about the boy. I saw him in a prep school blazer yesterday. He looked a bit down in the dumps.'

'So?' Elm was uncomfortable with his family's casual snobbery and was enjoying his moment of self-righteousness. 'What are we meant to be?' He gave a slight, despairing shrug. 'Perfect?'

'Well, they're probably saying the same things about us.' Daphne was quietly brooding over Asp's hospital confession, uncertain what to tell Henry and Elm. She was not indifferent to her son's distress. They were alike in so many ways, but she was worried that she would have to stop counselling the developers who had uncovered Nasty's remains. They'd been sent to her by the inspector for trauma therapy, and as her only other patient was PC Petrovich who didn't really count, at this rate, she'd have none left and no income.

Elm caught his father's eye in the rear-vision mirror. 'A pity they've missed out on a dead body in the garden. They might have heard Asp as Lady Macbeth in the potting shed.'

'What did you say?' Henry honked a cyclist in front and passed him out of habit.

'The new neighbours. They might have heard Asp rehearsing Lady Macbeth in the potting shed. Except she shut all the windows.'

'What have the windows got to do with it?'

'Acting.'

'She's always acting.'

'She shut the windows so they wouldn't hear.'

'I was **not** playing *Lady Macbeth.*'

'Who then?'

'Jocasta. After she's married Oedipus. Don't you know anything, Elm? Let's play I Spy.'

Henry passed a hand across his forehead and thought of his plane in its separate parts under the bed. 'How old are you meant to be, Asp?'

'You know how old. Aunt Rose told me to rub my womb and imagine I gave birth to my husband. Not too old to fuck a son.'

'Nice one.'

'I'm the mother round here. Ask me what it's like.'

'And I'm the son.'

Ever since the family gathering at the Putney Crematorium and the discovery of Nasty's remains, followed by Asp's voluntary admission to hospital, Aunt Rose had insisted on staying to help the family look after Leaf. Uncle Hamish was keen to know if all the body bones had been found in the bin bags. He was hoping the police would let him join in the search should any be missing. Meanwhile, Elm had begun to acquire tit-bits of feminine attire without the family registering the changes. Being on weekend leave, Asp was the first to comment.

'Is that a diamond I can see?' She spoke as they paused at a traffic light. They were still only halfway to Tate Modern. A small, glittering stud lay on the outer tip of Elm's ear. A touch of *Oberon. It was typical that he would wear the real thing,* thought Asp, who was also wondering how he'd found the money.

'Yes. Want it?' Elm fiddled with his hair and blushed again.

'No. Have you had streaks, Elm?'

She was looking suspiciously at some blonde strands amongst the red, but Elm refused to reply. The whole family appeared to be studying the traffic, but out of one eye, Asp was noting the five other changes in her brother.

He smelt of apple ripple instead of sweat. His fingernails were varnished pearl grey and matched his trousers. The nails were cut, not bitten. He'd shaved the orange fuzz from his neck, and on his wrist, he wore a silver bracelet with a heart-shaped lock. It was woven into his watchband so you didn't notice it at first, but when he raised his hand, the chain flopped with a faint sound like maracas. The cumulative effect was arty and incipiently exhibitionist.

'That's it. We're here. Turn left at the next corner,' he said to change the subject. 'I saw the chimney.' The family was queuing at the entrance when Henry discovered he had forgotten to swap his prescription sunglasses for his clear. There was a general feeling they had got off to a bad start if he were going to view all the exhibits through a glass darkly.

'Is that PC Petrovich over there by the entrance?'

'He comes and goes like the Cheshire cat.

'Or the goat lady.'

'That's not him. He's taller and thinner.'

'It's just a guard.'

'It's an art installation.'

'We should start from the top and work our way down.'

'When we finally get in.'

Daphne complained that by the time she'd sorted out which information card belonged to which work, she'd forgotten the contents. Henry told her to shut up, which she did, with the cunning trick of sending Elm away to discover who had done what.

There was no compulsion to admire. It just crept upon them as they stood above the Turbine Hall and were bathed in a beam of sunlight. If anyone remembered how Asp had thrown a fit the last time she was in a gallery, they kept quiet about it.

'I don't want to leave yet.'

There was a video of a woman in labour, a man who was weightless underwater and someone so old and dying there was no discernable sex in his organs. They stayed for the birth of the baby, and Asp insisted the writhing of the mother gave her ideas for her role as Jocasta.

A day of looking at art brought a tolerance of each other – nothing so galvanising that it would change the way they'd feel or think forever, but a memory lodged that could be summoned up for comfort when required.

As Henry and Daphne faced each other on their pillows that night, instead of turning away out of habit, one of them, it doesn't matter who would reach out to pat the other on the arm in a moment of fleeting solidarity.

Elm could discuss the indescribable elegance of a circle, and they would see it through his poetic prism and not as evidence of some oddity.

Asp was able to count the faults of her father when looking in the mirror and reflect that some of them were hers.

It was Leaf, the overlooked, absent-mindedly adored Leaf, who remained the solitary figure outside the group, resisting all fetters of spirituality at all times.

***

'But stay, what noise?'
Hamlet

CHAPTER 40

The inspector arrived early for his second unofficial interview with Asp. The doctors were finishing their ward round as he waited outside in the corridor, tasting the toothpaste that lingered in his mouth because his wife had insisted on shutting him out of the bathroom before he had finished cleaning his teeth. It meant he arrived at the hospital just in time to see PC Petrovich leave a small private room on the left and to wonder why his underling was there on the spot before him.

'Ah, Porfiry. A private visit?'

PC Petrovich turned. His voice was defensive. 'Following a hunch, sir. Checking something out. For my own satisfaction.'

'Not on duty then?'

'Not exactly, sir.'

The inspector understood how his constable believed he'd been sidelined. He had sympathy with his need to pursue other threads in his own time. As long as their territories remained separate, it was not the inspector's business to pry into his constable's private life. On the other hand...

The talk that followed was strained, desultory. They were embarrassed by their lack of interest in each other's ideas and uncertain how to extricate themselves without being rude as the doctors swirled past, and Asp, still in her dressing gown, stepped out of her private room and into the corridor.

'I spy Nemesis with my little eye. Are you a ghost, or are you real?'

She sounded cheerful for the first time in a long time, thought the Inspector as Asp beckoned him to follow.

The constable was fiddling nervously with his watch. 'I'm running late. Sorry. Must go. Bye, Inspector. Bye, Asp,' and he dived between them, hurrying away out of sight in his embarrassed, slightly clumsy way.

'A mirage,' smiled Asp. 'He disappears the moment you get close.' She could have been describing her own father.

Asp had telephoned Henry the night before to say he must remember that she loved him. It was an impulse she couldn't ignore – like wanting to avoid every crack in the pavement and having to turn round, go back and start walking or hopping all over again if she missed by landing on a crack.

'No, I'm not going to lend you any money,' Henry replied in a sour voice and put the phone down without bothering to say goodbye.

***

'FOR BONNY SWEET Robin is all my joy.'
Hamlet

CHAPTER 41

'Been to any more concerts since I last saw you, Porfiry?' Daphne was arranging some pink tiger lilies that PC Petrovich had brought to show her he thought she was wonderful.

'One. But I wish I hadn't gone.'

'Was the music so dreadful?'

'It was mine.'

'But Porfiry, that's a shame. You should have said something, and I would have come.'

'I didn't want anyone I know to be there.'

'Only strangers are allowed to hear your music?'

'Yes.'

'Why?'

'Because they won't lie.'

'Well then.' Shocked, she placed the vase of flowers in the middle of the table and plucked at the stalks. 'What was it about?'

'It wasn't about anything. There were no words.'

'What were the instruments then?'

'There weren't any. It was electronic.'

'Ah,' she said quietly.

It had been a genuine discussion with genuine pauses to find the words. She was momentarily in thrall to the idea of PC Petrovich as an unrecognised musical genius. She remembered her plans for her ceramic sculpture. She would create these perfect egg shapes that were hollow, and when you picked them up, the warmth of a person's hands would trigger the sounds of music. His music. Her art. Their musical egg boxes. 'Shall we go upstairs?' she asked. Her voice had a catch in it. A small thrill of happiness.

'Why not?' He said in his morose way. He had woken up that morning with a feeling that a cold was coming. When he caught a cold, he got asthma. Increasing his gloom further, he'd decided to end his sessions with the only woman he desired, his life consultant.

'Mrs Thrush... Daphne.' He closed the fire door behind him. As it was the only door still in use within the house, the decision to close was analytically significant.

'Yes, Porfiry?'

'Can we make love?'

She thought of Henry and felt the child kick inside her.

'But Porfiry, I'm pregnant.'

'Are you?' He faltered. 'It doesn't matter.'

'I wish I weren't. I would love to lie on the floor with you right now, but I can't.'

She observed the swelling underneath her waistband and tried to smooth both it and the material stretched tight across her stomach. *The queen is never seen with a rumpled skirt,* she thought. Her womb ached. Like Jocasta. Except she hadn't married her son.

'It really doesn't matter, if you don't mind.'

'Maybe I'm not pregnant. Perhaps it's just fat.'

'It's fine.'

She'd been standing with her back to him up until then. 'Fine. Is it?'

Taking hold of his hands, she lowered her head so he couldn't see her eyes. 'This is quite common, Porfiry. You've heard of transference. Patients fall in love with their therapist. That sort of thing.'

'But I haven't. I haven't, really. I just thought... you might say yes.'

'Oh.' She grabbed hold of an empty hat stand and rattled it against the floor. 'Why? How? Tell me, Porfiry.' More flabbergasted than insulted, and when the rattling stopped, curious. 'Do I look as if I want to have sex with you? Is it something about my eyes? Do I send out signals saying, 'fuck me?'

'No, it's not like that.' He took the hat stand out of her hands and placed it carefully beside a pyramid of beer cans that she was in the process of glueing together.

'What's it like then, do you mind telling me?'

She was standing behind her desk with one hand on her hip, an ample Venus on a plinth but to Porfiry, a nymph. She took one tissue from the box she'd finally remembered to buy for her patients to use and blew her nose. Since she'd sent next-door's developers to another therapist to avoid conflict of interest, there was only one patient, not three. 'Go on.' She thrust her bosom to its zenith and smiled at him encouragingly. 'Explain.'

'I don't know. I thought if I had sexual intercourse with

someone who understands me, I'd feel better. I do fancy you, Daphne.'

'This is original, Porfiry,' she said, scrunching the tissue into a small ball. 'But of course, it's out of the question.'

'I'm sorry.'

'It's unethical.'

'But I'm not your patient. I decided that on my way here.'

'You are naive, Porfiry. This is ridiculous.'

'That's why...'

He stopped and looked around the room. Unfastened his trousers quickly so they slipped to the floor and, because they were loose, stepped out of them easily and kicked them into a corner. She came from behind the desk and stood in front of him, the last of the summer fruits. A single bead of sweat ran down one side of her face. He kissed the line it made and put his hands on her shoulders as she put hers on his.

They moved around the room like that. Sashaying between the hats and the scarves. Fox trotting. When they reached the door, she leaned against him, and as his fingers discovered the buttons on the back of her skirt, the patient gave a small, discreet moan.

'Is that it? Is that it?'

The anxiety in his voice touched something in her so that she hesitated, considering her next action. Then clumsily, she slipped to the floor, pulling him with her.

'Not quite,' she answered softly, and in their huddle, he saw and was transfixed by the dark red petals of Daphne's vulva.

'You look for something beautiful in a place where you think it's least likely to be,' he whispered into her ear when she was still.

'That's insulting, Porfiry.'

'No, it's perfect.'

***

'The houses that he makes last till doomsday.'
Hamlet

Chapter 42

There had been three significant changes in the last five years that suggested the Thrush family's neighbourhood was becoming richer. One was the inescapable wail of burglar alarms. Not for the cars but for the houses. The sound became so commonplace that nobody bothered to discover if there was a burglar about. The second was the cars themselves, being either larger, flashier, or else urban jeeps crammed with baby seats for the school run.

There was also the matter of the local sports club. When they first moved into the area, no one could afford its membership. Now, half the street could be seen jogging daily in the direction of its gates, towels over their necks, last week's tennis rackets in their hands, hell-bent on achieving an exclusive sweat. It was a sore point with Daphne, who belonged to the other half that would have liked access to the pool but couldn't afford the fees.

The house alarms were ringing when Daphne finally told Henry that Asp had confessed to the murder of Nasty. As he listened to her voice above the clamour and understood that his daughter, his own flesh and blood and not his wife was (possibly) guilty of the crime, he took one of the axes from the cellar and chopped down the elderflower, the magnolia, the small acer and the holly trees next to the foxholes at the end of their garden.

It seemed like a belated fit of empathy after years of not knowing how to live in someone else's shoes. It seemed that, at last, Henry cared about his daughter even if it were only as an extension of himself, and so, probably, he was looking in the mirror.

With each swing of his arms, he hoped for relief, but none came. The next morning, he paced throughout the house with his hands over his ears so he wouldn't have to hear the flapping of the startled wood pigeons or Daphne digging in the replacement shrubs she had begged from an old neighbour further up the street.

While she was still in the garden hanging up strings soaked in wine as decoys for the moths, he saw a hand-delivered letter pushed through their letterbox. It came from those whose alarm was the largest, the most penetrating, the most frequently heard across two streets, and the letter, like their alarm, was wind driven.

Dear Mr Thrust,

It is necessary to put in writing now the sheer ***anger*** *we feel at what you have done to the privacy of our home and garden by removing your trees. Every room on this side of the house is now exposed to* ***your*** *scrutiny and we are aware of this exposure every hour of the day. We cannot sit in the lounge, be in the kitchen, be in any of the upstairs bedrooms or enjoy any part of our garden without your windows overlooking us. It is quite unbelievable that you have inflicted this on your neighbours. How can you possibly want to live like this – do you* ***enjoy*** *staring across at other people's* *property? Do you realise that you have robbed a family of foxes of their natural habitat?*

The plants you have put in place of the trees are so inconspicuous as to be a joke. They are in the wrong place to produce any sort of cover, which they will not be capable of anyway, given their pathetic size. You have ***totally*** *ruined the entire aspect of the rest of our house and garden.* ***I*** *could never inflict such distress on my neighbours. We all have a right to privacy in our homes and gardens and you have no right to remove what we previously enjoyed. If you want to remove your trees in an act of vandalism, it is your duty to repair the damage you inflict. You obviously could not care less about anyone around you. If this is the selfish and un-neighbourly way you all behave in this neighbourhood, I am appalled to think we have left behind the more mannerly close we inhabited up until recently.*

We *will now have to spend a considerable amount of money to restore what you have taken away from us. We are tempted to build a 25 feet wall, which is completely within our rights – and may you relish staring at that. We can also plant several leylandii to replace the trees you have uprooted. Unfortunately, not even leylandii can grow fast enough to do the trick. We are totally unconcerned about what you will feel about our choice of remedy, as you were so unconcerned by what you have done to us. You will receive a copy of our bill very shortly so that you can see what you will have cost us – I know you do not care, but you should at least know what we will have been* ***forced*** *to pay out because of you. We shall, of course be seeking ultimate recompense through the courts.*

In short, we will be suing you for wilful destruction of our mutual environment.

Finally, I don't think anything in the history of our various homes has ever made us quite **so** *angry as this. I would like to think you can't sleep easily at night, knowing what you have done to neighbours who have never been an ounce of trouble to you since they moved in. I am glad that life has its own way of dealing with inconsiderate, selfish people and so your turn will come in due course. May the foxes whose homes you have ruined seek their just revenge.*

Yours sincerely,

Cain and Rosemary Mint

Daphne passed the letter to Henry before lunch.

'I'm not pregnant, you know.'

'So?'

'I just thought I should tell you that you were right and I was wrong.'

'Fine.'

'I've cancelled the reservation for the water birth.'

'And this? What am I meant to do about this boring piece of shit?' He tore the letter into jagged bits and tossed the lot into the waste bin. 'There. Bugger the neighbours. Bugger their leylandiis. I don't give a toss. What are we going to do about Asp?'

In his distress, he'd been secretly crying and examining her baby photographs all week, searching for signs of murderous tendencies or obvious resemblance to himself. Daphne was worried enough about his sanity to raise the volume on *The Ride of the Valkyries* to sit beside him and to hold his hand in the depth of her lap until it had finished without once asking him to turn the volume down.

'She wants her cat and her violin.'

Henry shook his head. 'They won't let her have the cat.'

'The violin then. And her *Bach Unaccompanieds.*'

'Elm can take them up. I'm not going.'

Henry disliked all hospital visits and considered this reason enough for his avoiding them. They stirred emotions which he felt he couldn't handle. For this reason, too, his exchanges with Daphne tended to be short and efficient, even when they were alone in the attic.

Neither of them could forget that Aunt Rose, Uncle Hamish and Elm were never far away. That they were unable to discuss Asp openly within the house was just as well. Each blamed the other for what had happened.

Elm agreed to go in Henry's place and discovered that Asp had been moved to a ward with a dozen other patients. Most of them seemed to be lying on top of their beds in their dressing gowns.

His appearance might have passed for normal until you noticed the cheekbones heavily rouged on white flesh, green shadows under the eyes, red dots inside the nostrils and the cuffs of his trousers rising above his orange hairy ankles to reveal a pair of silver sandals with kitten heels. More Kabuki *Barbie* than strappy Roman as he hobbled to her bedside. He had brought with him a bag of cherries, which they promptly shared. Could have been chatting on a train in the rush hour instead of sitting on two grey, hard-backed plastic chairs in a psychiatric ward.

'Things come around.'

Elm shook his head at her. 'You mean the way I look.'

'Suppose so,' she said, coughing to muffle her surprise and twisting on her seat. 'Did anyone see you come?'

A grave-eyed boy of about seventeen shuffled past. He paused to stroke the top of Elm's head, bending over him from behind, sneaking in the occasional stroke whenever Elm leaned backwards.

'I changed in the loo and chucked my trainers in the bin.'

'You came out of the closet.'

He laughed and filled his mouth with cherry. 'Feet first.'

'Did you bring my cat?'

'No. But I brought your violin. I left it in the sister's office.' Elm stood up and the boy was obliged to let go of his hair.

'The music?'

'It's in the case.'

'How's Leaf?'

'He's a pain. He's missing you.' The boy passed on. 'I think he's a borderline personality disorder.'

'You can never tell with Leaf.'

'He's stuffing himself with junk food.'

'He's on solids?' She covered her face with her hands in disbelief.

Any development in Leaf was received as a miracle.

'He's moved on from mashed banana and mother's milk – though he still has both.'

'He'll get fat.'

'He's gross. Did I tell you that he broke Granny's coffin?'

'He didn't.' Asp was genuinely shocked. 'You're making it up.'

'He did. I'm not.' Elm stretched and rotated his feet slowly in opposite directions. The sandals sparkled as they revolved. 'You were way over on the other side of the church. I put him down on the lid to rest because he was getting heavy and I heard this loud crack.'

They lowered their heads as brother and sister in a moment of intimacy. They chatted animatedly about a crane that would lift Leaf through the window if he became too fat to squeeze through the door.

'Did anyone tell you why I'm here?' she asked when she'd tired of the fantasy.

'He split the wood. A whole plank. He was so huge and blubbery it split from top to bottom. He's – I tell you – some developmental mutant.'

'Did anyone say why I'm not coming home yet?'

'I covered the crack in the coffin with lilies.'

'Elm?'

'Nobody knew.' Elm had swallowed the bob of cherries in his mouth whole. There was a choking sound from the back of his throat, followed by silence. 'Why the fuck, doesn't he grow?'

'Watch out. You'll grow trees in your stomach.' Asp really had no idea why Leaf failed to grow upwards.

Elm was quiet for a minute or two before pulling a packet of cigarettes out of his pocket. 'Let's go visit my rooms at Cambridge, Asp. Now.'

'What about my cat?'

'Not in a hospital. You can't have a cat in a hospital. Let's go.'

'Not yet. The inspector's coming to see me again.'

'Leave him a note.'

He offered a cigarette to the boy, who accepted it shyly. Elm noticed that on the lapel of his jacket was a badge with the words: *'I enter this day with a peaceful heart.'*

The boy gave Elm the sweetest of smiles – a smile that can only happen when the mouth is loose, and there are no uptight or ungenerous feelings.

'I haven't any matches,' mumbled Elm.

'You're not allowed to smoke here.' Asp then wished she'd kept quiet.

The boy continued smiling and slowly bit the end of the unlit cigarette, rolling it from left to right with his tongue while his wide apart eyes followed them out of the ward.

Asp was free to leave whenever she liked. The inspector had been quite clear about this, just as the doctors had washed their hands under the automatic taps and said nothing.

'I didn't know you smoked ciggies,' she said as she put an arm around Elm.

'I don't. I just carry them.'

***

'I have shot mine arrow o'er the house,
And hurt my brother.'
Hamlet

CHAPTER 43

Asp liked the way she could feel the cool of the stone steps through her shoes as she climbed the staircase to his rooms. The Bridge of Sighs was visible through the mullioned window, and she could hear the lapping of the water against the outside walls, the droning of the guides as they punted tourists up and down the river.

'Tea?' Sunlight spilt onto the sofa, and a mote of dust made a halo above his hair. *It is the place,* she thought, *where everything seems implausibly beautiful or distant, where time was altered in such a way that the wall clock moved backwards as soon as it moved forwards.* There was no waiting for her to say yes or no when he disappeared into the kitchen to put the kettle on.

'I can't imagine how it will be at Oxford,' she said, following him about with a tense look on her face.

'Like Oxford. Don't anticipate anything.'

Sometimes Elm sounded wise when he was being stupid. Of course she would try to predict what it would be like when she got there. She'd dilly-dallied in her mind between Oxford and Cambridge and then settled for Oxford because Elm was at the other place. She'd spent months choosing her college, agonising over which one might not reject her, which one might want her, which one she wanted, which one she could afford.

Her English master had pronounced her an X girl after reading her essay on *Hamlet.* Uncertain if this referred to a perceived brashness or the literary nature of her opinions and too afraid to ask, she applied and was accepted. Later she would say it was the library, the beautiful renaissance library with its black pillars, gold filigree, bunches of grapes, artichokes and roses in between and the squares of different pastel colours on the ceiling. Of course she would anticipate.

A tall blonde girl blew into the room, her thin green shawl wrapped around her twice and billowing from behind as she crossed the floor in springs. Asp thought she had never seen anyone so boldly exaggerated.

'Elm baby! Where were you? I *love* the sandals.' She hugged him from behind. 'Are they for me?' Dropped onto her heels and tugged at the narrow silver buckles on either side of his ankles. He lifted one foot after the other to shake her off.

'Fuck off.'

She tossed her mane of hair behind her neck and laughed, her teeth the only things about her that were small. No false embarrassment, accustomed to her own beauty and its effect on others, but in such a way that you admired the honesty and were flattered that she was your friend. This tall, white-haired goddess.

'I *have* to try them on, and you *have* to say yes because you're coming to my room for pancakes. You can't refuse. Can he?' Twisting her face, appealing to Asp. 'You'll come too. Don't tell me. I know you're sister and brother. It's *so* obvious.'

Asp prised – yanked the Jimmy Choos off his feet as Elm arranged three mugs on a tray. He was shuffling barefoot to a coffee table with three legs and a column of dictionaries propping up the lid. The mugs had long lost their handles and the chips were as brown as their glaze. Asp glanced at the ceiling, half expecting to find a gargoyle.

'I want my footwear back when you've finished. And they're not yours. That is Asp, by the way.'

'Me, Jasmine. Sweetpea.'

She shot up from the floor and hooked the kitten heels over the tips of her fingers so they swung violently with the least movement. It was bound to happen. This goddess of the garden crashed into Asp, standing against the wall looking startled and reluctantly amused. 'Come in half an hour exactly.' And she was gone before she'd sipped her tea.

'Asp?'

'What?'

'Let's play Truth.'

'No.'

'Yes.'

'You start.'

'In the market, there's an old man dressed in a tailcoat with a peaked cap and tap shoes. He's got this crummy radio. It plays 1940's music all the time. He's arthritic and moves with little side steps on the spot, hardly lifting his feet off the ground.' Elm was stirring two of the teas simultaneously with a knife and fork. 'Your turn.'

'Miss Sweetpea...is very beautiful.'

He looked pleased.

'You again.'

'There's a second old man who busks outside the bookshop. Turns up at four in the afternoon with his harmonica, but he doesn't bother to play a tune.'

'Are you shagging then, Elm?'

They swallowed their tea and eyeballed each other.

'Not finished. He runs his lips along the edge. No blowing, mind. Nothing that you can hear clearly.' Elm wiped the tea stains off his mug with his sleeve. 'Just a feeble sort of whistling noise. Never *tries* to play a tune. He was a student a long time ago. My bedder told me all about him.'

'Are you shagging?'

'Next week.'

'Are we going for pancakes?'

'We're so *not* having this conversation.'

Asp flung her arms above her head in exasperation.

'It's all so fucking twee.'

'What is? *Truth*? Pancakes? Punting?'

He eyed her from across the top of his mug. It was impossible to know what he was thinking. He stayed like that, not drinking, touching the rim with his lips.

'Phoney. Whatever.'

'No. *What* is phoney, whatever?'

'Oh, everything. Tea in chipped mugs. The view through the window.'

'And you, not.'

'You asked me.'

'Okay. So what about the busker?'

She fingered the bits of braid falling off the corners of the cushions. This was a new thing. Stories. She preferred it when they used to lock themselves in the bathroom, and one of them would start by saying what was bugging the other and follow it up with something consolatory. There was a lot of skill in playing the game without bust-ups. He'd changed the rules without telling her. Good one.

In the end, she decided it must be a college thing, a whole sophisticated world of people chatting in parables to each other, exchanging profound thoughts in college rooms and libraries before swallowing their chips and ale in basement bistros. She put her feet up on the corners of his chair and locked him in with her toes.

'Tell me what your bedder said about the busker then.'

Elm was still watching her, sucking at his empty mug with the tips of his teeth and making up his mind whether to continue. 'The bedder cleaned for another college about thirty years ago.' He pushed her feet away from his chair and stood so that he had his back to her and she wouldn't see his face as he talked.

'Apparently this guy used to work in his room a lot. He always left his bin outside for the bedder if he didn't want her to come in. Once he forgot, and when she knocked on his door, he called out and said he was too down in the dumps for her to come in, and so she said, "it doesn't matter, I've got a key, and I've got to come in anyway, or I'll lose my job". So she went in, and they had a talk.'

He paused to open the window, and Asp became restless.

'Go on,' she said.

'Well, things stayed like that for a while – with him leaving his wastebin outside each morning and having talks.'

The sound of lapping water from outside seemed louder, the guide belting out a potted history of the college. Elm stopped to listen through Asp's ears.

'There must be an ending to this story.'

'It's an ending, I suppose, if you think he's busking at the bookshop right now.'

'So when did he become one?'

Elm studied her through the curve of his arm and she caught a glimpse of his face that reminded her of Daphne. She'd tell him he was just like her if it was ever her turn, even though she had no desire to play.

'One morning, the bedder came to his room, but there was no bin in the corridor. He didn't answer when she called out, so she tried to unlock the door with her key. She couldn't open it because his key was in the other side. The caretaker had to come and force the door open, and they found him lying in bed under the sheets with an empty pill bottle and a half-open bottle of brandy on his bedside table.'

Asp listened with her eyes shut, knowing where this one was going and resenting it but wanting to hear just the same.

'They got him to hospital just in time. The bedder had to take a week off after that. She was so upset. When she came back, he had disappeared, and years later, long after she'd stopped working, she saw him again, busking outside the bookshop.'

Asp stood up and moved to the open window. 'Like me. When

I busk. I just pretend to play sometimes.'

'No, it's not. Not like you at all.' He pulled her round by the shoulders until she was facing him.

'You've got a life, Asp... and...' He held out her arms with his and stood on her shoes with his bare feet, 'you play the violin really well. You'd earn lots of money if you busked properly. But you're going to be an actress. After Oxford. Okay?'

'I think I'll go home now. I don't fancy any pancakes.'

'I'll see you to the station then,' He looked disappointed. 'When I've found something to put on my feet.'

'Some more sling-backs?'

'Just smelly old trainers.'

It was impossible to explain how she knew then that Elm had come to the end of his cross-dressing phase. She heard him banging doors in search of a pair of socks. His experiments with who he was, when they occurred, seemed more extreme or perverse because of their rarity.

A strident female voice was calling out from the bottom of the staircase. 'Edie? Where's the mop? Shit. Can you bring the fucking mop?'

They walked to the station and shared a double choc, choc-chip cookie, gossiping about CDs or films they wanted to see. Once, perhaps twice, Asp questioned Elm about Jasmine Sweetpea, and he answered with half-baked replies or by switching to another topic. When she finally remembered to ask how he could afford to buy a pair of Jimmy Choos, the train was pulling out of the station. Words floated back to her above the hubbub.

'Off a lorry. I got them off the back of a lorry.'

She settled into her seat, her face smiling and frowning alternately as she wondered if Elm had turned to crime. Then she forgot what she was thinking and spent the rest of the journey unaware that she was the only passenger in her compartment, feeling uncertain how she came to be there in the first place. The knock on her door by a guard at King's Cross reminded her of where she was and where she was meant to be going.

***

'Be thou familiar but by no means vulgar.'
Hamlet

CHAPTER 44

Since the arrival of the letter from Cain and Rosemary Mint, Daphne felt her neighbours had a point. The end of the garden was an eyesore. The only arguable gain was the light that flooded onto her castor oil plants and the lilies next to the pond. Even the frogs appeared to have changed colour. She had no interest in seeing Cain or Rosemary Mint eat croissants at breakfast, but it was difficult to miss. When she raised the blinds at the back of the house every morning, she found herself staring straight into their kitchen. From a distance, to be sure. It was not as if she got out the binoculars, although perhaps they did.

Daphne could already hear the piccolo whine of Rosemary Mint from Asp's bedroom. She was becoming pally with Wellies Two across the fence at the corner where all three gardens joined. Words like 'arboreal devastation' and 'ecological ruin' kept coming back again like hiccoughs. She was tempted to stick her head out the open window and risk a rant from Wellies Two against Henry. At that moment, she heard her own name mentioned and changed her mind.

'Of course Daphne never suspected anything. Though she really should have stopped to look in the mirror and see what a mess she

was. All those frumpy smocks that make her look fatter than she is. And, of course, now the skinhead look. I'm not exaggerating. Henry won't leave me alone these days, though I try to turn him away. And he knows I'm her ***friend****.'*

'REALLY?'

'*Whenever Daphne's out. He goes into the garden with the secateurs. Haven't you noticed?'*

'Well, they both seem to like cutting things. First it's her hair (maybe not first), then he goes and chops down all these trees...'

The voices merged with a flock of geese honking overhead. Daphne strained to pick up the thread and, as soon as she did, wished she hadn't.

'... Cut in pieces like a Sunday joint. Which one did it, I ask myself?'

'It was their lodger.'

'You mean the murderer?'

'No. The victim. The body. It was their last lodger. I read a description in the paper. Didn't you see? Front page headlines. It was her exactly, right down to the dyed hair and the leggings.'

'Before my time. Sorry.'

'Who? Nasty? We called her the common one.'

'Didn't know they **had** lodgers.' Mint's voice was precise with its regret.

'As I said, Daphne and I are **friend**s...'

'Bitches. Uptight, miserable, cow-frigging bitches.' Betrayal is the most painful truth, or else there's none. Daphne wept and slammed the window shut because she couldn't bear to hear any more. A sudden hot flush made her dizzy as she leaned against a corner of the sill and licked a tear at the side of her mouth. 'To hell with them,' she shouted upwards in the direction of the window.

No more would she curl and duck or scratch herself into heightened anxiety. She took a deep breath instead and slid to the floor in a solitary re-enactment of her meeting with Porfiry, savouring his farewell to his beautiful tiger lily. Below the window, she set about constructing a to-do list that was a shortcut version of all her attic tirades. Scribbled it down in a black, spiral-bound, indexed book of green, pink and yellow pages like the one she had bought Uncle Hamish last Christmas. All written in her untidy hand so that only she could read it back.

1. Must email Cedric:

   Dear Cedric,
   I know this will come as a surprise, but I have become dependent on your good advice. I realise what professional dilemmas our friendship may have caused you in recent times, but hopefully, all may be resolved soon.
   Yours, Daphne.

2. Be firm with Porfiry and feign a venereal disease for the sake of tact.

3. Collect mother's ashes. Enquire about will.

4. Insist Henry finds job or no more buying model

aeroplanes. Local bank requires teller. Henry should enquire.

5. Place an ad in the *Richmond and Twickenham Times* as a Life Transition Consultant along following lines:

   'Are you stressed, depressed, anxious or bereaved? Do you have panic attacks, psychosomatic illnesses, sexual problems, depression or suffer from uncontrolled aggression? Why not try INTEGRATIVE PSYCHOTHERAPY? Do unto others what they do unto you. Fuck them for a change. Ring 001122 and restore your self-esteem in ten easy sessions.'

6. Ask the French Institute to send another lodger:

   Ma chère madam,
   Je voudrais avoir un autre étudiant en logement aussitôt que possible, s'il vous plaît.
   Cordialement,
   Daphne Thrush

7. Keep Asp in hospital and not in prison – somehow.

8. Ask Cedric to choose best lawyers should she be charged; tell Uncle Hamish to research legal precedents and act as clerk; suggest Aunt Rose pay costs.

9. Advise Elm to remain at Cambridge until worst is over.
10. Write to all our past lodgers, requesting them to sign statements on how much they enjoyed living with us.

Dear Anne-Marie, Phillipe-Alexandre, Saulange, Violette, Anjelica, Pierrette,
Assume all is well. May I tell the authorities that you intend a return visit chez Thrush... **a bientot biensur*?***
Much love etc,
Daph
P.S. We are thrilled that Asp has had her place at Oxford confirmed.

11. Swimming on Mondays, Wednesdays and Fridays.

12. Do unto Wellies One whatever it is that Henry has been doing unto Wellies Two.

13. Invite Rosemary and Cain Mint to attend a life-threatening barbeque.

Daphne had managed to reopen the window at the bottom without sacrificing her position on the floor. A faint breeze stirred the stubble on her scalp. Inhaling the lemon and vanilla scents of crushed magnolia floating up from the refuse sacks that were bursting with branches, twigs and the cream-cupped flowers after a fit of gardening. Her voice startled her with its force.

'Bin bags!' Fifty or more rolls of black plastic sacks were stacked neatly in rows against the conservatory wall below the window. 'Bin bags,' she said again as her eyes expanded with understanding and horror. 'Stuffed bin bags. Good God, Henry, why?' It was a Belshazzar moment – her turn, her illumination followed by waves of uncontained anger and a leg shooting out from underneath her body in a violent reflex as she fathomed the enormity of what she believed was Henry's crime.

***

'...O, horrible! Most horrible!
If thou hast nature in thee, bear it not.'
Hamlet

CHAPTER 45

'I can remember the moment of revelation as if it were yesterday. When I recovered from the shock of thinking it had been Henry all along, my next thought was that husband and daughter were in it together. Sharing their X chromosome, I have no doubt.' Daphne was in the middle of her next voyeuristic fantasy.

'That baby in the pram...'

Wellies Two was rabbiting on full pelt, and much as I wished that I didn't have to listen, I couldn't pull myself away.

'The one they call Leaf, not 'Tree?''

Rosemary Mint and her sniggers – her mealy-mouthed, malignant sniggering.

'Strange how he never looks any older. Really strange.'

'Have you seen him up close?'

'No. I'm not interested in babies.'

The funny thing was, I didn't have to look through the window to know that Wellies Two was bored stiff by what Mint had to say about Leaf. My sweet Leaf. I sensed it as a mother does.

'You probably won't have noticed that he never looks you in the eye the way most babies do.'

'Really.'

'He doesn't look at you with his eyes wide open.'

'Just sideways with his lids half shut.'

Like a pigeon? My poor Leaf.

'Like Henry.'

'I wouldn't know about Henry. (Chuckle.) But it's true that the head doesn't point in the same direction as the one in which he's looking.'

'Sort of sneaky looking.'

'I know what you mean.'

'Sort of sideways, like a cow.'

I heard their trite little conversation by sticking the top of my head above the windowsill and listening and watching carefully. Wellies Two was applying her lipstick without any mirror. *Quelle* slag. Mint was running her fingers through her part like a dog's hind leg on a greasy scalp.

'Sneaky? He's a dirty old man, except he's a baby.'

'Like Henry.'

I would have shot both (with a rifle if I'd had one.) Wellies' lips made a perfect target, pursed for either kiss or bullet. I watched her as she slid the lipstick back into her pocket. Everything she did was slimy, slippery and inflammatory.

'I think we'd better change the subject.'

Mint decided to whisper. A bit late for tact.

'There's that peculiar old aunt of theirs with her peculiar husband. They're all odd, you know.'

Stitch up their mouths with crooked bits of string. I was about to lean out the window and tell them what I thought when my

Aunt Rose began quoting Virgil's 'Georgics' into the wind.

'I, Virgil, at that time lay in the lap
Of sweet Parthenope, enjoying there
The studies of inglorious ease, who once
Dallied in pastoral verse and with youth's boldness
Sang of you, Tityrus, lazing under a beech-tree.'

Auntie slumped in her wheelchair, drowned by emotion. Uncle Hamish pushed her back and forth in a state of happiness because Henry had asked him to calculate how many plastic sacks of chopped wood could fit in the red van and how many trips to the dump would be necessary to get rid of them all. To the nearest square centimetre.

'I must ask Henry to plant a beech tree, don't you think?' said Aunt Rose.

'You interrupted me. You interrupted me.' Hamish slapped the sides of his head in distress. 'Was I on forty-seven or forty-eight?'

'Cubic feet or bags, Hamish?'

'What did you say?'

'Take me to the potting shed.'

Aunt Rose pointed to some rotting wood covered in honeysuckle. Uncle Hamish began to count again as he wheeled her towards some upturned pots.

As a pair, they were a deaf old man and an elderly aunt of blameless social habits who went to bed each night after the nine o'clock news. I looked down at them fondly from above and shut the window for the second time that morning. Rosemary Mint and Wellies Two had disappeared inside their smug, grey, cement-rendered homes. I decided to walk to the park to find

Henry. I took Leaf and the cat with me in the buggy, and as I pushed them up the hill, my heart was beating inside my ears. Would I, when I, at last, found my dear husband, would I be able to come to the point straightaway? Would I be even wise to try? I had to be cunning about this. I couldn't exactly say: 'Henry, I know that you killed Anastase Besoin. I have irrefutable proof.' A bell jar would come down on his head and stay there. I had to trap him or shame him. As I kept on walking, I tried to sort out which it would be.

***

'I am but mad north-north-west;
when the wind is southerly
I know a hawk
From a handsaw.'
Hamlet

Chapter 46

The grass was acid dry when we passed through the gates. Red and fallow deer were grazing on opposite sides of the road. Geese were waddling in amongst the two herds, pecking at the insects on the scorched ground. Leaf insisted that we stop for a few minutes while he examined a stag beetle lying in the middle of the path. The cat lay curled up in his seat on the roof of the buggy, purring with his eyes closed.

Across a small bridge and on the left beyond the playing fields was the triangle of land where Henry and his friends were allowed to fly their model aeroplanes. Wheeling high above their heads, making no audible sound while they swooped, turned or narrowly missed one another and slipping and sliding as they landed on the grass, their wings as wide as an albatross.

'Henry,' I said, pulling him to one side when his plane was down. 'Henry,' I stalled, just for a second or two. 'Don't pick up the plane. Leave it. Your friends will bring it back for you. I know you murdered Anastase Besoin. I have proof. In a very little time, you will confess to the inspector and release our daughter from her purgatory.'

The bell jar descended as he caught my eye, a sob from the back of his throat. I saw the other fliers on the field looking at us quizzically, and I pulled him closer to me because I was afraid he was going to fall. The bell jar lifted as quickly as it came down. I put his hands on the handlebars of the buggy and waited for him to speak. I had never cared for Henry quite so much.

'I'm not sure where to begin.'

'Just begin,' I begged. We were walking without purpose in the direction of some gnarled oaks.

Henry, still gripping the handlebars, began.

'It was the first time – you've got to believe me, Daph. It was the very first time I'd ever done anything like this. I was so angry. I grabbed the wretched girl with both hands because I remember she was laughing at my model planes, and I shook her whole blubbery body. I couldn't stop shaking her. I know it must seem ridiculous or pathetic, but sweet Jesus, that was it. Then I dragged her onto the ground with me. We were on our own outside in the garden and I'd been polishing my wings.

'You were out with the children getting suncream for our French holiday. I can't remember exactly what happened next. I have...I suppose...some amnesia.' Henry swallowed, or maybe he gulped because he was uncertain where he was going with this new revelation. He shut his eyes and squeezed the lids tightly shut as if cudgelling his memory.

'When I snapped out of it, she was giving a sort of death rattle cry, and I realised she was a corpse. I couldn't feel any pulse in her.

The next thing I know I was cutting her up into lamb chop-sized portions with my electric saw and hosing down the lawn to get rid of the blood.'

Henry paused to wipe the sweat off his forehead with both hands, releasing the buggy. I screamed and grabbed the handlebars before it rolled down the hill we were standing on. At that moment, I, Daphne Thrush, was afraid I might vomit. We gag a lot in my family. Henry didn't look at me once. His voice was so low that when he finally continued, I had to lean across the buggy roof to catch what he was saying.

'Do I go on?'

'Please.' We were holding our breaths.

'I hate remembering.' He turned his head to watch some deer stampede across the road with a spotty dog at their heels.

'Henry,' I pleaded.

This time he turned to look at me. 'OK. Here we go.'

'Yes, Henry. I'm listening.'

'I stuffed the lot into some of those heavy-duty dustbin bags you bought for the garden, do you remember?'

'I remember.'

'I lugged them down to the cellar. With a bit of juggling, I managed to fit every bit of her into the freezer. I don't know why I did that. And when we came back from our holiday, you remember that smell? That putrefying smell? It was Nasty decomposing. She'd defrosted along with the peas and all the ice cubes. I must have knocked the plug out of the socket before we went away. I had to think quickly. You'd stormed off. I don't remember where to.'

'The coffee shop in Clapham. I'd gone there with Leaf.'

'Well, I had to clear it all up before you came back. So I put the wet bags inside some fresh dry ones and carried the lot up the cellar stairs and through the house and into the back garden and then - you know what I did. You can guess. I emptied everything over the fence into next-door's wilderness.' He hesitated before he added, 'And that's it.'

'We must tell Cedric, Henry.' I grabbed hold of his arm, holding it so tight that the veins twitched underneath his skin. 'You must tell him exactly what you've told me.' The nausea vanished as I realised what we must do, and I said, 'We'll let him decide what happens next.' And because I was afraid that he might not have told me everything, I added, 'Henry darling, you're not holding anything back, are you? I mean, you're sure this is what happened. You're not making this up to protect Asp?'

Henry shook his head slowly and pushed my arm away from the buggy as we returned to the field. He was bending low over the handlebars so that his hair brushed against Leaf's hat, and the cat stretched out a paw to push him away.

'No. There's nothing more. Nothing that I can remember.' He unbuckled Leaf from behind and lifted him easily into the air, tucking him at waist level under his arms until the fat baby legs were flying parallel to the ground. Leaf gurgled and kicked like any ordinary baby as he surveyed the parched earth of the park on a late summer's day.

Henry's mates had already moved further away to re-launch their planes. I started packing up Henry's tools, disassembling all his planes and storing their parts in his trolley so we could leave as quickly as possible. He appeared traumatized, for he said nothing at all. Unthinkable normally. But nothing was normal anymore. Our lives were unravelling like one of those batty conspiracy theories on the internet – you believe some of it, and then the doubts set in.

We walked without talking towards the car park, the cat still strapped to his buggy bag and Leaf singing in his father's arms. It was mostly 'Ah' or 'Ooh' in a continuous loop, the rhythm changing slightly as we stumbled over some rabbit holes. The tune was sliding up and down between the same notes over and over again in a quest for melody.

Leaf enjoyed being carried when his nappy was dry, which miraculously, it was. He also felt comfortable with the swishing sound of our feet walking across the grass. When I saw the red van glittering in the morning light, I realised the sunshine was being reflected in the front windscreen and that a moment of beauty was able to exist when some things were at their ugliest.

My belief in Henry's word was of crucial importance. If I believed what he had said, then he had a chance of convincing others. It is true that I was a fool to think for a moment we had solved anything.

***

''Tis a quick lie, sir, away again from me to you.'
Hamlet

CHAPTER 47

'Once we know ourselves, we have the power to change who we are, though obviously there are other forces apart from insight that shapes lives and cause problems.'

Asp's psychiatrist had said this to Henry before the scene in the park. He had also said that if they were looking for a diagnosis to pin things on, Asp showed some of the signs of an obsessive-compulsive disorder. Henry held it in his head. At last, he had a name he thought he understood. It explained – he thought – her squirrelling of Roman nails and old pipes from the river, the round stones, the smooth stones, the muddy old pebbles and discarded rubber bands that she brought back and hoarded in pretty patterns underneath her folded T-shirts.

It was much the same with opinions or fears. She would start with a list. Her fears were anything from the old man hiding under the bed to grab her feet when she got in it to a fatal illness that would strike her down if she didn't open and shut the Venetian blinds above her bed half a dozen times before she got out. It all depended on how much she could function, despite those fears.

'There is more to it than that, but you get the idea.' The

psychiatrist sighed as if he really had nothing more to say.

'I had a ghost under my bed once, but I kept it a secret.' Henry wanted to show solidarity with his own child and not because it was true.

'Ah, I see.' The psychiatrist massaged his own neck very slowly with both hands as he thought to himself, like father, like daughter.

Henry wanted to hit him.

'These things are often familial.'

It was the word 'familial' that sparked off Henry's plan. His heart and mind were stuffed with thoughts of tribal loyalty after a lifetime of denying their importance. The idea was so simple, so soothing, if not elegant. It no longer mattered that he couldn't find a job or that his post these days consisted only of rejections to all his applications. It wouldn't really matter if a bank or a betting shop refused to take him on. In fact, any rejection was convenient, given that he would have to be in jail for quite some time. His heart leapt into his mouth and his head no longer felt like an empty bucket.

'What... I mean, what if the things she says to you are fake, Doctor? How do you know when something's real?' Not, 'What if everything is fake, like the hair you've sprayed with gunk to cover a bald spot?'

'You learn to distinguish what is real.'

How supercilious in his certainty – this psychiatrist with the hair problem, with the arty corduroy suit and leather patches on his arms, leaning back in his swivel chair and pointing to all the medical books on his shelves, boasting the erudition of others. Henry shook his head, in pain over the psychiatrist's words, but also to conceal a sudden shaft of cunning and illumination. He could hear the words of prosecution thumping through his head:

'Members of the jury, it's as plain as the nose on your face that this man is guilty.' It would be followed by a column in the *Putney and Barnes Gazette:*

'HENRY THRUSH, a retired banker of 56 years, has been arrested after the discovery of new evidence in the case that has become known as 'The Butcher in the Back Garden.' Improved DNA techniques have identified him from several stains on the garments of the severed body found in his neighbour's eco-friendly wild garden. Thrush did not dispute that the DNA was his... The Crown Office issued a statement that no further investigations are currently being carried out while adding that if new evidence emerged, the police would, of course, pursue it.'

The day after Henry's encounter with the psychiatrist was the day he took his aeroplanes to the park. Daphne's delusion would prove a gift on the spot. There would be no surprise when he heard himself confessing to the murder. It would be a redemptive sacrifice from father to daughter. He had licked away the sweat of fear, sucking the salt from his skin. Just like Leaf. He had carried his youngest child in his arms as if he were a feather through the park, and he had listened to his childish singing with feelings of such tenderness. In a few hours, he would be alone in a prison cell, and Daphne would be weeping in the waiting room outside.

***

'The chariest maid is prodigal enough
If she unmask her beauty to the moon.'
Hamlet

Chapter 48

Nothing happened as quickly as Henry dreamed it might. Driving through the park gates, Daphne announced she wanted to swim in Richmond outdoor public pool and collect her mother's ashes so she could face Cedric with a clear head.

'Drop me off.' She had woken with a sense of hysteria that morning and could barely look at her husband as he turned the wheel. 'And take Leaf home. I've just remembered that PC Porfiry Petrovic is due at twelve for his final session. Make him a coffee or something if I'm held up. Maybe he can drive us to the police station, as I assume you won't be coming back.'

Henry's reply was as muffled as hers was pitiless.

'Why not?' she continued. 'There's a certain irony about it. Porfiry as the policeman and your wife as his therapist.' She reached into the back seat for her swimming bag and before Henry had braked, she had leapt out at the traffic lights.

He watched her weave between cars, carrying her recklessness with her across the road, disappearing behind bumper bars and lorries. For a brief second or two, he was consoled by a vision of her death before imagining his own in prison.

She swam in the nice and easy lane because there was a jam of bodies in the un-cordoned section of the pool. An elderly man with colourless hair and no fat on his bones was floating like a dead man in water. He was causing consternation for all the swimmers who wanted to pass in their relentless pursuit of fitness.

The elderly man refused to paddle or move from his spot, and despite her disturbed state of mind, Daphne was tempted to advise him to hang on there and if he wanted to float in choppy waters, well then, he should float. She might do the same herself, except that no one floated in the nice and easy lane. They just ploughed up and down quite slowly and never paused unless it was to get out at the other end.

The feeling of weightlessness was soothing, and the water was the same temperature as her body. Daphne remembered she had been moved by Henry's confession in the park, and she mustn't lose her sense of that. She vowed she would be kinder in their remaining time together.

***

'How should I your true love know
From another one?'
Hamlet

CHAPTER 49

'I'm so sorry I'm late, Porfiry. I was collecting my mother's ashes from the crematorium. Did Henry explain, I hope?' It was almost one o'clock when Daphne placed a small ten-inch urn on her desk next to her computer. PC Petrovich was ignoring his cold coffee in the attic.

He studied the floor. 'It's alright, Daphne. I've had time to think about things,' he replied.

'Oh?' She drew her chair closer to her patient. 'What things, Porfiry?'

'I like your pots,' he said, pointing to three ceramic bowls, each one of different size and colour.

'We'll talk about the pots some other time, Porfiry.'

'This is my final session,' he said dully.

'Yes,' she said. 'You told me.'

'And,' he paused, 'although I said that last time, I'm not happy about it.'

'It's up to you.'

She crossed her legs slowly, and he was able to see her thighs settle underneath her skirt. They were sitting in striped armchairs in front of her desk for what Daphne had planned would be a cosy chat. The cat had taken over the futon, spoiling her half-baked attempt at a neo-Freudian setting.

'I already know about Asp,' he confided. 'Henry told me what happened.'

'You keep changing the subject, Porfiry,' she said impatiently. 'Is that what you were thinking about when I came in?'

'No.'

'What then?'

He held his breath the way people do before exhaling quickly. It was the act of speech that frightened him. The forming of the words would weaken the power of his ideas.

'It wasn't just a foxtrot, was it?' he whispered. 'I mean, there was more to it than that, wasn't there?'

'I'm sorry?' Asking but not pausing. 'I don't think so.' Pulling prudishly at her skirt so it stretched across her knees. 'Although I think you think so, which is different.'

He reached out from his chair towards the ceramic pots on the floor under the skylight, picking up the smallest one. A sound like wind chimes came out of the mouth at the top. It was faint but distinct, and it reminded him of rain with its continuous jingling as he rolled it back and forth in his hands.

'I'm impressed. Why don't I have ideas like that?'

'You're full of ideas, Porfiry. But I made these for you. With some help from a potter's wheel.'

He drew the bowl to one eye and squinted deep down inside. He could see a small chain of silver bells lying in a loop at the bottom. The hollowed walls had a blood-red, crinkled glaze on the inside. Outside was as smooth and pale as an emu's egg. A delicate, bluish-green by contrast.

'You could insert a mini-disk of your music,' she added as he examined it.

'I prefer the bells.' Replacing the pot on the floor, he leant across the gap that was between them and placed his hands over her crossed knees. 'Do you think anyone would want to listen to what I write?'

'I'm sure they would.' Daphne removed his fingers one by one by pushing each tip backwards towards the palm. 'You are far too tough on yourself.' She leapt from the armchair, chased the cat off the futon and threw herself down on the hard black mattress with her arms stretched above her head. 'Okay. One last time, Porfiry. One last fucking time.'

In a silence that could have lasted no more than five minutes, there was a loud tapping on the door. PC Petrovich succumbed to a flood between his legs. He tried to stand and pull up his trousers, but instead, he knocked over the largest of the pots and fell backwards as he tripped over the cat. The pot rolled with a rippling sound against the other two smaller pots until all three lay in brittle shards across the floor.

'Are we going to the police station?' Henry was standing in the open fire door with his hand still on the knob, observing the mayhem. There was a strange glitter in his eyes. Daphne was jiggling her hips as she stood in front of him, pulling up her knickers with her skirt rucked up to her waist. For once, she seemed in control of her actions. Either that, or she didn't care.

'I think I'm going to be sick.' This was Porfiry.

'No, dear. You're not. It's just shock.' Daphne straightened her skirt and slowly rebuttoned it. She didn't say – 'no, you can't be sick'. Nor did she say, "you are a fully grown, physically robust and emotionally fit police officer who is used to handling unexpected domestic crises", though it was on the tip of her tongue.

She displayed no sense of urgency at all as she eyed the shattered pots or took in her husband's excited face. Instead, she turned away from both men and gathered up her notes from her desk. 'You will not vomit, Porfiry. Breathe. Breathe deeply. I haven't got a bucket. Henry, do something helpful please. Open the window.' And turning to Porfiry, she said in cold tones, 'You'll feel better in a minute, I promise.'

Husband and wife propped poor Porfiry's head against the wall so the world around him was spinning, but he felt too shocked and ill to protest. Henry went away in search of brandy while Daphne managed to do up Porfiry's zipper.

He had no desire to hurry up a passage of time that was so exquisite and was surprisingly without shame. For Porfiry, the zipping of his trousers by the woman he adored was the greatest consolation. He heard the arrival of his own breaths with wonder. He saw lights the size of pinpricks, and smelt the fumes of alcohol as Henry held the bottle of cognac to his lips. When he turned to move his legs, accidentally kicking a chain of silver bells, he knew he was listening to the opening of his next composition.

'Are you comfortable?' asked Henry.

'I have some money in the bank,' he replied and closed his eyes.

Daphne was already sitting at her word-processor, occasionally stroking her mother's urn of ashes with the back of one hand while typing with two fingers:

Elm Darling,

Can you get the next train home? Your father needs your support. This may sound terse, but it is not unfeeling. He is, quite simply, mad and says he killed Nasty. God knows she deserved it. I will expect you.

Mummy

***

Dear Cedric,

Henry has some important news for you. There is no need to ring or e-mail back. Some things are better face to face. Expect us en famille, although sans Asp, who, I think is better left where she is for the moment. Elm is coming down on the next train. PC Petrovich was going to drive us, but he's not feeling well and has gone home. We should be with you by late afternoon.

Yours,

Daphne

***

Ma plus chere Pierrette,

A lot has happened since we saw you last. It would be extremely helpful if you could write and tell me about your time spent with my mother. Things you did together – the fun you had etc. What was her exact financial state at the time of her death and do you know if there were any arrangements for a will? Will say no more for now, except please convey my best wishes to your family,

Toujours,

Daphne

***

Dear Violette etc,

Thank you for confirming that all was well while you were here. We are experiencing a rough patch right now, so forgive me for being brief. More later,

Gros bisoux,

Famille Thrush

***

Dear Camilla – Mother,

I haven't mourned for you the way a daughter should. Things come in fits and starts. This is perhaps because you died twice in my thoughts. But now I know you're really dead (your ashes are in an urn in front of me), I expect I'll feel differently soon enough. I've got used to the idea that you're gone, but I'm not sure how old you have to be before you're too old to cry about something like this. I don't understand how you managed to exist without obvious means of support like money. If you have a secret stash some place, it would be useful to know where. This is, I suppose, a case of God wot.

Your loving daughter,

Daph

***

PC Petrovich lay with his head resting peacefully on Henry's lap.

'Henry? Can we go now?' whispered Daphne.

***

'Call me what instrument you will,
Though you can fret me,
Yet you cannot play upon me.'
Hamlet

CHAPTER 50

'I want to know what you remember as a child.'

Asp curled into her ball shape on a nursing chair next to a gas fire with artificial coal. She had no desire to go backwards to come forwards.

'Start anywhere you want.'

'Jesus, Mary, Joseph and the wee donkey.'

Her head tucked low into her legs. She was laughing at his banality. The only way she could stop laughing was by reading the pre-admission pamphlet for the psychiatric ward upside down, where she'd dropped it on the floor.

A woman was walking in a garden with the shadow of a nurse behind her. *Not a good start,* she thought, looking up briefly before she ducked down again and remembered his ten tips for preserving sanity, beginning with *'Accept yourself for who you are.'* The laughter returned. She would have to discover her own image to escape from it. How could she explain this to a psychiatrist with a bird's nest on his head, whose notion of self must be located in a tin of hairspray and who believes that childhood memories are at the seat of the human soul?

She had always regarded suicide as a consolation or an option. It wasn't something to be picked over with another person in the event of her survival. The laughter died in her throat.

'On a scale of one to ten, how happy are you?'

'Minus fifteen.'

'Feeling worthless, hopeless, bored, depressed?'

'Tick, tick, tick, tick.'

He filled in the boxes until he was yawning more than his patient. On his orders, Asp had been placed on suicide watch, which meant a nurse kept coming into her ward every fifteen minutes to check she was there, following her to the occupational therapy room, the cafeteria, the bathroom, the lavatories or the psychiatrist's door. The fifty minutes of consultation were almost over, and it was time to move away from his questionnaire before she was reunited with the nurse. She would comply to please herself.

'I was in the garden with my brother once. I must have been about five.'

She sat up as he looked down at his fob watch and popped it back inside his waistcoat.

'We were OK in the garden together. There were slugs crawling all over the grass and leaving a trail of silvery paste on the grass.'

'It was slug slime.'

She flashed her old death stare right back at him – couldn't help feeling that the people who stepped into her life were characters out of *The Wizard of Oz*, the way they were revealed in unstable refractions - the inspector, the goat lady, the psychiatrist

– all of them, distorted by her reflection and lost in some liminal space.

'I ate one. I ate it as a dare. Elm'd never eat a slug.'

'Do you remember the taste?' He looked bored.

'No. It stuck to my tongue. Then I swallowed it and thought how smooth it was. Like an oyster – just some revolting phlegm on your plate, and you don't want to eat it, but you still do because you don't want to lose face. And you're surprised when you like it, and you think about swallowing some more and suddenly it's silky and slippery – like swallowing a goldfish.'

She was faltering as she tried to be accurate, remembering George, the family goldfish. This was the first significant pause.

'That's because you *think* you should have been disgusted.' His eyes were level with hers. 'It feels worse because you aren't.'

'Oh, please.'

She fiddled with the badge that her friend in occupational therapy had given her and which said, *'Fuck it.'*

'Did you eat any other slugs?'

Silly man, she nearly said aloud.

'Just the one.'

Saw they were going nowhere and that it was largely her doing. Decided she'd prefer a game of ping-pong in that temple of ashtrays, the OT room, with the nurse breathing down her back.

'I only killed one, okay? One slug and one person. Mind you, I used to think I'd murdered my own grandmother.' Sitting on the edge of the nursing chair, wishing he'd hurry up and turn off the gas fire. It was early September and she was feeling hot.

'That's all I remember.'

'And your grandmother…?'

I'm not really interested in the past, you know.'

The psychiatrist turned halfway round in his chair until she couldn't see his face. 'You have confessed to the murder of your grandmother. Your father says the only murder you ever committed was in your mind. He says he murdered your grandmother. What do you think about that?'

'That's crap. My father lives in a fantasy world – not me. She died in France of natural causes. He's saying that to protect what he *thinks* I am.'

He swivelled halfway back again. 'And your brother? Do you know if he is also going to join in with some sort of confession to let you off the hook?'

'Elm? Elm confess?' She leapt up from her chair. 'To what? That's fucking ludicrous. That would be another lie. If he does, Inspector, I'm telling you he's making everything up to protect our father.'

'And not you. Not to protect you?'

She hesitated. 'Ask Elm. But if he did, it'd be another big whopper.'

'And your mother? Has she told you what she says? Because she thinks she's responsible for the death of your ex-lodger.'

'You're joking.'

'I'm not.'

'That's… That's crazy. It's her martyr thing. It's rubbish. Everyone loathed Nasty. But only one of us killed her.'

'OK, Asp, I've got something I want you to watch on video.'

'What did you say?'

'Actually, it's a DVD. I want you to watch it.' He spun his chair so that it moved backwards and grabbed the zapper off the mantelpiece. 'Go on. Do me a favour. Just have a look at this.'

She wanted to say, 'piss off. You may think I have a chronic, neurobiological disorder of the central nervous system caused by an abnormality in my neurotransmitters, but that's just your opinion. Give me Prozac. Is that okay with you?' Instead, she was silent, drawn by flickering on the monitor to yesterday's news. The arm of his chair and the window behind were reflected on the screen alongside the grainy footage of police dispersing crowds with tear gas.

'Today, at a London Youth Court, a Canadian student with British nationality was sentenced to six months imprisonment as a result of her involvement in anarchist riots in the city.' Cut to newsreader in artistic tie. *'The nineteen-year-old, who cannot be named, showed no remorse when sentenced. Prosecution described how she attacked police during a riot to reclaim the streets, throwing bottles at officers while resisting arrest.'*

Close-up of obese female with candyfloss pink hair, dressed in lumberjack shirt and black leggings with a patch over one eye, hitting a city stockbroker with a banner saying 'FUCK RULES.' Recognisably Anastase Besoin alive and kicking.

'On leaving the courtroom, the student was seen to make obscene gestures in the direction of the presiding judge and was heard to cry, 'Hurry up and die, Your Honour.'

In his summing up, the judge said, "Nothing short of a custodial sentence could possibly be justified in a case of wanton violence in a public place".'

Zap. Nasty and the newsreader shivered in the reflected furniture. Zap-zap into a diminishing pinhead of light.

'So what are you going to tell me now, Asp?' The psychiatrist dropped his zapper on the desk and cupped his hands behind his head, crossed his absurdly short legs and revealed a pair of odd red socks, one bobbly, one smooth, one bright scarlet, the other more a wine colour. 'Whose body was it in the garden, or don't you know?'

'Oh, give me extra medication. Of course it's Nasty. Good riddance, I say. How could she *not* be dead? I should fucking know.'

'And who is in the news report we've just watched?'

'The Duchess of Blackpool.'

'I see.'

'So get me out of here, will you? I've been left to rot forever in this place. One more week and it's time for discharge. I'm no more acute than the hair on your head. All I want is some human warmth, a fundamental kindness, not a fucking DVD that's obviously fake and a load of condescending questions.'

Asp watched the psychiatrist's hands creep slowly round from the back of his neck and cover his face for several seconds. She didn't like the way he peered at her through the slits of his fingers, but she couldn't pin it down any more than that.

'I've got nothing to say,' she said aloud. Except...'

'Except?'

'Your socks don't match.'

'Does it bother you?'

'Does it bother *me?* Yes actually, it does bother me. It's crap because it means you didn't look properly when you put them on.'

She shrugged her shoulders. 'And while we're at it, I don't see why it's a crime not to like yourself.'

'Sometimes you see things that might not be there.'

The psychiatrist began turning in his chair. He kept turning until he felt that the world was spinning and not himself. *It was true about the socks,* he was thinking. He rearranged the hairs on his head to cover his bald spot and inhaled deeply several times until the blood coursing round his body revived his thoughts. He saw that the fake coals in his gas fire were no longer flickering, that the mantelpiece was flat and solid, not moving in waves, and got up from his chair and went over to his desk, retrieved the zapper and pressed *re-play.*

***

'So shall you hear
Of carnal, bloody and unnatural acts,
Of accidental judgements, casual slaughters,
Of deaths put on by cunning and forc'd cause.'
Hamlet

CHAPTER 51

Inside Leaf's head, there was a crowd of thoughts with no space to move around. To say what he really thought was not an option. That he had chosen to remain mute for his entire life did not mean he was without frankness of thought. He never at any stage deceived himself, although his decision not to make an effort to speak or grow was a kind of tactfulness. By not expressing himself out loud and bottling everything up inside, he was expressing concern for what others might think, his own thoughts being generally of a morose and pessimistic nature.

In some darkened way, he had grasped from the beginning that self-expression was the beginning of corruption. He believed that he could stave it off by willfully clinging to his silent, permanent immaturity. Babies are not expected to speak in sentences. Only saints and fools can speak their minds without being accused of malice or pettiness, and Leaf, the baby, knew that he was neither.

As he sat strapped into his car seat, sandwiched between Uncle Hamish and Aunt Rose with his mother and father in front, he was content to keep his thoughts to himself. It is easy to be outspoken when a person's frankness is selective. He wondered if his parents had considered how much candour a confession might bear, how much could be omitted before it ceased to be frank.

One confidence invites another, bringing with it all sorts of related discoveries and in this way, Asp's confession had brought on Henry's, which would induce Daphne's, which would leave him, Leaf, the all-seeing savant baby, ripe for contamination. And not forgetting Elm. Surely Elm would have a confession up his sleeve to complete the circle? Or maybe not, now that he had the blonde goddess to think about.

Leaf, had he been able to express the thought out loud, would have said he liked the axiom, the whole truth and nothing but the truth, but he doubted if anyone in his family would understand its implication or be capable of the preparation that is necessary when spilling all the beans.

'How old am I? Eight years or nine an' a half? All those years of bottling up everything I know. I'm perceived as an idiot. It has its advantages.'

He unbuckled his belt slyly while his aunt and uncle were looking out the window. His chubby hands rested on his stomach, and as he breathed in deeply, he expanded infinitesimally – a fleeting moment of growth, which he allowed to happen once in a while to shift the distribution of his baby fat. It was as if, with that small shudder, he carried in every fibre of his being the knowledge that he would have to change – as if he had eaten some magic mushroom or swallowed a microdot of LSD and his consciousness had expanded willy-nilly.

***

So. I was hanging on a hook in my papoose at the top of the cellar stairs next to the cloakroom. So that big blubbery girl came down the steps and pulled my nose as she passed. *'Come on-n-n,'* she yelled to the other blubby bag that was supposed to be her friend. *'Come 'n' see what they've got down here. Hurry up.'*

Both of them, beetroot punkies, side by side an' me hanging on the wall like a peg bag, there wasn't that much room for me to swing. I covered up my face in case they took another swipe, yelling at each one in turn. *'If you don't shut up, I'll cut you up,'* snarled Nasty.

I have a terrible temper, but I know when to be quiet, and everyone needs friends. Besides, the possibility of eavesdropping was as tempting as it was frightening. Asp was cleaning out the pond while I was meant to be having a nap. There was no one else inside the house except her and me an' the other blub that Nasty called 'Sea' and we always called 'the ex-drug dealer'.

You'll get yours, I thought between hiccoughs, my nappy brimming from the sudden shock. *The net is cast. Beware.* It wasn't a matter of inner vision or prophecy on my part, but I believe that the sum of a person's actions is taken into the next life, and Nasty was stockpiling her sins.

'Crazy baby,' said Sea. 'You crazy baby. You know what? You're a poisonous toad that's swollen up. Crazy baby. Cray-zee.' She went on like that until Nasty interrupted.

'Eeughh. Watch it.' That was directed at me. As if I could do anything else, hung up on the wall and forgotten by my family as per usual. The sad fact was that no one ever gives me much thought at any time. It was hours before Asp collected me and meanwhile, I had to live with these two making whoopee.

At first, they just looked round and poked at the coal heap. I could see Nasty pick up one of the old shoes that belonged to my granny. It must have been buried under some coal and not been seen until this moment. I know it was Granny's shoe because there were holes for her bunions to stick through. They laughed and Nasty stuck her fingers into the holes and said:

'I bet the old girl's buried under there,' meaning the coal heap. Sea was more interested in pulling stuff out of the freezer; bags of ice, frozen peas and an old bucket of ice cream. 'Want some?' she said, looking straight up at me.

It was raspberry ripple, and I did. It was my favourite at the time, but she just punched me in the tummy and kept on laughing in her creepy way. Sea was creepier than Nasty. She said things that eventually came true, like, 'You want to kill me, don't you?' She said that to Nasty. I heard her. She said it lots of times when she wanted Nasty to kiss her.

'You really want to kill me,' she kept saying, and Nasty shook her head an' smiled and picked up a trowel from a box of ol' tools and started dancing on the spot, holding it close to her chest, seeing there was no room to wave it about. Sea had found Asp's old fairy dress made of petticoats from Oxfam.

Anyway, she put it on her head and started dancing too. Both of them lifting their fat legs and shaking their bodies while Sea was singing 'Crazy baby, you cray-zee.' They were sweating and banging into each other. Then Nasty stopped dancing and said they could use the trowel as an ice cream scoop.

I pretended to close my eyes so they wouldn't notice me. I watched them guzzling, and I could see they were kissing with their tongues wiggling round inside each other's mouths. Sucking up the drips like they were starved for it. I was practically asleep when Sea bit Nasty on the lip, and they both started screaming into each other's throats. Reason may be the first thing to go, but I wasn't sure if this was part of their lovey-dovey stuff or if they were really mad at each other.

'Chomp, chomp, wham, bang, scrunch, ping, saw, yuck.'

'Shut up, you blubbers,' I shouted, except they didn't hear.

Nasty tried to grab hold of Sea's tongue, but she couldn't get a hold, and her fingers ripped the inside of Sea's cheek instead. 'Fairy faggot,' she kept on yelling. There were red bubbles on Sea's teeth.

'Double-crossing fairy faggot. Give me back my money.'

Sea had dug her thumb in Nasty's eye, and the blood got mixed up with the raspberry. They swayed from side to side, groaning, all pink and red looking. Nasty held something in her hand that looked like liver but was probably a lump of Sea's cheek.

I knew the axe was sure to follow. Nasty got it off the wall, you see. She struck so hard the axe broke in two separate pieces, and the grip was still in her hands when Sea folded over in the middle like a load of old washing.

I reckon she was dead before she hit the floor. Scrunch, thud, yuck. Nasty pulled out the freezer plug and wired up the electric saw. Z-Z-Z-Z-Z. It buzzed like wasps, only louder. Z-Z-Z-Z-Z. Drilling in short blasts. That's when I screamed blue murder an' she yelled back at me. She'd got that mean look in her eye, and I wanted so hard not to yell, but I couldn't help it, could I? I'd never felt so alive.

'Shut up,' she shrieked in my ear with the saw in her hand. Her eye looked awful. It had closed up tight and stuff was leaking out the sides. She went back to her sawing and stuffing and once or twice I saw her good eye looking up to see if anyone was coming. How she managed to clean up, I'll never really know.

When Asp finally stuck her head into the cloakroom, it was dark and Nasty had switched off the light. She was banking on Asp not bothering to turn anything on, and that's exactly what happened. Asp just leaned over the top of the stairs to unhook me like she always did.

She wouldn't have seen Nasty behind the freezer, and I could hardly open my mouth to cry, 'Help, help murder. Watch out.' Asp thought I was asleep anyway. They always think that when I half shut my eyes. It's why I spent our whole holiday in France with my lids down, trying to forget what I'd seen.

Sea, I solemnly swear, was bludgeoned to death with an axe. She was sawn into bits and stashed away in transparent doggy bags inside the freezer. I am a witness, and what I saw sank into my subconscious and stayed there until the last week or so when it came out again from necessity.

'Can you tell me a little more?' the inspector will say when I decide to speak up at last. 'So far, I have at least three confessions and must examine each one carefully before I can decide which is true.'

And I will reply, 'Well, yes, I suppose so. Three confessions do seem rather a lot. But ask Nasty. Go find her. She's not been murdered. Ask her to tell you what's true and what's not. Make the detecting part a bit easier for yourself.'

And he will say, 'Given her propensity for whoppers, I'm not sure she's capable of telling the truth.'

'Maybe,' I will answer, 'there is truth underneath the lies. Maybe she lies, not obviously for the sake of truth, but for herself.'

And the inspector will nod his head in agreement and mutter something wet like, 'out of the mouths of babes,' and, 'that's where the detective work lies – in sorting out what is and what isn't fact.'

My greatest problem has usually been that as soon as someone speaks the truth, I suspect a lie. So I nod my head in sympathy, but really (because all this talk about veracity has given me a headache), I think that if I shake my head or suck hard on my dummy, it will get rid of it. I can't help but feel that he's engaging me in a game of teasing by inviting me to discuss things seriously. As soon as I do, he retreats into his own intransigent thoughts because I've said something that doesn't fit in with his theories.

That's the moment when my family (except for Asp, who won't be at the police station because she's still in hospital) will turn to me with amazed eyes as if none of 'em has ever seen me properly before this moment.

Now – if disorder of the mind comes out of the trauma of such relationships, will my family recognise that we're all nuts as a result of our respective traumas? What will Asp think when she hears that I've spoken my mind out loud? Perhaps everyone will expect me to grow up, be my age.

Of course, alternatively, I might choose to be like Uncle

Hamish. Detached by numbers. What I'd choose to say would not necessarily reveal what I think. Or... and this is me, Leaf, playing Tantalus and salivating over a bowl of raspberry ripple but unable to eat it 'cos I'm in Hell. I could, instead, just go on being silent and immature to my grave.

I expect we're already late for our meeting with the inspector, being stuck in a traffic jam because Hammersmith Bridge is shut again, and we have to turn back on our tracks. My father is hugging the car in front from frustration, and my mother looks up at me through the rear-vision mirror to remind herself that she's a good mother.

To while away the time, Uncle Hamish is singing, 'One man went to mow, went to mow a meadow, one man and his dog, went to mow a meadow.' It's his favourite song, next to 'Nine Green Bottles.' Why is it no one in my family can sing in tune except me? Aunt Rose is reading a book on physics called, *Why We Exist.* Maybe Inspector Love will have gone home by the time we get to the station. I am, of course, an optimist.

***

'The readiness is all.'
Hamlet

CHAPTER 52

Daphne was preparing for the winter before autumn had settled. She dealt daily with the anticipation of her own decline. Lately, she had started to lose balance when she got up from a chair, would lie down on her bed and, without intending to, roll over to the other side. Her family assumed she had drunk one glass too many. The truth was she had never recovered from Wellies One's rejection of her offer of free sex by moonlight.

'Thank you, my dear,' he wrote in immediate reply to her loving note of the previous week, 'although perhaps another time.' *The shit,* she thought, tearing the page of obscure medical scrawl into a thousand pieces and thinking the smug-faced, hoity-toity shit as her blood pressure shot to the top of the glass tube at the point where death intervenes.

A different letter had brought a glimmer of hope and reprieve. It arrived in Monday's mail by return of post among the unpaid bills. It was Pierrette's extensive reply to her brief note. In French.

Ma plus chère Daphne,

I suppose you didn't ask about the will on the telephone because you were afraid of execrable taste. Don't worry. I refuse to believe in good, bad or any such definitions of human behaviour. And please don't feel guilty. We should all live in America, where they want you ***not*** *to feel guilty about* ***any****thing. Of course, money is important, and I hope you will understand when you read what I have to say about your mother's legacy that I too, deserve a part of it. (Asp may have mentioned my plans for a sex-change in Colorado next Spring?)*

A single moth flew out of the duvet cover she had spread across her bed. Not Angle Shade, nor Old Lady, but a common moth so small it could have been a midge. It hovered like a piece of starved fluff before it disappeared against the distempered yellow of the walls. It wasn't enough that they sucked the wine from the strings of hessian hanging in the garden, but their larvae must suck the lanolin from out of her clothes.

Your mother's actor friend paid our fares to Paris on Eurostar. I earned some pocket money by busking with my violin, which kept us going for a while. Our life was made up of hotels, travel and trawling in dustbins for leftovers. I'll leave it at that. There weren't many laughs when we were getting started.

In Moscow, we met up with some oligarchs after bonding with the beau monde in the Café Mussorgsky on the Tverskoi Boulevard. It was a night of vodka with blinis and cranberry marmalade, and more vodka. Boris, the leader of the oligarchs, asked us to be their couriers. We were to help them with a spot of money laundering by carrying their cash to places like Cyprus and Borneo.

Daphne scratched a red weal on her leg and resolved to buy fresh mothballs and blinis.

I admit that your mother had the idea first. She was, you understand, despite her difficulties with communication, a natural-born blackmailer. We knew exactly how the oligarchs had acquired their billions – the way they dug into the coffers of the Kremlin and bought state assets for a fraction of their cost from corrupt ministers.

We understood that a word in somebody's ear had fixed the past elections and I'm not meaning Chechnya. Of course we knew about oil wells in Siberia. We uncovered the plotting, scheming, privatizing, sharp practices of at least seven oligarchs controlling 50% of the economy of Russia. We knew about the various car bombs and the chauffeurs who were found dead in mysterious circumstances. In Russia.

But towards the end of last year, we made a series of property investments in former eastern bloc countries and lost a lot of money. To you, she was your mother. To the oligarchs, she was tough in business, hating to lose money and locked in a quarrel that was clearly getting nasty.'

Daphne could feel the woollen fibres of her vests and tights worming their way into her skin, inflaming the pores so that when you scratched them, they moved somewhere else. She would have liked a modest inheritance to buy silk underwear and enough vitamins for a comfortable life.

We knew too much and were in it too deep. We realised it was time to go and vanished to the south of France with the remaining money. Mme Pod had our few jewels sewn into the hem of her fur coat (not mine).

But it was my idea to head for the Riviera. I knew they'd follow us there. We eventually lost them between Cannes and Monte Carlo and that was a stroke of genius on my part. They fell in love with the blue skies, the casinos, the ease of money laundering and the beaches. They stayed to admire the view and mingle with the other mobs. We didn't. Not one of them thought of looking for us in the tiny village of Peyruis.

The worst of psoriasis, thought Daphne, *was its visibility – the itchy, burning, inflamed patches on her shedding skin.* She reached for a tube of cortisone and slapped it across the angry weals of her face until she gleamed like a phantom in the dark and was sufficiently soothed to go on reading.

Your mother's health began to deteriorate with stress and age. Before the final stroke, she indicated her needs through a series of nods and grunts or notes. She told me she preferred Jean-Pierre to Pierrette and that she had no intention of funding an operation for Pierrette. She had, without my knowledge at the time, posted her fur coat to her actor friend with instructions to place the contents of its hem in brown envelopes in a Harrods deposit box.

Before she left England, she left instructions for what should happen in case of an accident, ill health, death etc. This, my dear Mrs Thrush – Daphne – is a true account of what happened.

It was the same with the woolly bears or moth larvae in her

bedroom curtains and almost all the other drapes and flummeries within the house. As tattered and as full of holes, Daphne recognised that her life had degenerated into a world without expectation of anything pleasurable and good. Until that is, she made the decision that all shampoos are paint strippers and by not using them, her head didn't itch anymore.

There was nothing I could do about it except try and make her see my point of view. Your mother sold the majority of the diamonds, but she did have a few roubles left, and these were converted into euros by her actor friend. Not a lot, but she left it all to Asp in her will. It is quite straightforward, I think, but how the money should be dispersed is up to Asp, n'est-ce pas?

As I said before, a small amount of money would pay for my proposed operation and would, I think, be fair recompense for my role as your mother's carer over the last few years. I found a copy of the will under her mattress in my parents' house, which I enclose with this letter.

A bientot, gros bisous,

Pierrette

Daphne slipped off the edge of the bed and without losing her balance once, did a little jig before rethreading her needle and settling down to read her mother's testament. She smiled at her reflection in the mirror. 'How much exactly is not a lot?'

***

'The ears are senseless that should give us hearing,'
Hamlet

Chapter 53

The Thrush family trip to the police station had been a farce. PC Petrovich had declined to come with them because he said he was still feeling unwell. Inspector Love looked right through Daphne and beyond to Henry, saying that he didn't believe Henry's confession one little bit and certainly no more than he did Asp's. The case of the dismembered body in their next-door neighbour's garden remained unsolved as DNA samples and dental examination had not revealed an identity as yet, and there was a need for more evidence before any conclusions could be drawn.

Henry drew into himself, deeply wounded, sitting in a far corner of the room. Daphne was lost alternately in anticipation of Asp's inheritance or gloom about Asp's future. Aunt Rose appeared confused but wasn't at all, while Uncle Hamish, who was on a sweeter planet, sang his counting songs next to Leaf, who was impenetrable as usual and stuffed into his new pushchair at the end of the row of seats.

Elm had arrived separately at the police station with the dried crumbs of breakfast on his shirt and the girl, Jasmine Sweetpea, clinging to his arm as he launched into one of those hearty games of virtual Cluedo that sometimes shy people introduce to spice up the party. The result was a familiar, competitive braggadocio from each member of the family, each contributing in their noisy, boastful, exhibitionist way. As a group, they gave the inspector one of his worst headaches for that week.

'It was the ex-drug dealer. The ex-drug dealer was the corpse, and Nasty was the murderer.' (Elm.)

'Yes, Inspector. Had you thought of that?' (Henry.)

'Of course. They wore the same clothes, didn't they?' (Daphne.)

'Tweedle-dee and Tweedle-dum.' (Asp.)

'Their shirts never buttoned up properly.' (Daphne.)

'She means they didn't button up the same way.' (Asp.)

'What have buttons to do with the price of eggs?' (Henry.)

'And those black leggings.' (Daphne.)

'She means the legs were fat.' (Asp.)

'Gross, egregious, gargantuan.' (Elm.)

'Three men, two men, one man and his dog went to mow a meadow.' (Uncle Hamish.)

'Golly-golly-golly.' (Leaf).

Elm was sorry for the inspector, who seemed clearly out of his depth.

'It all happened in the conservatory. That's where the bin bags are kept.' (Henry.)

'Do you feel cheated, inspector?' Aunt Rose came into the fray.

No, he thought.

'It wasn't the conservatory. It was the cellar.' Henry looked quite excited. His cheeks were abnormally flushed and he behaved as if he had been drinking vodka at 11am. 'There's an electric saw down there.'

A little man, unknown to anyone else, had settled inside Henry's head to whisper that there was an arrangement between his wife and the detective, but he couldn't put his finger on it more than that.

Inspector Love was chewing his lower lip to help him stay awake. 'If,' he began cautiously, 'I have an idea about a case and I can't prove it, then I feel cheated.' His brown suede shoes tapped anxiously on the floor. 'It happens sometimes.'

'Maybe the ex-drug-dealer had a criminal record. Maybe,' Elm was cautiously enthusiastic. 'Perhaps you have her fingerprints.'

Leaf roared and Uncle Hamish sang his own descant.

'We've already met Miss Anastase Besoin.' There were small gasps from everyone that sounded like a row of corks popping one after the other. The inspector stared at Jasmine to relieve his headache, seduced by the yards of blond hair and her youth in that order. He was breathing heavily. 'PC Petrovich managed to track her down,' he continued. With difficulty.

Daphne's mouth opened and shut several times. In shock.

'Nasty not dead yet? Where is she, Cedric?'

'Under medical observation.'

The inspector slipped his hand in Daphne's, patting it gently, warmly, almost lovingly. Henry, still flushed in the face, walked out of the station reception room without a word.

'Is she in prison?' Elm twisted the new badge on his T-shirt until he could read its message by closing one eye. *'Find that which shines and is beyond corruption.'*

'Or perhaps a police cell?' Jasmine Sweetpea jumped up and moved into Henry's place next to Elm. She stroked the red-gold crest that was Elm's hair. 'Well done,' her fingers seemed to say. 'My emperor penguin.' His fairy queen had spoken.

Daphne dropped the inspector's hand, clung to the edge of her seat and saw that the world was slowly turning over in front of her eyes, and she was hurtling towards her own grave with the inspector not far behind.

'Anastase Besoin is neither in a cell nor in prison – but she is in hospital – the same one that is looking after Asp. When her treatment is complete, she'll be returned to her detention centre.' The inspector was feeling exhausted and short of temper with his little group.

'Detention centre?' Elm rose to his feet. 'Has Nasty been sentenced? What for? Pissing people off or maybe for murdering her best friend in *our* cellar?'

He was glad that he'd distanced himself from the general balminess of his family by telling his beloved Jasmine on their way to the station that he'd been adopted at birth. (It was the first conscious lie he had ever told.)

Aunt Rose suddenly lost her temper and told Uncle Hamish to shut up or stop counting – he had moved on from 'One Man Went to Mow' and was halfway through 'Nine Green Bottles'.

'Sorry.' The inspector covered his face with his hands. 'The matter's confidential. I'm sure you'll understand why I can't say any more. But...' His words were progressively slower until the gap between each one made it hard to follow the sense of what he was saying. 'Please...'

He tried to breathe deeply. 'No more... false confessions, please. No...no more inventions.' He was reluctant to say 'lies'.

The day he needed a machine to guide him on this one was the day he retired. 'Or... I'll be... ... obliged... an arrest... on ... grounds... of... police... ...time... wasted.' He thought this must be how it is when you are about to have a stroke.

Daphne heard her friend's halting speech with a mixture of pity and disappointment. *What perverted justice was this,* she asked herself, *that allowed Asp and Nasty to be thrown together in the same hospital?* She sat on the edge of her seat, alternately feeling dizzy and brooding about the implications. There is a thin line between an atmosphere of fear and one of anger.

Nasty was the main target of Daphne's anger, and Asp the object of her fears. Time evaporates when a person is concentrating on an idea, an issue or a set of circumstances, and she didn't notice when the inspector moved the rest of the family out of the room with its posters of wanted criminals on the walls and into the corridor, saying that he was sorry, but he was not feeling well. She barely noticed when he turned to speak to her.

'Thank you for your e-mail, my dear – I mean the one before last – where you mentioned the idea of friendship as it affects us both.' He drew Daphne to her feet and steadied her so his breath stirred the fuzz of hair above her ears. 'Like you, I hope it's been resolved.'

He felt a nothingness in him as a man. It was always like that when he became too close to someone. In his thoughts, he was standing in a black sea with the water up to his armpits. The girl, Jasmine, was walking towards him through a wrinkled line of moonlight that spread in ripples on the surface of the water. Her hair was wrapped around her body until it dipped into the sea where it floated outwards from her head in a fan of luminous green seaweed.

The pleasure he felt was so intense that, for one brief moment, he forgot how much his head was hurting. Sadly, the woman in front of him was not the monochrome dream of an old man's lust but a weary and disappointed middle-aged woman. Such a small space that existed between reality and fantasy. 'Goodbye, Daphne,' he said at last, closing the door behind her as she led her family out of the police station and into the afternoon light.

***

'There's matter in these sighs, these profound heaves;'
Hamlet

CHAPTER 54

It was from that moment that Daphne had been misted in a small sorrow. She understood that whatever passionate feelings might exist were separate from what she felt between her thighs. It should have been a moment of catharsis, but instead, she pricked her thumb with her needle, darned the last of the bedroom curtains and waited for the blood to appear. It seeped into the cloth, where it would remain as a memory.

She made no attempt to staunch the flow but watched its redness spread deeper into the fibres. PC Petrovich had telephoned to say she was to meet him in an hour's time in the hospital foyer. She could tell from his voice that he was triumphant, although he refused to say why they should meet. She tucked her mother's will inside the letter from Pierrette and slipped both under her pillow.

Henry and Uncle Hamish had biked to the park for a spot of flying. Leaf and Aunt Rose came with her to the hospital and gave comfort by demanding her attention from time to time. Had Leaf been more conventional in his growth patterns, she could have sworn he was showing signs of precocious adolescence.

The smell of budding maleness in his room, the sullen way he turned his cheek if she bent down to kiss him in his shiny new pushchair, or the tantrums if she forgot were all developmental milestones once looked for in vain. His spirits would lift with the distraction of a ride in Aunt Rose's wheelchair, but by the time she had stashed the damn thing in the red van, put away her sewing box, wiped the milk stains off his baby-gro and cleaned out the nappy bucket, she knew they were going to be late for their appointment.

'Porfiry?' PC Petrovich was standing with his back to Daphne, chatting to a bloated figure behind a stack of wilting rubber plants in the main hospital entrance. Another step, and she realised the figure was Nasty with a black patch over her right eye. Her left eye was squeezed between the folds of her flesh, and she looked uglier than Daphne had remembered.

'Oh,' she said, glaring at Nasty. 'It's you.'

'Yes, me.'

'Daphne.' PC Petrovich seemed anxious on Nasty's behalf.

'Porfiry,' sighed Daphne.

'What a fucking surprise.' Nasty made no attempt to back away. She was like a cat with a mouse in its mouth. Wanting approval but not knowing how to get it.

'Why are you here?' Daphne lifted a howling Leaf from Aunt Rose's lap.

Nasty: 'I'm in a meeting.'

PC Petrovich: 'We're discussing her therapy.'

Daphne, startled: 'Oh? What's it like?'

Nasty: 'Pills mostly... To make us sane.'

'Not better yet, dear?' Aunt Rose whispered from the safety of her wheelchair, though no one heard.

'I saw Asp through the window of P Ward this morning. That's *P* for potty.' Nasty stopped and looked around nervously as if expecting someone to appear from behind.

Fiddling with the gold locket on the gold-plated chain around her neck (it was a parting gift from her father), Nasty's words sounded defensive. 'Either Asp was avoiding me, or she couldn't hear when I called out to her. I nearly smashed the glass, but I decided not to because I didn't want any more of their piss injections to calm me down.' A pause. 'Is Asp deaf or something?'

Leaf squirmed and struggled, bawling in his mother's hold, his head pointed towards the floor.

'What sort of injection, dear?' Aunt Rose looked interested.

'You hear me. That baby needs one. Right now.' Nasty bent down until she was frowning at Leaf and was looking at him from the same height. 'A double dose of blockers would do the trick,' she said with malevolence and laughed.

Leaf wrinkled up his nose and roared until he became one of those trumpeting angels by Della Robbia – all puffed up cheeks and round bottoms, kicking at the air as he tried and failed to connect.

'Do you have any experience then?' Daphne tugged at his collar, forcing him to lie still, to the point of choking her own child because she couldn't do the same to the huge, wobbly, ugly person in front of her. 'Do you have a needle on you?' she asked.

'We're all crackheads in my ward. I thought you'd fucking know that.'

Leaf's face had turned a darkish blue, and Daphne restored him quickly to Aunt Rose's knees. She became aware of the ease and control of PC Petrovich within the group. It was a touch of Napoleon, with one arm crooked and the hand touching his heart. She had lost interest in Nasty. Nasty had lost interest in her.

'Talking of piss farts.'

Asp burst through the swing doors behind the rubber plants. Pushed to the front by her psychiatrist, she stumbled past her mother, Leaf, Aunt Rose, PC Petrovich and collided with Nasty.

The psychiatrist dragged her back.

'Where is she?' Asp was shouting with her eyes shut. 'Show me where she is.' Her hair was wet from an interrupted shower, and there was a great deal of soap in her eyes.

Nasty smirked and waved two fingers in the air at Asp. "I'm here, slimeball. You blind or something?'

Of course there were precedents for Asp falling to the floor in a faint when cornered. This time, she tucked the strands of wet hair behind her ears and waited for her breath to come. The world she saw was clad in a bubble. She felt brilliantly cool.

'I thought you were dead.' Asp's face was unreadable as she spoke.

Nasty grinned. 'What a fucker.'

'Yes.'

'Can we go somewhere we can talk?' asked PC Petrovich.

'We *are* talking.' Aunt Rose's smile was sweet.

'All of us?' Nasty leant towards Leaf and squeezed his nose. 'Some of us *can't* talk.'

'Follow me.' The psychiatrist, who was beginning to look more and more like the inspector, inclined his head, taking care not to disturb the strands of hair that he'd sprayed with his usual gunk into parallel threads.

Asp was the last to follow. She had made her plan. The soap bubbles in her eyes gave everyone coloured stripes down the middle of their bodies. As they marched through the longest corridor in the hospital and the wheels of Aunt Rose's wheelchair creaked for lack of oil, Nasty banged the wall nearest to her with her fists and said she felt she was Hansel or Gretel on her way to the witch's house. Those fists, glowing purple and covered with translucent splashes of light, crashed down with the weight of fury and her own fat.

Clots of plaster were dislodged by the blows, and for a split second, they paused mid-air as if deciding where to fall. A freak blast of wind blew across from an open door on the other side. It carried about a million confused lumps in a mini blizzard, and one of the larger ones landed on Leaf's head.

Though he lay concussed and whitened in Aunt Rose's lap, it was assumed by everyone that he'd fallen asleep. It had been difficult enough for Aunt Rose to accept that Aristotelian laws were invalidated by Newton's theory that any mass, whether astral or terrestrial (and in this case not only the lump of plaster but Leaf's head as well), is subjected to the same force of gravity. But no one, not even Nasty, in a malign moment of wishful thinking, could have predicted the effect of the push of the wind with the pull of the earth.

'Isn't it interesting that there are always twice as many little lumps as there are big ones?' Aunt Rose mentioned this in an aside to PC Petrovich after the dust had settled on all of them but mostly on Leaf.

Nasty had agreed not to pummel any more walls, or she would be sent back to her room on Meditation. They walked, or in Aunt Rose's and Leaf's case, they were wheeled past wards named after emotions and beliefs. Resurrection. Serendipity. Tranquillity. Peace. Optimism. They passed X-rays, pathology, reconstructive facial surgery, orthopaedics, the burns unit and the staff cafeteria.

Somewhere between Happiness and Reincarnation, they turned left, and as a nurse approached from behind, wheeling a trolley with a bedpan on top, they hesitated and shuffled to one side to allow her room to pass. The psychiatrist was softly humming a tune by Handel when the nurse stopped to empty the contents of the bedpan on top of Nasty's head.

'Think of what it is as what you've done. Unfortunately.' The nurse's voice was surprisingly gentle.

Nasty groaned and slid down the side of the wall onto the green linoleum floor at a particularly wide junction that was linked to all the other corridors.

'Or what is done cannot be undone.' Asp smiled at the nurse.

She, Nasty, lay flat on her back, dividing the group into two flanks. There was no attempt to remove the giblet-like lumps from her hair, face or body as she lay staring up at the ceiling with her one eye so fixed and strained it looked ready to pop out of its socket.

'Why you're Sister Bonaventure from the nunnery.' Daphne peered into the nurse's saintly face.

'You're Mimi-Saulange without your flute,' exclaimed Asp.

'Fortunately...' The nurse was wiping the bedpan with neat,

short strokes, using a box of tissues from her trolley.

'No, it's the nurse with the bobbing watch.' The psychiatrist looked at her with disappointment and added, 'Except it's not bobbing.'

There was just the slightest hesitation as the nurse twisted her neck sideways to read the time on her now motionless fob. The psychiatrist was not sure where his refrain was meant to fit with the rest of the aria, but he could hear someone in the distance whistling the passage in between the part of the tune that he liked best. The inspector was walking slowly towards them from the other end of the corridor with his mouth pursed in an 'O'.

'Yes,' said the nurse, standing to attention as he passed, satisfied her bedpan was spotless, 'unfortunately, it is time.'

***

'This is mere madness,
And this a while the fit will work on him.'
Hamlet

CHAPTER 55

'I ask you, did Beethoven die of lead poisoning? Or was it syphilis? And do we need to know? Does it change the way we listen to the last quartets? The medical evidence is in the hair, not the air.'

The inspector's mind was wandering in between bursts of whistling. He heard the psychiatrist's version of the Handel aria, and the differences had made him philosophical or mad, depending on the listener's point of view.

'Ombra mai fu...'

'Was that all it was? A *da capo,* back to the head? You mean the *tune* returns once again, just like the vision of my mother-in-law? Look here, Miss Besoin. There are rigorous procedures to match the criminal's fingerprints to the crime. Very well Miss Anastase Besoin. *Nasty* indeed. I have in my hand, as you can see, a piece of axe. No. Not the head. Just a splinter of...'

'...di vegetabile care
ed amabile soave piu...'

'...the Handel.' Sorry. I mean, as in the *handle.* I have found sixteen points of agreement in the loops, curves, breaks and ridges on these remarkable scraps of wood and on your toothbrush. In other words, the fingerprints are yours, Miss Besoin.'

'Ombra mai fu...' He gave up whistling and hummed instead.

'Actually, I didn't find the axe. PC Petrovich found all three pieces of it under the eaves of Mr and Mrs Thrush's attic, plus the blade. Thank you, Sister. I would be most grateful if you would perform the last rites. For whom did you say? For Anastase Sybille Amour Besoin, my *daughter.* Didn't you know?'

Still humming (although this time around, it is an extract from Mozart's *Marriage of Figaro*), the inspector removed the gold necklace with its locket, lifting it above Nasty's head and slipping it into his pocket at the precise moment that his newly acknowledged daughter sat up with her back propped up against the wall. There were small fissures where the grime had caked itself against her skin and where Nasty's cochineal hair spread outwards like the ears of a koala.

'My father?' *(Nasty to the inspector, patting at her bare throat in bewilderment or shock.)*

'Your father.' *(The inspector to Nasty.)*

'Her father?' *(Daphne to the inspector.)*

'My daughter.' *(The inspector to Daphne.)*

'Your daughter?' *(The psychiatrist to the inspector and the inspector to the psychiatrist.)*

'His daughter?' *(Asp to PC Petrovich.)*

'His daughter.' *(PC Petrovich to the floor.)*

'Her father?" *(Aunt Rose to Leaf.)*

'My father.' *(Nasty to the inspector and the psychiatrist.)*

'Well, bugger me,' said Leaf.

Aloud.

And so, once in a while, there are strange and unsettling forces at work. A superannuated baby speaks against the odds. Poltergeists throw a beam of light across a room, or occult gobbledygook screws up the hard disc. Premonitions of doom and paranoia creep into our souls.

Some people visit the devil every day, and when an image or message is threatening, when there is no logical explanation for the unsettling crossover between the rational and the mystical, between the scientifically plausible and the murkily psychological, it discombobulates. On the other hand, certainty can be a damp squib.

Leaf, waking up from his concussion and a lifetime of concealment, realised he had to accept responsibility for his actions. As a tubby-tummed prophet in the effing wilderness, if he could speak and be understood, he'd be expected to conform in other ways, the chief of which was to grow up and appear normal. But that was in the future, and this was still the beginning of his articulacy and what, in his mind, amounted to a quasi-religious crusade.

Those present in the hospital corridor listened to him in their surprise and made no demands, did not question his quiddity, and, if necessary, would obey him like stunned sheep.

'You catch me in a bad moment. You really do.' The voice was lower, gruffer than he'd expected, more pigeon than piglet. 'And I'm not ready for exposure in a public hallway.'

His world was spinning without consent. 'It's like the shit on Nasty's face. I can do without it. Why kick a bully when it's down?' he asked without any sequence to his thoughts. 'I'm not some dodgy geezer speaking for your benefit. Anyway, it's not convenient to see you all staring at me when we've something more important to think about than my ability to speak. I'm no bleeding miracle, you know. I've just had a major head injury.'

He felt he had come out of a burrow into the light. The space around him was shivering in an unstable red, and the figures on either side of him were similarly blurred. The only things he saw clearly were the hairs on Aunt Rose's chin. As his eyes adjusted, he noticed that the inspector/psychiatrist, who had morphed into one and the same person, was on his knees, wiping the stains from Nasty's face with the end of his shirttails.

'Cripes. I'd bet you'd rather be diverted from this mess than think about the implications of it. Everyone knows there's more than one way to do a hatchet job – you don't have to have an axe.' He rubbed his head as a baby does with its whole fist.

'S'obvious, isn't it? The inspector's daughter is a psychopathic murderess. The inspector is mad with grief and suffering from an identity crisis. The police constable has to accuse his ex-boss of covering up the evidence. The nun has to bring retribution in the form of a bedpan. My family has to confront its own insanities.

God had to create a blizzard to reveal the entropy. Yet you'd rather stop and gawk at me and think how the cat got my tongue at birth. Did God give me back my speech with a plaster thunderbolt?' He was out of breath, his roly-poly body heaving in Aunt Rose's lap and splintering her brittle bones. 'Let's go to Occupational Therapy.'

PC Petrovich was the only one who seemed pleased. For several minutes, Nasty picked at the bitten nails of both hands. Tears drenched the cheeks of Daphne, Asp, Sister Bonaventure and Aunt Rose. The inspector and the psychiatrist stared at Leaf impassively.

Leaf closed his eyes. 'Oh, all right then.' He continued to speak with his eyes tightly shut. 'Cripes. You're wondering why I never said a blind thing in the first place. Well,' his voice dropped another octave, 'I'll tell you once and for all.'

'I was nine months old and lying in my pram in the sun when the ol' girl's cat jumped on top of me and fell asleep on my face. When I woke, I knew I'd lost the power of speech before I'd shown I had it. Will that do?'

'OT's this way.' The psychiatrist, or maybe it was the inspector, jerked his head towards the ceiling. He was having problems hauling Nasty to her feet until the inspector, or was it the psychiatrist, leant forward to take an arm. At first, it seemed as if all three were bowing to Leaf.

'Follow me,' he crowed, still speaking from the depths of Aunt Rose's lap.

And so the motley crowd did follow the baby with the old lady in the wheelchair that was being steered by Daphne with great recklessness towards OT. As for the last rites, everyone seemed to have forgotten they had been requested, including the inspector, the psychiatrist, Nasty and Sister Bonaventure, who would have carried them out. PC Petrovich walked behind Elm and Jasmine Sweetpea, who, in turn, were behind everyone else. Pride had settled in the constable's throat and tickled the back of his nose. He was buoyed up at having passed so convincingly into manhood in the last week, and his confidence showed in the way he strode, imagining the grand opera he would write. His dreams were full of *deus ex machina* and the counterpoint of voices, rich with mead, harmony and honey.

Porfiry Petrovich was relieved to have solved a crime on his own initiative. He was surprised to have restored a daughter to her father and vice versa by dint of DNA results and intuitive understanding of the purpose of a crap piece of jewellery. (Nasty's locket contained a recognisable photo of the inspector with Nasty's mother on the inside.) Most importantly, in a few minutes, he, Porfiry Petrovich, would establish his credentials as an avant-garde composer with an audio-visual display in Occupational Therapy, not that anybody knew that yet.

Asp and Daphne had turned around at least twice to look at him with admiration and to check that he was following them. As he willed the straggling group ahead to hurry up, his movement acquired even greater swagger, and for the first time in a long time, Porfiry was almost content.

***

'To draw apart the body he hath kill'd,
O'er whom, his very madness, like some ore
Among a mineral of metals base,
Shows itself pure and weeps for what is done.'
Hamlet

CHAPTER 56

Blame must lie, not with the intemperance of a violent man but with the compassion of a father who saw that the law's punishment for his child was going to be so drawn out and unforgiving that she'd be better dead. The motley crowd, which had expanded ad hoc as they progressed, was now grouped inside the OT room with its orange walls, its hard grey plastic chairs, the vomit-patterned carpet, cigarette stubs and empty tins of coke lying in darkened corners.

Uncle Hamish and Henry joined them there, puffing from their exertions in the park. PC Petrovich put out the lights and took his place beside some figures wearing masks. They were sitting in silence at the other end of the room next to some computer equipment, a monitor, a projector and a tangle of wires.

No one noticed when the inspector slid his hands around Nasty's naked throat from behind and, in a spot where the skin was exquisitely soft, squeezed out her life without a sound from her lips as she fell to the floor for the second and final time.

A pinkish light spread across the edge of the ceiling, spilling onto the bare wall to the right. The image of an ear crept past a curtained window. An eyebrow and an eye hovered above a central heating pipe, and one nostril and half a mouth settled into the space that was left – a pallid ectoplasm, a cropped phantasmagoria or some blanched and disembodied freak, although to those who knew her, the projected face was unmistakably that of Nasty. No one turned around to examine the real thing lying in its pathetic huddle on the floor. Everyone was gripped instead by her illuminated ghost.

Apart from a whirr on the computer – so low-key that most people present would have sworn there was no sound at all – the room was silent. In the beginning - in the beginning, it was silent. But as the half-lips went on writhing, it became apparent that the visual pulse had an equivalent in sounds. Short, detached clicks matched the movement of the image. They were without obvious pitch, and there was nothing that you could hum back – just this percussive purr that came in blasts and was the slowed-down call of a posse of bats. The pitch came later with a sustained whistle followed by a human voice from the dead. Nasty's voice with an echo added to it – a sort of gangsta rap with lines like:

'I've done a crime an' 'l have to do time. It was her or me an' that's my plea, for choppin' up Sea. What a fucker, what a sucker...I've done a crime...'

Then back to the whistling sound in a chromatic descent. A fanfare on tenor trombone blew the notes *D-E-A-D*.

Fortissimo. For an overture, it was not great. Had it been understood that PC Petrovich wanted to wake the un-living, his audience might have been more sympathetic. Except that nobody knew his intention and anyway it failed. The non-spectral, stiff-as-a-dodo Nasty lay on the floor in the darkness between people's feet.

Not even six tubas and an electronic drumroll caused a twitch of her corpse. Her screen image had faded *a niente* from the wall, and her rubbish rap was drowned by bass guitar. *Dum-de-dum-de-de-dum.* The masked figures slowly turned from green to red to blue, and the yellow teeth through the cardboard lips mocked what was real. Asp thought she saw Elm running back and forth in the shadows between different bits of computer equipment. An amplified moan, not Nasty's, but sounding suspiciously like Pierrette, came and went in waves.

'AAAAA-VOOOO-CAAAA-DOOOOOO.' The displaced and strangled voice of a belly speaker or a man-sized doll with a drag queen face. Elm tweaked the reverb button and caught the cry in a loop. He mixed it with a roll of miniature bells that was beautiful in its way. PC Petrovich stood before the double row of masks and raised his hands as a conductor, shaking them in an exaggerated way, extracting his last climax from a row of open throats.

'AMEN, A-A-A-A-A-MEN, A-MEN! A-MEN! A-MEH-H-N!' cried the living dolls. The anthem, by its clamour, signalled they were near the end. The solo trumpet returned with the notes *D-E-A-D* played backwards. This was the haunting part. No longer declamatory, but muted and as mournful as a fox that cries out because it has lost its den. The composition was over, finished. PC Petrovich returned to the mound of equipment and muttered something to Elm. Someone, perhaps it was the inspector or the

psychiatrist, switched on the wall lights.

Sister Bonaventure, looking increasingly like Mimi-Saulange, was the first to applaud. Everyone, except PC Petrovich, who was bowing and Nasty, who was dead on the floor, clapped until their hands ached and they couldn't clap any more, except Leaf and Aunt Rose, who continued for another minute as the people with masks removed them one at a time. There was a synchronous gasp from those who watched. It came again with each new revelation like a prolonged coda.

Pierrette was the first to reveal herself. It was a chance to show off her powers of gestural and expressionist performance as well as the benefits of recent surgery. 'Look at me, look at me!' she cried, which everybody did.

She kept plucking at the wisps of her feather boa and flicking those that came adrift into the air like the magnificent, human stick of candy floss she was. Laughing, waving at Elm and Asp and anyone whose eye she caught. The slip of skin beneath her nose had been miraculously restored, her figure was sensational, and Elm was the first to congratulate her on her crimson wet-look boots with fifteen-centimetre heels.

More cheers as Monsieur, Madame Levin, Doctor Oblonsky and the goat lady stood up to raise their masks, one by one in canon as a tight little water ballet. It was slightly more haphazard when Anne-Marie and her beekeeper, having flown all the way from New Zealand for this, tried to do the same, as did Violette, Anjelica, Jasmine Sweetpea and the man from the furniture shop who sold Daphne her curtain remnants.

The boy from the psychiatric ward was standing with the Mint and Wellies families in the row behind, next to an elderly actor wearing a long knitted scarf, a red carnation in his buttonhole and a badge that said *'I love wankers'*. They created a more sedate sequence, their smiles fixed, as if the removal of their masks had restored their sense of self.

PC Petrovich motioned for them to sit down and, pressing his hands together across his lips, thanked them silently.

'I confess to the murder of my daughter, Anastase Sybille Amour Besoin.' The inspector found his voice at the moment that Leaf and Aunt Rose stopped clapping. He moved their wheelchair to one side and stepped back to expose Nasty's body. *This was,* he thought to himself, *the final confession of this case.*

'She looks happy like that,' remarked Leaf.

'Congratulations. About time. Felicitations. Bravo.' Aunt Rose wiped away a tear from her chin.

PC Petrovich continued bowing.

***

'Why, all this while I ha' but play'd a part,
Like to some boy that acts a tragedy...'
Antonio's Revenge by Marston, from which
Shakespeare drew ideas for Hamlet

CHAPTER 57

Magic may be the result of will to effect change. Asp argued with her family, with Pierrette and everyone else in the room, that it was human will, not science, when the inspector and the psychiatrist managed to carry Nasty to the hospital morgue without any interference, returning within minutes to tell the tale.

It would be Asp's will, not science's, when the four-foot candle placed next to Nasty's body by the inspector would melt during the night, setting light to Nasty's hair and causing not only her spontaneous cremation but also a fire in the morgue that would extinguish itself as quickly as it had begun, leaving no cinders and burning nothing apart from her corpse and such entrails that had splattered against the ceiling or the walls as solidified gobs of spit, erasing all memories of her physical existence.

It was Asp's will, her combustible testament – not the inspector's and clearly not Nasty's. She would have reported the inferno if something else had not happened, which was also a type of magic. She was sitting alone on a weary sofa in the OT room after the others had left. Her violin was on her lap, and her bow in her hand, moved from side to side like a cow's tail swishing flies.

The inspector came into the room as grey as one of the plastic chairs on which he sat to have a brief chat with her. He ran his fingers through his hair, puffed up the strands, drew attention to his baldness and, with such small gestures, morphed into her psychiatrist.

'I have something to show you,' she said.

Asp leaned down to the floor and placed her bow back in its case. She was afraid to stir from the sofa or lose sight of him for a moment in case he changed his appearance again.

'Yes?' The psychiatrist sounded pleased.

Asp's eyes were fixed on his strands of hair, wet from sweat against his skull... 'Yes. But not right now. Another day.'

He looked disappointed as she wrapped her old silk scarf around the instrument, tucking it in with quick darts at the sides. He could see the anxiety on her face and thought he understood.

'I'll come back later,' he said.

'As you...'

Her voice trailed to nothing.

***

Epilogue

A baby pink laptop sat on the desk alongside the forgotten clobber of PC Petrovich and Elm. The laptop had been bought with the inheritance left to Asp by her granny and which had been divided evenly amongst the family and Pierrette. A part of Asp was sorry she hadn't asked the psychiatrist to stay. She would have liked someone to feed her a spoonful of raspberry jelly and to sit with her until she had cracked the beginning of what she wanted to write.

Start. New file.

A row of words to bring her closer to the real thing, not too much, in case she dug herself in as she typed:

'On the afternoon of the pigsty, a bald-headed monk sat on a lily pad...'

Crash. Warning: You have performed an illegal action. Cancel. Okay. aspthrush.blog.com.

The following winter, Henry decided to sell their house and move further down the road to the one on the corner, which was divided into two flats and was, therefore, cheaper. He and Daphne would occupy downstairs, and the children would live on the top. The only disadvantage was that its front door faced the main arterial road through South London, and so was more directly under the flight path to Heathrow airport than their present home.

The windows of both flats were permanently shut to avoid any fumes. A paling fence, which divided the garden from the main road's footpath, had been knocked down by a truck and left to rot on the grass. There was an air of neglect about the place, but Henry saw that as a positive in negotiating the price.

The first Daphne knew of Henry's plan was at eight o'clock on a Friday morning when Leaf was suckling at her breast. She had heard the sounds of sawing wood. Realizing that it was not the noise of her son's devotion to her nipples, she peered through the curtains of their front bay window and spied the stick of an estate agent's sign being honed at the point and dug into the earth by the front path. It said 'House for Sale.'

Is there any more to say before I close my file? The typeface on the screen blinked twice as it switched automatically to sleep mode. Something private and profoundly personal was tucked away in there – something for Asp to re-read after hours of sitting on her own in the OT room when the objects on her desk – the pink laptop, a copy of *Hamlet and Antonio's Revenge* – were imperceptibly robbed of their colours by the darkening light. She pressed a key by mistake with her elbow and glimpsed the opening paragraphs of her novel:

'CURTAINS'
by Aspen Thrush

CHAPTER I

Jean-Claude, our lodger, returned to France after his final school exams to become a monk. Without his support, I had no intention of explaining to the policeman at our front door that Granny had disappeared, not because she joined the Salvation Army to wear the bonnet, which she was always promising she would do, but because she was lying under the coal heap in the cellar. Jean-Claude and I had buried her there one Sunday afternoon, tucking away her feet under lumps of coal next to a pair of shoes with holes cut for bunion comfort.

The fact that Granny and the shoes disappeared at the same time was the primary evidence my family needed to be sure she had left the house. These particular shoes were always worn when she went out for a walk – with, of course, the gloves. When arguments grew after a Sunday lunch, she would tug at their blue nylon tubes, flattening them out like tentacles of jellyfish, drawing them onto each finger before announcing she would walk as far as the pond and back.

'The rest is silence.'
Hamlet

Printed in Great Britain
by Amazon

32711991R00212